2-99
15/2

The Origins

The Ossians

DOUG JOHNSTONE

VIKING
an imprint of
PENGUIN BOOKS

VIKING

Published by the Penguin Group

Penguin Books Ltd, 80 Strand, London WC2R ORL, England

Penguin Group (USA) Inc., 375 Hudson Street, New York, New York 10014, USA

Penguin Group (Canada), 90 Eglinton Avenue East, Suite 700, Toronto, Ontario, Canada M4P 2Y3

(a division of Pearson Penguin Canada Inc.)

Penguin Ireland, 25 St Stephen's Green, Dublin 2, Ireland (a division of Penguin Books Ltd)

Penguin Group (Australia), 250 Camberwell Road, Camberwell, Victoria 3124, Australia

(a division of Pearson Australia Group Pty Ltd)

Penguin Books India Pvt Ltd, 11 Community Centre, Panchsheel Park, New Delhi – 110 017, India

Penguin Group (NZ), 67 Apollo Drive, Rosedale, North Shore 0632, New Zealand

(a division of Pearson New Zealand Ltd)

Penguin Books (South Africa) (Pty) Ltd, 24 Sturdee Avenue, Rosebank, Johannesburg 2196, South Africa

Penguin Books Ltd, Registered Offices: 80 Strand, London WC2R ORL, England

www.penguin.com

Published in 2008

1

Set in 12/14.75pt Monotype Dante
Typeset by Rowland Phototypesetting Ltd, Bury St Edmunds, Suffolk
Printed in Great Britain by Clays Ltd, St Ives plc

A CIP catalogue record for this book is available from the British Library

ISBN: 978-0-670-91743-3

www.greenpenguin.co.uk

For Trish, for everything

The happiest lot on earth is to be born a Scotsman. You must pay for it in many ways, as for all other advantages on earth. You have to learn the Paraphrases and the Shorter Catechism; you generally take to drink; your youth, as far as I can find out, is a time of louder war against society, of more outcry and tears and turmoil, than if you had been born, for instance, in England. But somehow life is warmer and closer; the hearth burns more redly; the lights of home shine softer on the rainy street; the very names, endeared in verse and music, cling nearer around our hearts.

Robert Louis Stevenson, *The Silverado Squatters*

It's shite being Scottish.

Irvine Welsh, *Trainspotting*

I

Edinburgh

'I know that we've been drinking
But I've had a great idea
Let's drown this land tomorrow
Let's wash it all away'

The Ossians, 'St Andrew's Day'

'Connor, I don't know why I let you drag me to the stupidest places.'

Connor watched Kate peer over the edge of the stonework, pulling her heavy coat tight against the biting wind. A tousle of black hair whipped across her sharp, pale face, a couple of strands catching in her mouth which she pulled at, briefly irritated. She looked tall despite leaning into the wind, her slim frame lost in the dark folds of her coat.

Behind her, the regimented north of the city sloped down towards the water where oil tankers made their way serenely up and down the firth. A small shaft of light pierced the claustrophobic cover of cloud, reaching down to Fife, like something from a biblical epic. Strange, thought Connor, surely God has better things to do with his time than make Fife look good.

Two hundred feet below, buses chugged down Princes Street, the strain of their engines merging with bagpipe wails, rackety drills and dull, throbbing hammer sounds. The pavement was a crush of shoppers.

Connor examined the graffiti on the crumbling black gargoyle next to him. Japanese, Icelandic, Italian, Spanish – it seemed like every nationality except his own had climbed the monument to leave a mark.

He looked down. Workmen bustled about in the gardens below,

raising tents, assembling metal frames and spreading flooring, preparing the city's Christmas fairground for its onslaught of spangle and glitz. It wasn't even December, yet Edinburgh had festive fever.

'Because you're my sister and you love me,' he said, waving his half-full bottle of gin and tonic airily. He took another swig.

'Yeah, right,' said Kate, brushing more hair away from her face. 'Explain this one to me again?' She swept her hand around the view. Spots of rain began to fall.

'Don't go into a huff. I just thought I'd create a vibe or something. Bring a bit of momentousness into our lives. What with the record release, the launch party, the tour and everything.' He paused to take another hit from the bottle. 'Is "momentousness" a word?'

'How drunk are you?' said Kate. 'We're not on until ten tonight.'

'Just soak up the view,' said Connor, ignoring her question. He started to walk round the cramped third tier of the monument and Kate followed grudgingly.

Southwest lay the castle on its hunk of volcanic rock, then the distant solitude of the Pentland Hills. As they turned east, the big plug of Arthur's Seat then the fake Greek columns of Calton Hill came into view. A plane glinted briefly as it banked high above, heading west.

He looked at the leaflet he'd been handed.

'Guess how many steps we just came up.'

Kate frowned. 'I don't know. Too many.'

'Two hundred and eighty-seven to be precise. Says here it's the largest monument to a writer in the world. And the architect drowned in a canal before it was finished. Think he was steaming?'

'Not everyone drinks like you.'

Connor looked at the giant Ferris wheel erected twenty feet away for Christmas revellers.

'Look at this thing,' he said, waving his bottle at the wheel. 'What a fucking joke.'

'What's the matter with it?' said Kate. 'It's just a big wheel. A bit of fun, you know?'

'This monument is higher, has better views and is a hundred and fifty years old, plus you get a bit of exercise climbing it. That's just a piece of modern, flashy tat.'

'So what?' said Kate. 'And since when did you give a shit about getting any exercise?'

Connor was silent. He felt another headache creeping up on him and gulped down two large mouthfuls. Not enough gin in the mix.

'Modern life is rubbish,' he said, smiling.

'Great,' said Kate, sweeping his chaotic fringe away from his face to expose tired green eyes and a pallid, taut frown. 'Now you're quoting Blur. You must be drunk.'

The familiar malty smell of the breweries swirled around them. Down below, Edinburgh had an air of anticipation as the city prepared for the festive season. Connor saw the shaft of light over Fife disappear, plunging the north into gloom.

'Come on,' he said, heading for the stairs. 'There's something else I want to show you.'

They emerged minutes later from the dark, dizzying spiral of the Scott Monument's stairway, blinking in the fading light, Connor two steps ahead. He turned left, pointing with the bottle.

'This way.'

'Where are we going?' Kate sighed.

'You'll see.'

When he acted the fizzy little kid with innocent, puppy-dog eyes, it somehow forced her into the grumpy, funless older-sister role. She never felt dour or dowdy with anyone else, just him. Although only half an hour separated their entries into the world she'd always thought of Connor as years younger, and often wished he would grow up. She sometimes wished she hadn't grown up quite so much.

They walked through the German Christmas market, a collection of stalls selling overpriced crap, Connor goading the stall owners and waving his bottle recklessly about.

Kate wondered whether things would've been different if Connor had been first out the womb. But that wasn't his style. Let his big sister go first, let her take all the responsibility, let her get all the pressure, and then he could play the runt-of-the-litter role. Did that nasty big sister starve you of oxygen in the womb, did she? Aw, diddums.

Connor stopped at a stall selling dreamcatchers and other new-age junk and began hassling the owner.

'Can we just go where we're going, then meet the others?' said Kate. 'I need a drink.'

Connor offered up his gin and tonic, now barely a fifth full.

'A proper drink, in a pub.'

'I get the message,' said Connor, heading for the exit. 'We're about to visit an invaluable part of our country's heritage, something with particular relevance to today. And' – he made a shushing motion with finger to lips and his voice dropped to a whisper – 'no fucker knows anything about it.'

Kate shook her head as the rain thickened, then followed her brother down the darkening street.

Connor pushed open the heavy oak doors and tiptoed in, cartoon style. They were inside St Mary's Cathedral at the top of Leith Walk. The distant grumble of traffic was the only sound apart from their clacking footsteps across the cold marble floor.

The church was dark except for strips of weak daylight from the high windows. Two prim-looking girls were lighting candles and praying at a small shrine near the main altar. The high, vaulted roof made every sound resonate, and the girls looked round at the sound of Kate's and Connor's footsteps before turning back to their prayers.

Connor led Kate past the confessional booths to an empty bench beside another small shrine. As they sat down, a grey-haired, middle-aged man in jeans and a jumper came out a side room carrying a stepladder and cloth. He set the ladder in front of the first booth, climbed up and began dusting the top.

Connor and Kate watched him for a moment then turned back to the shrine. In the alcove was a small altar. An arrangement of thistles in a vase stood on the altar beside a modest wooden statue of a man carrying a cross. Below that, set into the marble, were two spotlit glass display cases. In the middle of each was a small object like a pebble, flanked by two six-inch golden angels.

'Know what we're looking at?' Connor said in a hushed voice.

'You know I don't. Let me guess – the Holy Grail? Two rocks?'

'These are the actual remains of St Andrew. Or at least some of them. A bit of shoulder, I think, and something else. Maybe a toe.'

'Really? Just sitting here?' Kate was irritated she hadn't hidden her surprise. She looked around the cathedral. 'Shouldn't there be security or something? Or tourists, for that matter?'

'That's the thing,' said Connor, animated. 'Typical of Scotland, isn't it? Our patron saint's relics, on our patron saint's day, in the capital city of the country, and there's no fucker here. No one even knows about it. There's hardly any song and dance today, just a half-arsed celebration at best. OK, we're not all Catholics, but still. Look at what Guinness did for St Patrick's Day. That bogtrotting alkies' piss-up is known all over the world, and St Patrick was just a fifth-century ex-Roman with a thing for snakes. St Andrew was one of Jesus' best mates. And what are we known for? Sean Connery and Billy Connolly. Tartan and golf. Whoopee.'

'Bogtrotting alkies,' said Kate, smiling. 'What does that make us? Heather-munching, haggis-chasing smackheads?'

'Maybe.' Connor picked up a leaflet from a pile next to them and examined it. He let out a laugh, making the praying girls raise their heads and frown.

'Sorry,' he stage-whispered. He looked at Kate and prodded the leaflet. 'It says here that St Andrew is the patron saint of singers and sore throats. How cool is that? My very own patron saint. What else' – he ran his finger down the leaflet, reciting in a singsong voice – 'the patron saint of Russia, fishmongers, spinsters and gout. A strange bunch, eh? Here's another one – the patron saint of women who want to get pregnant.'

'How about the patron saint of irritating arsehole brothers? Is he that?'

'Now, now.' Connor folded the leaflet into his pocket and put his hand on her arm. 'That's no way to talk to one of the rising stars of the country's thriving indie rock scene, is it?'

Kate playfully punched her brother on the arm. 'I wish you'd never seen that review. Shows what journalists know.'

'Hey, don't forget you're the sultry, Amazonian bassist, cooler than an iceberg and hotter than hell, if I remember rightly.'

'Exactly my point.'

The man had finished cleaning the booths and was folding down the ladder.

'I see you're examining the relics,' he said in a soft Edinburgh accent. 'And what do you make of them?'

'Are they really bits of St Andrew?' said Kate.

'We believe so.'

'We, as in . . . ?' said Connor.

'As in the Catholic Church,' said the man. 'I'm the priest here, Father William.'

'I'm Connor and this is my lovely sister, Kate. Care for a drink, Father?' Connor offered the bottle to the priest, who shook his head.

'And what brings you to see these old bones?' he asked.

'Him,' said Kate, pointing at Connor.

'I thought it would be good to see them,' said Connor. 'Today and everything. I thought there would have been more interest on St Andrew's Day.'

'I suppose,' said the priest, 'but we're happy enough to look after them whatever their wider appeal.'

'So you consider them a Catholic treasure rather than a national treasure, do you?' Connor took a last swig from his bottle and wiped his mouth with the back of his sleeve. Father William eyed him thoughtfully.

'Both, son,' he said slowly. 'I take it you're not of the faith?'

'No, but I am of the nation.'

'What's that supposed to mean?' said Kate.

'Fuck knows.' Connor turned to the priest. 'Sorry. No offence.'

'None taken,' said Father William. 'I think I'll leave you to it. No rest for the wicked and all that.' He gave Connor a measured look.

'I hope you find what you're looking for,' he said, picking up the stepladder and heading off.

'Almost a U2 quote,' said Kate. 'Scary. What next, someone quoting Abba at us? The winner takes it all?'

'There's nothing wrong with Abba, Kate.'

Connor put on a comedy pout for her benefit. Kate looked at him closely for a second.

'Connor, why do you always assume that you're right and everybody else is wrong?'

'Because I'm an egocentric, introspective, self-absorbed, narrow-minded bigot?' he said cheerfully, getting up sharply and heading down the aisle. 'At least, that's what my therapist says.'

'You don't have a therapist,' said Kate, turning away from the bones. 'You could do with one, though.'

'Pub!' shouted Connor, making the praying girls jump. 'Sorry!' he cried, then opened the doors and was outside.

When Kate caught up he was standing on the church steps, looking at the building's Gothic façade. The roar of traffic on the Greenside roundabout filled their ears. The last rays of weak sunlight had disappeared and the cars had their headlights and windscreen wipers on.

Kate turned to follow Connor's gaze. Hanging from the front of the cathedral was a large banner with the words:

ACT JUSTLY

LOVE TENDERLY

WALK HUMBLY.

'Good advice,' shouted Connor over the noise. 'I'll need to nick it for a song.' He got the leaflet and a pen out his pocket and scribbled for a moment.

'Right,' he said. 'It's quite definitely time for a drink. Let's meet the others.'

★

The Barony was dead. Two Australian girls in matching black polo necks, bar aprons and neat ponytails stood at the end of the bar, arranging cutlery into paper napkins. The coal fire at the back was nearly out, and the scatter of wooden tables around the L-shaped room contained some studiously casual twentysomething and thirtysomething slackers, too old to be young, too young to be old.

Hannah was walking to the bar as Connor and Kate came in, her small frame revealed in a tight T-shirt, suede skirt and boots, her bobbed red hair pulled away from her face on one side by a kirby grip. She was two years older than them, but her petite body and sweetly relaxed features made her look a good deal younger.

'Hiya, babe,' said Connor, kissing her on the cheek. 'You getting them in?'

'Looks like it. What you after?'

'Gin and tonic? Stretch to a double?'

'Suppose so.' Hannah turned to Kate. 'The usual?'

Kate nodded.

'Danny's round the corner,' said Hannah, and Connor sauntered off. 'What have you been up to?' she asked Kate.

'Don't ask. He's in one of those moods. Plus he's half-cut already.'

Hannah pressed her lips into a line and paid for the drinks.

At the table Danny was swigging the last of his pint. The glass seemed lost in the unruly growth of his dark beard. He was wearing a zip-up hoody, tatty black combats and a pair of beat-up Golas, and he smiled as he spotted Connor.

'Hey, big man,' said Connor, slapping him on the back. 'How's it going?'

'Sound,' said Danny in a low Belfast rumble. 'What's happening?'

'Me and Kate have just been seeing the sights, getting in the mood and all that.' Connor sat down and the girls brought the drinks over. 'We should probably have a toast,' he said, scraping his stool forwards and leaning in over the table. 'To The Ossians, a successful third EP and a cracking fortnight of adventure on the open road.'

They clinked glasses and started discussing how they'd each wangled time off work for the tour. As a teacher Hannah had the most trouble, resorting to two weeks' unpaid leave from Marchmont High. Kate was using up valuable holiday days from her engineering job at an avionics company, while Danny had just jacked in his crappy temp programming job, hoping to pick up something else when they got back.

Connor was drumming on the table absent-mindedly. His home-made bottle of gin mix had loosened his headache, eased the pressure and created a warm glow in his chest, but the drink in front of him wasn't nearly strong enough.

He looked at the other three round the table. His sister, girlfriend and best friend – the perfect set-up for a band. He wondered how they'd get along, being on the road together for the next fourteen days. The other three had been dubious when he said they were touring the north of the country, but he'd insisted. They'd played Edinburgh, Glasgow and London to death, and he was sick of it. He wanted to see what else was out there. He'd only ever lived in the dead-end fishing town of Arbroath and here in the capital. The trip ahead would be a real life experience, Scotland was out there to be discovered. How many people think they know their country, when nine-tenths of it lie outside their experience? He'd had twenty-four years of pampered, middle-class living, with scarcely a story to tell down the pub. No wonder he got depressed. A year studying maths at Edinburgh University had ended in disillusion, and since then there had been a bunch of useless jobs. Pubs, a library, a museum and now he worked in a poxy little record shop, dealing all day with skinny indie kids in tight tank tops until he felt like ramming Belle and Sebastian CDs down their annoying throats. He sure as shit wasn't going to miss that place for the next two weeks.

He'd been in plenty bands before, of varying incompetence, but things seemed different with The Ossians. In the last two years they'd steadily built up a following around the toilet circuit of central Scotland, and they'd worked the MySpace thing cleverly, too. Their first two EPs received critical acclaim – journalists liked them but they sold squat.

This third record would be the breakthrough. The *St Andrew's*

Day EP was a leap forward. The band were finally beginning to sound like he always imagined they could. Record companies from down south were showing interest, requesting meetings and details of forthcoming gigs. But Connor wasn't going to bite at the first hook. Let those London bastards come up here, see what we're about. If they want us to move south, they can get to fuck. This is a band with character and independence, not some bunch of Scottish, kowtowing London-industry arse-lickers, the likes of which were ten a penny in the fucking charts. They would succeed or fail on their own terms. Let the A&R guys come, waving chequebooks and buying dinner, and let's see who ends up getting their own way.

At the table, Danny was asking him a question.

'Sorry?'

'When's soundcheck?'

'Not till six,' said Connor, downing his drink and standing up. 'Still time for a wee snifter. Same again?'

Feedback squalled around the Liquid Room until Hannah stamped on her scuffy yellow Boss overdrive pedal. A faint electric hum continued to buzz around the room. Connor approached his microphone, shielding his eyes as each bank of lights flashed in turn.

'Sounds fine up here,' he said to the loose-limbed, afro-haired kid in a Mogwai T-shirt behind the mixing desk. 'Can I get a bit more of Kate's vocal through the monitor, and that's it.'

'OK,' said the engineer. 'You wanna try another one?'

'Not arsed,' said Connor. 'Anyone else?'

The rest of the band shook their heads, and the four of them downed their instruments and wandered off as the support band lugged their amps and guitars onstage. Doors opened in an hour. Hannah checked her watch and followed the rest as they walked out the back door to the Portakabin that served as their dressing room. That was a pretty slick soundcheck, she thought, compared to some of the shambolic efforts they'd had in the past. Her AC30 might be a beast to lug about, and it was a pain in the arse buying new valves every time one blew, but Vox knew how to make amps, all right, and it sounded great onstage, creating a warm, throbby sound when she played her faithful, scuffed old burgundy Gibson SG through it.

Inside the Portakabin, a gas fire flickered uncertainly and a large fridge in the corner thrummed. Zebra-stripe fur covered the walls and a small, rickety table was spread with sandwiches, a bottle of Jack Daniel's and a bottle of gin. The fridge was stacked with lager, Coke and tonic water. Kate and Danny got themselves beers and slumped into a threadbare sofa in the corner where Danny started to skin up, while Connor went to fix himself and Hannah drinks.

The door opened and a short, sturdy, stubble-headed man wearing a black denim jacket and jeans bustled in waving a handful of paper at them. He had an air of comic menace, like a spoof East End hardman. Paul was their manager. He'd come to Edinburgh ten years ago as a stand-up comedian at the Fringe and never left. These days he ran a promotions company, but still liked to put on a show, even in a zebra-stripe dressing room.

'People,' he declared in a thick London accent. 'Don't ever say that Paul doesn't look after you. I have here a schedule covering the next two weeks.'

The four of them raised their eyebrows.

'Schedule?' said Danny. 'Oooh, la-de-da.'

'Shut it, Irish fuck,' said Paul.

'Northern Irish fuck to you.'

'Whatever, you'll be praising me in a fortnight when everything's gone smoothly and you haven't even had to scratch your arsehole for yourself. All gigs, accommodation, travel, riders, support bands, interviews, payments and piss stops have been sorted.'

He handed out sheets, which they scanned casually. There were ten gigs in fourteen days on a route which saw them skirting round the country anticlockwise.

'Any questions?'

'We finish in Glasgow on Friday the thirteenth?' said Danny. 'Nice touch.'

'Where the hell is Durness, and what exactly are we going to do there?' said Kate.

'Northwest tip of the country. It's a long drive from Thurso to Ullapool, so I thought we should break it up. I've been up that way a couple of times – bleak bastarding landscape. Still, it's what your man wanted.' Paul gestured to Connor. 'His odyssey of self-discovery into redneck, pig-squealing country, or whatever it is. Anyway, all the gigs seem solid enough, there are good local supports to boost numbers, and we're getting decent money.'

'Sounds great,' said Connor. 'We get to see our own country, find out what the fuck's out there, and get paid for the privilege, right?'

'We should come out with a tidy profit,' said Paul. 'Oh, and while I remember, I've had half a dozen guarantees that London labels are sending people up to the Glasgow gig, and a couple are meant to be coming tonight as well. Which should mean that maybe, if we're lucky, one fucker will bother his arse. Whatever, just make the most of these gigs to get up to ramming speed, so you can blow their bollocks off on the thirteenth.'

Paul's mobile started ringing and he flipped it open as he strode out the door, waving as he left. Danny sparked up his joint, took a toke and passed it to Kate as they started chatting about the tour schedule.

'How you doing, honey?' said Hannah, approaching Connor at the drinks table.

'Fine.' Connor pressed the heel of his hand into his eye socket.

'You don't look fine,' said Hannah, massaging his shoulder. 'Is it another headache? I told you to go to the doctor. Christ, I hate nagging you, but you've got to look after yourself. You can't go pissing off round the country with splitting headaches and insomnia.'

'I'll be OK,' he said, taking a swig from his plastic cup.

'That's not helping.'

'Fucking hell, love, give it a rest. Everyone drinks.'

'Not like you.'

'I'm the troubled artist, amn't I?' said Connor, wagging a finger. 'The old Cobain syndrome, nobody understands my torment and all that pish.'

'Don't joke about it,' said Hannah, letting go of his shoulder. 'Don't even joke about it.'

Hannah stood there as Connor downed his gin, gave her a quick kiss and turned to fix another drink. He was drinking too much, but she didn't know what to do about it. They all drank a lot, a shitload in fact, but he drank differently. They all relaxed when they got pissed, but Connor only became tighter and tighter with every gin. She would have to keep an eye on him on this tour, as per usual.

The Liquid Room was typical of Edinburgh's sprawling, labyrinthine Old Town, full of old stone nooks, crannies and cubbyholes. A recent makeover failed to hide the centuries of damp that permeated the dingy, subterranean club.

It was filling up. Connor and Danny stood outside the open loading doors to the side of the stage, smoking an alfresco joint and watching the support band. The Hydraulics were a gang of pale-skinned, teenage glamour pusses with backcombed hair, spangly Danelectro guitars and self-righteous anger as their weapons of choice. It all screamed early Manics to Connor but he liked them, they were supremely confident despite a lack of talent. They ended in the obligatory shriek of feedback, contemptuously eyed up the crowd, and strutted off as if it was Wembley Arena. Connor laughed, took a last drag from the joint, flicked the roach in the gutter and headed backstage. Danny looked miffed at not getting a final toke but followed Connor without saying anything.

The Ossians played a stormer. Connor teetered on the brink of being shapelessly drunk and incoherent during their fifty-minute set, but held it together. Through the gin haze, he stared out at the five-hundred-strong crowd, soaking up the admiring looks. For some reason his attention kept being drawn back to one particular face, a young guy at the far edge of the crowd, half-shrouded in darkness. Connor thought he recognised him to begin with, then smiled as he realised that in the half-light the kid actually looked a bit like himself. A younger, taller, thinner version of him. Jesus, they were even modelling how they looked on him – that was fucking scary. He looked again later in the set, but the face was gone. Around him, the rest of the band pushed the songs into vibrant new shapes in a show that was edgy and wired, with The Ossians always just in control. Danny was a clattering maelstrom of rhythmic energy at the back as he battered away on the vintage white marine pearl Ludwig kit he'd bagged dirt cheap at a car boot from a fellow drummer who had no idea what he was selling. He and Kate made a perfect rhythm section, Kate sauntering about with her sunburst Gibson Firebird bass like she owned the place, when she wasn't helping Connor out with vocals. But it wasn't all full-on rock attitude, the band could do quiet and atmospheric as well as bash out killer riffs. They finished with a relaxed stroll through 'My Evil Twin', the simple country melody and sweet harmonies belying the dark humour of the lyrics. Connor gently strummed his black Tele, the sound shimmering as it resonated from his Fender Twin Reverb, while he and Kate shared a microphone. Hannah, abandoning her usual guitar to knock out hypnotic little lines on a noddy eighties Casiotone keyboard, drifted off into her own wee world, while at the back Danny put down his sticks, slugged on his pint and slapped a set of sleigh bells in time. The crowd loved it.

Afterwards, Connor hung about out front, taking slaps on the back, pretending to be modest about the attention but secretly lapping up every indulgent second. He was bought drinks at the bar, doubles on his own insistence. The rest of the band came out from a brief rest backstage and the praise renewed. Shy teenage boys hovered a distance away from Hannah and Kate, besotted and scared. The girl fans were much more brash, rushing up and kissing Connor, asking him to sign CDs, all exposed midriffs and cleavages. Connor looked awkwardly at Hannah, who just smiled. She didn't mind, it was innocent enough. She had plenty of worries where Connor was concerned, but infidelity wasn't one of them.

Looking around, she noticed a couple of familiar faces in the crowd from fifth and sixth year at Marchmont High. Some were underage drinkers, but she couldn't be bothered worrying about it. She got grief when she first started teaching, mostly from bitchy girls who felt threatened by her looks, but when they found out she played guitar in a band that wasn't lame, grudging respect took over. She wasn't back in the classroom for the next fortnight, so she could forget about all that shit for now. When she was up on that stage, she felt like a different person playing the guitar, the history-teacher part of her subsumed completely. But then, that's why she did it, wasn't it?

A Franz Ferdinand classic kicked in over the PA and the dance floor began to fill. The Ossians found a padded leather booth and sat down.

'Well?' said Hannah.

'Fucking great or what?' said Danny. 'That was one of the best we've ever played, easy.'

'Yeah, it was pretty cool,' said Kate, smiling.

'It was good, right enough,' said Connor. 'A great start to a fucking brilliant tour.' He looked at Hannah, touching her hand on the table. 'What were you on, love? What was that solo in "RLS" all about? You went off on one. And the end bit of "Justified Sinner", too. Fucking superb.' He kissed Hannah's cheek and she smiled.

'Maybe she was just trying to keep up with you, Mister Unpredictable,' said Danny. 'You were all over the place tonight.'

'But in a good way,' said Connor. 'Just keeping everyone on their toes. Right, I'm off for a single fish.' He looked at Hannah. 'And I'm having a dance when I get back, OK?'

He headed to the Gents, pushed open the heavy door and went into one of the two cubicles. He finished pissing, zipped up and took a speed wrap out his pocket. He licked his finger and stuck it in the speed then sucked it clean, repeating the move four times before folding the wrap up and sticking it in his pocket.

As he came out the cubicle he was grabbed by a massive pair of bear mitts and thrown hard against the far wall, banging his head against the cold tiles.

'What the fuck?' he said, shaking his head. In front of him was a tiny man, not much more than five feet, with a bald head and heavily creased face. Behind him loomed a big bastard mountain of a guy, rubbing his hands together like a kid eagerly awaiting his dinner.

'Nick, I was going to come see you tomorrow,' said Connor to the smaller guy. 'Honestly, I just had to get this gig out the way then . . .'

The short man held up a hand gently as if trying to flag a bus.

'Save it, Con,' he said in a high-pitched Highland accent. 'You're just embarrassing us all with that bullshit. We both know you've been avoiding me, and we both know why. The little matter of thirteen hundred quid for drugs which, I assume, you either gave away when you were cunted, or just took yourself, with no intention of ever paying me back. It's my own fault, of course. I should never have let you run up a fucking tab. Stupid really.'

'I've got the money, Nick, I just need to get it . . .'

Nick held up his hand again, this time gesturing slightly to the big lump of meat behind him, who strode forwards.

'Shug, wait . . .' said Connor as the big guy punched him square in the face, making his head crack off the tiled wall again.

'Jesus fucking Christ,' said Connor, holding his nose. Blood seeped through his fingers.

'Hold your head back,' said the big guy in a friendly voice, handing Connor a tissue. 'And pinch the bridge of the nose, that helps stop the bleeding.'

'Listen to Shug, he knows what he's talking about.'

'Fucking cheers,' said Connor through his hands, but tilting his head back nevertheless.

'Now,' said Nick. 'What are we going to do about this debt?'

Connor kept quiet. Pain throbbed back and forth across his face and his forehead as he dabbed at his nose and lip with the tissue.

'Initially, I was just going to have Shug here put you in hospital, teach you a fucking lesson,' continued Nick. 'But then as I was scooting around the Internet I read on your site that you were planning a tour of the Highlands. A quick email exchange with your helpful manager gave me the details. Which led to an idea. I need to conduct certain transactions, as it were, outside Edinburgh, but I'm having trouble moving around at the moment, because those twats at Drug Enforcement are watching me. The transactions I'm talking about aren't exactly legal. I'm sure you understand. For a while I've been wondering how to get round that. You see where this is going, don't you? Suddenly here was good old Connor, who happened to owe me quite a lot of money, and who also happened to be in a band about to tour round Scotland. So I thought, why don't I get you to conduct these transactions for me? No cunt suspects you of anything, except being a gobby wee shite, and the tour is the perfect cover. So. What do you think so far?'

'I'm not getting involved in any fucking drug deals,' said Connor, his head still tilted back. 'Are you mental?'

Out of the corner of his eye Connor saw Nick signal again to Shug, but before he could prepare himself he felt a powerful fist to his stomach, knocking the wind out of him and making him double up.

'Sorry,' said Shug.

Just then the toilet door opened and a gangly student came in. Nick stared at him, blocking his path. The student quickly took in the situation, turned and left without a word. Connor was still trying to get his breath back, wheezing a little as he tried to get air into his lungs.

'Don't be an arsehole all your life,' said Nick. 'All I'm asking is that you take care of a wee bit of business for me, and we'll write off that money you owe.'

Connor saw Nick's hands move, and looked up from his crouched position to see a Stanley knife pointed at him. The wee nutjob had arrived in Edinburgh a few years back from somewhere up north, and had started working the door with Shug at one venue or another. Like all these shortarse hardmen, Nick was the psycho of the pair, but somehow it was Shug who did the donkeywork. Pretty soon Nick realised that dealing a bit on the side at clubs and gigs could double the money they earned as bouncers, and gradually the dealing took over, until eventually the pair went into it full-time. Connor had been buying off Nick on the sly for over a year now, without the rest of the band knowing. He knew Nick well enough to know he would use that fucking knife if it came to it.

'I don't think you have much choice,' said Nick.

Connor looked at Nick and the knife for a few moments in silence. 'I don't suppose I do,' he said eventually.

'Good,' said Nick, smiling and putting the knife away. 'So here, take this.'

Shug took a small army surplus kitbag off his shoulder and slung it at Connor.

'Inside are four packages,' said Nick. 'Each one has got written on it who it's for, and where you'll meet them. There's also a mobile in there. Keep it on you and switched on at all times. The folk you're dealing with will get in touch before each deal. And I'll be keeping tabs on you as well. At each drop they'll exchange packages with you. Just bring me back what they give you. Think you can manage that?'

'Jesus,' said Connor.

'Is that Jesus yes, no worries, Nick. Or Jesus, no fucking way, I'm a fucking moron and I can't even tie my own shoelaces?'

Connor looked from Nick to Shug then back again.

'Jesus yes, no worries, Nick.'

'Good. Now just to show that I'm not totally heartless, here's a little something for your trouble.' Nick pulled a plastic bag of white powder out a pocket and threw it at Connor. 'Speed. You're not worth coke, and I know you prefer the cheap shit anyway. Consider it an extra wee bonus to keep you going on the road. One last thing, don't be tempted to open any of the packages. I find out that anything's missing, or any of these deals have gone tits up, and you'd better never show your sorry fucking face in Edinburgh again. Understand?'

Connor nodded as he pocketed the speed and shouldered the kitbag. The blood was still dribbling slightly from his nose, but he felt a little better.

'Right,' said Nick, 'I think that concludes our business. Remember, keep the phone on, I'll be checking in from time to time, OK?'

Nick opened the toilet door and headed out. Shug went to follow, then turned back at the doorway.

'Nice gig, by the way,' he said. 'Great band.'

'Thanks,' said Connor as Shug left. He waited in the toilets a few minutes, touching his nose tentatively, and wondering what the fuck he'd just got himself into, then made his way out into the sweaty darkness of the venue. When he reached the table he could tell by the looks he was getting that his nose hadn't stopped bleeding.

'What the fuck happened to you?' said Danny.

'Just a wee altercation in the bogs,' he said, nonchalantly sliding the kitbag under the table. No one seemed to notice, their attention drawn to his bloody face. He waved his hands around and tried to smile. A little blood dripped into his mouth.

'Christ's sake,' said Hannah. 'What kind of altercation?'

'Just some punter had a problem with something I said onstage.'

Hannah passed him a tissue which he held to his nose.

'You think we should get this looked at?' she said.

'Don't be daft, it's just a bloody nose,' said Connor. 'Anyway, we've got partying to do.'

Paul came over to the table, clearing a way through the crowd for a lanky, spindly young man in an expensive leather jacket, the pair talking as they came.

'Jesus, been chasing parked cars again?' said Paul, looking at Connor's face.

The beginning of a black eye was already visible, and a trickle of blood lay just under Connor's swollen nose. He discovered that his upper lip was bleeding, and he sucked the ferric taste into his mouth.

'Danny gets upset when I muck about with arrangements on-stage,' he said smiling at Paul, then Danny, who just shook his head.

'Anyway,' said Paul, 'this is Jerry Gould, he's the A&R for K2 records, flown up specially to see you.'

The man offered a thin, cautious hand to Connor, who shook it aggressively, then he nodded acknowledgements to the rest of them. He seemed nervous and excited.

'I thought you guys rocked!' he said. 'I mean, totally fucking rocked. I've got the three EPs and they're great and everything, but The Ossians are just amazing live, really.'

'Thanks,' said Hannah. 'Glad you liked it.'

Paul butted in. 'Jerry says K2 are very interested in working with The Ossians. He's bringing the label boss up for the Glasgow gig.'

'He's not really like a big boss,' said Jerry. 'He's just a guy, you know? I'm definitely going to recommend that we sign you, but he always likes to see what's going on for himself. When he sees you in Glasgow, he'll be fucking blown away. It's just his kind of thing – music with bollocks, but also with brains. I can't wait to hear what else you've got coming up.'

'The next EP's already half-written,' said Connor, fidgeting with the bag strap under the table. 'It's called *Argentina '78* and it's about Scottish national identity.'

'First we've heard about it,' said Kate.

'It's a work in progress.'

'I think we need to talk about shit like that,' said Kate, 'before you go shooting your mouth off.'

'Easy,' said Paul. 'Jerry's just saying that K2 are totally into the band.'

'Look, I'll leave you guys to it,' said Jerry, as Paul placed an arm on his shoulder and gently angled him away from the table. 'But we'll talk more at the Glasgow gig, yeah? And you can meet the boss. It's been good talking to you.'

'Yeah, good meeting you, Jerry,' said Connor sarcastically, but Jerry and Paul were already out of earshot. He turned to the table. 'What about him, eh? What a corporate fucking dicksplash.'

'What's your problem?' said Kate, glaring. 'He was just saying he liked us. You seem to be happy enough taking praise off fifteen-year-old girls, but not grown men who work for record labels.'

'I just didn't trust him.'

'You only spoke to him for two bloody seconds, what are you on about? You've got some serious problems dealing with people, you know that?'

'I deal with you lot OK, don't I?'

'I wouldn't ask that if I were you,' said Kate. 'And anyway, we know what you're like. We're used to it. I'm not sure the wider world is ready for your little quirks.'

Connor was desperate to look inside the bag. He assumed he was carrying drugs or money, or maybe both, but who knew with Nick Simpson? That guy was fucking trouble, and now Connor was up to his arse in the shit along with him. Jesus. He needed a drink.

'Whose round is it?'

'Mine,' said Danny, raising his bulk out the booth. 'Same again?'

Connor took Hannah by the hand. He had to try and calm down.

'Right, about that dance we were going to have,' he said.

'Are you asking?'

'I'm asking.'

'Then I suppose I'm dancing.'

Even at four o'clock on a winter morning, the sky above Edinburgh wasn't dark. Bulging orange clouds raced overhead, bouncing streetlight back down to earth as the leafless trees in the Meadows swayed hesitantly.

A stream of drunk people headed through the park down Jawbone Walk, away from the city centre. A trio of girls in short skirts were clinging to each other and singing Kylie. Two teenage boys stood by a large cherry tree, one resting his hand on the other's back as his friend puked up the night's intake. Over to the west a Gothic church spire split the purple edge of sky, as eerie white steam from the breweries drifted upwards behind it.

The five of them made their way home like twigs in the stream of people around them. Danny and Kate walked arm in arm sharing a bag of chips, while Hannah toked a joint alongside. Behind them Connor and Paul were propping each other up and moving as much sideways as forwards.

Connor felt peaceful. His headache was gone and his face had stopped hurting. He felt his lip with his tongue, it was swollen and raw but there was no pain for now. He saw his sister, best friend and girlfriend up ahead and felt a skelf of love jab his heart. He knew exactly how to wind them all up and could never resist doing so. They'd come to expect this, which made him subconsciously conjure up new ways of pissing them off.

He knew he drank too much, but he didn't have a drink problem.

It became a problem when you couldn't handle it, right? When it was affecting your life and your relationships for the worse? All his mates got drunk all the time, just like him. Kate had told him recently that he didn't drink for fun. He was having fun now, wasn't he? She'd also accused him of thinking too much. How the hell do you think too much? That's like saying you breathe too much. But then you *can* hyperventilate. So could you hyperthink? Better to think too much than too little. He realised he was thinking about it too much.

'What're you thinking, Boy Wonder?' Paul whispered loudly.

'Just thinking about thinking too much.'

'Eh?'

'Something Kate said.'

'She's dead right, you do think too much.' Paul squinted at Connor. 'Hey, have you always had that bag?'

Connor clutched the kitbag closer to his shoulder. When they'd got chucked out the Liquid Room at closing he'd almost forgotten about it hidden under the table, which would've been a fantastic way of fucking up this whole ridiculous thing before it even got started. He was desperate to look inside. He felt nervous carrying it, keen to get home and stash it safely. Up until now, the rest of them had been too drunk to notice him carrying it.

'Yeah,' he said. 'Got my guitar shit in it – leads, pedals and stuff. Plus my lyric notebooks. Didn't want to risk leaving them in the van overnight.'

Paul shrugged. Connor looked across the park at the steeple needling the sky. Patches of low cloud sped overhead but beyond that he couldn't see the moon or stars.

'That's the problem with this fucking city,' he said, pointing upwards. Paul followed his finger.

'What, the sky?'

'See the stars?'

Paul stumbled forwards.

'No.'

'Exactly. Sometimes you just want to look at the stars, don't you? But you can't cos of all this fucking streetlighting everywhere.

If you go to the countryside the sky's jam-packed with fucking stars, but here you can't see shit. All those alien civilisations millions of light years away, and what do we do? Block it all out. What if they're trying to contact us right now, and we can't detect it because of some stupid fucking street lamp? How shit would that be?'

'You think that's happening?'

'Probably. How the fuck would we know? That's the real reason I want to get out of here – to see the stars. To see millions of years into the past. To see all those other fucked-up worlds and find out if they're as useless as we are. Fucking streetlights.'

He lashed out a foot and booted the bottom of the light they were passing. It rattled a little. Something caught Connor's eye – a black, shadowy shape on the unlit grass moving parallel to them.

'What's that?'

'Just a dog,' said Paul, following Connor's gaze.

'Looks more like a big cat to me,' said Connor. 'There are loads of big-cat sightings in Scotland, you know.'

'Yeah, but not in the Meadows,' said Paul. 'That's up in the mountains and shit.'

The dark figure turned and paced alongside the path twenty feet away. It came forwards, its quick feet and flat, downward tail flickering at the edge of the shadows as it was exposed. A fox. It stood and looked at them for a second before trotting off towards some nearby bins.

'Maybe we'll see some wild animals up north,' said Connor. 'Lions and tigers and bears, oh my!'

'I don't know what you think this tour is going to be like,' said Paul. 'Scotland's not exactly a fucking jungle. What are you expecting, a bloody safari?'

They were walking under the arch at the bottom of the path, heading towards the Marchmont Road flat that Connor, Hannah and Danny rented between them. The arch was twelve feet high and made of a whale's jawbone. It had stood there for a hundred and fifty years and it looked worn and tired.

'Reckon this is the real Moby Dick?' said Connor, slapping the bone. 'Old Father Abraham, or whatever his name was, searching all those years for the white whale and here it is, sitting at the arse end of a park in Edinburgh, rotting away and no one gives a flying fuck.'

'Father Abraham was with the Smurfs,' said Paul. 'You mean Captain Ahab.'

'That's what this tour is, our search for Moby Dick,' said Connor as they closed on the other three. 'You think I'll make a good Captain Ahab?'

'Didn't Captain Ahab die?' said Paul. 'You'd be better off as Father Abraham.'

'Come on, there's more bevvying to be done,' said Danny as they left the Meadows. He looked at Connor and cocked his head sideways. 'Hey, you always had that bag?'

'Yeah,' said Connor. Fuck's sake, he thought.

'What have you two been talking about?' said Hannah, falling back in line with Connor and Paul.

'The stars, big cats and Moby Dick,' said Connor.

'And the Smurfs,' said Paul.

'Just the usual, then?' said Hannah. She leant in, kissed Connor softly on his swollen lip and passed him the remains of a joint.

'Yeah,' said Connor. 'And we're not even properly stoned. Yet.'

2

South Queensferry

'Beacon, guide us through the winter dark
Linger in our souls, cling around our hearts'

The Ossians, 'RLS'

Connor woke with his hands folded across his chest like an Egyptian mummy in a tomb. Thin light filtered through the curtains giving the room a washed-out, fuzzy look. He'd thrown the duvet off in his sleep, and Hannah lay curled up next to him in black pants, her pale knee bent over his leg, her head nuzzling into his shoulder. He looked at the clock. 10:33 blinked at him. He'd slept for two hours.

A siren sounded far away and quickly faded, leaving only the sound of Hannah's breathing and the faint peal of church bells. He felt crushingly tired, yet couldn't sleep. He hadn't slept well for months now, and in the morning sometimes felt like he was encased in a coffin of cotton wool.

He was still drunk, stoned and speeding. He reached for a half-smoked joint in the ashtray next to the bed, lit it and inhaled. He looked at Hannah. Her sedate face was more human than anything he'd seen in the mirror recently. She'd always had a sense of calm; that was one of the reasons he was drawn to her. They'd met five years ago, when he was nineteen and she'd just turned twenty-one. Inevitably, it was at a gig – The Twilight Singers at the Venue. Connor was standing at the bar when he noticed her. Her red hair was longer then and her face slightly sharper, but her eyes were just as bright and her body just as tightly packed.

'Do you fancy him?' he said.

'What?'

'I was just asking if you fancied him,' he said, pointing at the stage. 'Greg Dulli?'

'Yeah,' she laughed. 'Do you?'

'Of course. How could you not?'

He bought her a drink, they got talking, she bought him a drink back. Later they danced and drank and discovered they were both in bands, and split an E between them. Later still, at a party in someone's flat, they spent several hours on a sofa with their noses almost touching, discussing which parts of their own bodies they disliked most, comparing them and laughing. By the morning they were buying trainers on Princes Street, spaced through lack of sleep, their eccy comedown and the new rush of feelings. He still wore the trainers.

Connor looked at her now in bed. Before he'd met Hannah he'd never gone for older women, but with her it was different straight away. OK, there were only two years in it, but at that age two years still seemed a big deal. Hannah had always been more mature, more honest and more purposeful than him. It made perfect sense that she was a teacher now, she'd always instinctively been drawn towards helping others, and good at communicating with kids. Some of that was no doubt down to growing up with a much younger stepsister and stepbrother. That was another thing – her resilience. She was an only child stuck in the middle of a divorce when she was ten, yet she'd never taken sides, and always got along with both her parents and their new partners. Her mum had chucked her dad out of their Leith Walk flat after one too many disastrous drunken gambling sessions but, following a spell inside, her dad had cleaned up, got his shit together, found a new woman and even held down a steady job. Her mum, meanwhile, had hooked up with a lecturer at the further education college where she worked as secretary, moved to a colony flat in Leith Links, and had two more kids. Hannah took it all in her stride. She was the first from either side of the family to go to college or uni, and her parents were immensely proud of that fact. She was faintly embarrassed by their enthusiasm, but at the same time kind of proud of herself, too.

One year of university had been enough to convince Connor that higher education wasn't for him. He'd been a little obsessed with maths at school, all those cryptic sequences, symbols and equations. He thought there might be a key to understanding the world in all that abstract space. He thought that imposing the structure of geometry on the universe might help it make more sense. He could never have expressed any of this, it was just there in the gloomy recesses of his mind, never enough to grab hold of. But hours of dry lectures and blackboard scribbles killed his interest, and he dropped out. Since then his life had been a masterclass in avoiding responsibility. All his jobs had been no-brainers, easy to perform, impossible to care about. Just the way he liked it. The band was the purpose, at least that's what he clung to for now.

He finished the joint, extricated himself from Hannah's limbs, pulled his jeans on and went through to the living room. Out the window it was a beautiful, clear winter day. The frost on the ground was slowly melting in the weak morning sun. He reached under the beaten-up old sofa and pulled out the kitbag he'd stashed when they got in last night. He unzipped it and started looking through the contents. There were three tightly bound packages a little smaller than shoeboxes, each with two words written on them in black marker. He flicked through them. 'Dundee – Jim'; 'Aberdeen – Kenny'; 'Kyle – Susie'. He weighed them in his hand. Definitely drugs, he thought, but what kind? His fingers were itching to tear them open and find out. He put them back in the bag and lifted out a smaller padded envelope with 'Thurso – Gav' written on it. It flexed a little in the middle. Money? How much? He sized it up in his hands for a few moments, then slung it back in the bag. He had a rummage around and pulled out a sleek new mobile. He switched it on. The battery was fully charged. In the address book were only five names – Gav, Jim, Kenny, Nick and Susie – all with mobile numbers. Jesus, this was really happening. He was a fucking drug mule. Unless he didn't go through with it. Unless he just phoned Nick now and told him to get to fuck, he wasn't going to get involved in this bollocks for anyone. But he didn't have the money he owed. And even if he did, Nick wouldn't accept it now. And if he just refused to do it, he had no doubt Nick would chase him down and fucking kill him. He could take the bag to the police. But Nick would surely just deny all knowledge, landing Connor in the shit. And even if they believed him, and somehow nailed something on Nick, it wouldn't be long before he was out again, looking for Connor. He was over a fucking barrel. Jesus. So. Drug mule it was, then.

He put the mobile in his pocket, zipped up the bag and pushed it back under the sofa. He went through to the kitchen to make a start on breakfast. He wasn't hungry, but he knew Hannah would be, and he wanted to have something ready for her.

As he put the bacon under the grill, Hannah appeared in the kitchen doorway in just a short, tatty old Wilco T-shirt, her legs goose-pimpled as she stood watching Connor, who had his back to her, oblivious to her presence.

Hannah recognised the addictive side of Connor's personality as something she'd seen in her dad's shambolic, drunken days down the dog track, the bookies, getting chucked out of casinos and winding up crying on the sofa at home, begging forgiveness. Maybe she hung in there with Connor because she'd seen her dad come through all that bullshit.

He turned as if sensing her.

'Hey, sexy.'

'Hey, sexy, yourself.' Hannah tiptoed in on the cold tiles and kissed him gently on the lips. She tasted the mixture of tobacco and hash from the joint he'd finished. She looked at his face. Apart from the bruising and cuts, there were tired lines criss-crossing his forehead and under his eyes, but despite all that, somehow, he was still a good-looking boy. 'How's that bashed face of yours this morning?'

'Not as bad as it looks.'

'Just as well, cos it looks pretty bad.'

'Thanks.'

'Did I miss much after I went to bed?'

The five of them had sat up for a few hours drinking cheap whisky, skinning up and talking shite, all of them buzzing from the success of the show and looking forward to the tour. Hannah wasn't sure what to expect from the whole thing, and she wasn't convinced about Connor's motives either, but she felt a small thrill thrumming in her belly when she thought about being on the road for two weeks. In the end, Hannah had gone to bed first, leaving Paul crashed out on the sofa and the other three jabbering away about Christ knows what.

'Nothing exciting,' said Connor, cracking an egg into a frying pan. 'Paul was out for the count, and Danny walked Kate home shortly after you went to bed. I had a quick joint for the road and came through. You want coffee with this?'

'I'd love coffee,' said Hannah. 'Bring it back to bed, will you? It's freezing in here.'

'Sure.' Connor watched Hannah skip out the room, his eyes drawn to her arse cheeks poking out from under that old T-shirt. He smiled, shook his head a little and turned back to the cooker.

The Hawes Inn knew how to make money from the past. A chalkboard outside the whitewashed South Queensferry pub declared 'Inn Keeping with Tradition, established 1638'. They were offering a set-price lunch called Robert Louis Stevenson's Choice. Whether Stevenson would really have opted for Caesar salad and lasagne was open to debate.

Inside, the walls were covered with prints of Stevenson and Walter Scott, alongside photographs of both Forth bridges under construction. A small red lamp hung in each window, partially blocking the extraordinary views over the firth. Swirls of flowery red dominated the carpets, chairs and curtains, and a thin aquamarine wash coloured the walls. Every few minutes the rumble of a train on the bridge overhead was like a grumbling, ghostly reminder of the past.

Connor, Hannah and Kate sat at a table while Danny got the drinks. Connor smiled as he looked out the window. This place was perfect, he thought. A boozer with literary tradition dating back three hundred and seventy years, where some of the greats of Scottish writing had hung out, and now it was habituated by anodyne Sunday-driving families and aimless, lonely travellers. It felt a bit like those fake pubs you got in airports, he thought. The only difference was the view.

Outside, the *Maid of the Forth* bobbed uncertainly on its moorings, clanking occasionally against a jetty. Small gulls huddled on the swirling, murky waters of the estuary, hunched into the wind and looking as if they'd rather be anywhere but there. Their tiny bodies rose and fell helplessly in the swell of brothy water that bubbled into froth as it hit the shore.

Behind the ferry, stretching ominously into the distance, was the overbearing figure of the Forth rail bridge. The massive structure was like a giant rusty snake that's swallowed three eggs, stretching its body in and out of the incessant wash, its continual degradation from the onslaught of wind and wave covered by patches of clumsy scaffolding, rough bandages wrapped around the snake's underbelly.

To the left was the sleeker presence of the road bridge. Like a scale model of the Golden Gate Bridge, the sorry, pale construction looked like it knew it was a poor imitation of a grander design. Connor smiled again as he thought of all the clumsy metaphors he could drop into the interview about to take place. He imagined the journalist rolling his eyes as he thought he had another pretentious rock musician on his hands, not realising that Connor was one step ahead, playing him and the media at their own game. Or was he? Playing them at their own game was still playing the game, wasn't it? Connor massaged his brow as he felt himself sobering up and grains of speed disappearing from his bloodstream. Thinking too much. He was getting himself tied up in knots. Where was Danny with the drinks? Danny appeared on cue, clutching two pints and two shorts.

'First drink of the day,' he said. 'Sun's past the yardarm, so you're all safe from becoming alkies.'

'Where's this journalist?' said Hannah. 'Don't tell me we're actually on time for once.'

'Nope, he's just later than us,' said Connor. 'How unprofessional. I must remember to write a letter of complaint to the editor.'

Just then a slight man about their age approached the table. He had a long thin neck that made it look as if his head could flop off at any minute, and he wore thick-framed, oblong glasses, a stripy work shirt and a tank top with a diamond pattern on it. He looked like he'd get blown away in a breeze.

'The Ossians, I assume,' he said, holding out his hand.

'How could you tell?' said Connor, looking round the pub. The place was full of young families, old folks and a handful of Mondeo-driving couples in matching waterproofs, all contemplating the lunch menu. He wondered how many were considering Stevenson's Choice. 'You trying to say we stick out in this homely environment?'

'Exactly,' said the journalist. 'I'm Andy Turnbull from *The Scotsman.*'

'I'm Connor, this is Hannah, Kate and Danny.'

'Pleased to meet you all. I take it you're all right for drinks?' said Andy, scanning the nearly full glasses on the table.

'Double G and T, cheers,' said Connor. 'And get yourself something.'

Andy returned with two glasses, pulled up a chair and started rooting around in a school satchel.

'Right,' he said, 'this is a general piece for the arts section of the paper. It'll be an introduction to The Ossians – how you formed, what you're all about and what you're into. I'm pretty interested in the whole Scottish identity thing, and the fact you're touring up north. I'd also like to chat about what you hope to achieve with this EP, the tour and further ahead in the future. How does that sound?'

'Sounds like you've already worked out what we're going to say,' said Connor.

A smile came over the journalist's face. 'Not at all. Say what you like. That's the whole point.'

He pulled a notebook and a small tape recorder out the satchel, put the machine on the table and started flicking through the pages of the notebook. He switched the machine on and a small red light glowed at them.

'Ready to go?' he said.

'Is a photographer coming?' said Danny.

'Should be here in a while,' said Andy. 'Shutter-monkeys are lazy bastards. He'll get here eventually.'

Danny finished his pint. 'Do you need all of us for this?' he said.

'Up to yourselves,' said Andy. 'I'd prefer at least two of you.'

Danny pushed his chair back and got up.

'I fancy a walk. Anyone else?' He was looking at Kate, but Hannah replied.

'Yeah,' she said. 'Let's leave the siblings to it. We'll see you in a bit.'

She got up, smiled at Kate and Connor, and left with Danny.

'OK,' said Andy, leaning back in his chair. 'Let's start with the unusual band name.'

'Ossian was a third-century Scots Gaelic poet,' said Connor, rubbing his hands as if about to give a lecture. Kate sipped her drink and looked out the window. She knew she wouldn't be speaking much. Connor continued. 'A bunch of his work was discovered by a guy called James Macpherson in the eighteenth century, and published to great acclaim. Napoleon was a big fan. He was described as the Scottish Homer, and I don't mean Simpson.'

'So you're saying you're part of some legacy of Scottish story-telling?'

'Not as simple as that. Most folk thought Macpherson made it all up, and he was discredited as a fake. It's typical of Scotland that our oldest history and literature might not even exist. It might be an eighteenth-century fabrication, like tartan for lowland families. Everywhere you look, Scotland is made up of stupid myths and romantic ideals, most of which are fake, or more likely a mixture of falsehoods and reality. Tartan and shortbread for tourists. Fucking Brigadoon. And this place.' Connor waved a hand around the pub. 'Just a tourist haunt now, whereas once it was a place where our greatest writers hung out.'

'Sounds like you hate Scotland.'

'Not at all.' Connor was getting more animated now, and occasional glances were being thrown in his direction from nearby tables. 'I fucking love being Scottish. But it's that whole corny Jekyll and Hyde thing, isn't it? The dual nature of Scotland, blah, blah, blah. James Hogg and his justified sinner. Scotland's always had this double life, the Deacon Brodie syndrome, so much so that it's a terrible fucking cliché these days. But clichés are clichés because they're true. I just thought Ossian was another side to that. People reinventing an early history of Scotland to give them something to be sentimental about. I see us as part of that schizophrenic heritage.'

'This isn't the kind of stuff you'd expect from a rock band,' said Andy. 'Is it the kind of thing your fans give a toss about?'

'You think we should just stick to "Baby, I love you" or some-thing? People underestimate the intelligence of music fans. We all love a shit-hot guitar riff, but you're allowed to have a brain as well. I love bands that say something about the human condition, bands that are trying to find answers. But it's not as if we spend every waking minute wondering about the nature of our nationality, or what life's all about. We drink and sleep and screw and swear and argue and talk shite like everyone else. And only a couple of our songs are about Scottishness, anyway. There are also songs about relationships, politics, observations, stories, depression, insecurity, joy, happiness, all that pish. The stuff of life, you know?'

'The *St Andrew's Day* EP seems to be in a different league in terms of quality from the first two records, *The City of Dreadful Night* and *RLS*. What are you hoping to achieve with it, and with the tour of the Highlands?'

'It's not about achieving anything. It's just about putting our music out there, hoping to entertain people and make them think a bit more than they did before. We like telling stories and we like loud guitars and we like making people think about their lives. As for the tour, why not go up north? Apart from anything else, we'll be following in the footsteps of James Macpherson – maybe we'll unearth our own semi-fabricated Scottish legend, who knows? I'll let you into a secret, Andy, I've never been further north than Aberdeen before, in my own country for fuck's sake, and frankly I'm disgusted with myself. There are things to experience, places to see and people to meet up there, just the same as anywhere else in the world. It's always the stuff on your doorstep that you never notice. Like this place – I've lived in Edinburgh for five years and I've never been here before. How many people spend their whole lives in Edinburgh and never even see the sea close up? Look at that bridge out there. The sea, the sky and the coastline, the smell of salt air and the sound of trains overhead. It's living, you know? Experience.'

Connor was shouting and waving. People were looking at their table. He stopped to catch his breath.

'How about another drink?' he said.

'Yeah, sure,' said Andy. Kate nodded and Connor went to the bar.

'Is he always like this?' said Andy.

'Pretty much.'

'And you're twins.'

'For our sins.'

'How is that? I mean, how do you get along?'

'We argue all the time,' said Kate. 'He acts up, I slag him off. And round it goes. Just the usual brother–sister shit.'

'Is there tension in the band, then?'

'Probably a lot less than in other bands, because we know each other so well. It might be Connor coming up with ideas for songs, but the rest of us back him one hundred per cent. If we didn't all love him, and the music, we wouldn't be here, would we?'

'I read that you all live together, Monkees-style, is that right?'

'The other three share a flat, but I've got my own place.'

'Why's that?'

'I just like my own space. I always have. Maybe it's a twin thing. When Connor and I came to Edinburgh we didn't live together, or really hang out together all that much to begin with. I guess we just wanted a bit of distance from each other and from our schooldays. Connor knew Hannah and Danny for a while before I met them, but we're all pretty close now.'

Connor returned with a handful of drinks.

'Been getting the inside track from Kate? Very wise. Don't listen to a fucking word I say, it's all bullshit.'

34

'I'm interested in the kind of music that influences you. Some people might think it's strange, if you're so into Scottishness, that the stuff you sound most like is all relatively underground American music of a certain flavour. I'm thinking of Sparklehorse, Bright Eyes, Midlake, Rilo Kiley or The Hold Steady.'

'All good bands but, no offence, Andy, I hate that fucking question. The assumption is that because we're Scottish we have to sound like Jimmy Shand or some Runrig piss-take or the fucking Proclaimers. Fuck that. Look, I love loads of bands and artists from all over the world, not just American ones. There's Biffy Clyro, Mogwai, Boards of Canada and King Creosote among plenty others here in Scotland, but then there's also dEUS, Super Furry Animals, The Arcade Fire, Sigur Rós and a hundred more around the world. But there is something about the American alternative rock aesthetic that predisposes me to it. Don't ask me how or why, it just does. So it seems perfectly natural for us to sound the way we do. And anyway, I think The Ossians' sound is pretty diverse. "Declaration Of Arbroath" is pure punk noise, whereas "The Sleepwalker" is a lo-fi, psychedelic thing. And there's everything else in between.'

He glugged his pint and smiled.

'I take it you've read a lot?' said Andy. 'You seem to know a bit about Scotland's history and literature.'

'A bit,' said Connor. 'I guess a lot of that comes from Hannah being a history teacher. I'm just a fucking pleb with no higher education, but there's always interesting shit worth reading lying about our flat.'

'How did you and Hannah meet?'

'Me and Kate moved to Edinburgh five years ago, and I met Hannah and Danny in my first week here. They're my two best friends. We were just hanging around at the same gigs and parties and stuff and we got to know each other. We were all in different bands at the time, the usual bullshit, and eventually we got together. But I started going out with Hannah straight away.'

'And how is it being in a band with your girlfriend?'

'Not a problem. We get on great. I probably save all my arguments for Kate.' He glanced at his sister who made a tight-lipped,
sarcastic face. 'And Hannah's a shit-hot guitarist, so there's no
problem there.'

'Sometimes you seem to have as much to do with literature as
music. Are you a fan of modern Scottish authors?'

'Absolutely, and not just modern authors. I've always been a fan
of Scottish literature, ever since I fired through a copy of *Kidnapped*
I picked up from the local library as a kid. From there I read other
Stevenson stuff, which led me on to loads of other writers –
everyone from Hogg to Kelman. At one point I thought about
studying literature at uni, but a dickhead English teacher in my fifth
year put me right off the subject for a while. Stupid really. Nowadays
Scottish literature seems healthier than ever, with plenty of great
writers emerging in the wake of the whole *Trainspotting* thing. But
it's not as simple as "It's shite being Scottish". The truth is, it's both
shite and great being Scottish, often simultaneously. I suspect
anyone with a fucking brain thinks that about wherever they're
from, don't they?'

'So what's next for The Ossians?' asked Andy. 'I hear there's
plenty of record-company interest down south. Do you see yourself
signing to a major London label?'

'Only if the terms are right,' said Connor, finishing his pint.
'There's no point in prostituting ourselves to some bunch of fuckwit
record company execs who have no idea what we're about. We
have to be allowed to do exactly what we want, where we want.
And that definitely does not mean moving to London to be where
the supposed action is. That can get to fuck.'

Connor put his empty pint to his lips and realised there was
nothing left.

Andy looked like he was about to ask Kate something when a
short, squat man of around twenty lumbered in carrying several
bags of camera equipment.

'There you are,' he said, panting. 'Sorry I'm late.'

'Connor, Kate, this is Dominic, our esteemed photographer for
the day,' said Andy.

The man nodded briefly and stood there with a bead of sweat running down his forehead.

'Maybe we should find the others and get our picture taken,' said Connor, leaping out his chair. 'Fading light and all that. Isn't that right, Dominic? If you've got enough for the piece, Andy?'

Before the journalist had time to reply Connor was heading for the door and out into the blustery, salty air.

Hannah and Danny had been walking along the front for a couple of minutes before Hannah noticed the big smile on Danny's face.

'What are you grinning about?' she asked.

'What do you mean?'

'Come on, you look like the Cheshire Cat sitting in front of a bucket of bloody cream. Tell me.'

'I don't know what you're talking about.'

'Like hell you don't. I know you, Danny McIntyre, and I know when you're sitting on something. Come on, tell your Auntie Hannah.'

Hannah linked arms with him and leant into his bulk as they strolled along the prom, blown about by the swirling breeze.

'OK, but promise not to say anything just yet.'

'Of course, what do you take me for? My lips are sealed.'

'Me and Kate kind of . . . snogged last night.'

Hannah stopped in her tracks, pulling Danny to a halt in the process.

'What do you mean? What kind of snog? When? Where? How? Answers, please.'

Danny laughed. 'When I walked her home.'

'And?'

'And what?'

'Come on, I need more information. Was it just a mistaken drunken fumble kind of thing, or a could-be-going-somewhere kind of thing, or what?'

'Well, we were both drunk, obviously. And there was some fumbling going on. But I don't think it was a mistake. It might be going somewhere, I suppose.'

'And what does Kate think?'

'Don't know. Hopefully the same thing. We didn't really discuss it before I left this morning . . .'

'Woah, woah. Stop the bus. This morning? You stayed over?'

Hannah was smiling widely and Danny was shuffling about a little awkwardly, looking at the pavement, then out to the water.

'Yeah, but not like that. I mean, we didn't . . . we just . . .'

'OK, spare me. This is fucking huge, Danny. You and Kate? This is totally massive. Is it completely out the blue?'

'Not exactly,' said Danny, starting to walk again, as Hannah caught up. 'We've kind of been hanging out a bit, outside the band. Just mates to begin with, but things have been different between us recently, and last night, well . . .'

'You and Kate,' said Hannah, shaking her head. 'I can't get over it.'

'What do you think?' said Danny.

'I think it's bloody brilliant, is what I think. It's just a bit of a shock, that's all. I didn't see it coming. Wow.'

'Tell me about it. I'm probably jinxing the whole thing by telling you. God knows what Kate thinks.'

'I'm sure she'll be well into it,' said Hannah.

'You think?'

'She doesn't do or say anything she doesn't mean.'

'I suppose.'

'So even if you were both totally steaming, I'm sure she knew exactly what she was doing.'

'Maybe,' said Danny. 'You can't tell Con, though. Not yet.'

'Come on, he'll be well chuffed.'

'You reckon?'

The truth was, Hannah didn't know how Connor would react to the news. He had no reason not to be cool about his best friend and his sister getting it on, but you never knew what he was going to do at the moment.

'I'm sure he'll be fine,' she said. 'But I won't mention it if you don't want me to.'

'Thanks,' said Danny. 'You know how he likes to wind Kate up all the time. If he finds out and starts on her, that could kibosh the whole thing before it gets going.'

Hannah patted Danny's arm. 'Don't worry,' she said. 'You keep me posted, all right?'

'OK.'

'Jesus, you and Kate, eh? I can't get over it.'

They walked further along the esplanade, Hannah shaking her head, both of them with big smiles on their faces.

Forty minutes of rough sailing on the *Maid of the Forth* took them to Inchcolm Island, the 'Iona of the East' according to the leaflet in Connor's hand. He'd insisted on their photos being done on the small, rocky outcrop in the Forth. It was stunning. A twelfth-century abbey occupied the centre of the small kidney-shaped island, with a tiny sandy bay alongside. Raised hummocks lay at the two extremes of the island, decaying Second World War battlements perched at one end and a host of nesting gulls at the other. Behind the gulls' home of thick grass was a breathtaking view of both bridges, the low sun hanging anaemically behind.

The four band members stood on the beach throwing stones into the sea and pretending to look disinterested as the photographer snapped away, taking a handful of shots at a time before changing lenses. An old, deflated football lay on the sand, and Connor and Danny started kicking it about as Connor produced a hip flask and offered it round.

The pant of the water as it lapped on the shore was drowned by the frantic squawks of seagulls hanging in the wind, then diving for fish. A few tourists, dressed as if going on an Arctic expedition, traipsed dutifully around the abbey then back to the meagre little gift shop at the jetty.

The photographer gave the band vague instructions, which they ignored, so he just kept taking pictures of them as they walked along the beach. Driftwood, plastic bottles, tyres and other tidal junk were scattered along the sand and a black mongrel dog barked at the gulls.

Connor was amazed at the quiet beauty of the place, and felt a sense of disgust that he hadn't even known Inchcolm existed until recently, and yet you could see Edinburgh from this very spot. If there was beauty like this only a few miles from where he'd lived for five years, and he never knew about it, how much more was there to discover in a whole country? He was struck by how sheltered his life had been. In the interview he'd surely come across like a spoilt, pseudo-intellectual, middle-class kid, playing at rock 'n' roll. He had much more to say to the journalist now, and wished he'd explained things better back in the pub. He probably *was* a spoilt, pseudo-intellectual, middle-class kid, playing at rock 'n' roll. But what was wrong with that? Was he supposed to work down the fucking mines or something, just to have some credibility?

He had another hit of single malt and took a few quick dabs of speed from the bag in his pocket. It made his brain fizz and he wanted to go over and make the journalist turn on his tape recorder. But he knew better than to act in the initial rush, so instead started playing keepy-uppy with the football, singing a melody that he was working on.

Ahead of him, two gulls were taking it in turns to swoop down at the barking dog, shrieking as they came. The dog ducked and cowered, but started barking again as soon as the gulls' dives were over. The rhythm of squawking and barking continued, and Connor thought it sounded like a needle stuck on a record. He wondered if there was a mathematical relationship between the dog and the gulls, a set of simultaneous equations to be solved. Once you found the solution you could release the animals from their eternal loop, their forever-repeating purgatory.

He knew he was thinking this way because of the speed and the whisky, beer and gin in his bloodstream. He could feel the synapses snapping and the neurons murmuring. All that complex biology to create a bunch of idiotic thoughts in the pathetic little mind of a human, standing on a tiny rock in a small estuary of a poxy country at the arse end of nowhere. The stuff of life, indeed.

Connor could hear a mobile ringtone cutting through the barking and squawking, and after a few moments realised the sound was coming from his pocket. A tinny version of the opening chords to 'Smells Like Teen Spirit'. He grimaced, pulled out the phone and looked at the display. Nick. He answered it, moving away from the others.

'Hey, how's my favourite messenger boy?'

'"Smells Like Teen Spirit"? Is that the best you could do?'

'I thought you'd like it.'

'What do you want, Nick?'

'Just checking up on you, like I said I would. Wanted to make sure you managed to get the bag home OK last night. You didn't accidentally throw it at a copper or something.'

'I'm not happy about this.'

'I'm not asking you to be happy about it, just fucking do it.'

Connor sighed. This was going to be a long fucking fortnight. 'So, these guys will ring me, yeah? And I just meet up with them, swap packages, and that's it?'

'Pretty much. Easy, isn't it?'

'What about the police?'

'What about them?'

'What if they've worked this out and are following me.'

'Trust me, they haven't worked anything out. This is the fucking pigs we're talking about here. Thick as shit in a bottle.'

'What if they do?'

'Look, just keep an eye out, that's all. The only way the police will bother you is if you act like a suspicious twat. So don't.'

'Christ.'

'Christ doesn't come into it, Connor. Just keep a cool head, do what you're told, and everything will work out fine.'

Nick sounded confident, but Connor was a long way from sharing that confidence. He thought of the kitbag full of fuck knows what sitting underneath the sofa back at the flat and felt like chucking the mobile into the sea in front of him.

'Is that it? Can I go now?'

'Sure. You'll get a call from Jim in the next day or so about the Dundee thing. Just stay cool, OK?'

Connor ended the call without replying.

'You got a mobile?' said Danny from behind him, making him jump.

'Jesus, Danny, I nearly shat myself. Don't creep up on folk, eh?'

'Just asking. Thought you didn't like them. Aren't you always on about not wanting to be contactable the whole time?'

'Yeah, but I thought it would be useful on tour, just in case we get into any trouble on the road.'

'You planning on getting into trouble?'

'I'm not *planning* to.'

'So who was that?'

'Just Paul checking up on us.'

'He's got your number?'

'I gave it to him this morning.'

'What's he saying?'

'He wants to meet us in the Earl later for a pint.'

'He already told us that last night, didn't he?'

'Yeah, right. I think he'd forgotten, though, steaming and everything.'

Danny looked at Connor closely.

'You OK?'

'Just needing a drink, is all. Warm us up. It's a bit parky, isn't it?'

The journalist caught up with them. 'I think Dominic's had enough,' he said. 'His poor little fingers are getting cold, and besides, the light's about gone.'

Connor looked at the darkening sky behind the bridges. Andy followed his gaze.

'You know that thing about them forever painting the rail bridge?' said Connor.

'Yeah,' said Andy. 'By the time they finish they have to go back to the beginning and start painting again.'

'Apparently, that's a load of bollocks. Just another stupid myth about this country. I suppose it makes a better story that way. And everyone loves a good story. So does it matter what the truth is?'

They stood looking at the bridge as the sun gave up the struggle and died, and clouds took over the sky, bringing in the night. Of course it fucking matters, thought Connor in reply to his own question, but he said nothing.

They stumbled out the Earl of Marchmont at closing, giggling like schoolkids. Danny offered to walk Kate home through the Meadows, avoiding looking at Hannah, who was watching the pair of them and smiling.

Connor and Hannah walked the short distance to their flat arm in arm, stopping to snog twice on the way. After the second embrace against Scotmid's doorway they separated.

'You're gorgeous, you know that?' said Connor.

'Yeah, course I do. You're not so bad yourself,' said Hannah, pressing up against him.

Connor thought he saw something out the corner of his eye. He turned and seemed to sense movement at the shop's bins, but wasn't sure. It didn't help that he was half-cut again, as per.

'Did you see that?' he said.

'What?'

'I thought I saw something. Over by those bins.'

'Probably just rats.'

Connor looked for a few more seconds, but didn't see anything. He toyed with the idea of heading back towards the bins, but Hannah pulled at his arm.

'Come on,' she said, 'let's get home. I fancy shagging your brains out.'

They were soon at the front door, then stumbling down the hallway and into the living room without putting the light on, simultaneously trying to walk, snog and undress each other. Connor had his hands underneath Hannah's short denim skirt, stroking her arse with one hand, pushing her pants aside and slipping a finger inside her with the other. She was already wet and let out a little gasp. She tugged at his belt to get his trousers off, then pulled his T-shirt over his head, Connor kissing her breasts all the while. She unhooked her bra and he started sucking her nipples. They were naked now, apart from Hannah's skirt pushed up to her waist and her knee-length leather boots. She couldn't be bothered trying to take them off, and besides, she knew they turned him on. He lifted her up on to the dining table in the corner of the room and slipped easily inside her while still standing. After some slow movements they speeded up, rocking in unison for a few minutes, her knees raised and his buttocks clenching, her hands stroking the tight muscles of his stomach, until she felt Connor go rigid and come inside her, then felt the shiver of her own orgasm as he collapsed on top of her.

They lay like that smiling at each other for a couple of minutes, not speaking, just kissing occasionally, before Connor climbed off her awkwardly, and she got down from the table. It was dark except for light spilling in from the hall, and in the half-light Connor watched as Hannah pulled her skirt down and put her T-shirt back on.

'You fancy skinning up?' she said as Connor put his clothes back on.

'Sure. Get us a drink?' he replied as she headed towards the kitchen.

He went over to the window, only now realising that the curtains were open. Oh well, he thought, give somebody a wee show, if they could see anything in this darkness. He began to draw the curtains but stopped. He thought he saw movement outside, in one of the doorways down the street. He peered hard out the window for a few minutes. Nothing. The only motion now was a tree swaying a little in the breeze. There was no one out there. He was sure he'd seen something, and earlier, over at the bins. But was he sure? He was fucking drunk, and speeding and stoned, so maybe he was letting his imagination get ahead of him. He thought of the kitbag under the sofa. He thought about the police. How could they know what he was up to? They couldn't. Could they? Fuck, he was losing it with the paranoia already, and they weren't even on the road yet. He had to try and chill the fuck out.

'Get anywhere with that joint yet?' said Hannah, coming into the room with two large whiskies, and switching a lamp on.

Connor took one last look out the window, but all he could see now was his own reflection. He closed the curtains.

3
St Andrews

'Give me a sky full of stars and a telescope
And I'll be a happy man
Give me a woman to love and a hand to hold
And I will throw it away'

The Ossians, 'Stargazing'

The atmosphere at the rehearsal room was oddly schizophrenic, their childish excitement at hitting the road tempered by the suppressing weight of their hangovers. Connor stayed quiet while the rest of them nervously prattled and fussed over loading up the gear. As they drove over the Forth, the skittish energy in the van was still palpable, Connor imagining the life being blown back into him by the wind that funnelled down the firth and swirled around Inchcolm before heading out to sea. He tentatively felt his throbbing face. His black eye had turned a browny green colour and his lip had scabbed over. A couple of his lower teeth seemed a little loose and he instinctively flicked his tongue over them. They listened to The Flaming Lips as Paul drove north into the kingdom of Fife.

The road into St Andrews was lined by several miles of golf course. That most gentlemanly of sports was born here and they knew how to capitalise on it, with rows of exclusive, five-star hotels providing for loud Americans and camcorder-wielding Japanese. The population of St Andrews was made up of rich golfers, rich housewives and rich English students. It had never been a place for poor people, but since Prince William did his time there at uni, everyone but the idiotic elite had been priced out.

The student union was the only ugly building in town. Surrounded by eight hundred years of crumbling scenic history, the union was a sixties breezeblock of grey concrete slabs and scratchy

45

windows. In the bar, televisions blasted out MTV over the soulless expanse of blond wood and wrought iron. The three pool tables were busy and a handmade sign in a wacky typeface asked that drinks not be placed on the table.

The Ossians were the oldest and poorest people in the place. Girls in rugby tops and boys in baseball caps with jumpers tied around shoulders oozed southern English superiority, their healthy skins and correct posture suggesting better breeding and bigger purses. Scottish students were spottable by their persecuted looks and pasty complexions. Paul had gone off to find the promoter, leaving them with drinks beside the pool tables.

'I fucking hate students,' said Connor loud enough for the pool players to hear. They pretended not to.

'What a surprise, something you hate,' said Kate. 'Change the record. Most of our fans are students, so what does that make you?'

'Just because we're popular with the cunts, doesn't mean I have to like them.'

'In case you'd forgotten, everyone in this band was a student at one time, so it's hypocritical to turn round and say you hate them. Also, you know we're staying with Keith tonight – a friend of mine, please try and remember – who happens to still be a part-time student, and who is very kindly letting a bunch of drunken strangers sleep on his floor on a Monday night. So stop with the angling-for-trouble routine. I suppose you won't be happy until you've provoked someone into hitting you in every town we play?'

'It might improve the face,' said Connor, wincing as he smiled. 'Anyway, I'm not trying to provoke anyone. If I was I'd be calling these wankers here a bunch of upper-class English toff fuckwits or something, wouldn't I?'

The two nearest pool players turned to look at Connor. They were the size and shape of rugby players. The one about to play straightened up.

'Look, mate,' he said in a Home Counties accent, 'we're just having a quiet game of pool here. Why don't you leave it?'

Connor put on a mock surprised look, as Kate and Hannah rolled their eyes and Danny started rubbing his forehead.

'What do you mean, *mate*?' said Connor. 'I was only pointing out – in a private conversation, I might add – what I would be saying if I was looking for trouble. I didn't expect any nosy cunts to be listening in.'

The pool player sighed, took his shot and missed. His shorter, stockier mate came to the table and missed. Connor downed some more of his drink.

'Fucking hell, Danny, I reckon we could wipe the floor with these posh bastards. What do you think?'

'Connor,' said Danny, as the stockier pool player turned to face them.

Hannah got up and pulled Connor out of his seat by his coat sleeve. 'I'm not sitting through this crap,' she said firmly. 'Come on, arsehole, you're taking me for a guided tour.'

He wore a surprised look but let himself be led away from the tables, downing the remains of his pint on the way out and chucking the glass nonchalantly on the floor, where it smashed.

'Sorry about that,' said Kate to the pool players. 'He's my brother and he's a complete dickhead.'

'Don't worry about it,' said the first player. 'Fancy a game of doubles?'

Kate looked at Danny, who shrugged in agreement.

'Why not?' she said, taking a cue from the rack. 'Two shots don't carry, one shot only on the black, name your black bag and you have to stick to it, yeah? Play for drinks?'

Danny looked at Kate, smiled and picked a cue.

Outside, Hannah was fuming and Connor was laughing. She stared hard at him.

'At the risk of sounding like your mother, I don't know why I fucking bother.'

'Not sure my mother has your potty mouth.'

'Of course she does. Is this what it's going to be like for the next fortnight? You picking fights with strangers, me hauling you away before you get a doing? I should just leave you to get the shit kicked out of you.'

'Why don't you?'

'Christ's sake, is that all you think of me?'

'You're lovely when you're angry,' said Connor.

She punched his arm.

'That's the most annoying thing anyone can ever say,' she said. 'Except maybe "good girl". I should dump you on the spot.'

'I promise never to call you a good girl. Anyway, if you dump me, who'll give you the guided tour of St Andrews?'

A cold wind blew down Market Street as they stood in silence. After a moment Hannah spoke with a surprisingly cheery tone.

'Let's have the bloody tour, then.'

They walked to the east end of the street where the cathedral had been decaying since it was built eight centuries before. It was making a decent stab of surviving considering the exposure to the elements, as it clung to the promontory above the town's harbour where the university elite paraded in ermine every year. The two ends of the cathedral remained standing, slowly crumbling in a swirl of rain and sea spray amid a ramshackle scattering of grave-stones, the odd angles and layout of which suggested a recent landslide. To the right, the monolithic St Regulus tower remained intact. Connor and Hannah wandered round the ruins, hunched into the weather like pilgrims grimacing at the wrath of God. The place was deserted except for a single wet figure across the other side of the ruins, examining tombstones studiously in the hardening rain.

'Is there any point to this?' said Hannah. 'Apart from catching pneumonia?'

Connor led her to the entrance of the tower where they sheltered, shaking off the rain. The fake fur collar of Hannah's charity-shop suede coat had flattened along with her hair. Connor, with his collar up and lighting a fag, looked as if he thought he was James Dean.

'This is supposedly where some of St Andrew's remains were kept,' he said, passing the lit cigarette to Hannah and lighting one for himself. 'But then they got lost. What is it with Catholics and old bones? You'd think they'd be too busy mounting crusades. That was the Catholics, wasn't it?'

'Just cos I teach history doesn't mean I give a shit about it,' said Hannah. 'And anyway, how do you know all this stuff?'

'Read a book once. Probably one of yours. Want to go up the tower?'

'Four quid? Na,' said Hannah. 'At student-union prices that's at least two pints. Honey, as tour guides go you're a pretty shit one. This town got anything going for it apart from a crumbling cathedral and a street full of tea shops and Pringlewear?'

'Well, we can go and see the university full of twats, or the golf course full of different twats?'

'Tempting, but why don't we just head back. This may come as a surprise, but I never really wanted a tour of this shithole anyway, it was just a diversion tactic.'

'Hey, this is the poshest shithole in the whole of Scotland, you know.'

'Still a shithole. Come on, let's get back. The others will have a head start on the bevvy if we're not careful.'

Connor produced a hip flask. 'I think you'll find no one gets a head start on Connor Alexander in the drinking stakes.'

She wrapped her arms around him and kissed him.

'Oooh, I love it when you talk boozy.'

'Yeah, yeah. You love the fact I've got some single malt in here.'

'Not at all,' she said, grabbing the flask. Connor wasn't quick enough and in a moment she had the top off and was glugging from it.

'Why I oughta . . .' said Connor, waving his fist in a cartoon wobble. She handed the flask back and licked her lips.

'If I didn't know better, Mr Alexander, I'd say you were trying to get me drunk and have your wicked way with me.'

'There's nothing wicked about my ways.'

'No? Let's just see how many fights you start on this tour, shall we?' A pensive look came over Hannah's face. 'Seriously, you are going to stay out of trouble, aren't you? I mean, you say you hate all that self-destructive rock-star crap, but then . . . you know? I worry.'

She stroked some of the wet hair away from his eyes and looked at him. He seemed a little lost, a look she both hated and found attractive despite herself. She knew he put it on. She knew he manipulated her and everyone else around him all the time, but there was still a little boy in there who needed to be shown the way.

It hadn't been love at first sight or any of that corny crap. She thought he was cute and funny and probably the least laddish boy she'd ever met. After a stretch of beery, leery Britpop fans traipsing through her teenage years, he was a welcome change and something of a challenge, a whirlwind of nervous energy. The challenge was to step into that storm and not get swept away. She couldn't work out what made him the way he was. She'd met his parents plenty of times and got on better with them than either he or Kate did. They seemed like average, middle-class, hippy parents, nothing to get angry about. But Connor resented them for reasons she couldn't fathom. Maybe he just resented them because they were his parents. In comparison she loved her own parents in an uncomplicated way, despite everything that had happened between them. They'd each made sacrifices for her, and she respected and admired them for it. They'd been through a tough time with the divorce, but they'd come out the other side. For Hannah, family meant peace and contentment. But for Connor everything was a fight, everything was a struggle against unseen forces. His flunk out of uni, his aimless jobs, his drinking and drug-taking, the band, the tour, his parents, his friends, his sister and her – he tackled it all like he was defending the keep of his soul against enemy forces. What made him that way? Was he born with the seeds of it already in him, or had the world shaped him? Better not to get into the whole nature versus nurture thing, she thought. Maybe people were just the way they were, and that was that. She wanted to show him there was a different way to live your life, but she wasn't entirely sure how, so she just tried to look after him. But wasn't it about time someone looked after her for a change?

She noticed he hadn't answered her about behaving. He seemed distracted and was looking over her shoulder at something in the distance.

'That guy's watching us,' he said.

'What?'

'That guy, over by the gravestones. He's pretending to look at the stones, but really he's watching us.'

Hannah turned to look. A tall, lean figure was walking slowly among the tombstones, stopping to examine each one in turn.

'Don't be stupid. He's just looking for a grave. Why the hell would he be watching us?'

Connor seemed to hesitate. 'You're right, why would he?'

'Maybe he's a fan of the band, and recognises us.'

There was another pause, Connor keeping his eyes on the stranger in the distance.

'Yeah, maybe that's it,' he said eventually.

She kissed him on his wet forehead.

'I think you're smoking too much blow, my little paranoid android,' she said, turning into the rain and wind. 'Come on, droopy drawers, time to head back.'

Connor followed her out the graveyard towards the gig, but couldn't resist looking back over his shoulder at the tall, thin figure in the distance, still standing examining the gravestones a little too closely for his liking.

After a fraught soundcheck with a hapless student sound engineer, plus a hefty kick of whisky and amphetamine, Connor sat down backstage with Danny to be interviewed for a student-run Internet radio show.

The show's presenter fumbled with a minidisc recorder and mic. Connor was quickly on a rant. Starting with the myth of Ossian, he rattled through the life of St Andrew, the role of pi in the building of the pyramids, the music of Wilco and Sufjan Stevens, the idiocy of Kurt Cobain, the state of the Scottish football team, the Declaration of Arbroath and anything else that sprang to mind. The presenter, struggling to keep up, flashed pleading looks at Danny, who just smiled and supped his pint. Having grown up in a big family with half a dozen brothers and sisters, Danny had learned early on in life to stay out of things, only butting in when he really had something to say. This made him the perfect partner for Connor in interviews, because Connor never let anyone else speak. After half an hour the student switched off the minidisc.

'Have you got enough?' said Connor.

'I think that'll do,' mumbled the presenter, looking shell-shocked.

'Anything else, just grab me.' Connor was holding the front of the student's expensive-looking shirt. He seemed intent on not letting go.

'No, no, I'll get out your way. Let you get on with the gig. Thanks a lot.'

He extricated himself from Connor's grip and shot out the door.

'What's his problem?' said Connor. 'I was just getting going.'

Danny grinned at him. 'You wee daftie,' he laughed.

Connor's eyes narrowed as he looked at Danny.

'You big shite,' he said slowly. 'You've started on the pills already?'

Danny snorted a laugh and drank some more of his pint.

'Bastard!' Connor's eyes were wide. 'Right, I'm having one as well, then. Can't have you coming up on your own, can we?'

Danny produced an E from his pocket and Connor necked it, washing it down with the end of the whisky from his hip flask.

Kate poked her head round the dressing-room door.

'You pair. Support band are on. Want to take a look?'

The place was mobbed. Despite being a Monday night most of the three hundred kids in the place were well on their way to paralytic. Gangs of large lads crowded down the front of the stage. Pockets of girls who looked like they'd be more at home at a debutantes' ball giggled in the seats scattered around the perimeter of what looked like an old gym hall.

Hobbes were a student band and boy did they suck like one, thought Connor, I bet they're named after the cartoon tiger, how fucking depressing. They were five laddish blokes with rosy cheeks and buttoned-down shirt collars, churning out a vaguely funky derivative blues rock that was totally without soul, style, attitude or originality, yet which still sent their mates and girlfriends into an unaccountable frenzy.

Halfway through the set, just as Connor was getting suicidal, he felt the first eccy rush kick in. He still knew the band were shite, but he wanted to forgive them, take them away somewhere quiet and explain the world of decent music to them.

Hannah was standing next to him.

'Crap, eh?' she shouted.

'They'll learn.'

She looked at him carefully for a second.

'What?' he said, grinning stupidly, his head bobbing slightly in an involuntary response to the bass drum. She smiled through a look of disapproval.

'I thought we were waiting till after the shows before taking anything?'

'Is that the royal "we"?' said Connor. He laughed and kissed her cheek. He felt a surge of love for her, a pain in his chest. He was proud to know someone as beautiful as her. He revelled in the cornball sentiment for a moment, knowing full well it was chemically induced, but justifying it to himself as an enhancement of a feeling he really did have inside him.

Hobbes finished to ecstatic squeals and raucous roars, followed by the usual murmured chatter before the sound engineer stuck on a record.

'Right,' said Connor as he strode towards the stage. 'Let's rock the fuck out of these wankers.'

Their show was blistering and the crowd were completely apathetic. With their mates' band finished, the booze kicking in and valuable pulling time disappearing fast, most of the students were concentrating on getting their tongues inserted in other people's throats. In spite of the Ecstasy, Connor was raging. He was drunk enough on whisky, gin and beer to let the anger overcome the chemistry, and he turned sarcastic and offensive between songs.

'This is for all the yah rugby pricks out there' and 'This is for all you pashmina-wearing James Blunt fans' received rowdy boos and drunken heckles. The Ossians thrived on the bad feeling now emanating from the audience. Danny and Kate pummelled away through the set with conviction, occasionally throwing glances and smiles at each other, while Hannah tore shreds out of her SG, breaking a string at one point but playing on regardless. They ended with 'Declaration Of Arbroath', Connor turning his overdrive way up and letting his guitar crunch and feed back the whole way through the song before throwing it against his amp in disgust.

'There's another rock 'n' roll cliché for you, kids.' He stumbled over a guitar pedal, picked up an empty bottle of Beck's and lobbed it into the crowd. 'We've been The Ossians, you've been a bunch of posh English cunts, cheers.'

When he got backstage Connor saw Kate greeting a large, fresh-faced blond guy with a rugged chin and bulky muscles underneath a tight T-shirt.

'Con, you remember Keith,' she said, 'one of those posh English cunts you hate so much.'

Connor felt his hand squash under a firm handshake.

'Hi, Keith. No offence with the English cunt thing. I came over a bit McGlashan back there, that's all.'

'Sorry?'

'Never mind. I wasn't referring to you, obviously.'

'No offence taken,' said Keith in a cut-glass English accent. 'This uni *is* full of posh cunts. I hate them.' He laughed a booming laugh. 'I really enjoyed the gig. You guys are amazing. That's the best bit of entertainment we've had here in years, if you don't mind me saying.'

'Mind? Keithy boy, I can always take a bit of ego massage. Why don't we get you a drink, and you can tell us how fucking great we are.'

Kate watched as Connor guided Keith towards a crate of Beck's, only just able to reach around the big man's shoulders. Keith was an ex of Kate's, one of those early uni experiences that was as much about getting laid by someone seemingly exotic as it was anything else, for both of them. For Kate, after a childhood fumbling around in Arbroath with underfed boys, the affluence and self-confidence of Keith was utterly alien, as was his thoroughly toned, muscular body. To Keith's eyes, used to a parade of perfectly manicured and curved blonde types, this tall, dark, sinewy and intelligent Scottish girl with a mind of her own was as fresh as a North Sea breeze. All too quickly, though, the exotic became normal, and there simply wasn't enough there after the lust to keep things going, and the relationship petered out after a few short months. These days Keith was doing well for himself, designing software part-time for a marine research centre down the East Neuk coast while trying to finish a computing PhD, and the two had stayed friends after uni, somewhat to the surprise of them both.

'What did you make of the show, then?' said Hannah, approaching Kate with two beers and handing her one.

'Wasn't exactly our kind of crowd, was it?'

'That's putting it mildly. Still, I think we played OK.'

'Yeah, apart from laughing boy over there, winding everyone up.'

'Can't really blame him, the reaction we were getting.'

'Maybe.' Something occurred to Kate. 'Where's Danny?'

'Dunno, I saw him with Paul a few minutes ago.' A mischievous look came over Hannah's face. 'Why? You missing him already?'

Kate looked at Hannah and realised she knew.

'He told you?'

'I weaselled it out of him.'

'How much?'

'Everything.'

'Nice try. How much?'

'Just that the two of you snogged the other night.'

'Last two nights, actually.'

'Wow. Two nights on the trot, eh? That's serious.'

Hannah was laughing as Kate shoved her gently on the shoulder. Kate started laughing, too.

'It is *not* serious.'

'I'm only winding you up.'

'Well don't. I've no idea where this is going, or where it's come from, but . . .'

Kate tailed off, not knowing what else to say.

'Funny, that's almost exactly what Danny said about it,' said Hannah.

'Really? I don't want to sound like a silly schoolgirl, but what else did he say?'

Hannah smiled. 'Just that he really liked you, that's all. And that you were taking it easy.'

Kate smiled too, downed some of her beer and looked round the room again. Connor and Keith were in cahoots over in a corner. Hannah followed her gaze.

'He's pretty fit,' she said.

'Who?'

'Keith. In that buffed-up, posh kind of way.'

'Yeah,' said Kate. 'A bit too buffed-up and posh, in the end.'

'I know what you mean. I prefer the scrawny Scottish indie-boy look,' said Hannah, laughing again.

'I'm more of a big, hairy Irish teddy bear girl myself,' said Kate, joining in.

'Christ,' said Hannah, as the two of them leant on each other and laughed. After a moment something occurred to Kate.

'Does Connor know?'

'No. But you should tell him.'

'I will,' said Kate, 'it's just that we don't really know where we're at yet, so there might not be anything to tell.'

'That's what Danny said, sounds like you two are made for each other. You'll be finishing each other's sentences next, and wearing matching outfits. Seriously, though, you should tell Con.'

'I will,' said Kate. 'Honest.'

Paul bustled in with Danny ambling behind.

'Fucking Ents Committee or whatever they're called aren't happy,' he said. 'Reckon you were inciting racial hatred, Con. They say it was offensive and they're talking about not paying us.'

'Racial hatred?' said Connor. 'Fuck off. I was just letting off steam. How the fuck can they not pay us? Bunch of inbred yah eejits.'

'Don't worry, I'll sort it, but it might be best if we get the gear out of here sooner rather than later.'

'Fuck's sake,' said Connor, his eccy high long gone. 'Fine.' He gulped down the best part of a bottle of Beck's and headed towards the door. 'Let's just shift the stuff and get the fuck out of here to a proper pub.'

Within fifteen minutes the gear was loaded. The band and Keith hung about in the corridor by the emergency exit waiting for Paul to get back with the money. Half a dozen students came out the entrance of the performance hall into the strip-lit corridor in a flurry of laughs and swearing. One of them spotted Connor.

'Hey, it's that lippy little twat with the chip on his shoulder,' he said. 'What's your problem, Jock?'

'Leave it, Tom,' said another one. It was one of the guys Kate and Danny had played pool with. 'They're all right. Let's just go.'

'Hang on. Let's see what this guy has to say when he's not onstage. What have you got to say for yourself, Jock?'

'How about fuck off, poof? Something like that?'

'Poof, is it? How about I treat one of these lovely ladies to a proper English shagging, show you I'm not a poof?'

Connor lunged at the guy and ran straight into a right hook. He didn't think it was so easy to be knocked off your feet by a punch, but he found himself on the floor and felt dizzy. The guy stood over him.

'Next time, try not fighting like a girl, as well as shagging like one, eh, Jock?'

The guy from the pool game pulled him away, and they headed off down the corridor towards the main bar. Connor had blood streaming from his nose and the cut on his lip had opened up again. He felt something in his mouth and spat a tooth into his hand.

'Think the tooth fairy will find me in this dump?' he said as Danny and Keith helped him to his feet. 'We could probably do with the money if we're not getting paid.'

Paul came round the corner waving a pile of notes at them and saw Connor's face.

'It seems like I'm always saying this, but what the fuck happened to you?'

Connor just looked at him, felt round his mouth with his tongue and spat blood on the floor.

'Look,' said Keith, 'I know a decent pub round the corner. Why don't we get out of here.'

'You're my kind of guy, Keithy boy,' said Connor. 'Despite your upbringing.' He laughed but nobody joined in. They all just looked at him. 'Come on, the pub waits for no man. Or woman.'

He looked pointedly at Kate and Hannah but they both just strode out the emergency exit into the night.

The six of them clattered out of Aikman's at midnight. The rain had stopped and the wind had given up. Keith suggested a walk along the beach so they stocked up on booze from the van and headed towards the West Sands. The path to the beach went straight across the eighteenth fairway of the Old Course. Danny and Paul pulled branches off a tree and swung them like golfers up the fairway towards the clubhouse shouting 'fore'. Up ahead Kate and Hannah were chatting, while Connor brought up the rear with Keith.

'So what is it you've got against us English?' asked Keith, smiling.

'It's not the English *people*,' said Connor, pointing a finger. 'It's not *you*. It's the arrogant, self-important Englishness we constantly get shoved down our throats on television, in the papers, in films and books. Scotland's such a half-arsed country that most of our media is made in London for an English audience, and the handful of garbage we do produce ourselves is even worse. But it's either that or the morally superior crap from down south, continually rubbing our noses in how fucking inept we are.'

'It sounds like you've got a problem with Scotland, not England.'

'You're not the first person to say that.'

'So what are you going to do about it?'

'Change. Find a new Scotland. Invent a better country. It's that easy. Other fuckers do it all the time. Look at those Scandinavian bastards, they're always so bang up to date, all shiny and liberal and open-minded. Makes you sick. I reckon it would be cool to be Swedish. Or Icelandic. Look at Björk, she's fantastic. Now there's a true original who does what she likes and doesn't give a flying fuck what anyone thinks. Who have we got in comparison? Sharleen Spiteri or Simple Minds? Jesus.'

By now they were on the beach. The long expanse of the West Sands looked like a ruffled amber tablecloth in the spilt light of the town. Only the white noise of the waves could be heard. Paul and Danny had caught up with the girls and Connor looked at them, then at the distant, twinkling lights of Carnoustie across the water.

'Did you know this is where they filmed that scene in *Chariots of Fire*?' said Keith. 'The slo-mo running at the start.'

Connor looked around, but in the semi-darkness he couldn't make the connection.

'Really?' he said. 'I suppose there must be hundreds of places in Scotland that appear in films, eh? Except not in *Braveheart*, of course.'

That ridiculous film was probably the most famous piece of Scottish history in the world, thought Connor, and yet it was inaccurate, jingoistic drivel, starred an Aussie and was filmed in Ireland as a tax dodge. Classic. He'd read that they'd erected a William Wallace statue somewhere that looked like Mel Gibson. Christ Almighty.

The others had stopped. When Connor and Keith caught up they were standing around a dark, oily mass laid out on the sand. Danny handed Connor a joint and tipped the body over with his boot.

'Dead seal,' he said. 'Doesn't look as if it's been here long either, there's no decay.'

In the dark they couldn't make out much, only the glassy eyes and oily skin now half-covered in sand. The eyes seemed full of tears, and Connor couldn't pull his gaze away. He felt the joint top up his level of stonedness, which was combining with the smacky aftermath of what had turned out to be a pretty dodgy E. In turn, the alcohol was taking the edge off the stoned feeling, and the speed was sharpening up the boozy fuzz. On top of it all he'd snicked a couple of Feminax off Kate for the pain in his mouth and this bloody headache, and they were starting to ooze through him. Just another night in the drug cocktail cabinet of his body.

'Should we do something? Tell someone?' said Kate.

'No point,' said Keith. 'They get washed up here quite regularly this time of year. Something to do with homing instinct gone wrong or the changing tides. Someone will find it in the morning and call it in.'

They stood looking at the body of the seal for a long time, passing the joint and then another between them. Connor wondered what kind of God gave animals instincts that would end up killing them. Did He change the currents and the tides to fuck with them? Or was it all chance?

They turned and headed back to town, wrapped up in their own thoughts. At Keith's flat, a trendy and expensive one-bedroom place with a massive living room, they drank and smoked some more, gradually winding down and dropping off to sleep, until only Connor was left awake at eight in the morning, the first hints of a lightening dawn sky out the window.

He was a mess. His vision was blurry and his eyelids drooped as his gaze switched from out the window to the joint in his hand, which had gone out. Packed too tight, he thought as he searched for a lighter. He looked around the room. This living room was about the size of the whole flat he shared with Hannah and Danny. In the corner was a state-of-the-art hi-fi, which was making noises like angels talking to whales or something, as far as he could make out. Out of the fog of his brain he eventually recognised it as Sigur Rós. He smiled. In the other corner of the room, a surprisingly small television was on with the sound muted. It was already showing breakfast programmes, the news and markets for the early riser. Or the late sleeper, in his case. As he tried to focus on it he thought he saw something he recognised. It was footage of Edinburgh, somewhere quite posh-looking, perhaps near his March-mont flat. Then there was a face on screen, and Connor seemed to wake up a little. He shook his head from side to side to focus his eyes on the screen, but it was swirling in front of him as he reached for his whisky and sucked on the remains of the joint. The face looked familiar, definitely someone he knew, or that he'd at least seen before. But where? His scrambled brain couldn't work it out, and he hunted about the sofa looking for the remote to turn the sound up. But just as quickly as it had appeared, the face was gone, replaced by the inane smiling, prim, air-brushed do-goody features of a BBC breakfast presenter. Shit. What the hell was that all about? He would have to try and remember this in the morning. Wait a minute, it was already morning. And he needed to sleep. God, he was tired. He was already struggling to remember what the face looked like. Thin, pale, young – a teenager, maybe. It was a boy, wasn't it? He thought so, but he wasn't even sure of that now. A girlish boy? Or a boyish girl? Jesus, he had to get to bed. He'd worry about it in the morning. But it was already morning. Shit, hadn't he already been through this?

Eventually he fell asleep where he sat, and dreamt fitfully about swimming in the sea, followed by vacant-eyed, androgynous seal-like corpses with vaguely familiar faces, who disappeared whenever he turned round. He woke two hours later, before anyone else was up, had three painkillers, the remains of the joint and a hit of gin and tonic for breakfast.

It was Tuesday. Next stop Dundee.

4
Dundee

'All we need is whisky to drink
A fire in the grate
And a roof that doesn't leak'

The Ossians, 'A Roof That Doesn't Leak'

The Tay was a useless river, too shallow for ships, large spreads of sandbank appearing at low tide. The road and rail bridges hugged close to the slapping, silty water as if trying to pretend they weren't bridges at all but causeways.

The Ossians drove over the river gazing at the rail bridge curving towards them, no hint of the ghosts that haunted it from its predecessor's collapse almost a hundred and thirty years ago. The leaden sky above was sullen and huffy, as if it would rip apart and piss down on them any minute. They felt a strong westerly rock the van, Paul angling the steering wheel into it.

Hannah and Kate sat up front with Paul, Connor skinning up behind them and Danny reading a newspaper. Connor had filled a large lemonade bottle with gin and tonic, which he'd liberated from Keith's drinks cabinet before the rest were awake. He swigged it occasionally and the others pretended not to notice because they couldn't be bothered getting into it.

Danny laughed. 'It says here that Britain's about to be hit by the remains of an American hurricane called Hannah.'

'Really?' said Connor, his head twitching up from the arrangement of fag papers. 'That's a good omen. What do you think, love? You feel like laying waste to the country, leaving death and destruction in your wake?'

'Yeah, why not?' said Hannah. 'Nothing better to do. Is this one of the cool hundred-mile-an-hour hurricanes, or just a jumped-up rain shower?'

'It's died down over the Atlantic. Caused a lot of damage up the eastern seaboard but a lot weaker now. Should still blow over the odd tree, though.'

'Sounds about right,' said Connor. 'By the time we get it, it's diluted and boring, yet everyone'll still make a massive fuss about it. Especially if it's anywhere near London. You know what a fuss they make in bloody Hampstead, every time the BBC pundits can't get into work for a bit of a breeze. Arseholes. Every time it snows they cancel all the programmes and moan about it. It's just a bit of fucking snow, for Christ's sake.'

'I hate to interrupt your bullshit, but the last thing we need on this tour is snow,' said Paul. 'Remember we're heading into some remote places with shitty roads and we don't want to get stranded.'

'It'll be fine,' said Connor. 'They're used to snow up north.'

'Yeah, they stay indoors, that's how they deal with it.'

In front of them lay Dundee in all its ugly office-block glory. An array of boxy grey and brown buildings were strewn across the town centre, with high-rise flats arranged at sporadic intervals further up the hillside. Above them rose the Law Hill, its stone war monument dominated by the radio repeater station behind it, towering testaments to the past and present.

'Wasn't it up Dundee Law that Billy Connolly recited that shite poetry on his show?' said Danny.

Connor sparked up the joint and swigged more gin and tonic. 'Yeah, William McGonagall,' he said, becoming animated. 'Reputedly the worst poet in the world. His *Tay Bridge Disaster* fucking rules, by the way.'

He started waving his arms about dramatically and tried to stand up as the van lurched forwards. He tumbled into Danny and took another toke.

'Beautiful Railway Bridge of the Silv'ry Tay! Alas! I am very sorry to say, That ninety lives have been taken away, On the last Sabbath day of 1879, Which will be remember'd for a very long time.'

He sat down with a bump as Paul accelerated away from the bridge and Kate laughed.

'That is brutal,' she said. 'Maybe we should have called ourselves The McGonagalls instead of The Ossians.'

'What are you saying about my lyrics, exactly?' said Connor.

They drove past the *Discovery*, Captain Scott's ship that a canny tourist office had used to rebrand the city. A tiny Christmas tree sat on the prow of the ship, dwarfed by the vessel's elaborate rigging and three masts.

'The city of discovery, eh?' said Connor as they headed away from the river. He passed the joint to Danny and took another hit from his bottle.

The gig was in the basement of Drouthy Neebors, a pub opposite the art college on Perth Road. One of a chain of Scottish theme pubs, it was named after a line in Robert Burns' 'Tam O'Shanter', but that's where the poetic tendencies of the place ended. Nevertheless it was a tight wee live venue with a decent reputation.

As they loaded in the gear, Connor heard that Nirvana ringtone and felt his stomach tighten. He'd put all that Nick stuff to the back of his mind in St Andrews, now here was tinny little Kurt Cobain riffing away like a maniac in his pocket. Shit, shit, shit.

He glanced into the van and saw the kitbag in a pile of stuff in the corner. He'd decided to bring it as his main bag, using his clothes to cover up the packages inside. The only other thing in there was a copy of the James Macpherson collection of Ossian's epic poetry, which Connor had bought a couple of years back and never got through. He'd first heard about Ossian a few years ago at an art exhibition full of strange, moody collages about the myth, and he'd become kind of besotted with the idea. When he finally managed to track down a copy of the book, he discovered he was more in love with the story of Ossian than the actual poetry. To be honest, he couldn't make head nor tail of the flowery, overblown language. He'd brought the book in a final attempt to get to grips with it, at least that's what he told himself, but he knew it wasn't even going to get opened in the next fortnight.

A farty drumkit sound had kicked in on the ringtone as he took the phone from his pocket and moved away from the van. It said 'Jim' on the screen. He answered it.

'Connor?' The voice was relaxed and surprisingly well spoken.

'Yeah.'

'Jim here. I believe you're expecting my call?'

'Yeah.'

'You've got something for me?'

'Yeah.'

'Do you say anything except yeah?'

'If there's something worth saying.'

'Fair enough. Where are you?'

'Drouthy's. You know it?'

'Meet me at the *Discovery* in half an hour.'

'The ship?'

'Of course the ship. You think there are two *Discoveries*?'

'Just checking.'

'You know where it is?'

'Think so. We came past it on the way in.'

'Good. So, half an hour?'

'What if I'm in the middle of something?'

'Are you?'

'Not really.'

'Well. See you then. And don't forget the package.'

'I'm not a fucking idiot.'

'I don't know that, do I?'

'Wait. How will I know you?'

'You think I'll have a carnation in my buttonhole? Maybe I'll be carrying a rolled-up copy of the *Financial Times*?'

'I don't fucking know, do I?'

'I'll be the one hanging around in the freezing cold, looking as if he's waiting for someone to arrive with a package for him.'

'Right.'

He put the phone away. The rest of them were coming and going, loading stuff in from the van. This was doing his head in, having to sneak around and think of excuses to disappear. He waited until it was just him and Danny at the van then announced that he was nipping along the road for fags. He waited for Danny to lug his kick drum inside, shouldered the kitbag and headed down the road to look for a taxi.

After a few minutes no cabs had passed, so he resigned himself to hoofing it. He knew roughly which direction to head and, as he walked, he rehearsed in his mind what he would say. What did people say at drug deals? Was there an etiquette involved? A set of social rules he knew nothing about? This guy Jim had seemed all right on the phone, but what if he turned out to be an arsehole or a psycho? What if he wanted to open the package, or if he didn't have anything to give Connor in return? As he walked down Perth Road then Nethergate the pavement got busier, mostly with students. It was dark already, and Connor kept turning round and looking behind nervously. What if someone was following him? What about that figure he'd seen in St Andrews at the cathedral? Could Drug Enforcement or the police or whoever it was really be following him? If so, would they pounce as soon as he met Jim, or wait and nick him later? Jesus, his heart couldn't take all this. He still had some gin left in the plastic bottle, and he slugged it as he went. He stepped out to cross the road at the bottom of Nethergate and a sleek blue Beamer swerved to avoid him. What kind of cars did undercover cops drive? Surely nothing as flash as a BMW.

By the time he reached Discovery Point he was sweating despite the cold. A thin rain had started and the temperature must've been kicking around freezing. Teatime on a Tuesday in December wasn't exactly prime tourist season, and the *Discovery* was deserted, both the ship and the rotund visitor centre alongside. Connor was impressed by the size of the ship, its triangulation of masts and ornate tangle of rigging. At the other side of the closed visitor centre was a small car park with a few shiny executive cars in it. Standing in the shadows of the visitor centre was a short, round figure smoking a cigarette. Connor approached him, and as he got closer he saw the man was smartly dressed in an expensive leather jacket, dress trousers and leather shoes. He was middle-aged, with a friendly face, thinning white hair and chubby fingers.

'Jim?'

'Hello, Connor,' said the man, switching the fag to his left hand and holding his right hand out. Connor shook it. 'Can you believe they took this thing to the Antarctic?' he said, pointing his cigarette at the ship.

'When was that?'

'Hundred years ago. Must've been bloody freezing.' He crushed the fag end under his shoe. 'The package?'

Connor unzipped the bag and rummaged around inside, pulling out the correct parcel on the second attempt and handing it over. Jim briefly checked that it had his name on it, then put it in a holdall by his feet.

'Nick said you'd have something in return,' said Connor.

'What's he got on you?'

'Sorry?'

'What's he got on you? You don't exactly look like this is your usual line of work, so I'm assuming that he's got something over you, making you do this.'

'That would be about right. Now, you have something for Nick, yeah?'

Jim looked at him, then slowly removed a thick brown envelope from his jacket pocket and handed it over. It was obviously money, thought Connor, as he stuck it in his bag, but how much? And for what, exactly? He decided to ask.

'What have we just given each other?'

'Come on. I think it's best that you don't know.'

'You're probably right. Can I ask you something?'

'You can ask.'

'How did *you* get into this? You don't exactly look like the drug-dealer type.'

'Who mentioned drugs?'

'You know what I mean.'

'You think I should be a greasy little working-class smackhead?'

'Not exactly.'

'Everyone takes drugs these days, Connor, I'm sure you're aware of that. You know Nick, after all.'

'I suppose.'

'You're in a band, is that right?'

'Yeah.'

'Any good?'

'We do OK.'

'You going to be famous?'

'I doubt it, at this rate.'

'Shame. If you did, this would make a great wee story for dinner parties.'

'Yeah, hilarious.'

Connor looked around him. He could hear the waves splashing against the *Discovery*'s hull, and the noise from the riverside road as cars swished past in the gloom thirty yards behind him. Above, a small twin prop was coming in to land further along the waterfront. There must be an airstrip along there, thought Connor. He suddenly remembered the gig.

'Shit. What time is it?'

Jim looked at his watch. 'Six o'clock.'

'I'm late for soundcheck.'

'I'll be seeing you, then.' Jim held out a hand, which Connor quickly shook. 'Good luck with the gig. You'll get a taxi at the train station, just over the road there. I'd give you a lift, but it's hardly wise.'

With that, Jim headed towards one of the expensive cars sitting in the car park, its lights blinking as he unlocked it. Connor watched him get in and drive off. He looked around again, and couldn't see anyone on foot, just the blur of cars on the nearby road. So that was it, he was a drug dealer now. Fucking great. He lifted the kitbag and headed towards the taxi rank at the train station, picturing himself getting on the first train out of this fucking place instead.

Considering it was a wintry Tuesday night, Drouthy's was surprisingly busy with uni and art-college students, as well as a gang of underage skater kids blagging drinks on fake ID. Connor tried to put all memories of the meeting at the *Discovery* behind him as he thought about the show, helped on by a couple of large sherbet-dab fingers of speed in the toilets after soundcheck. The gig was a double header alongside a Dundee band they knew called The Lithium Sea Monkeys. Connor didn't much care for their heads-down, indie thrash punk but they were nice guys, and the fact that three of them were from Belfast meant Danny automatically bonded. Dundee University seemed to be mostly populated by Northern Irish. Kids left Belfast in their droves, tired of being surrounded by all the bullshit. Sectarian Glasgow wasn't an option and Edinburgh was seen as the home of snooty yahs, so a small expat student community had grown up in Dundee.

Connor was a little jealous of the community spirit he heard about at Dundee Uni, it was small enough for people to know each other but not so small that it was claustrophobic. Then again, he'd bombed out of higher education after a year – and it would've been sooner if his tutors could've found him – so what the hell did he know about it?

Most of the two hundred kids rammed into the sweaty basement had come to see The Lithium Sea Monkeys and they put on a fine show, thrashing, flailing, shouting and being a whole heap of fun. Unlike the previous night, the crowd were at least interested enough to pay attention to The Ossians. The sight of a guitar band with two women in it was still a rarity in indie world, and it was a fact that always gained The Ossians extra attention from guys. Kate and Hannah tended to shrug it off, used to being objectified since hitting puberty. But it drove Connor mad, not just because they were his sister and his girlfriend, but because it was another example of how fucking annoying men were.

The crowd's reaction changed from vague interest to enthusiastic cheering as The Ossians did their thing. Connor was swept up in a familiar contradictory feeling of self-satisfaction and mild panic at his band's apparent popularity. As they approached the end of their set, Connor introduced 'RLS'.

'Today is the anniversary of Robert Louis Stevenson's death,' he said. 'This song is dedicated to him.'

As he picked out the first gentle chords, a shout of 'tits out' came from the front, clear as a slap in the face. Connor glared into the crowd and saw a couple of skinny teenagers with stringy arms and shaven heads laughing to each other, not even looking at the stage. Without taking his guitar off he launched at them and landed with an elbow in one guy's ribs and the guitar headstock in the face of the other. The jump pulled his guitar lead out, which lay buzzing loudly on stage.

The crowd separated as the three of them sprawled to the floor, Connor thrashing out with his right fist and using his left hand to bring the guitar neck down on them. After a moment of surprise the two guys started throwing punches back, and one of them quickly had Connor in a headlock while the other punched him in the face and stomach. Everyone around them was frozen with shock. Suddenly Danny was on them, flooring the smaller of the two guys without breaking stride. The other guy looked warily at Danny and backed off. Danny dragged Connor to his feet and round the side of the stage. By now Hannah and Kate had walked offstage, flicking amp switches as they went. It was all over as quickly as it had begun. Two bouncers from upstairs made it down, but since there didn't seem to be anyone obviously misbehaving they just stood around, staring hard at punters and puffing their chests out.

'What's the matter with you?' Hannah shouted in Connor's face. 'You think you're defending our honour or some bullshit? You're just as bad as those wankers, you bloody idiot. Macho bollocks. We women are very impressed with your ability to fight with strangers who shout at us. Do you want to club me over the head and carry me back to your fucking cave now? Sometimes I wonder what on earth goes on in that head of yours, if anything goes on in there at all, which I very much doubt.'

She stamped her foot and raised her face to the ceiling.

'Han's right,' said Danny. 'You're not helping. The girls get shit all the time, you just have to rise above that crap. Besides, you can't fight for shite, so you always get beat up and I have to rescue you.'

'Thanks for your opinions, but I'll do what the fuck I like. What, now I'm not allowed to object to a pair of cunts disrespecting two of my best friends?'

'That's not what it's about and you know it,' said Hannah. 'If they were shouting something about Danny you wouldn't go off the deep end. Or if they were shouting something about you, you wouldn't be half as annoyed as you are now.'

She crouched down in front of him.

'Look, it's not as if it doesn't piss us off,' she said, her voice softening. 'But you've got to get it in perspective. Of course we want to smash their faces in, but they're not worth it. That's what you have to keep telling yourself, idiots like that aren't worth the time or energy.'

Kate was standing over the pair of them, arms folded. 'Well, little brother, that's three gigs and three beatings. This tour is working out swell, isn't it? At this rate, by the time we get to Glasgow you'll be a basket case. I can't even be bothered telling you what an arsehole you are.' She looked around the crowd. Some people were watching them, others pretending not to. 'I need a drink. Shall we?'

Connor watched her disappear through the crowd, her long black hair bobbing from side to side as she strode towards the bar. He felt like a basket case already.

Later that night, the heavens opened and a bitter rain lashed the streets. They were at a party in the student flat shared by two of The Lithium Sea Monkeys, a large bay window looking out over the river at the dim sodium speckle of Fife. Arab Strap played in the background and a simmering tension from earlier hung in the air.

Connor's face was a punchbag. His left eye was swollen with bruising, as was his upper lip, which now had several gashes along it. His nose had patches of bluey brown colour and seemed looser than a nose should be, and he had a large scrape down the right side of his face from the corner of his eye to his jawline. He moved his fingers over his face and was reminded of the Elephant Man. He smiled at the thought. He was visiting his parents tomorrow and the sight of him in this state would drive his mum mad. Perfect.

One of the Lithium lads produced some coke, which Connor

snorted two lines of despite a searing pain in his misshapen nose. He pinched another handful of Feminax from Kate's handbag and took them in the toilet, washed down with a hefty glass of whisky. He was starting to feel all right. He was looking at his injuries in the bathroom mirror when he heard that 'Teen Spirit' ringtone, and the smile left his face.

He took the phone out his pocket, only now realising he still had his coat on. It was Nick. He pressed reply.

'How did it go with Jim?'

'Do you know how to change the ringtone on this phone? It's doing my head in.'

'I asked you a question.'

'And I asked you a question.'

'Don't get smart with me, Connor, or I'll break your fucking legs.'

'How are you going to do that, if I never come back?'

'Sorry?'

'If I never come back to Edinburgh, and you can't leave because you're being tailed by the fucking FBI or CIA or whoever the fuck it is, then how are you going to do anything to me?'

'I take it you're drunk?'

'Well?'

'Connor, you little prick. I know people. All around Scotland. Don't ever forget that. All it takes is a phone call. So sober the fuck up, and tell me how the meeting went.'

Connor gently prodded his swollen eye and winced.

'Fine.'

'He gave you an envelope?'

'How much is in there?'

'Don't be stupid, Connor.'

'Don't you think I should know what I'm carrying around, so I know how careful I should be?'

'You should be very careful, believe me.'

'I could open it and find out.'

'I wouldn't do that if I were you.'

'How would you know if I did?'

'You really must be steaming. Remind me to call you earlier in the evening next time.'

'Or I could go to the police.'

'We both know that's not an option.'

'Do we?'

'Yes. We do.'

'I'd still like to know what I'm carting around.'

'Connor, let me make this clear, so that it gets into even your retarded, drunken skull. If any envelope or parcel is opened, or anything is missing by the time you get back here, you're a fucking dead man. If I hear from any of my associates that their packages have been tampered with, you're a fucking dead man. If you fuck this up in any way, you're a fucking dead man. Got it?'

'I'm a dead man, got it.' Connor ran his finger down the scratch on his cheek. 'Now, are you going to tell me how to change this fucking ringtone?'

'Goodbye, fuckwit.'

As Connor put the phone back in his pocket, he felt something else in there. He pulled it out. It was a neatly folded piece of paper. He unfolded it. It was a flyer for the gig they'd just done. He turned it over, and on the back was written 'your secrets are safe with me' in neat handwriting. What the fuck? Was this meant for him? Maybe he'd lifted the flyer off a table somewhere, and this was a random note meant for someone else. But he couldn't remember doing that. And if he hadn't, then someone had deliberately gone into his coat pocket and put it there. Jesus. When had he not had his jacket on since they arrived in Dundee? He struggled to remember through the booze, then realised that he hadn't been wearing it for the gig. It was lying at the side of the stage in a pile of bags and guitar cases. Had someone put the note in his pocket then? Fucking hell.

He turned the paper over in his hands. He couldn't fathom what it meant. Had someone been following him? He'd been imagining someone following him since Edinburgh, but he'd put it down to drug-addled paranoia. Then again, what about that guy in St Andrews at the gravestones? If someone really *was* following him, then why? And had they seen him down at the *Discovery*? Oh,

Christ. But who would be doing this? If it was the police, why would they leave a note in his pocket? That was just stupid. Maybe Nick had arranged it, to put the shitters up him? That didn't really make sense either. Shit.

He couldn't handle this, not the state he was in. He sat on the toilet, still looking at the note. The handwriting was neat, almost pristine. He didn't recognise it. What did it mean, 'your secrets are safe with me'? Everyone had secrets, but the only thing he could think of was this drug-mule business. Did someone else in the band suspect? If they did, why write a note? Why not just confront him? And anyway, it wasn't any of their handwriting.

There were too many unanswered questions. His head ached. He wasn't going to solve anything sitting on the toilet, and he needed another drink, so he got up and headed back to the living room, folding the note and putting it back into his pocket. In the living room, Kate, Hannah and Danny were chatting and laughing around a small table with Dave and Sean, The Lithium Sea Monkeys' guitarist and drummer. They were second-year art students who made short films in their spare time. Paul was on a sofa chatting to two bohemian-looking girls, all bangles and lace, and another dozen or so people were hanging around drinking and filling the room with smoke and noise.

'Here he is,' said Danny, as Connor entered. 'Quasimodo. How's the face feeling?'

'It's my Michael Jackson look,' said Connor, trying to smile but unable to move his mouth muscles far enough. 'You like?'

'The lads here were saying we're invited back anytime if we can guarantee entertainment like that,' said Danny.

'If Con tries that again we'll not be going anywhere with him, right Han?' said Kate. She looked at Hannah, who just dragged on her Marlboro Light, stubbed it out and got up.

'I'm getting another drink,' she said. 'Anyone else?' There were nods all round. She turned towards the kitchen but Connor held her arm.

'Something up, love?'

'You know what's up,' she said. She turned to face him and her voice lowered. 'I'm really fucking angry with you, so it's probably best if you stay out my way at the moment.'

'But I was only trying to . . .'

'I don't think you know what you were trying to do,' she said. 'Whatever it was, I don't think it had anything to do with me or Kate. There's stuff going on up there' – she made a tapping motion with her finger towards his head – 'that needs sorting. Trouble is, you're always too bloody loaded to do anything about it. Just let me know when you've straightened out a bit, and you want to talk about it.'

'I'm not loaded all the fucking time,' he said, still gripping her arm. 'All right, I'm not sober at this precise moment, but we're at a party, on fucking tour. We're a rock 'n' roll band, for Christ's sake. We're supposed to be drinking and taking drugs. I didn't realise this was a teetotal fortnight or I wouldn't have signed up for it.'

'And I didn't realise your drinking was going to be such a fucking problem,' said Hannah. 'Now let go of my arm, I'm going to get a drink.'

'Wait, Han,' Connor pleaded. 'Look, there's stuff going on, weird stuff that I can't explain.'

'What sort of stuff, exactly?'

Hannah stood there, a look of anger and sadness on her face. Connor thought about the note in his pocket, the kitbag, the *Discovery* and the shadowy figures. Even in his drunken stupor, he knew he would sound like an idiot if he came out with any of it. He looked at the ground and shook his head slightly.

'Nothing,' he said.

She headed out the door. He slumped down at the table, and took a hit of whisky. The others were watching him.

'What?' he said. 'You all think I have a drink problem as well, is that it?'

Dave and Sean looked down at their beers, and Danny tried to put a hand on Connor's shoulder, but he shrugged it off.

'You just seem a bit all over the place at the moment,' said Danny. 'Everyone likes a bevvy, Con, me more than most. But you do seem to be taking everything a bit seriously. Like you said, it's a tour, we're in a band, it's supposed to be a bit of fun. I think we all just need to chill out a bit. And with that in mind, I'm going to skin up.'

Connor sat under a cloud. He felt like a kid being condescended to by his parents. Conversations started up again and his mind drifted. He looked out the window at the pummelling rain, caught in the yellow street-light glare as it pinged off the pavement. The clouds were so low you couldn't see where they ended and where the river started. They were only a few miles and a couple of days away from Edinburgh, but Connor felt lost. But then didn't he feel lost in Edinburgh as well? Didn't he always feel fucking lost?

Faces flitted across his mind – Nick's twisted smile as he showed Connor the Stanley knife, the fan at the Edinburgh gig gazing at him from the half-darkness, Jim wishing him luck as they shook hands. Once they got some distance between themselves and Edinburgh, then things might settle down, might relax. Christ, he needed to relax. But how could he, with all this shit going on?

Later, after more drink, grass and coke, he and Hannah argued again. Connor couldn't even work out what they were arguing about. Doors were slammed. He couldn't sleep. He sat up on his own drinking whisky, his eyes unfocused and his hands too shaky to skin up.

He went to the toilet, banging into one wall, then the other. He didn't recognise the swollen face in the mirror. It began to take the shape of a fat woman's face with too much make-up on, and a nose which couldn't decide which way it wanted to point. As he stood there trying to focus, he heard noises coming through the wall from the bedroom next door. As he listened, he realised it was the sound of a couple shagging. There were whispers and female moans, grunts and the rhythmic thump of a headboard on a wall. He stood there, captivated by the sound of it, trapped by the intensity of emotion. The moans and grunts and thumps gradually sped up, building in Connor's ears as he looked in the mirror at a face he barely knew. The intensity of the sounds kept growing, and Connor felt a slight flicker of tension in his cock. He stood there wondering when the noise was going to stop and release him, he couldn't walk away while it was still going on, he was caught up in it, helpless. Just as he thought it was going to go on forever, there was a loud final bang of headboard on wall, a female gasp, then a male voice saying 'Jesus'. Shit, he recognised the voice – it was Danny. He'd know that accent anywhere. So Danny was getting his end away, good for him. Who the hell with? He tried to remember the girls who'd been kicking around the flat earlier, but couldn't picture any of them. As far as he could remember, Danny had only been talking to the Belfast guys, himself, Hannah and Kate. He must've got speaking to someone else later on. Connor couldn't remember seeing him chat up anyone, but he'd been lost in his own wee world for the latter half of the night, drowning in a sea of booze and paranoia, and arguing with Hannah over Christ knows what. Well, good for Danny, he deserves a break. Connor staggered out the toilet, glancing at the closed bedroom door. He would have to try and remember this tomorrow, quiz Danny about it. The lucky dog.

He returned to an empty living room. He eventually fell asleep in a chair in front of the large bay window with a glass of whisky still in his hand, and dreamt in black and white that he was the Elephant Man being chased through the air by legions of dark, winged beasts.

5

Arbroath

'Blood red and backwards
The past will claim us all'

The Ossians, 'Declaration Of Arbroath'

It was one of those miserable days when the sun never had a chance. The sky was full of low fuzzy clouds that couldn't even be bothered raining; they just sat there bored and tired.

Connor had woken up after three hours' sleep. He looked at his glass of whisky then downed it. He finished making the joint on the table next to him and smoked it. Then he rubbed a finger of speed on to his gums. He had a sore face in too many places to bother counting and a blinding headache. He raked through the kitchen drawers, found some Nurofen and took four, washing them down with lager. He put the rest in his coat pocket. Once everyone was up he tried frying some bacon and eggs, by way of an apology for his arguments with Hannah, but made a mess of it, and besides, no one was hungry.

Hangovers and lethargy washed through them, and they sat mostly in silence with the television on for an hour or so, just the occasional burst of Paul's prattle breaking the monotony. Connor kept glancing at Hannah, but she ignored him. Danny and Kate kept smiling at each other, but no one else noticed. Connor felt like he was trapped in a bubble, cut off from the rest of the world by a thick chemical film.

With daylight disappearing fast, they dragged themselves out to the van. They eased into the vehicle like pensioners on a bus. They were due at the Alexanders' house for tea and Connor couldn't think of a single place in the world he would less like to be. Then again, at least they didn't have to play a gig with these hangovers.

They drove up the coast, The Zephyrs on the stereo. The road passed through rolling farmland, at this time of year barren, muddy and depressing. The occasional tree stood lonely on the horizon, bare branches a tangle of nests. Screeching crows circled the trees and once or twice they saw a rusty tractor ploughing a field for no apparent reason.

About halfway there, Paul broke the silence.

'Look,' he said, 'Con, Han – why don't we forget about last night? Drink was drunk and things were said that shouldn't've been. It doesn't mean anything. Christ, if everyone was held accountable for their drunken actions the world wouldn't get anywhere. Just remember we're all mates and we have been for a long time. We've got a long way to go on this tour, so why don't we just put it all behind us and get on with things. OK?'

Connor looked at Hannah, who was just staring out the window. No one said anything.

'OK?' said Paul, more pointedly.

'Fine by me,' said Connor. 'Look Han' – he was talking to her back – 'I'm really sorry about last night. You were right. About everything. OK? Can we just forget about it?'

'Fine,' said Hannah, still facing forwards.

The road into Arbroath was flanked by a golf course then football pitches on the right, factories and a caravan park on the left. Connor hadn't been down this road since last Christmas and he felt nauseous. He hated his parents. OK, maybe not hate, but he resented them, at least. And he resented this town, for all the usual bullshit reasons that people hate the suffocating small towns that shape them. He looked at Kate. She didn't look too comfortable back in Arbroath either. She was fidgeting with the door lock, and picking at invisible threads on her jeans. Neither of them had been keen on stopping here on the tour, but Paul had pointed out they weren't exactly rolling in cash, and they had to take advantage of every free bed and meal they could if they were to make any decent money. It was a year since either of them had been back, so the arguments and constant bickering that seemed to pepper every Alexander family gathering had faded from their memories a little. Now, on the road to their parents' house, it was all coming back.

What made it worse was that the rest of them got on so well with Jean and Alan. They'd met them a few times in Edinburgh, and Hannah had been up to Arbroath a couple of times. In fact, Hannah got on with them best of all, and couldn't understand Kate and Con's problem. They seemed perfectly nice to her, if a little eccentric in a jaded, bohemian way. At least they were still together, she'd pointedly told Connor once.

They approached a filling station.

'Can we stop?' said Kate. 'I need to get a few things.'

'We're almost there,' said Paul.

'Just pull over and let me out.'

They pulled into the forecourt and Kate and Hannah went into the shop. Hannah started flicking through magazines while Kate absent-mindedly scanned the shelves of chocolate and crisps. She was thinking about last night, which had been pretty fucking great. She could've guessed Danny would be attentive in bed, then again she'd gone out with plenty of guys who'd seemed nice enough until you got them into the bedroom, where they became selfish bastards. But for all Danny's tender touches and thoughtfulness there was also something pleasantly raw about him, the sheer bulk of him. They'd shagged twice in quick succession, the first time with him on top, the second time more slowly as Kate took control, playing with his cock until it was hard then sitting astride him and moving up and down on him gently for what seemed like an age until they both came again.

No matter what happened now, she and Danny could never be just friends again. She wanted him now, and she wanted to be with him in the future, too. The thought scared her a little, because things were so unformed, so precarious between them, but she had a gut instinct that Danny was worth holding on to, that one day she could love him, if all the breaks went their way. The thought shocked her. She didn't fall in love easily. She'd been in and out of plenty of relationships since school, none of which felt like this one.

Mostly she'd just been playing around, without investing much emotion in what was going on. Maybe it was different this time because she knew Danny as a friend first. That was why she didn't want to tell Connor, or anyone else for that matter. She hadn't even discussed it with Danny, for Christ's sake. To mention it, to have it spoken of, was to expose it to possible destruction, and she wasn't ready to take that chance yet. What if she fucked it up? What if he didn't feel the same way? What if, what if. Why had Danny told Hannah? She wasn't happy that anyone knew and, although she trusted Hannah, she *was* Connor's girlfriend, and it put her in an almost impossible position.

'Putting it off, huh?' It was Hannah next to her.

'Sorry?'

'The parental visit. I assume this is a delaying tactic.'

'Yeah, something like that. I just don't feel up to all that stuff. Not with this hangover. Plus I think my period is coming on and I've run out of painkillers. I'm sure I had some, but I can't find them.'

Kate wasn't happy being back in Arbroath but, unlike Connor, who seemed to rage against the whole town for whatever reasons, Kate's gripe was specifically with her mother, who always knew exactly which buttons to press.

'How are things going with Danny boy?' said Hannah. 'Anything to report?'

Kate was disgusted to find that she was blushing like a schoolkid, the blood unstoppably rushing to her face as she remembered last night and the feel of Danny inside her.

'Look at you, you've taken a total beamer!' said Hannah. 'What is it? Have you shagged?'

'Last night.'

'Oh my God! And?'

'And what?'

'How was it?'

'I'm not going into details, for God's sake.'

'No, but, you know, generally, how was it?'

'Great.'

Hannah squealed and Kate found herself smiling widely.

'This is so exciting,' said Hannah. 'You and Danny are getting it on! You really need to tell Connor now. I mean, how am I supposed to keep a secret like this?'

'I'll tell him, I just need to find the right time. Maybe tonight.'

'Good idea, cos if you don't, I'm probably going to blurt it out drunk.'

'Please don't. Anyway, I thought you were hardly talking to him after last night.'

'Oh, I'm just making him sweat a little. Let him know what he's missing out on if he keeps pissing me off.'

'What were you arguing about anyway?'

'To be honest I was pretty steaming, and I can't really remember. Stupid really. I probably owe him an apology.'

'I doubt that very much.'

'Maybe not, but it takes two and all that, and I probably didn't help by flying off the handle.'

'You've got nothing to be sorry about, it's Con who keeps doing idiotic shit.'

'He's not that bad, just a bit highly strung.'

'That's one way of putting it. He's lucky to have you, you know.'

'Maybe,' said Hannah quietly before perking herself up. 'Right, let's get stocked up on comfort food and painkillers.'

Back in the van Connor had finished skinning up and Danny was eyeing the lit joint.

'Sure that's a good idea?' he asked.

'I'm just smoking it now so my fucking hippy parents don't hog it all,' said Connor, passing the joint across. 'They'd probably think they were being all decadent and wild. Bastards.'

Connor watched as Danny inhaled deeply. There was something nagging at the back of his mind, something from last night he was going to ask Danny about, but he couldn't remember what it was. He pictured the last time he'd seen him, sitting across the table late into the night, Danny skinning up expertly with one hand. Maybe all this grass was knocking his short-term memory to fuck. It would come to him later on, once he'd had a few more drinks.

The girls returned with crisps, chocolate, juice, painkillers and a couple of newspapers.

'There's a review of last night in the local paper,' said Kate.

She flung the folded paper at Connor, who quickly scanned it.

'Not bad, only three factual errors,' he said. 'Apparently we're a Glasgow-based band; Kate, you were playing guitar last night; and at one point we played a song called "My Evil Sin". How does this shite make it into print? Fuck's sake.' He passed the paper to Danny, who read through it carefully.

'Fucking hell,' he shouted. 'Big Country! Big fucking Country! Do we fuck sound like Big Country.'

'I know,' said Connor. 'I didn't want to mention that. Some folk have no clue, do they? Obviously this twat has never heard a decent record in his life, so it's hardly worth getting het up about.'

'Hey,' said Hannah, 'that *Scotsman* piece is in today. Look at us all arsing around on the beach. You look great, Con, with your black eye and wonky nose. Mind, you look a lot better in this photo than you do at the moment.'

'Thanks, love,' he said, noticing the thaw in her voice. 'Give it here.'

He read through the article. It was the main feature on the page under a large windswept band picture.

'It says here I'm pretentious . . . egotistical . . . ranting . . . and . . .' his finger ran along the lines as he spoke, '. . . passionately confused. Not a bad haul.'

Kate took the paper from him and read it. 'At least they've left all your swearing in, that's something I suppose. What d'you think, Paul?'

She passed the paper to him and he glanced at it briefly.

'You didn't say anything racist, did you?' he asked Connor.

'Only about the English, probably.'

'Well, there's no such thing as bad publicity.' He started up the engine and pulled his seatbelt on. 'Any chance we can get moving to your folks' place? I'm starving.'

The van pulled away from the forecourt with a squeal of tyres and they were heading for the family showdown.

They hadn't made it past the hallway and it'd already started. Jean Alexander was a trim, short figure at fifty-four and she wore a tight white blouse with several buttons undone exposing a pale, freckled breastbone, along with skintight jeans and thin-heeled boots. She'd already mentioned Kate's hair (split ends, needed conditioning), lack of make-up ('Just to bring out your eyes, dear') and clothes (apparently black wasn't the camouflage some people thought it was). Then she noticed Connor's face, held up her hands and shrieked.

'My baby,' she wailed, with just the tiniest hint of the Highlands left in her accent. 'What have they done to you?' She went to put her hands on his cheeks but Connor flinched away.

'Hi, Mum,' he said in a heavy voice, yet with the beginnings of a smile on his lips. 'It's nothing. Just a little argument with a fan.'

'Some fan!' Jean squealed. 'Have you had it seen to? Come on, let's clean it up.' She tried to hold Connor's hand but he pulled away.

'Leave it, Mum,' he said. 'Stop fucking fussing.'

'I see your language hasn't improved,' said Jean. 'But you really must have those cuts seen to. Come on.' She tried again to take his hand but he slipped her grasp.

'Honestly, Mum, forget about it. It's just a bit bruised.'

'Hey,' said Kate, 'weren't you in the middle of having your usual go at me, anyway?'

'No, dear,' said Jean, distracted away from Connor. 'I was just trying to help you look your best. It's important to look your best.'

'Tell that to the Elephant Man over there,' said Kate, laughing. 'Where's Dad?'

'He'll be pottering about somewhere, probably, you know your father. Try the study, he's mostly in there these days.' She turned back to Connor. 'My baby, look at the state of you. How did this happen?'

'I told you, a disagreement with a punter,' said Connor. 'Now can we at least get in the fucking door. And how about offering us a drink? Some host you are.'

Hannah, Danny and Paul remained tight-lipped. They'd seen this performance a handful of times before, and it didn't pay to get involved. Only now did Jean seem to spot them.

'Hannah, darling, come in,' she said, ushering the three of them to follow Kate and Connor, who had already walked through to the kitchen. 'It's Paul, isn't it? And Danny?'

'Mrs Alexander,' said Danny, making to shake her hand and getting a kiss on each cheek.

'Fuck that, Danny,' she said. 'I'm not a grandmother yet. And I never will be at this rate. Call me Jean, everybody does. Go on through, I'm just in the middle of getting dinner ready, but I'm sure there'll be something to keep everyone going until then.' She called up the stairs, 'Alan! The kids are here. Stop faffing and come down. Wait till you see Connor's face!'

She hurried through to the kitchen where Connor was already handing out beers from a case on the floor.

'You've found the beer,' said Jean. 'Good, good. Would anyone prefer wine? There's plenty in the rack through in the pantry or I've got a bottle of Merlot open here if anyone wants.' She took several mouthfuls from a large glass and waved the half-empty bottle at them.

'We're fine with these, Mum,' said Kate.

'I do wish you wouldn't drink lager, Katherine,' said Jean. 'You know how it affects the stomach. You'll have a beer belly in no time, if you haven't already under all those baggy clothes. No wonder you never seem to have a boyfriend.'

'Fuck's sake,' said Kate, glancing at Danny.

'I'm just saying,' said Jean.

'No, you're not,' said Kate. 'Any psychology student can see you're just projecting your own faded youth and a lifetime of disappointment on to the shoulders of your only daughter.'

'Yes, very clever, dear,' said Jean. 'You're not the only one who went to university, you know. Or watches *The OC*, which seems

85

to be the same thing these days. And I'm not doing any such thing, I'm just looking out for my children. A mother is allowed to do such things, you know.'

'And while we're at it, your pathetic golden boy act with Connor is wearing pretty thin,' said Kate. 'I got a degree, a decent job, a flat and I'm paying off my student debts, and all I get is abuse about drinking beer. Con bombed out of uni after two minutes and has done nothing but get loaded for years and borrow money he'll never pay back . . .'

'Hey,' said Connor.

'. . . and what does he get? The fucking prodigal son treatment. I'm surprised we're not having fatted calf for dinner.'

'If you're quite finished,' said Jean, stirring a large pot of chilli while pouring herself more Merlot. 'Perhaps you'd like to help out around here and show everyone to their rooms.'

'Fine,' said Kate, picking up her bag.

'And track down your father while you're up there, dear. I think he's going a bit deaf.'

'Maybe he chooses not to hear you, Mum. Christ knows, I would.'

Kate headed out the door with Hannah, Danny and Paul traipsing silently behind. Connor opened a second beer from the crate.

'I wish you wouldn't have such a go at Kate all the time. She's got a point, she does get the shit end of the stick.'

'Connor, you're such a sensitive boy, but you know how mothers and daughters are. That's all it is. We're too much alike, that's the problem.'

'I don't think so, somehow,' said Connor. 'And never, ever say that to Kate, or at least make sure there's nothing throwable in the vicinity if you do.'

'You're both so young,' said Jean. 'You'll understand when you're older and you've got kids of your own. Whenever *that's* going to happen.'

'Jesus,' said Connor, laughing. 'Do you know what a cliché you are?'

'Why, of course, dear,' said Jean, swigging more wine. 'But what a delightful cliché I am, don't you think? Now come here and give your mum an Oedipal cuddle.'

Connor just stood looking at her and drinking his beer.

The Alexanders lived in a gently sprawling, beaten-up four-bedroom house that had skulked in unkempt gardens for a hundred years. They'd come into a small inheritance courtesy of Jean's grandmother and bought the place just before the twins were born. They hadn't done much to it since, except the odd bit of painting here and there to cover up garish, swirly wallpaper. The house overlooked the Keptie Pond – a man-made, sludge-filled former boating pond with a small island full of nesting ducks, swans and wiry bushes. Behind the pond sat a fake medieval castle known as the Water Tower, built around the same time as their house, which had originally been used to store the town's water supply. When Connor and Kate were at primary school the Water Tower was where the older kids went to sniff glue, drink cider and fumble around in each other's pants.

A soft, feathery snow fell, coating the landscape in an early Christmas sheen. In the light from the street lamps the snow looked a pale, leathery yellow colour, like jaundiced skin. Connor sat on a broken bench in the front garden smoking a joint with Danny. Hannah and Kate were upstairs and Paul had been roped into helping in the kitchen, where a well-sauced Jean was flirting heavily. Connor and Danny took turns at a bottle of Merlot, swapping it for the joint.

'I used to fall in that pond every winter,' said Connor. 'When it iced over we used to be down there like a shot, daring each other on to the surface, or breaking up the edges and doing chicken runs across the pieces. Sometimes we'd play this game, Sieg Heil, where a bunch of us stomped across the ice in a row, like stormtroopers, gradually getting faster and faster. As you stamp harder and faster the ice behind the line gets weak and bends, so if you fall behind too much you disappear through the weakened surface. You'd think we'd fucking learn. But every year when it got cold we'd be back down, breaking up the edges and falling in. It's only about four feet deep, and half of that is stinking mud, so there's not much danger of drowning. Mum used to send me round the back of the house and hose the shit off before I could go inside. Surprised I never caught hypothermia. Sometimes I wonder how none of us ever got killed, the way we played back then. It was like we were testing how far we could push it, you know?'

Danny took a toke from the joint and swapped it back for the bottle.

'Everyone does that when they're nippers,' he said. 'It's all that rites of passage guff. If we were Aborigines, we'd be off into the bush to wander about for a month eating witchetty grubs. Instead we piss about near lakes, railway lines, harbour walls, electricity pylons and shit like that, just trying to get the kind of kicks our ancestors used to get hunting bears or whatever.'

Connor laughed and handed back the wine bottle. They were silent for a while. They could hear Jean laughing inside and the radio playing something classical and soothing.

'Your mum's pretty friendly,' said Danny after a while.

'That's her game,' said Connor. 'She's always loved sticking it in folks' faces, especially when she's had a few, which is pretty often.' They were quiet again for a moment. 'Must be where I get it from. Do you think you can inherit being an alkie?'

'Nah, I don't go in for all that genetic crap,' said Danny. 'Seems to me you make up your own personality as you go along. There's no use blaming genetics for being fat or stupid, so I've no excuse. You've just got to get on with things.'

'Is that some sort of life philosophy?' said Connor, raising an eyebrow.

'Could be,' said Danny. 'I don't think too much about it, Con, that's your job as the tortured artist. I just sit at the back, drinking and smoking and playing drums. While also looking out for the rest of you hapless buffoons.'

'I meant to say, thanks for jumping in for me yesterday at the gig.'

'No problem.'

They swapped the joint and the bottle.

'Shit,' said Connor. 'I just remembered, I knew there was something I wanted to talk to you about. Last night, you dirty dog, I heard you.'

'What?'

'I heard you shagging through the bathroom wall. You jammy bastard. Who the hell was it? I couldn't remember you chatting to any of the girls at the party later on.' · ·

Danny looked uncomfortable. 'It wasn't me, Con.'

'But I heard you,' Connor laughed. 'It was definitely you.'

'Which room?'

'The one next to the bathroom.'

'I was across the hall, mate, sorry.'

'But I recognised your voice.'

'Remember Dave and Sean are both Belfast boys, must've been one of them.'

'Shit, I could've sworn it was you.'

'Were you steaming, by any chance?'

'Of course, but I was sure it was your voice.'

'Don't you think I'd own up if it was me? I don't exactly get much action, so if I was shagging you'd be the first to know about it.'

'I suppose.' Connor punched Danny's arm gently. 'Maybe you'll get some before the tour's over, eh?'

'Maybe,' said Danny, finishing the last of the wine, as Connor ground the dead roach into the gravel with his toe.

'Food's up!' came a high-pitched voice from inside the house, followed by laughter then the clatter of a pan lid hitting the floor.

'Let's face the music,' said Connor.

Danny let out a deep breath as he watched Connor head in, then looked out across the road. The snow had stopped and the pond surface looked like a waxy, black mole on the snowy skin of the land. He shook his head as he got up and headed inside for dinner.

Seven places were set around a scuffed beechwood kitchen table, candlelight throwing shadows on to pine-panelled walls. Jean was talking and gesticulating, making sure she was centre of attention. She sat at the top of the table and motioned to Danny as he came in.

'Sit here, Danny, next to me,' she said, waving theatrically at the chair next to her. 'I want all the handsome young boys next to me, and I've already positioned young Paul here on my left.'

'Hey, what am I?' said Connor.

'Please, dear,' said Jean. 'We're not that incestuous yet, are we? Sit down and tuck in, everyone.'

Connor and Danny sat down in front of plates of steaming chilli and rice. Hannah and Kate came in a minute later followed by Alan Alexander, a quiet, serious-looking man in his fifties with trim white hair like a Roman emperor and small, oblong glasses perched on the end of his nose.

'Hello, Connor,' he said carefully, as if peering under a stone at the slaters beneath.

'Hey, Dad,' said Connor. He turned to Hannah and Kate. 'And what have you ladies been up to? Talking about me behind my back?'

'Get over yourself,' said Kate.

She took a seat next to him and Hannah moved round the table to sit opposite, with Alan sliding into place at the opposite end from Jean.

'What *have* you been up to, Alan?' said Jean. 'Honestly.'

'Just working upstairs, dear,' he said, almost whispering. 'Then chatting to the girls for a bit.'

'I might have known. A pretty girl like Hannah in the house and you're straight in there.'

Everyone pretended to ignore this except Kate.

'Actually, Mum, at least Dad had the fucking decency to ask how I was getting on. You know, how my job's going, life in general, stuff like that? Instead of just harping on at me the minute I'm in the door about my lack of fucking lip gloss.'

'Let's just eat,' said Alan. 'Kate, I'm sure your mother wasn't having a go.'

'Why do you always defend the old lush?' said Kate.

'I beg your pardon,' shouted Jean. 'How dare you call me a lush, you prissy little madam.'

'Mum, just shut up, eh?' said Connor.

'That shows you know nothing about me at all,' said Kate. 'At least I flirt with men my own age, not boys twenty years younger than me.'

'Look!' Connor was standing up, wobbling. 'Can we all just shut the fuck up and eat!'

There was silence. Danny, Paul and Hannah picked up their cutlery and started on the food. Connor couldn't touch his. He tried a couple of mouthfuls but the speed had ruined his appetite. He couldn't remember the last time he'd had a decent meal. Or the last time he hadn't had a headache. His jaw was throbbing in time to a jabbing pain across his forehead. He downed the glass of wine in front of him as polite small talk stuttered up around the table, mainly between Hannah and his folks. Connor couldn't fathom why Hannah got on well with Alan and Jean. Maybe it was just easier to talk to other people's parents than your own.

He looked across at her now and was pleased to find he still thought she was fucking sexy. What wasn't to fancy? She was wearing a tight, chocolate blouse displaying a perky cleavage, a short fawn skirt and knee-length boots. Her red hair framed her soft, smiling features perfectly. If only he hadn't been taking so much amphetamine, he could've had a hard-on right now under the table. As it was, his body felt like a limp, washed-out bag of bones – beaten, bruised and asexual. He really had to cut down some of his drink and drug intake. At least he was thinking about it, that was a good sign, wasn't it? The first step of twelve, or whatever it was. In the time it'd taken him to think this he'd necked another glass of wine and the speed bag in his pocket felt tingly hot against his thigh. He couldn't concentrate because the pain in his jaw had spread to his ears, and a roaring sound drowned out the conversation around the table. He could see lips moving but couldn't make out anything.

He got up and went to the bathroom. Raking through a mirrored cabinet full of pill bottles, he was amazed at how many medicines you could accumulate simply by getting older. There were pills for all sorts of conditions he'd never heard of. He examined each label in turn, emptying half the pills out of each bottle into his pocket. If they weren't painkillers, he thought, they'd be something similar, so what was the difference? Four bottles he just emptied completely – Vicodin, Valium, Prozac and something with a long name that ended in barbiturate. He'd heard of them, that was enough. He took a Valium and a Prozac, figuring that they'd even each other out but leave him more chilled, and headed back to the kitchen where, after the solitude of the bathroom, it seemed like everyone was shouting through loudhailers at each other.

'I really don't know where you get this complex from,' Jean was saying. 'I obviously love you and Connor equally, as does your father.'

'You *know* that isn't true.' Kate was exasperated. She looked at Connor, pleading. 'Back me up here.'

Connor sighed heavily as he picked up a fork and pushed some rice around his plate.

'Kate's right,' he said quietly. 'Mummy's boy and Daddy's girl, that's always the way it's been around here. Dad's got no more time for me than you have for Kate, Mum. But for some reason the pair of us can do no wrong in the other parent's eyes. Just your average family set-up, I wouldn't get too worked up about it.'

Silence hung in the air like fog.

'Why don't we talk about something else,' said Danny eventually, with little conviction. The pain in Connor's head was dissipating a little, spreading itself thinner and thinner as it moved to his skin's wafer-thin surface then floated away into the flickering candlelight.

Conversations started up again tentatively, as if everyone were walking on ricepaper. Connor poured another glass of wine. He tried to remember the first time he ever got drunk, but couldn't get the dates right in his head. There was the time he'd mixed up a little of everything from his folks' drinks cabinet into an old Irn-Bru bottle, then got wasted on it with two mates – Christ, he couldn't even remember their names – up at the Water Tower one summer afternoon. When he tried to cycle home he fell off several times. He would have been about ten years old. Or there was the time on holiday in Brittany, when he and a girl from Cornwall – what the hell was her name? – smuggled some cider away from their parents' party and got legless on the beach, holding hands and looking at the stars. Was that the same summer? Or the one before? Or after? How the hell did anyone ever write memoirs, thought Connor, without making it all up? He couldn't even remember people he'd met a month ago, let alone his first kiss, his first pet, or who used to beat him up most at school. Then there was the Hogmanay where he sneaked a bottle of Malibu upstairs to his room and shared swigs with the Henderson girls from next door. At least he could remember their names. Emma and Louise – neither particularly pretty, looking back, but he was besotted with one or other of them for two years. An infatuation which was completely one-sided, he found out after embarrassing himself by asking first one then the other to be his girlfriend without really knowing what it meant. Was that the same year as the French summer or the mixy at the Water Tower? If only he'd kept a diary then he'd know his exact drinking history – a saga of pukings, fumblings, fights, dares, games and humiliations. Probably just as well he never kept a diary.

It was strange that, despite being twins, he and Kate never really hung out together much at school. Maybe it was because they *were* twins, and sick of the sight of each other twenty-four hours a day. People always assumed they had a sixth sense, and were disappointed when they revealed they were just like any other brother and sister. They argued, they had a laugh, they knew far too much about each other and they sometimes used that knowledge to get their own way. Despite the hapless slacker image his folks had of him, and their impression of Kate as a proper grown-up, they were secretly quite alike, thought Connor. Kate had a whole history of fuck-ups and disappointments and minor triumphs and pathetic weaknesses, like his, that their parents would never know about or understand. They were the same age and grew up in the same house, that was enough to keep them close to each other, looking out for each other. No telepathy, no sixth sense, no magical powers, just proximity of age, place and family. What else was there?

Everyone else had finished their food. Connor hadn't touched his. Kate was clearly itching to leave, although she remained tight-lipped. Hannah looked at Connor and motioned at Kate's fidgeting. Connor got the hint and stood up.

'Anyone fancy a pint?' he said.

'Why can't we do a cover of "Ally's Tartan Army"?'

The tension of earlier had gone, or at least they'd all drunk enough to forget it for now. They were in the bar of the Thistle Hotel, a skanky old place dumped in the middle of smart, detached houses, with a gravel car park made for handbrake turns. The bar was filled with long-haired, thirty-something metalheads and pubescent nu-metal skate kids, all getting primed for the appearance of an AC/DC tribute band in the function room down the hall. The Thistle was one of those small-town hotels that wouldn't know what to do if you actually asked for a room. An easy scam for a late licence, it was no more a working hotel than Holyrood Palace. They were on the edge of east central Scotland now, and there were Export and Special taps on the bar instead of 80 Shilling pumps. The lager was the same shit wherever you went.

The Ossians didn't restrict themselves to beer. Their table was full of empty shooter glasses, tumblers, pints, discarded lemon wedges and salt cellars.

'It's the best fucking football song ever written,' Connor declared to hoots of derision. 'All right, maybe "I Have A Dream" is up there, too. But "Ally's Tartan Army" makes a much better point, even if it's sung by Andy fucking Cameron.'

'You weren't even born when it was out,' said Paul, laughing.

'So what? It's still a cracking tune.' Connor started singing loud enough to attract looks from surrounding punters. 'We're on the march wi' Ally's Army, We're going tae the Argentine, And we'll really shake them up, When we win the World Cup, Cos Scotland is the greatest football team.' He waved his drink around. 'Conjures up images of Archie's goal and all that. Better than sex, just like they said in *Trainspotting*. No wait, it was heroin that was better than sex, wasn't it?'

'Don't know, I could never watch it cos of that Blur song on the soundtrack,' said Paul.

'Ewan McGregor was fit as fuck, though, for a supposed junkie,' said Hannah.

'Hey, watch it,' said Connor, laughing.

She gave him an innocent look. 'Don't worry, love, that heroin chic thing is *so* ten years ago. Ah, the good old days, when Edinburgh was exposed as the smack capital of Europe.'

'Wasn't it the AIDS capital as well?' said Connor, downing a whisky.

'And, of course, Scotland is the heart-attack capital, the alcoholic capital and the dumb-as-fuck capital of Europe,' said Paul. 'Seems like the only thing you don't top the table at is football.'

'And music,' said Connor, wagging a finger at him. 'But The Ossians are going to do something about that, aren't we kids!' The rest of the table let out a half-hearted cheer. 'But only if we get to do a cover of "Ally's Tartan Army"!' Connor was up out his seat and singing again. 'And England cannae dae it, Cos they didnae qualify, oh!'

'Sit down,' said Hannah, grabbing him. He stumbled and landed on her lap.

'You trying to tell me something?' he said.

'Yeah, you're pished. Now come here and give me a kiss.'

Connor smacked an exaggerated kiss on her lips then turned to the table.

'How about a round of flaming Drambuies, then?'

Without waiting for a reply he got up like a shot, causing Hannah to make a heavy oofing sound.

'You pair seem to have sorted things out,' said Danny to Hannah.

Hannah ruffled his beard with her hand.

'Unlike your good self,' she said, 'Connor can be a complete arsehole at times, as I'm sure you're only too aware. A self-centred little shit, wrapped up in his own manic, demented, sick little world.'

'Is there a "but" coming?'

Hannah laughed.

'But his heart is in the right place. Deep down, he's one of the good guys. As you are, big man, the main difference being that you're able to take care of yourself, something His Highness over there seems thoroughly incapable of doing.'

'What do you pair think?' interrupted Paul.

'About what?' asked Danny.

'I thought "Tomorrow" from the *Annie* soundtrack would be a good song to cover, Kate thinks maybe something from *The Wizard of Oz*.'

'Going for the gay market, are we?' said Danny.

'I don't mind either,' said Hannah. 'As long as we don't have to listen to Con singing "Ally's Tartan Army" any more.'

Connor clunked a handful of nip glasses on the table and got a lighter out. They poured the Drambuies into their mouths, swilled them round, then tipped their heads back and opened their mouths. Connor went round with the lighter, sparking a cool blue flame into life in each mouth, then his own. They sat there for a few seconds, the flames flickering in their open mouths like pyres on a windy hillside before Connor made a noise in his throat, and they shut their mouths and swallowed the hot, sickly sweet liquid. They smiled at each other. Connor rubbed his hands together and leant forwards.

'So, back to this "Ally's Tartan Army" cover we're thinking of doing.'

Outside the Thistle, thick snow fluttered down from a heavy sky, straight out of *White Christmas*. They piled outside having spent the last two hours heckling the AC/DC tribute band to play a series of decidedly non-AC/DC songs including, naturally, 'Ally's Tartan Army'.

They started a snowball fight, buoyed by booze and memories of childhood winters. Bikers and metalheads joined in as they drifted out the hotel. Pretty soon thirty people were shouting, swearing and pelting each other with snowballs. Danny grabbed Connor several times and shoved snow down his collar, getting a fistful of snow in the face in return. After ten minutes everyone was knackered and they all gradually slipped away, the bikers making the most dramatic exit on low-slung roadsters with souped-up engines and silencers removed.

Shivering as they walked home, Connor and Hannah hugged each other so close they had difficulty moving forwards.

'Wish we weren't going back to my folks' house,' said Connor.

'They're not so bad,' said Hannah. 'Besides, they'll be in bed, won't they?'

'Hopefully. The less we see of them the better.'

'What a drama queen you are.'

They came round the corner and saw the inky ripples of the Keptie Pond.

'Han, did I tell you about the games we used to play on the pond when it iced over?'

'Yeah,' said Hannah, pretending to yawn, 'Sieg Heil, chicken runs round the edge, etcetera, etcetera.' She laughed as he tried to pull away, faking a huff.

'You know, if you weren't so cute, I could hate you,' he said.

'No you couldn't,' she said in a babyish voice, 'you could only wuv me vewwy much, honey-woney.'

'Yeah, and don't you know it.'

She looked him in the eye for a moment.

'Yes,' she said and hugged him closer. 'I know it.'

The Alexanders were still up. The Ossians tumbled in drunk and cheery and set about the drinks cabinet with a vengeance. All the arguing of earlier was forgotten as Alan and Jean – both seriously drunk by this point as well – played their old records to a barrage of ridicule.

This was all role-playing. It was Jean and Alan's job now to be ageing hippies living in the past, even if that's not what they felt like. Equally, the rest of them were obliged to be the mocking younger generation. Everyone played their role well enough, happy to go along with it. It beat having a real conversation. They'd tried that earlier and ended up fighting like toddlers, so wasn't this better?

Every time another slice of the faded hippy dream came on the turntable (still playing vinyl for fuck's sake, thought Connor), Paul did his best impression of Harry Enfield doing his impression of Dave Lee Travis. A third-hand joke they all laughed at for the simple reason that they all recognised it. The past was eating them all up, it was eating everything up in the world around them. Nostalgia was a joke, but a highly lucrative and popular joke. Television programmes reminded people what sweets and crisps they used to eat, what television programmes they used to watch and what toys they used to play with. Fashion was recycled with barely any new twist at all.

They listened to The Doors. Connor wondered whether it had always been this way. Had people in 1890 harked back to the days of 1870? What about the eighteenth century? Or the Stone Age? Were kids always embarrassed by the elderly, just as the old were disappointed in the young? Was any of it even unhealthy? You have to push things forward, he was always saying in interviews about The Ossians' music. But wasn't their stuff just a blend of all the bands they liked, a rebranding of bits of musical heritage? There was nothing new in rock 'n' roll, someone had once said, but didn't that just mean everything was new? Isn't that what James Macpherson had done with Ossian? Taken scraps of oral storytelling, myths and legends that he discovered on his travels, and knocked them into a shape palatable for the times he lived in? Wasn't that all anyone did in music or literature?

He felt his headache returning, mixed with a buzzing feeling in his stomach from what he guessed was a speed comedown. He reached into his pocket and dabbed some white powder on to his finger then into his mouth. Nobody noticed. Then he remembered the pills he'd stolen. He put his hand in his other pocket, feeling the folded-up note from last night next to the pile of pills. Your secrets are safe with me. No, he wasn't going to think about that shit, not tonight. He took a random pill from his pocket and popped it, washing it down from a pint of gin and grapefruit. He felt better instantly. Psychosomatic, he knew, but hey, feeling better was feeling better, right?

His folks were dancing now – more of a drunken stagger, really

– to what sounded like Jimi Hendrix. Certainly wanky enough guitar-playing, thought Connor. That hippy thing was so fucking fake, just guys with guitars for dicks, spreading it around and pretending it was part of some new free-love bollocks. Did women really fall for that shite back then?

Part of him thought his folks looked kind of sweet, grins plastered across their faces, and part of him was disgusted by the sight. A joint was going round, and Jean and Alan took a small toke each, then had to sit down.

'I'm not used to this,' said Alan, out of breath.

'Aye, we're not as young as we used to be,' said Jean.

'There you go with the clichés again,' said Connor.

'Connor, dear,' said Jean, slurping from a wine glass. 'The older you get, the more you realise that life is made up of clichés and precious little else. That's why they're clichés.'

'Not my life,' said Connor.

Jean let out a laugh and stroked her son's face.

'We'll see,' she said.

Hannah woke at six. She and Connor had stumbled into bed at half four, haphazardly removing each other's clothes and licking, kissing and gently biting each other's exposed flesh. As Connor lay on top of her, sucking her nipples, Hannah could feel that his cock was only half-heartedly stirring between her thighs. He moved downwards, kissing her belly, then her pubes before settling in down there, licking and kissing with his mouth and rubbing with his fingers. She pulled at his hair, playing with it as he flicked his tongue in and out of her until eventually she came, tensing her whole body as her legs shook and her hands gripped at his scalp. After a few moments he emerged smiling above her. She playfully pushed him over on to his back. 'Your turn,' she said as she started moving his semi-erect cock in and out of her mouth, stroking his balls as she did. His dick became properly hard for only a few brief moments, then almost immediately softened again as he came in her mouth. She swallowed the warm, salty stickiness then lay on top of him, kissing him on the mouth, letting him taste his own spunk. She got off him and they both lay there breathing in the darkness before dropping off to sleep in each other's arms.

Now, she was on her own. Something had disturbed her. Connor wasn't there. Nothing unusual in that – he'd hardly slept at all recently – but there was something else troubling her that she couldn't put her finger on. She heard the sound of breaking glass from downstairs. She got up, blood pulsing in her ears, pulled her jeans on and walked slowly downstairs.

The kitchen light was on and the back door was open. She moved cautiously into the room and noticed pieces of broken pint glass on the floor. No one was about. She stepped carefully over the glass and looked out the back door, folding her arms against the cold. Outside, the moon hung low and heavy in a clear sky spangled with stars. Light from the kitchen spilt gently out the door and window, making the snow-covered grass look like soft cotton sheets on the earth.

A noise came from the bottom of the garden. In the moonlight she could just make out a low, four-legged silhouette that seemed to be pawing at the frozen earth. As she got closer she realised it was Connor on his hands and knees, wearing just a pair of boxer shorts and digging in the dirt.

'Connor, what the hell are you doing?' she asked. He didn't respond. His movements seemed robotic, like he was receiving instructions. She called out again, but he just kept clawing at the earth, getting precious little purchase on the rock-hard soil. She walked up next to him and saw that his eyes were closed. He was sleepwalking.

She didn't know what to do. She'd read somewhere that waking sleepwalkers was a very bad idea, it could psychologically disturb them or something. But here he was in the moonlight trying to bury a bloody bone in the back garden, so surely he was disturbed already? Plus his fingernails were beginning to bleed, an inky dribble coming from his hands. She couldn't let him continue.

Alan appeared at the back door and came over.

'What the hell?' he said. 'Connor?'

He looked at Hannah, confused.

'He's sleepwalking,' she said. 'Well, sleepdigging. What should we do? You're not supposed to wake them, isn't that right?'

'So I've heard.'

They just stood there watching Connor, his ridged spine visible beneath his taut, pale skin, without a clue what to do.

'Has he done anything like this before?' said Hannah.

'The odd bit of sleepwalking when he was little, but most kids go through that.' Alan stood with his hands on his hips. 'This used to be our dog's favourite spot for digging,' he said after a while. 'Damn thing used to bury all sorts of crap down here. Connor would've seen him do it hundreds of times. Maybe he's dreaming about that.'

'Look at his hands,' said Hannah. 'We have to do something.'

She knelt down, rubbed his back gently and held one of his wrists. He let himself be guided away, his eyes still closed as he walked like an old, infirm man slowly up the soft, white slope of the garden and into the kitchen, Hannah on one side of him and his father on the other.

Inside, they sat him down carefully at the kitchen table. Alan closed the door and Connor's eyes fluttered open. He looked around, confused, like a young animal searching for its mother. He stared down at his hands, frozen and bloody, caked in crystalline smears of icy dirt.

'What's happening?' he said in a weak voice.

'You were sleepwalking, honey,' said Hannah. She pulled out a chair and sat next to him. 'Out in the garden. We didn't know what to do. You were digging in the ground with your hands.'

Connor kept looking at his hands and stayed silent. Hannah saw a cloud of confusion pass across his eyes. He seemed to be trying to recall something, as if conjuring back his dream would explain it all.

'I can't remember,' he said.

He started to cry. Small, sharp intakes of breath to begin with, growing into a heaving motion as tears ran down his face. He made almost no noise, and Hannah thought briefly that he was having a panic attack, not crying. She held him and rocked him gently, his head on her chest.

'Shhh, baby,' she said. 'It's OK now.' She stroked his hair and he tried to speak but nothing came out. His father stood watching, not knowing what to do. Gradually Connor's wheezing receded.

'I'm fine,' he said eventually. He wiped away wet patches from his cheeks with the backs of his hands, then noticed the bloody mess of his fingers again. He stared at them. He shook his head and smiled a thin, straight smile.

'Better get myself cleaned up,' he said as he moved to the sink. He winced as the hot water spilt over his hands. He rubbed them with soap and turned to smile at Hannah and his dad.

'Out damn spot, eh?'

Alan eventually pushed himself away from the worktop, keeping his eye on Connor the whole time. He patted him gently on the back as he walked past.

'Think I'd better put the kettle on.'

'Ah, the old magical cup of tea,' said Connor, turning off the tap and facing the room. 'Good idea, Dad.'

Hannah looked at him and felt like crying.

6

Aberdeen

'Who doesn't dream of a car crash?
The rip of steel through skin'

The Ossians, 'Melancholia'

The centre of Aberdeen looked as if you could buy it in a box. Neat granite buildings the colour of window putty lined Union Street, with turrets, clocks and spires sticking up at irregular intervals. Unlike Edinburgh's crumbling, scaffolded history, Aberdeen looked like it was built yesterday. Connor hated it. It reminded him of those terrible seventies kids' shows like *Trumpton* they kept repeating on telly. Expensive executive cars rolled impatiently down the city's main artery, exuding the earthy richness that oil money brings.

Connor had gone back to bed for a few hours and woken surprisingly refreshed, events in the garden banished to the back of his mind. They left the Alexanders around three, their journey up the coast flanked by a fat orange sun alone in a sharp blue sky. Hazy light washed along the sea's horizon like a distant fog waiting to come inland. The sunlight was warm in the van and they soaked it up like lizards, but stepping out on to Belmont Street they were smacked by an icy blast of wind.

The gig was in Drummonds, a ramshackle pub on the edge of the small, cobblestoned grid of streets that was a magnet for the city's students and slackers. Sharing Belmont Street with Drummonds were three churches, now converted into large, soulless chain pubs; two communist-themed vodka bars called Revolution and Stalin; a handful of swanky style bars with large glass frontages and neon signs; and a smattering of multinational sandwich and coffee-house chains. This was nightlife in Scotland's third largest city.

It was five o'clock on Thursday, not a kick in the arse off the weekend, and Drummonds had a handful of punters starting early. A drum kit was already set up at the back of the room next to a flimsy PA stack on a small stage. Danny went over and examined the kit, shaking his head and sucking his teeth.

Waiting at the bar was Gerry, a friend of Paul's who ran a club in town and was a small time dealer on the side. Gerry was kicking on for forty, but looked older, thanks to two decades of heroin addiction. Back in Aberdeen's boom time, Gerry had a promising career as a solicitor ahead of him, but a series of smack-related misdemeanours and dodgy dealings with minor criminals put paid to all that. He was a decent guy deep down, Paul said, but he'd always had trouble trying to detox. Last Paul heard he was mixing heroin with methadone, the odd ketamine pill on the side. He had greying curly hair and a deeply lined, baggy face, and he was chatting to a dark-eyed barmaid with a pencil stuck through the silky brown hair piled on her head. He looked relaxed but worn around the edges. Paul introduced them and got a round in. A fat, open-faced man with a fin haircut and a bunch of gold hoop earrings in one ear came up to Connor.

'Connor Alexander? The Ossians?' He stuck out a pudgy hand.

'That's me, and us,' said Connor.

'I'm Cary Jones, I present the *Northsound* alternative show on Thursday and Friday nights,' he said. 'We had an interview scheduled?'

'News to me,' said Connor.

'Oh yeah,' said Paul. 'Connor, you've got an interview with Cary Jones from *Northsound* at five o'clock.'

'Thanks,' said Connor.

He and Danny plonked themselves down in a booth opposite Cary, who fished a minidisc and mic out his bag and set it on the table. 'You can swear if you want to, but we'll have to bleep it out.'

Most of the interview covered the same territory as previous ones, with the band name as the launch point. Scottishness, the reasons for the tour, the *St Andrew's Day* EP, challenging lyrics in rock music and the lack of a structured Scottish music industry were all covered in the first ten minutes.

'You seem to write a lot about drugs,' said Cary.

'Do I?' said Connor.

'Well, yes. Are you advocating drug use?'

'We're not advocating anything, Cary, but I do take drugs. Probably more drugs than Danny here knows about. But I'll tell you one thing,' said Connor, leaning forwards. 'I'll tell you what the best drug of all is, shall I?'

Cary looked at him.

'Booze,' said Connor, waving the remains of his pint in the air. 'This stuff is absolute nectar of the fucking gods, Cary. It's ambrosia, too, and I'm not talking about that rice pudding crap you get in tins. Booze can do anything, Cary, abso-fucking-lutely anything. It's massively underrated. Everyone's always banging on about smoking this or injecting that, or what you can create under the influence of licking poisonous frogs or snorting Guatemalan cacti. There's nothing worse than these drug-bore cunts. Nothing. "I've taken more exotic microdots than you have" or "Ooh the mushies on the *south* side of the mountain have a much smoother trippy effect". Who gives a fuck? Drugs are supposed to get you fucked up, right? And what gets you more fucked up than booze? Nothing. And it's fucking legal, which is genius. It's amazing what the human body and mind can achieve fuelled by booze. Great works of art can be created and great pains can be numbed, and all you get is a wee hangover, and probably some chilli sauce stains on your trousers from a kebab on the way home. I'm not advocating that anyone dabble in kebabs, you understand. Evil, nasty things, kebabs. Never touch them.'

'Uh, right,' said Cary. 'Apart from booze, what else drives The Ossians?'

'Hate,' said Connor. 'Another vastly underrated commodity, and we plan to bring it back into the mainstream consciousness with a bang. I'm not talking about all that nu-metal or emo angst crap, I'm talking about real, true, bona fide hate. Everyone hates something, whether it's your wee sister, your boss, the way slow people get in your way on the pavement, the government, your shitty damp flat, your smack habit, your lack of anything interesting to say to the opposite sex. Whatever. But it's everywhere. There's a media-led social fascism in this country whereby people aren't allowed to admit that they hate things – car adverts, reality TV with so-called celebrities, piss-poor jobs or the neighbours' matching fucking tracksuits. Everyone's supposed to just knuckle down and endure it. No way. Hate is the answer. Hate and booze. A classic combination like Ant and Dec, or Ecstasy and grass.'

He finished his pint. Behind Cary, in the corner of the room above the bar, a gaffer-taped television was on with the sound down. On screen was a slightly out-of-focus photograph of a teenager. Connor stared at it for a few seconds, then realised where he recognised it from, it was the same picture he'd seen on television a couple of days ago – was it in Dundee or St Andrews? He definitely recognised the face from somewhere, but where? He hadn't been sure if it was a boy or a girl before, but it was definitely a boy, he could see that now with a clearer head. And maybe the kid wasn't as young as he'd thought – possibly around twenty – definitely nearer Connor's age than he'd thought before, in his stupor. But where did he know the face from?

Connor pushed himself out the booth and shouted at the barmaid, who was still talking to Paul and Gerry. 'Hey! Stick the volume up on the telly, will you?'

The barmaid looked as if she wanted to take the pencil out her hair and stab Connor in the eye with it. Connor stood next to the booth as Cary and Danny stared at him. Paul and Gerry, too, were looking at Connor with annoyance. He could see out the corner of his eye that Hannah and Kate were watching him as well, as were most of the punters in the place. The barmaid slowly turned and started rooting around next to the till for the remote. Connor looked up again at the television, which was now showing footage of the inside of the Scottish Parliament, MSPs waggling their fat fingers in the air. He sighed.

'Never mind,' he said to the barmaid, who was only searching half-heartedly anyway. Everyone in the place returned to their business, and Connor wondered what was so compelling about that kid's face, and why it was always on television.

'Did you see it?' asked Connor.

'What?' said Danny.

'There's some news report I keep missing. About a kid or something. I've seen it a couple of times now, and I definitely recognise the face.'

'It wasn't *Crimewatch*, was it? Could've been your own face, maybe.'

'Ha, ha. I'm serious. Whatever this kid's done, he's on the news, and I'm sure I know him from somewhere.'

'Where?'

'That's just it, I can't remember.'

'Maybe he's a fan of The Ossians,' said Cary.

'What?' Connor only now remembered Cary was there.

'Maybe he's a fan, that's why you recognise him.'

'Maybe,' said Connor. For a second he thought someone had put Nirvana on the jukebox, then realised the sound was coming from his pocket. Hell's teeth. He needed to put that fucking thing on silent.

'Are we done with the interview?'

'Sure, if you've had enough,' said Cary. 'I've got plenty of material for the show.'

'Cheers, then,' said Connor, shaking hands and heading towards the toilets. 'Gotta go.'

He hurried to the bogs, gripping the mobile in his pocket, trying to muffle the sound. By the time he got to a cubicle the ringtone was at the first verse, a nasal Stylophone sound replacing the melody. He pulled it out and looked at the screen. 'Kenny'. He pressed reply.

'What?'

'Connor.' The voice dragged out slowly.

'Kenny?'

'Yeah, man.' Shit, this guy sounded stoned off his fucking tits, or worse. 'You got something for me?'

'Yeah, from Nick.'

'Quality, quality.' There was a lengthy pause. Connor didn't know whether to speak or not. Eventually he heard, 'You at Drummonds?'

'That's right, we're playing in a couple of hours.'

'How about if I come down and meet you after the show, dude.'

'Don't know if that's a good idea. The rest of the band don't know I'm doing any of this.'

'Don't worry, man, I'll be cool. I'll come find you.'

The gig went well. A healthy crowd of students and locals pitched up, all sauced but not so far gone that they didn't pay the band at least a bit of attention. A couple of well-meaning local support bands – a chubby new rave outfit and a pasty-faced Radiohead bunch – brought plenty of mates. Connor was precariously pitched between the best part of a bottle of gin he'd lifted from his folks' house, a couple of anonymous pills and some furious weed smoking, and kept his provocative banter more or less in check. The band were relaxed and confident after a night off, and although playing well within their capabilities, they seemed to fit together more neatly than they had for the first few shows. Coming back on for a genuinely unplanned encore they sauntered through an old Thin Lizzy cover before finishing with a new tune, 'The Haar', which they'd been kicking around the rehearsal room for a while but never played live. Swaying to a sea shanty rhythm and with both Kate and Hannah playing keyboards which sounded like accordions, the song built to a shuddering climax of crashing drums and shredded, warped guitars before collapsing in a glorious mess. Everyone loved it, and the four band members left the stage with big smiles on their faces.

After the show there was back-slapping and a heap of nervous praise from a handful of seventeen- and eighteen-year-old schoolkids in indie wear, the girls with their hair in bunches, the boys hiding behind straggly fringes. The band lapped it up. Cary from *Northsound* appeared and added to the congratulations, saying the title track from the new EP was one of his most requested songs.

Connor was standing with Cary, Paul and Hannah, but only

half-listening. He scanned the crowd for someone who might be Kenny, at the same time searching for the face of the boy from the television news reports. There was too much weird shit happening: the face on television, the note in his pocket, the people he was seeing everywhere who seemed to be watching his every move, following him around. Just as he was gazing round the place he felt a tap on the shoulder and almost jumped through the ceiling.

Behind him was a tall, ungainly man, hunched over for no good reason, his long hair tucked behind his ears and a smoky look in his bulbous eyes. He looked like a Jim Henson creation. He held out a giant hand, which Connor shook, getting a surprisingly firm grip.

'Just wanted to say, man, that was a great set.'

Connor recognised the drawling voice immediately.

'Thanks.'

'I mean it, youse have got some fantastic tunes, mate.'

'Cheers.'

'My name's Kenny by the way.'

Connor had already moved to stand between Kenny and the rest of them. Paul and Hannah left him to it, assuming that Kenny was just a fan after a chat. Connor glanced round at them.

'I'm Connor.'

'I know.'

'Well?'

'I'm away to the toilets, man,' said Kenny, dropping his voice and pawing at the ground with one foot, a movement which made Connor nervous. 'I'll be in the first cubicle. Follow me in.'

Kenny lumbered off in the direction of the bogs. Connor waited a couple of minutes then wandered as casually as he could over to their gear behind the stage. He pulled the kitbag from the pile and made his way to the toilets. He looked round to see if anyone was watching. Hannah and Paul were still talking to Cary, and over at the other side of the room Danny and Kate were laughing and joking with each other, sliding out from a booth and heading in his direction. They hadn't seen him. He ducked through the back and into the Gents.

The toilets were empty, apart from the first cubicle door being closed. Connor pushed it open and there was Kenny, slouched and smoking a joint. There wasn't much room and Connor had to squeeze past his bulky frame to close and lock the door. He heard the door to the Gents open, then a pair of giggling, breathless voices followed by the sound of stumbling, a cubicle door closing and locking, then the grunts and gasps of a couple trying to have a quick, silent shag. Kenny shook his head while smiling, then pointed at the cubicle door, unlocked it and slipped back out the toilets. Connor followed, listening to the sounds from the other cubicle and being reminded of the noise through the wall the other night.

Outside the Gents, Kenny was heading down a flight of stairs to the pub's delivery door. He stopped at the door which, although a fire exit, appeared to be chained and padlocked.

'Thought it best not to do business to the sound of lovemaking,' said Kenny.

Connor thought it was an odd choice of word for a quickie in the bogs, but said nothing.

'Let's just get this over with. Folk'll be missing me. You got something?'

'Sure, dude, no worries.' Kenny pulled a thick brown envelope out his back pocket and held it up as if examining it for the first time. 'And you?'

Connor unzipped the kitbag and took out Kenny's parcel, handing it over in exchange for the envelope.

'Sweet,' said Kenny, secreting the package under his coat.

'We done?' said Connor.

Kenny laughed quietly. 'You're not used to this, eh, mate?'

'What?'

'You look nervous, man. I'm guessing you don't do much of this kind of thing.'

Connor looked up the flight of stairs, then back at Kenny. 'Correct. Now, we're finished, yeah?'

'Sure, man. Pleasure doing business with you.'

'Wish I could say the same.'

'Hope to see you around.'

'No offence, but I really hope never to see you ever again.'

'Harsh, dude, but I take your point.'

Kenny held out his hand again, but Connor was already taking the steps two at a time.

When he walked back into the bar he re-stashed the bag and headed back to Paul and Hannah, who were just being joined by Danny and Kate.

'Where have you been?' Hannah asked. 'Off having secret rendez-vous with amorous fans?'

'What?' said Connor.

'Only joking,' said Hannah. 'Just saw you chatting to that long-haired bloke, then the pair of you were gone.'

'Oh aye, he was just saying he liked the band,' said Connor. 'Then I went to the bogs.'

Danny spluttered into his pint and Kate seemed to go pale. They exchanged a raised-eyebrow look. Connor wondered how much money was now in his kitbag in those two envelopes, if indeed they were full of money, and what he could do with all that cash. He imagined jumping on a random plane and jetting into the sunset to avoid all this stupid cloak-and-dagger pish, but even as he did, he realised he was revelling in it all, perversely beginning to enjoy sneaking around, avoiding prying eyes and doing dodgy deals with fuckwits. He looked around, hoping to see a familiar face among the crowd. All he could see were fans of The Ossians, kids with futures ahead of them and a worry-free weekend to look forward to and none of this pish filling up their half-formed little lives. He stopped looking around and headed to the bar.

They were staying in Gerry's poky flat on a bleak stretch of road with the incongruously sunny name of Beach Boulevard. The street's frosty, spindly birch trees looked over them as they skited down the icy pavement and into the flat.

'At least you never got a punch in the face this time, Con,' said Danny, passing a joint around the small living room once they'd settled in.

'A first for the tour, eh? Four gigs and three beatings. I'll need to get the ratio back up tomorrow, maybe try to get two beatings in one night. What do you reckon, Han?'

'If it's getting late and you still need a slap, you let me know.'

They got more stoned, chilling out after the buzz of the gig. Gerry wasn't drinking or smoking much. He explained he would have to make a delivery soon and wanted to stay straight for driving. Just then his mobile went off.

'Yup,' said Gerry into the handset. 'No problem. I'll pop round now. See you in a bit.' He put his phone away then said to the room, 'Anyone fancy coming for a drive?'

'Can we get some munchies on the way?' said Danny, lifting his head from skinning up.

'No bother.' Gerry was already digging car keys out his pocket.

'I fancy a bit of fresh air,' said Connor, pushing himself up from the sofa.

'Don't know if that's a good idea,' said Paul, giving him a look.

'Paul's right,' said Hannah.

'Hey, there's no problem, people,' said Gerry. 'This delivery's for a mate of mine. I'm just doing him a favour. We'll be back in twenty minutes.'

'You heard the man,' said Connor. He glanced at Danny. 'You finished that doob for the road?' Danny pushed the roach in and nodded. 'Right, let's go. See you in a bit.'

'Reckon they'll be all right?' said Paul after they'd left.

'Danny'll look after Con,' said Kate.

'You'd know all about that,' said Hannah, instantly regretting it.

'What's that mean?' said Paul.

Kate gave Hannah a ferocious look before turning to Paul. 'She just means we're all good at making sure Con doesn't kill himself.'

Paul smiled as he took in Kate and Hannah's faces. 'That's not what she meant at all. Come on, what's up?'

Kate sighed, then swept her hand out, giving Hannah the floor.

'Kate and Danny are an item,' she said. 'I'm sorry, Kate, it just slipped out before. I forgot Paul didn't know.'

'How long's this been going on?' said Paul.

'A week or so,' said Kate, looking down and playing with the foil on her beer bottle. 'What do you think?'

'I think it's great. Is it serious?'

Kate just shrugged.

'What did Con say when he found out?'

'Ah,' said Hannah. 'He doesn't know yet.'

'Hannah's been hassling me to tell him.'

'Quite right,' said Paul.

'I'm going to, I promise. I've just been waiting for the right time.'

'Soon, eh?' said Paul. 'Especially now me and Hannah know.'

'I'll tell him tomorrow, OK?'

'Cool. It's great news, Kate, but you can't go keeping secrets from each other, not in this band.'

'I know.'

Paul stood up and headed towards the kitchenette. 'Now, let me get you ladies a refill.'

'What are we delivering anyway?' said Connor in the front passenger seat.

They were driving through cold, wet, empty streets, heading for the university area.

'Ketamine,' said Gerry. 'Want one? I've got loads spare if you're interested.'

'How much?'

'Don't worry about it. Just have one.' Gerry held out a large powdery-looking pill. 'Better just take half now, see how you get on.'

Connor took the pill, broke it roughly along the line and washed one half down with beer, offering the other half to Danny, who shook his head.

'I'm all right with this, thanks,' he said, waving his joint.

Connor put the other half-pill in his pocket. 'So how's Aberdeen to live in?' he said.

'All right,' Gerry replied. 'Bit of a craphole, but where isn't?'

'Isn't everyone meant to be loaded with oil money?'

'You think I'd be staying in that fucking dump of a flat if I had any oil money? Anyway, all that is running out. I reckon this place is heading for the shitter pretty soon. The smack's been kicking every cunt in the teeth for the last ten years now. Give it another few years and this place'll be dead on its feet.'

'There must be something good about it, though?'

'The talent's all right, with the uni and that. But then there's all the fucking hassle you get between them and the locals. Some folk just cannae seem to get along.'

Connor looked out the window and wondered when the pill would kick in.

'Same thing in Edinburgh,' he said. 'Fucking worse down there, cos all the students are posh bastards.'

'It's not so bad,' said Danny. 'Sure there's trouble, but you go out your way to find it, Con. In Belfast you learn to keep your head down, or you get in some serious shit.'

'What do you mean, I go looking for trouble?'

'You're always stirring it up. All I'm saying is, if you came from somewhere with paramilitary organisations, kneecappings, beatings, murders and fucking drug lords, you might not be so quick to shoot your mouth off.'

It was sleeting now, and the windscreen wipers squeaked backwards and forwards as Gerry swung the car into a side street and pulled over.

'I'll be two minutes,' he said, switching the engine off. 'You pair aren't going to start fighting are you?'

They both laughed as Gerry opened the door and got out, letting swirling sleet in, then disappeared into a doorway. With the engine off, they could hear the wind whistling. The sleet was thick now, and they passed the joint between them. After a while Connor said, 'Maybe you're right. But sometimes I can't help myself, you know? I don't mean to stir things up, it just happens. Before I know it, bam, my mouth's open and the bullshit is coming out. Maybe I'll bite my tongue from now on.'

Danny laughed, leant forwards and ruffled his hair. 'Then you wouldn't be you, would you?'

'Perhaps that'd be a good thing.'

Gerry opened the door and dived into the driver's seat, breathing out heavily and blowing on his hands. He had a thin covering of icy snow on his hair as he stuck the key in the ignition and pulled away.

'Another happy customer,' he said, then to Connor, 'How's that pill? Anything yet?'

Connor thought he could feel something, like he was being rolled in bubble wrap. Gerry's words seemed to be coming from further away than the width of a car, and when Danny offered him the joint it seemed to take an age for his outstretched hand to grab it.

Connor remembered a time when he was eight or nine, playing with Kate in the park. They were daring each other to do stuff like run across the railway line, or throw stones at a passing dog walker. It came to Kate's turn, and he dared her to jump off the high wall of the old folks' home. Without fear or hesitation she did it, but landed awkwardly on a piece of broken bottle, slicing right into her knee so that pinky white bone jutted out. She looked down at her knee and was silent for what seemed like ages, then started screaming for Connor to get help. He just stood there, paralysed, the whole scene appearing through a vaselined lens with the sound turned down. He ran away in the opposite direction from their house, running until he could hardly breathe, the burning in his lungs making him cough until he was sick. Then he wandered around the streets for hours worrying about his sister, too scared and ashamed to go home.

When she saw Connor run off, Kate had simply stopped screaming and hobbled home with a hankie wrapped around her knee. When Connor eventually got up the courage to head back, there was a note explaining that his mum had taken her to hospital. Kate told their mum she'd been on her own. She looked at him impassively when she got home, and he couldn't meet her gaze. He'd never got up the bottle to mention it to her since, and she'd never brought it up. It made him feel ill now, thinking about it.

'Hey, want to see something cool?'

Gerry was talking to them. He swung the car down a narrow one-way street and they emerged at the other end with a view of large ships to their right, a harbour entrance in front of them, and a long pier stretching out to their left.

'I didn't even realise Aberdeen had a harbour,' said Danny. 'Although thinking about it, that's pretty stupid.'

'A harbour and a beach and everything, my friend,' said Gerry. 'You fancy scaring some birds?'

'Birds?' said Danny.

'I'll show you.' Gerry turned the car left, and crawled out along the pier. He was hunched over the steering wheel, leaning forwards like an old man on a Sunday drive. A third of the way up the pier they came to a rusted iron gate sitting open with 'North Pier' in small ferric letters on the side. Gerry switched the headlights to full beam and stopped the car. It was snowing heavily now, and the flakes slapped the windscreen with a faint, fat sound before being wiped away. Connor and Danny peered into the light. They could see hundreds of grey and white shapes stretched out along the pier in front of them, starting about thirty yards away.

'What are they?' said Connor, feeling seasick from the motion of the wipers and the snowflakes on the windscreen.

'Sleeping seagulls,' said Gerry. 'They come here every night. I've been down here a few times before, it's funny as fuck. You rev up and bomb into them, and they scatter in a fucking panic, flapping everywhere. Two minutes later they're all back down, snoozing away like nothing's happened.'

They sat for what seemed to Connor a very long time gazing at the birds. Looking closely, he thought he could see the occasional feathered breast rising and falling. They looked so peaceful and snug, he wished he was out there sleeping with them.

'Why don't we just leave them?' he said.

'Yeah,' said Danny. 'Let's get back to the flat. I've run out of beer and grass back here anyway.'

'You sure?' said Gerry, looking at the pair of them. They both nodded.

They waited another few seconds, then heard the car's engine straining as Gerry ramped it up to full revs, shouting at the top of his voice, 'Fuck that! Come on you feathered fucks, let's see you fly!'

They felt a jolt as the car leapt forward, and Gerry whooped and screamed as he fired up through the gears. They were only a few yards away from the first bird and travelling at fuck knows what speed, then at the very last second Gerry realised the seagulls weren't going to get out the way, they weren't even trying, they were just sitting there, mostly still sleeping, the odd head bobbing up from under a wing, then whump! They hit the first row of birds, Danny shouting from the back, Con holding on to the dashboard, Gerry realising what was happening and lunging for the brakes.

But he wasn't quick enough. Crumpling thumps and sickening, muffled whacking sounds filled the car, as they steamrollered over bird after bird. In the distance some gulls had flapped off from the end of the pier in a faint fluster, and as Gerry slammed on the brakes the car skidded to the left, then the opposite direction, then back again as its nose brushed the small wall flanking the side of the pier.

Finally they stopped. The three of them sat in silence for a few seconds, but already they could hear distressed cries from outside the car, dying and injured birds frantically trying to take off, flapping broken and ripped wings helplessly.

'What the fuck!' said Danny.

'I don't understand it, I don't understand it,' Gerry was saying under his breath, gazing glassy-eyed at the steering wheel. 'They usually take off. I don't understand it.'

'Never mind that,' Danny shouted at him. 'What the fuck are we going to do?'

'We've got to get the fuck out of here,' said Connor, his mind snapping into focus.

'Shouldn't we help them?' said Gerry.

'How the hell do you propose to do that? Call the fucking RSPB?' said Danny. 'Con's right. Let's get the fuck out of here.'

'But we've got to reverse,' said Gerry. 'We've got to go back over them.'

They sat there with the engine throbbing, the windscreen wipers swatting away snowflakes to a beat, the cries of dozens of birds swirling in the snowy air outside. Eventually Danny spoke.

'Look, it's probably for the best. The ones that are still alive are probably fucked now anyway.' He sounded like he was trying to convince himself as much as anyone else. 'Don't think about it. Just get us out of here.'

Gerry sat motionless over the wheel looking lost.

'Come on,' said Connor, grabbing his arm and shaking. 'Let's go. Someone might hear them and call the police.'

Gerry looked up, then slowly put the car into reverse. They sat like that for a long time. Gerry's eyes began to clear and he shook his head as if trying to get rid of cobwebs.

'Right,' he said. 'Are you ready? Let's get this over with.'

He revved the engine, pulled the handbrake off and they bolted backwards. Like driving over a ploughed field, the car rocked from side to side as more sickening thuds came to their ears. Connor slammed the heel of his hand into his forehead trying to ignore the sound, except it wasn't sound it was juddering motion. He could feel the bodies being crushed underneath them and felt sick.

Then the rocking stopped. Gerry was still reversing as fast as possible, out past the rusting gate and into the nearly empty car park at the end of the pier. The car was now running smoothly. They turned and stopped, as Gerry opened his door and vomited on to the pavement, followed by a few spits. He closed the door, put the car into gear and slowly drove off, not looking at the other two. Connor slipped the other half of the ketamine into his mouth without saying anything.

Outside the flat, Gerry switched the engine off and they sat. No one had spoken since they'd left the pier.

'We never mention this, understand?' said Gerry.

'Yeah, like we'd go around telling every fucker about it,' said Connor.

'Fucking hell,' said Danny. 'Fucking hell.'

They left the car and went inside.

They'd only been away half an hour, but it seemed like years to Connor. The three of them put on smiles and eased themselves back into conversation.

'How was it?' said Paul.

'Aye, fine,' said Gerry, heading for the fridge. 'I could do with a drink now, though. Who's needing?'

'I thought you were getting munchies?' said Kate, looking at Danny.

'Oh yeah,' he said, laughing and sitting down next to her. 'Shit. Totally forgot. Sorry.'

'Too busy smoking and drinking, eh? Doesn't matter, not really hungry anyway.'

Hannah looked at Connor, whose glassy eyes shifted round the room, failing to focus on anything. He sat on a stool next to a worktop in the kitchenette adjoining the living room and propped his chin up on his hand. Gerry came back from the fridge with a handful of beers.

'What have you been doing to him?' said Hannah, pointing a Marlboro Light at Connor.

'How d'ya mean?' said Gerry, handing her a bottle.

'Look at the state of him. He can't even sit up straight. What did you give him?'

'I didn't give him anything. He took something. Just a wee half-K, he'll be fine in a bit, once he bottoms out.'

'Ketamine? Do you not think he was out of it enough?'

'Look, he wanted it, so I gave it to him. What's the big deal?'

Paul jumped in. 'No problem, Ger, it's just that Con's hammering it pretty hard at the moment, and we're looking out for him, you know?'

'Fine,' said Gerry. 'Whatever. Let's just start playing catch up, eh?'

He produced a large wrap of coke and started chopping out fat lines on a CD case with a credit card. He snorted the first two himself, then passed the CD and the rolled-up tenner around.

'Go on, then,' said Paul, crouching over the table and blocking a nostril before taking a hit.

'What the hell, eh?' said Kate. She followed suit, as did Danny and Hannah, before the CD went back to Gerry.

'Don't think laughing boy needs any of this, do you?' he said, nodding in Connor's direction. Hannah smiled nervously. Gerry snorted the last line and sniffed violently for a few seconds.

Connor was lost. Looking the wrong way down a telescope, he could see the rest of them away in the distance. He sensed they were talking to him, or about him, the body language pointing in his direction, but he couldn't make out what they were saying, and wasn't too bothered anyway. They were passing round lines of something, and he tried to say he wanted one, but his mouth wouldn't move. His legs felt made of fatigue and heavy as hell, like two long fishtanks full of murky water. He felt the edges of his mouth becoming moist, and wondered if he was drooling. Where the heel of his hand touched his jaw, he imagined it glowing like ET's finger. Connor wanted to phone home. He wanted his fingers to light up like ET's, and he wanted a bicycle that would fly, with a perfect full moon as a backdrop.

He thought about the seagulls, their hearts bursting inside their ribcages. Did birds have ribcages? He wondered if their tiny brains had any comprehension, as they saw the headlights bearing down on them, of what was happening. He wondered if their souls were fluttering up to heaven, a whole flock of them squawking and flapping and creating a stushie up there. Even in the state he was in, Connor realised this was ridiculous. He had to get back out the tunnel and into the room in front of him, fuzzy though it was. Even as he thought this, he imagined riding a flying bike with ET on the handlebars, alongside a noisy, cawing flock of seagulls, the face of Ossian, flowing white hair and blinded eyes, replacing the full moon behind them. Ridiculous pish. Get back to the room. It's not that hard, it's just a few hundred miles away. He decided the room could wait a while and closed his eyes, which made little difference since he wasn't focusing anyway.

After what seemed like a few hours he felt his brain come back together from the ends of the universe, opened his eyes and managed to get a bottle of beer from the worktop to his mouth. The coldness of the beer surprised him, and he almost choked. The room was only a few feet away, and he could hear voices. He was back. He got up and walked uncertainly over to where the rest of them were sitting.

'Back in the land of the living, eh?' said Paul.

'Aye,' he said slowly and sat down. Then after a while, 'Anyone got a joint?'

Danny passed him one and he felt his heart relax as he inhaled the sickly grass smoke.

'What did I miss?' he said.

'Usual pish,' said Hannah. 'Kate was telling us about the time the pair of you went joyriding.'

'I did explain it was our neighbour's car and it was only round the block once,' said Kate, taking a drag on her fag. 'And that we had the keys, and managed to get them back into their house without anyone finding out.'

'How old were we?' said Connor, shaking his head.

'Thirteen?'

Connor could hardly remember it. The event had become replaced by the telling of the story and he could no longer be sure that he saw the events in his mind as they'd really happened. He remembered the rush as the engine started. They managed to get the car to move, stuttering at first, then smoothly. He thought his heart would burst out of his chest with the adrenaline of it. He'd felt dizzy with excitement. How easy it was to get high back then. Fucking listen to yourself, he thought. You arsehole. You're only twenty-fucking-four, and you sound like an acid casualty from the sixties. It's pathetic. Then he thought, stop fucking analysing yourself so much, it's this that's killing you; the constant prodding and poking into the scabby wound of your mind. Then he thought, shut the fuck up.

His head was pulsing with pain. He went to the bathroom, sat down and swallowed a pill from his pocket without looking at it. His mobile rang and his heart sank. Must be Nick checking up on him. He pulled it out his pocket.

'It went fine, leave me alone,' he said.

No noise at the other end. Connor waited.

'What the fuck is this, the silent treatment?'

Nothing.

'Don't be a dickhead, Nick.'

Still no sound. Connor looked at the display. 'No Number'. He felt cold.

'Who the fuck is this? How did you get this number?'

'Your secrets are safe with me.' The voice was quiet, high-pitched and calm.

'Look, who the fuck is this?'

Silence.

'What fucking secrets?'

Connor thought about the note in his pocket with that same phrase written on it. If someone had gone into his pocket to place a note, maybe they could've got his mobile as well, figured out the number. He was momentarily impressed that he'd even thought of that. But who the fuck was it? He didn't recognise the voice at all.

'Look, I don't know who you are, or what you think you know about me, but you've got it all wrong. I don't have any fucking secrets, so there's nothing for you to know. Just leave me alone, you little shit.'

'I know about the drugs.'

'Bullshit. What drugs?'

'And I know about the gulls.'

Connor almost dropped the phone. That was only a couple of hours ago, how could the same person who left a note in his pocket in Dundee have seen them running over the birds two hours ago? A stalker? A guardian angel? A fucking psycho? The police? Why would they be playing this stupid cat and mouse game?

'I don't know what you're talking about,' said Connor. 'Leave me alone.'

He hung up and switched the phone off. Fucking hell. Fucking fucking hell. This was totally freaking him out. He couldn't even begin to work out what the hell was going on in his current state. He staggered to his feet, fumbled with the door handle and headed out, hoping to find a joint to calm his frazzled nerves.

★

They drifted to bed around five, Connor crashing with Hannah on a sofa bed in Gerry's lounge, but knowing he was never going to sleep. As Hannah's breath fell into heavy, regular washes of noise, he slipped out from under the duvet, pulled his clothes on, skinned up and headed out the door.

He found the beach at the bottom of the street. The tide was out and the snow had stopped. The lights of tankers blinked far out to sea – red, green then orange – and half a mile down the coast the light at the end of the North Pier winked accusingly at him every few seconds. There didn't appear to be anything happening over there, so the voice on the phone hadn't done anything about it. Why phone and say 'your secrets are safe with me'? Why tell someone you know secrets about them if you're not planning to do something about it? And how could they know about the gulls, the drugs and every other fucking thing he was up to? If he didn't already have a twin he might've thought it was an evil sibling, separated at birth, now stalking him, getting ready to pounce and reclaim a life that should've been his. He smiled at the absurdity of the thought then lit the joint, sheltering it from the wind off the sea, and inhaled deeply. This was the safety zone, the stoned comedown with the lapping of the waves as rhythmic, therapeutic massage for his mushy mind. He smoked the joint hungrily, letting the grass cover everything in a thick blanket of forgetting.

But he couldn't forget the gulls. It was terrible. He tried to tell himself it hadn't happened, that it was all a ketamine trip, but that was bullshit. He reminded himself it was Gerry who went for it, even though he and Danny had said not to. He still felt responsible. Someone had seen them, and phoned to tell him so. Which meant what? Fucked if he could work it out.

He looked again in the direction of the North Pier. There was a figure standing on the beach two hundred yards away. He froze. The distant street lamps left the beach mostly in darkness. He stared at the figure, who seemed to be looking back in his direction. He finished the joint and began walking towards the person, trying to keep his heart from racing. The figure remained motionless. He was tall and thin, Connor could see now. He moved faster, walking at speed and feeling his lungs start to burn a little. He was about a hundred yards away, the figure still standing there, hands in pockets, watching him approach. Connor broke into a jog, anxious to see the details of the figure's face, but there wasn't enough light. He could see a pale face and dark hair, but couldn't make out any features. He was about fifty yards away when the figure seemed to wake up from a trance, turning and bolting along the seafront. The wet, compacted sand was firm underfoot and Connor sped up, sprinting now, with the figure ahead of him, running away, coat flapping behind him. It was a similar long coat to Connor's. His lungs burnt as he ran, but already the figure was getting away, his long legs increasing the distance between them with every step. 'Who the fuck are you?' shouted Connor as he ran, the valuable air leaving his lungs with difficulty. 'Why are you following me?' He couldn't breathe any more and was slowing down. The figure was some distance away now, escaping effortlessly. As Connor slowed then stopped, doubled over and gasping, he watched the figure take the steps up from the beach to the promenade three at a time, before stopping at the top. The figure turned and looked back at Connor for a few moments, then got into a dark car parked at the side of the road and sped off.

Connor stood there on the sand, his heaving and wheezing matching the rhythmic slap of the waves on the shore. He sat down on the beach and looked out to sea, where the coloured lights of tankers were still blinking at indecipherable periods. He felt dizzy and confused as he watched the lights blink, each flash in the darkness frustrating him more as he failed to decode the message he was sure they were trying to send him.

His hands and feet burnt with the cold when he slipped back into Gerry's flat. He'd been looking behind him for the whole walk from the beach, but hadn't seen a soul. He now felt the urge to look back out from the front of the house, so from the hallway he opened the first door on that side of the flat. In the dark he could make out Gerry in a double bed with Paul on the floor at the other side of the room, both sleeping. He quietly closed the door and opened the adjacent one, which led to a spare room. He stumbled in and headed for the window. Outside the street was crystalline emptiness, the slippy pavements glistening up at him and the snow-streaked birch trees twinkling in the streetlight. There was no movement out there whatsoever. It was like the icy backdrop of a pantomime production, inert and lifeless. He didn't know how long he stood there, but he didn't see a single thing move.

Gradually, he became aware of a sound in the room. It was breathing. He turned, and now that his eyes had got used to the dark, he could make out a figure on the floor in the corner, next to a scabby sofa. He tiptoed across the room. He stood over the figure, looking at it for a very long time. It wasn't one figure, but two, tightly entwined and sleeping peacefully inside a single sleeping bag. Kate and Danny both had smiles on their faces, and their arms around each other, Kate cuddling into Danny's chest. They looked peaceful and happy. The sleeping bag had unzipped a little, and Connor could see that neither of them was wearing any clothes, on their top halves at least. He looked away from his sister's breasts quickly, and stared at their faces for a long time, thinking about events over the past week.

Eventually, he stepped carefully over the couple and headed towards the door, quietly closing it behind him as he left.

7

Inverness

'Two sides to everything, two sides to everything
We are a Saturday night, we are the Northern Lights
I am the evil twin, I am the state we're in'

The Ossians, 'My Evil Twin'

'How are my favourite little rock 'n' roll cousins, then?'

Murray stood in the doorway of his flat, arms spread out, a large joint hanging from the corner of his grinning mouth and his right eye closed from the smoke. A barrel of a man with a shaved head and wearing a paisley-pattern silk shirt, Murray looked every one of his thirty-nine years, and looked as if those years had been a heap of fun.

Kate and Connor's cousin lived in a street full of bed and breakfasts on the banks of the Ness, upriver from the city centre. Having spent the last two decades avoiding wearing a suit and tie for a living, Murray Alexander now worked as a graphic designer for a cool little company that bashed out sleek-lined brochures with fashionably chunky lettering for other cool little companies scattered around the north of Scotland. Twenty years in and out of bands in Inverness, Glasgow and London had given him a knowing look and a Buddha-like placidity of the been-there-done-that variety. At the height of the grunge years, his band The Clean Livers had been touted as the next big thing. Single of the week in *NME* twice, a tour supporting Mudhoney and a dozen interested record companies had ended in nothing. Now the grungy garage-rock they used to peddle was back in fashion, and Murray couldn't care less. Every Sunday night he played earthy country tunes down at the Market Bar for beer and fags, and was happier than he'd been in a long time.

He slapped Connor on the back and kissed Kate on the cheek as they came in, then held the front door as the rest trooped by, handing Danny the joint at the back of the line. The living room was open-plan with wood-panelled walls, and filled with piles of records, CDs and books in every available space. Two dirty cream futons and a green beanbag were arranged in front of a small portable television in the corner, and a large burgundy rug covered most of the floor. A beaten-up sunburst Fender Strat and a rose-coloured twelve-string Rickenbacker sat on guitar stands next to each other, facing into the room like an old married couple in the pub. A Tanglewood acoustic lay face down on a futon.

'Take the weight off,' said Murray, lifting the acoustic out the way and leaning it carefully against a wall. 'I'm just having a wee Friday afternoon G and T, anyone care to join me?'

They all said yes and he laughed.

'Shit. Bad crash. Who wants to help in the kitchen?'

'Come on, Uncle Murray,' said Kate, patting his arse as they made for the kitchen door. 'You can tell me all about the action up here in Inversneckie.'

'Hey, less of that uncle shit,' said Murray and laughed a big, throaty laugh.

Connor stood at the window. The Ness was being pelted by heavy rain, dimpling the surface as ducks bobbed their heads under, unperturbed. Well-groomed trees lined both sides of the water, strung together by unlit fairy lights, and the pink crenellated battlements of a twee Victorian castle could be seen in the distance. There was no hope of sun. The skies had descended over Inverness, and rain battered off the clean-looking streets as office workers bolted to pubs and cafés for Friday lunch, covering their heads with bags and newspapers.

Murray and Kate handed out tall glass tumblers of gin. Connor tasted his. Not nearly strong enough but it would do for now.

'And how are you, my troubled cousin?' asked Murray, clinking glasses and taking a swig.

'Oh, you know. Troubled.' Connor smiled back at him. Murray laughed.

'You do realise you take life too seriously, boy.'

'So people tell me.'

'How have the gigs been going?'

'Not bad. It's been three days since I've had a punch in the head, so things seem to be improving.'

'I was going to ask about your face,' said Murray. 'No offence, but you look like shit.'

'None taken,' said Connor. 'Isn't *Fight Club* chic back in yet?'

'Fuck that,' said Murray, patting his stomach like a puppy. 'Corpulent chic, that's the new craze. And I'm rocking that look right now.'

'Murray says this town is full of goths and hippies,' said Kate, plonking down on the beanbag. 'Doesn't exactly sound like our kind of place, eh?'

'Don't worry,' said Paul, 'you'll knock that shit out of 'em.'

'The kids are all pasty-faced and black-clad these days,' said Murray. 'I blame Marilyn Manson and My Chemical Romance. Most of the idiots my age around here are dropouts with rat-tails, knitted coats and flowers in their hair. Fuck knows where they get it from. When I were a lad' – he put on a Yorkshire accent – 'the kids round 'ere knew 'ow to kick out the fookin' jams, so they did.'

Hannah flicked through a stack of novels piled to waist height. 'How bad can it be tonight?' she said. 'It's Friday, after all. What's this place like that we're playing, Murray?'

'The Crow? All right, actually,' said Murray. 'A bit out of town and a bit seventies-looking, but they've got a decent reputation.'

'What about the support?' said Paul. 'Have you heard of The Stretchmarks?'

'You're asking the wrong man,' said Murray, sitting down and supping his gin. 'I haven't been to a proper gig round these parts for years. Not seemly for a man of my rapidly advancing years.'

Kate sat down next to him and cuddled up. 'Aw, come on now, Grandpa. Want me to get your pipe and slippers?'

'What a grand idea,' said Murray. 'I've got a pipe somewhere. And some decent hash for once. Hydroponic shit grown by a mate of mine.'

'Hydro what?' said Danny.

'Means it was grown without soil.'

'Bollocks. How the hell do they do that?'

Murray adopted a teacherly voice. 'It's not new, they've been doing it in the States and Australia for years. I don't know the ins and outs, they just grow it in some magic solution of pixie dust or something. It's all the rage up here in the sticks. Don't you southern folks know anything?'

'Sounds too healthy for our busy lifestyles,' said Connor. 'We like something a bit more artificial that'll fuck you up properly.'

'Don't you talk about being fucked up,' said Hannah, giving Connor a sideways look. 'Not after last night.'

'Oh yes?' said Murray, raising his eyebrows. 'Do tell.'

'Your man here was on the horse pills last night,' said Danny. 'Fucking shapeless.'

'I had a very relaxing time, thank you,' said Connor, meeting Danny's gaze. 'Just as well, after last night.'

'What do you mean?' said Kate.

Connor took a long slug from his glass before saying, 'Oh, you know, just the stress of not getting in a fight. I missed the adrenaline and testosterone kicks.'

Danny looked at Connor, who took another drink and turned away.

'Anyway,' said Murray, 'back to this hydroponic shit. I fancy a blast, so everyone stay where you are and I'll be right back.'

Connor could feel Danny looking at him. He wondered if Danny had told Kate about the seagulls. He wondered how long it had been going on between him and Kate. Why hadn't they said anything? Did everyone know except him? Were they all laughing at him behind his back? Did they think he was a maniac, and they couldn't tell him the news about his best friend and his twin sister? He thought about the stalker, the guy on the beach. Was he really being followed? Maybe it was just a punter on the beach, who ran off when some psycho started chasing him and shouting at him. What about the phone call? The note? His life was a mess of secrets and confusion, half-truths and half-seen faces. He wondered if he was going insane. But thinking about it meant he wasn't, right? Had he really seen Danny and Kate together? He was so loaded that he wasn't sure about anything he'd seen over the last week, now he thought about it. Maybe it had been entirely innocent. No, that was stupid, they were naked. Fuck, he just didn't know any more.

He finished his drink and went to the kitchen to fix another, stronger one.

Murray had the Crow's vibe bang on. A fudge-coloured, L-shaped building next to a petrol station near the edge of town, the Crow declared itself with a cheap, dirty-white seventies sign above the door, the low-slung bar area adjoining a dozen bedrooms that hadn't seen a lick of paint in a long time. Posters in the bar advertised some decent gigs, mainly from other bands on the Scottish indie scene like My Latest Novel, 1990s and Idlewild. While that might've indicated a reasonable amount of musical taste in the Highland capital, the band currently murdering their instruments on stage said otherwise.

Contrary to their standard garage-rock name, The Stretchmarks were a ghoulish goth-rock disaster, like The Damned on a very bad day or The Mission on a particularly good one. As their powder-faced singer writhed about on the floor, eyes tight shut and spit flying from the corner of his mouth, The Ossians crowded around one end of the bar in high spirits. Much of their buoyancy was down to Murray. Not only was the man a tonic in himself, but his hydroponic hash pipe got everyone giggling in five minutes flat. An afternoon of lazy smoking and drinking had gently propelled them into a good mood, if perhaps a little too relaxed to get psyched up for the gig.

Worried about being too chilled, Connor had spent the last few minutes rubbing speed on his gums in the toilets before popping a pill from his pocket. He was now illicitly pouring gin from a half-bottle he'd picked up into an empty glass, and swigging it straight down, only a slight grimace to show for the drink's strength. He remembered the phone in his pocket, took it out and switched it on. There were four messages from Nick. He went out to the car park and phoned. The call was answered on the second ring.

'Where the fuck have you been?'

'Switched the phone off.'

'You arsehole. I told you never to switch it off.'

'It's the ringtone, it's killing me. I couldn't take it any more.'

'I don't fucking care. Change it then, dickhead.'

'I don't know how.'

'Jesus Christ. Anyway, how did it go?'

'Fine.'

'You met Kenny all right?'

'He seemed a bit of a fuckwit.'

'What does that make you?'

'Fuck knows.'

'Exactly.'

'I think someone's following me.'

'Are you being careful?'

'Of course.'

'Then stop being paranoid. No one's following you.'

'Someone phoned this mobile.'

'Who?'

'I don't know. It said "No Number".'

'What did they say?'

'That my secrets were safe with them.'

'Shit. Really?'

'Yeah. Any ideas?'

'In a word, no. Let me think about it.'

'I also found a note in my pocket to the same effect.'

'What other secrets do you have?'

'None.'

'Yeah, right. A cunt like you always has secrets. What is it? Kiddie porn?'

'I don't want to do this any more, someone's definitely following me.'

'So that's what this is about. You want out, so you invent some shit to make it sound like you're being followed. Nice try.'

'That's not how it is.'

'Don't fucking bother, Con. You're going through with this, or you're fucking dead. How many times do I need to tell you? If the police were on to you, you'd be in chokey by now.'

'That's reassuring.'

'Just get on with it. Be a fucking man for once.'

'You certainly know how to motivate your workforce, don't you?'

'Fuck off. I'll be in touch.'

Dial tone. Connor wandered back inside. The Stretchmarks were finishing in a humdrum mash of feedback and crash of cymbals, skulking offstage to a spark of polite applause. About three hundred kids had arrived by this time, most of them dressed in black with pierced lips, small tattoos, dyed hair and pocket chains everywhere. The same goth kids you saw hanging around the top of Cockburn Street in Edinburgh, thought Connor, the ones that the local paper was always up in arms about. Kids hanging about in the street? What the fuck next? Kids drinking and smoking and fucking? Good.

Part of him had expected things to be different on tour. Wasn't that the reason he'd picked out these places? That, and the claustrophobia. Having been brought up in a poxy, run-down fishing town, Connor felt strangely claustrophobic away from the coast. He only realised when Danny asked him why there were no inland gigs on the tour. He had to be near the sea. So Stirling, Aviemore and Pitlochry were out and Thurso, Ullapool and Kyle were in. And, of course, Inverness. A television in the corner of the bar showed MTV2 with the sound down. The same channel could be picked up anywhere in the fucking world, thought Connor, so there must be little pockets of goth, emo and nu-metal kids scattered around the globe. So what? Part of him thought it was a shame to lose the individuality of different towns to the forces of globalisation, but did that really happen? Did it happen more now than in the past? Haven't kids in small towns always looked to other cultures, to American culture, for kicks? Connor found it hard to summon up any moral outrage about it. There were worse things in the world. Maybe he was just too stoned or tired to give a fuck. Or maybe he had other shit on his mind.

Their set started well. With Murray grinning side-stage, ostensibly acting as guitar tech but really just getting more loaded, the band were slow into the creepy menace of 'Melancholia', but picked up through 'St Andrew's Day'. When they got into a groove during 'Alcohol', Connor noticed Kate and Danny smiling at each other. He smiled a little to himself and looked away. Weaned on nu-metal, the kids in the crowd automatically went for the heavier numbers, but seemed to be getting some of the subtler stuff, at least that's the impression Connor got from the stage. Maybe it was that hydroponic shit from the afternoon, but his antagonism levels were unusually low, and he felt himself getting drawn in by the goodwill of the crowd.

Half an hour in they played 'Geometry'. Starting with a simple picky guitar part, they built up layer upon layer of noise, Connor and Kate's harmonies intertwining until the song exploded in a climax of guitars, Hannah firing out the kind of solo that sounds like all the right notes played in the wrong order. Only it didn't happen. Connor turned round. Hannah was standing still, the guitar hanging limply round her neck. She was pinching her brow, her eyes tight shut and her other hand was groping around for something to lean on. She started swaying, then she was on the ground. The guitar rang and clattered as Hannah lay there. A blinking red stage light made it look as if she was asleep in a bedroom with neon street signs outside the window. By the time Connor got over to her she was twitching violently, her whole body thrown into spasms. Her head banged off the wooden floor and her legs thrashed as if she was trying to shake her shoes off. Her eyes rolled back in their sockets and a thick spit appeared at the sides of her mouth as Connor tried to hold her head and stop it beating against the stage. Panicking, he thought he should get her on to her side, then somehow she was on her side anyway. He tried to get her mouth open, but her jaws were clamped shut like they'd been wired together. Connor could see the muscles in her neck strain, and sensed waves of rigidity wash through her body as he held her, trying to grapple with her left arm which waved around violently.

All of a sudden it was over. Danny and Kate had only just noticed what was happening and stopped playing to scramble over the stage to them. Hannah was slumped, her body loose in Connor's hands as if a terrible tornado had passed through her. Murray ran onstage and crouched next to them, unsure what to do.

'What the fuck happened?' shouted Danny over feedback, but no one answered. Kate went over and turned Hannah's amp off. The absence of noise was startling. The crowd didn't know what to do. They stood looking at each other, then at the stage.

Hannah's eyes opened and she looked around, confused.

'What's going on?' she whispered.

'Shhhh,' said Connor, stroking her hair away from her face. 'You've had some kind of fit or something. It's all right.'

She tried to get up but only managed to prop herself on to her elbows. She saw the crowd looking at her. She tried to get up further but her body was weak and she wanted to go to sleep.

'Let's get you to hospital,' said Connor. Hannah tried to wave this idea away, as if swatting a fly. She felt so tired she could barely speak and desperately wanted to get offstage, so she let herself be lifted to her feet and guided to the side, where she lay on a bench under the window and closed her eyes. After a while she opened them again and saw concerned faces.

'I don't need to go to the hospital,' she said, but even as the words came out she found them unconvincing, and thought of a big hospital bed where she could sleep for hours.

'I think you do, love,' said Kate, smiling. 'Hell of a way to get out of playing that solo.'

Hannah smiled a bleached-out smile.

'I never liked that bloody solo anyway.'

Raigmore Hospital was only a hundred yards down Old Perth Road but they drove it, immediately getting lost in a maze of roadworks, traffic cones, diggers, No Entry signs, car-park barriers and pay machines. After parking they had to walk about a hundred yards anyway, which had Connor fuming by the time they reached the doors of A&E. After being admitted and led to a painfully bright bed area screened off by a blue plastic curtain, they sat and waited for three hours while nothing happened.

Weekend nights in Scottish hospitals are awash with booze casualties. Several times while they waited someone stumbled into their area, offering garbled apologies or incoherently shouting at them. Singing, screaming and crying could be heard from the other side of the curtain, as harassed nurses and doctors hurried by with bloodied patients on beds or in wheelchairs.

Each time someone official went past Connor was up hustling, gesticulating and shouting until he got threatened with ejection. Each time he secured a promise that someone would be with them soon. On one wander in search of someone to harangue he found himself next to an unattended girl, maybe twenty, either asleep or unconscious and gently dribbling in a wheelchair. On her lap, her handbag was open and Connor could see two medication blister packs inside. Without thinking he pocketed them. The pulse in his throat became so strong that he realised he wasn't breathing. He walked round a corner and stood taking small, shallow breaths, waiting as his pulse gradually slowed and his head stopped swimming. He returned to Hannah, a stone in his stomach as he imagined how the others would react if they knew what he'd just done. Fuck them, secrets seemed to be order of the day at the moment.

Around half twelve Murray, Paul and Danny returned to the Crow to pack up the gear before they closed, while Connor and Kate stayed with Hannah. She drifted in and out of sleep, occasionally waking surprised and irritated by the brightness of the place. As she dozed, Connor and Kate sat quietly for a while until Connor spoke.

'How long?'

'Sorry?'

'How long has it been going on?'

'What?'

'I saw you and Danny last night.'

'Uh-huh?'

'Together.'

'We're always together. With you and Han being a couple we don't have much choice.'

'Kate, come on. I *saw* you. Together. In a sleeping bag. In Gerry's spare room.'

There was a long silence. Kate played with the button of her jacket.

'A week or so,' she said eventually.

'Does anyone else know?'

Another long silence.

'Danny told Hannah. And she let slip to Paul last night. I was going to tell you, but it never seemed like the right time.'

'What did you think I was going to do? Throw a wobbly?'

'No, of course not. But you've been a bit . . .'

'What?'

'Volatile, recently, I guess.'

Connor thought about the bag full of drugs and money, the note, the anonymous phone call and the figure on the beach. He thought about Hannah lying next to them in a hospital bed. She knew about Kate and Danny, and hadn't told him. He didn't exactly have a moral high ground on keeping secrets.

'Maybe,' he said. 'For what it's worth, I think it's great the two of you have got together. I always said you'd make a great couple.'

Kate gave out a relieved laugh. 'You never said any such thing. I bet the thought never crossed your mind. It never crossed my mind until recently. And anyway, I don't even know if we *are* a couple yet.'

They sat in silence for a while longer. Around two o'clock Hannah woke, and not long after a doctor arrived. He was tall and overly handsome with a square jaw and perfect teeth. He looked far too young to know his way around a human body. He insisted on examining Hannah in private. Connor, wary of this kid being left alone with her, refused.

'Go on,' sighed Hannah. 'It's fine.'

The examination was over in seconds. The doctor pulled back the curtain with a swish.

'As far as I can tell you're fine,' he said, half to Hannah and half to Connor and Kate.

'But what happened?' said Connor. 'You didn't see her, there's obviously something wrong with her.'

'I am bloody here, you know,' said Hannah, a thin thread of anger in her voice.

The doctor couldn't work out who to speak to, so addressed the space between Hannah and the other two.

'She's had some kind of fit but it's nothing to get too alarmed about. It could be epilepsy, but it could also be a number of other things. It could also very easily be nothing at all, just a one-off incident.'

'Can't you test for epilepsy?' said Connor.

'Well, yes, but not right now. For a start you have to wait twenty-four hours after a fit. Also there are a number of things to test for, and really her own GP should arrange it and go over the options. We recommend that she undergo a CT scan. Even if it is epilepsy, which is by no means certain, there are ways of managing that effectively these days. Again, her own doctor can go over all that with her in more detail after she's had the appropriate tests.'

'Isn't there any medication you can give her?' said Connor.

'Fuck's sake, Con, will you let me handle this?' said Hannah, her raised voice making them all jump. She turned slowly to the doctor. 'Well?'

'There really isn't anything I can give you that would make any difference at this stage. The best thing to do is take it easy. I strongly recommend you stay off alcohol and any other stimulants, legal or otherwise. Try to stay away from stressful situations. Make an appointment with your doctor when you get back to Edinburgh and try not to worry about it.'

'Is that the best you can do?' said Connor. 'Don't fucking worry? What kind of half-arsed kid doctors do they employ up here?'

'I really don't think that's necessary.'

The doctor was backing away slightly.

'Shut up, Con,' said Hannah wearily. 'He's just doing his job.' She turned to the doctor. 'Thanks. I'll take it easy.'

'Excellent,' said the doctor. 'You'll need to free up the bed, I'm afraid. If you could sign out over at reception, that would be great.'

He headed down the corridor leaving Connor fizzing, like he needed to punch something or someone. Hannah looked him in the eye.

'Let's get out of here,' she said, sighing for what seemed like the hundredth time that evening. 'I need to go to bed.'

'We should pack the fuck up and head home,' said Connor as Murray opened the door to the flat.

He wasn't sure why he'd said it. Maybe part of him thought it, but he was also aware that he said it partially out of obligation. Actually, now he'd made the suggestion, it seemed like quite an appealing prospect, to leave all this bullshit behind and sleep for a week in his own bed. But how could he go back to Edinburgh, and Nick? And anyway, he was aware Hannah wouldn't let this happen. He could predict the conversation they were about to have, as chess Grand Masters predict their opponents' future moves.

'Don't be so melodramatic,' said Hannah. 'We're not going anywhere. I feel fine, for Christ's sake, just a little tired. We've got a day off tomorrow, right? If it's all right with Uncle Murray, I intend to spend the next twenty-four hours catching up on some much-needed sleep.'

'Hannah's right,' said Paul. 'If she feels OK and gets plenty of rest, there's no reason why we can't keep going. We all just need to take it easy for a day or two.'

Paul looked at Connor when he said this, but Connor's eyes were following Hannah as she eased into the beanbag.

'Can I get you anything, love?'

'Just a beer,' said Hannah.

'But you heard what the doctor said.'

'Just get me a fucking beer.'

They sat without speaking, the icy shadows of The Breeders on the stereo. Conversation gradually started up, like a pressure valve being released. Hannah finished her beer and slowly got up. Connor went to help her and she let him.

'I'm off to bed,' she announced.

'I'll come too,' said Connor.

Hannah looked at him. He was still wired on whatever the fuck he'd taken, and he'd drunk three beers in the space she'd taken to finish one. She knew that he'd lie there because he thought he should, the loving boyfriend, twitching and drumming, his irritating energy buzzing round the room and preventing her from sleeping. She didn't need it.

'I'll be fine,' she said. 'You come to bed when you want.'

He kissed her twice, the first one quick, the second a slow apology, and she was gone. He breathed out, a mixture of relief and sadness, and went to the fridge for another beer. He wondered what the pills were that he'd lifted from the girl in the hospital, and hoped they might get rid of his goddamn headache.

'I didn't realise you were in a fucking rambling club,' said Connor, blowing on his hands as water squelched into his Converse. Ahead of him Murray strode along a thin, watery path through soggy moorland. Freezing rain swept across the moor and a pregnant, dreich sky hung overhead. Connor felt his cheek stinging from the rain and trudged on.

It was mid-afternoon. Despite drinking, smoking and pill-popping till seven in the morning, Connor had been fussing over an exasperated Hannah all morning as she tried to relax. Eventually, driven mad by his inept nursing, Hannah pleaded with Murray to take Connor somewhere, anywhere, so she could get some rest. So now they were freezing their bollocks off in a field on the outskirts of the city.

'You wanted to discover a bit of Scotland, well here it is,' said Murray, his words whipped away as soon as he spoke. Ahead of them a rough wooden flagpole stood twenty feet high, with a small red and white flag snapping violently on top. Murray stopped and looked at the view. In the distance, a string of miserable conifers sulked beneath a cover of low gunmetal cloud. The wind gusted erratically, one minute fading to nothing, the next blasting and making the pair of them wobble.

'I've been reading your interviews,' said Murray, watching his

139

cousin's small frame cower in the elements. 'Please tell me you're not sober when you do these things.'

'How do you mean?'

'You talk so much shite. Entertaining shite, I grant you, but I hope for your mental health that you've got drunkenness as an excuse.'

Connor gave a shrug.

'That piece in *The Scotsman*,' Murray continued. 'What was it? Trying to discover a national identity or the state of the nation or some guff like that. Really, Con, you should stick to "we can't be pigeonholed" and "we just make music for ourselves and if anyone else likes it, that's a bonus". I don't think music fans give a flying fuck for highfalutin ideas about nationhood, and Holy Grail-style quests for whatever the fuck it is you're looking for.'

Connor was hungover and so tired he thought he might puke. He couldn't muster the energy to speak. He was concentrating on not getting blown off his feet into a bog and covered in freezing Highland crap. Murray was still talking.

'Anyway, this is the Scotland that you're so keen to discover. Imagine this scene soundtracked by Runrig or a pipe band, and you've just about got it.'

Connor didn't get it. He was still drunk from last night and couldn't really remember how they came to be standing here.

'In a fucking bog?'

'Pretty much,' said Murray, looking up at the flag whipping and rippling above them. 'Haven't you worked out where we are yet? A big bit of open moor? Near Inverness? With a couple of old flags planted in it?'

'Euro Disney?' Connor felt like he might pass out soon if he didn't get a seat in the warm.

'It's fucking Culloden, you dolt,' said Murray. 'If that means anything to you.'

'Sure,' said Connor, looking around. 'Jacobites, Bonnie Prince Charlie, Scotland v England, all that crap.'

'All that crap indeed,' said Murray. 'The last battle ever fought on the British mainland. It was a waste of time on a miserable piece of shitty bog in the middle of nowhere two hundred and fifty years ago.' Murray looked at Connor, who really thought he might vomit. 'Do you even know what happened here?'

'Yeah, we got fucked, didn't we?'

'And who are "we", exactly? Here on Charlie's side there were four thousand Highlanders standing behind a wee French Catholic ponce. Over there' – Murray pointed to their right where, in the distance, Connor could just make out another flagpole with a yellow flag flying from it – 'was a pompous English duke with English, German and Dutch soldiers and several thousand Scots behind him as well. In fact there were more Scots fighting for the English that day, who were really Germans anyway, than there were for French dandy Charlie. So that's your fucking Scotland for you. Thousands of clansmen slaughtering each other in a god-forsaken shithole in the name of Germany versus France. Makes you think, doesn't it?'

'It makes me think I want to get out this fucking rain,' said Connor, although his mind was buzzing, imagining the miserable scene that must have played out here. What the fuck were they thinking? What was the point of any of it? Were people back then really so stupid that they thought the killing of a few thousand men here would make any difference to anything? And had it?

'Come on,' said Murray, turning and heading further into the centre of the boggy field, to Connor's dismay. Murray stopped after a few strides and shouted back, 'Don't worry, they've got a tearoom just past that other flag. There's a visitor centre.'

'Is it licensed?' said Connor. He felt his pockets crackle with pills as he shoved his hands deep into them and hunched his shoulders into the oncoming wind. He felt wretched. The rain was heavier now and his feet were soaked. As he walked, his shoes started to squeak like a clown's, and he thought how ridiculous it would've been if both sides at Culloden had been wearing clown outfits, racing at each other in baggy trousers, red noses, braces and bow ties, their claymores whirling above their heads as they whooped their battle cries.

★

Back at Murray's flat, Hannah insisted on going out.

'Look, it's Saturday night and I feel better than I have all week, plus I've been cooped up here all day. So let's see what this city has to offer in the way of action, eh?'

An hour later the six of them – the girls in front, Paul and Murray next with Connor and Danny bringing up the rear – were walking up the west bank of the Ness into a face-pinching breeze with clear, dark skies above. The water seemed to Connor like honey, the slowness of its movement and the citrus sheen from the street lights mesmerising him. The metallic crackle of the blister packs in his pockets had annoyed him so much earlier that he'd popped all the pills out into his pocket, and thrown the packaging away. Now he couldn't tell which of the pills in his pocket he'd lifted from his parents' bathroom and which he'd stolen from the girl in the hospital last night, and he didn't care. He couldn't even really remember doing either of those things too clearly. The more he reached back into his memory, the more he felt a slight panic at the lack of concrete events from the last seven days. It was only a week since they'd played the first gig of the tour, wasn't it? At the Liquid Room? Where he got accosted by Nick and Shug in the bogs? And staggered home under the whalebones? He told himself these things had happened, but it seemed now that they'd happened in some shitty film he'd watched late at night.

He tried to focus on the city around him. He liked what he'd seen of Inverness. It didn't smell of anything that air shouldn't smell of. No breweries, no pollution, no crap. He could feel the inside of his nostrils nip as he breathed in deeply, coughing as the burning reached his chest and lungs. They walked under bare branches draped with twinkling fairy lights, the sounds of the town centre coming to them from across the meandering river. Connor thought there was something odd about the view across the water, then realised it was the height of the buildings, or rather the lack of height. Nothing was over two storeys high, including the handful of sixties breezeblock buildings that stuck out like spare pricks among the older, more distinguished stonework. And it was mostly flat, too. After living in Edinburgh so long he found a flat, low-level town a strangely foreign experience. They crossed over a pale-blue steel footbridge with a European Union plaque bolted to its arch, the yellow circle of stars a declaration of community. The bridge wobbled as they walked across into the drinking zone.

Connor saw the same crap they'd encountered everywhere else. McDonald's, KFC and Burger King; chain pubs and newly opened vodka bars; already-drunk punters clinging on to each other as they zigzagged down the compact grid of streets that constituted Inverness's nightlife. What was he expecting? He couldn't keep being surprised that places like this – only a few hours' drive from Edinburgh in a decent car – had been infected by civilisation as much as the capital had. And what was he expecting anyway, fucking mud huts? This place had air you could breathe and pubs you could drink in. Wasn't that enough?

Danny was talking to him.

'Kate told me you spoke to her last night.'

'Yeah.'

'I'm sorry we didn't tell you, it's just . . .'

Connor waved this away. 'I know, I know. It's fine.'

'It's not like we were sneaking around or anything, we just didn't know if there was anything to tell yet, that's all.'

'Hannah and Paul knew.'

'That was a mistake. And you can't blame them for not saying anything, it wasn't really their place.'

'I don't. I don't blame anyone for anything. I'm fine.'

'You sure?'

'Of course. Forget it.'

'Aren't you supposed to tell me that if I mess with your sister you'll kill me or something?'

'You're not going to do that.'

'How do you know?'

'Because I'd kill you.'

They both laughed quietly. They walked on a bit, then Connor said, 'Did you tell Kate about what happened at the pier?'

'No.'

'Isn't it a bit early with you and Kate to be keeping secrets?'

'Probably. But I didn't think it would exactly show us in a good light. Even though it was that dicksplash Gerry's fault.'

'I suppose not.'

'Did you tell Hannah?'

'No.'

'You think we got away with it? I mean, is it that easy to do something like that and nobody find out?'

'It looks like it,' said Connor. He thought about the anonymous phone call from the other night.

'Doesn't seem right, somehow. That we just get away with it.'

'What do you suggest? We go to a police station and say, "Excuse me, two nights ago we accidentally ran over hundreds of flying rats on Aberdeen pier"?'

Danny shook his head as he finished a joint and stepped on the roach.

'But don't you feel guilty?'

'I'm not exactly thrilled about it,' said Connor. 'But with Hannah's fit last night I've got more important things to worry about.'

The bullshit just kept coming, didn't it? Sure, he was worried about Hannah, but mostly he'd been thinking about the stalker, the drug deals and his next drink, not about Hannah at all. He did care about her. Hell, he loved her, and she'd collapsed twenty-four hours ago. What the fuck was he thinking, letting her go out tonight? But he knew she was eminently more sensible than him and wouldn't risk her own health. Not like him. If he told her not to do something, wouldn't she just turn round and do it? Plus it was a Saturday night and he wanted to get loaded. So there it was, in all its glory. Connor was more bothered about getting off his face than about the well-being of his girlfriend. Hold the front page. But she wanted to go out and so did he and so did the rest of them. So what? So I don't know fucking what, he thought. Well done, boy, you've tied yourself up in knots again.

'Where's this pub of yours, Murray?' said Danny.

'Good timing.'

Murray stopped beneath a black wrought-iron canopy jutting

over the street, the words 'Victorian Market' embossed on the side.

'It's in here.'

He headed down a tiny alley that looked like a dead end, the whitewashed, pebble-dashed walls on either side filthy with grime. By an unmarked door, a couple of gnarly old buggers stood sucking on filterless fags. Murray nodded at them and pushed open the door, which led to some rickety stairs. The rest of them followed, and Connor wondered what a Saturday night in Inverness would deliver.

The Market Bar was full of drunks. Old drunks, cool drunks, arrogant drunks, unwashed drunks, kid drunks, pathetic drunks and gregarious drunks. Connor felt at home. The air was heavy with the stench of urine and cheap air freshener, thanks to the smoking ban. The small, square, pine-panelled room was heaving with the dregs of the city's drinkers. On a tiny carpeted stage opposite the bar an old man with a runny nose and the skin peeling from his hands sat on a bar stool, elaborately fingerpicking on an old, large-bodied Gibson that had definitely seen better days. He crooned and picked away through blues and jazz numbers, wiping his nose on the sleeve of his filthy jumper and using that sleeve as a guitar slide. Between songs an emaciated young barman with a messy ponytail and massive baggy jeans delivered pints of 80 Shilling to the old-timer, which he gulped down. A tatty, single-flame gas heater flickered away high on one wall surrounded by framed black and white photographs of anonymous musicians.

They sat around a table next to the stage and Danny got the drinks in. Nobody in the place seemed to be paying the old blues guy any attention whatsoever, but Connor was immediately mesmerised by those flaky old hands, skimming up and down the fretboard and over the strings like pond skaters on water. The others were talking away, the usual opening gambits of pub chat, but Connor found himself getting more and more sucked into the blues guy's world of heartbreak and lightning-fast fingers. Murray and Kate chatted to two loose-limbed, disjointed characters that Murray obviously knew. Paul, Danny and Hannah were talking to a couple of hippy-looking girls at the next table, one of whom had long, mousy brown hair pleated all the way past her arse, the other with bells in her blonde dreadlocks and dozens of silver bangles on each wrist.

'Is your mate not chatty, then?' Connor heard the hairbell girl say to Hannah.

'Nah, he's just into guitarists in a big way,' she replied, looking at Connor gazing at the blues guy.

'And what about you?' said Hairbell.

'I'm a guitarist,' said Hannah, laughing.

Connor felt dislocated from the conversation and liked the feeling. He couldn't deal with other people just now, and he felt grateful for the distraction of the blues guy. Everything seemed to be happening around him and he had no control over any of it. Kate and Danny were a couple, and everyone had known except him. He was a drug dealer or mule or whatever, and someone was spying on him, leaving notes and phoning him on a mobile hardly anyone had the number to. He felt like one of the gulls on the pier, his head tucked under a wing to protect him, only to be wiped out as easily as pressing a foot to an accelerator.

His brain was buzzing as he tried but failed to retrieve the feeling of being absorbed in the blues guy's guitar-playing. He felt the need for more speed and pills – whatever they were. He headed to the bogs to pop another couple. If he was honest, a lot of the appeal was in the fact that he didn't know what they were. When he got back, the blues guy had given up for the night, and was slumped in a corner on his own.

The night shuffled on. Connor watched Hannah as she chatted to Paul and Danny. She laughed at something, throwing her head back in what might've been a flirty gesture in other circumstances. Maybe it was a flirty gesture, he thought. Christ, what was wrong with him? He couldn't remember the last time he'd seen Hannah laugh like that while talking to him. It always seemed to be arguments, or resigned sighing, or words drifting past each other in the air. What the fuck could he do about it? He felt stuck in a moment that he couldn't get out of. Christ, now he was thinking in U2 lyrics, it couldn't get any worse than that.

'What are you smiling about?' said Hannah, watching him.

'U2 lyrics,' he said.

'Oh shit,' said Hannah, turning to the rest of them. 'Watch out, folks, Connor's having a breakdown.'

'What, more than usual?' said Danny.

The bell for last orders had rung ages ago, but no one paid any notice. A clock on the wall said two o'clock, and the bar showed no sign of closing, so they were well into lock-in territory. The two loose-limbed guys from earlier came over and started teasing Murray, cajoling him into something, but he resisted. After a few minutes of this, Murray glanced at the guy behind the bar, who nodded gently. Without ceremony, Murray got up on to the stage, picked up the blues guy's guitar and sat on the stool.

He picked out a plaintive country riff for a while, minor chords tumbling gently over each other, then began singing in a smoky, sonorous voice, his eyes tight shut. He was singing something about water arguing with itself, and the colour of whisky, and hope and sorrow, Connor couldn't make out the words exactly, but he was instantly captivated. He'd never seen Murray perform like this, on his own with just a guitar, and it was compelling. The sound of chatter in the bar gradually faded as more and more people began tuning in to what Murray was doing. Connor felt Hannah's arm linking with his own, and turned to see her smiling at him. It was the most beautiful thing he'd ever seen, a face full of kindness, tranquillity and love, a smile that made him feel nervous and contented all at the same time.

He turned back. Murray was playing gently, singing softly, holding the attention of the whole room. It was mesmerising. Chords looped round each other, falling and rising, falling and rising, never properly resolving, Murray repeating the same few lines, which somehow seemed to be imbued with more resonance and meaning each time round. Connor was struck by a mixture of awe and jealousy. Nothing he'd ever written was anywhere near as good as this song. He tried to think of the perfect word to describe what he was hearing. Grace. There was something graceful about it. A 39-year-old guy playing quietly in a room full of drunks, but he was somehow reaching deep into himself to deliver a sentiment that touched everyone.

Murray finished, the song fading gradually into nothing, and Connor sat motionless and silent as raucous applause exploded around the bar. All about him, people were shouting, whistling and clapping. Connor sat there feeling the presence of Hannah next to him. Murray smiled sheepishly as he took off the guitar and returned to their table, ignoring cries for more.

'That was amazing,' said Hannah, as Murray beamed.

'New song,' explained Murray, finishing his pint. He turned to Connor. 'What did you think?'

Connor shook his head. 'You don't need me to tell you it was fucking brilliant. You know it was.'

Murray shrugged.

'Listen, I'm beginning to feel things catching up with me,' said Hannah. 'Think I'll head up the road.' She looked at Connor. 'Walk me home?'

Connor looked at the pint and the whisky in front of him, then at Hannah. She was beautiful and selfless, thoughtful and caring, and she was his. Why had he been taking her for granted for so long? Why had he been treating her like shit?

'Sure.'

They grabbed their coats, said goodbye and headed out the door.

'That cousin of yours is quite something,' said Hannah.

They stood on the wobbly footbridge, leaning over the side, the Ness moving like syrup below.

'Yeah, he's something all right.'

'How do you think he gets to be so . . .'

'Talented?'

'I was going to say contented.'

Connor sighed. 'I wish I fucking knew.'

Hannah looked at him. 'You'll get there.'

'Will I?'

'Sure, when you're old and past it like Murray.'

Connor laughed. 'I feel old and past it now.' He turned to look at her, taking her hand. 'How are you anyway?'

'Oh, you know, surviving.'

They were silent for a while.

'I shat myself last night,' said Connor quietly. 'When you had that fit.'

'Really?'

'Yeah.'

'So did I, to be honest.'

'What would I do without you?'

'I'm not going anywhere.'

'I wouldn't blame you if you did. Leave me, I mean.' He felt Hannah squeeze his hand tightly. 'I've not exactly been easy to live with.'

'You're just a bit wound up, Con. You need to relax. Be more like Murray.'

'Maybe in fifteen years' time, eh?'

'If everyone took a leaf out of Murray's book, the world would be a better place.'

Connor sat there feeling the pressure of Hannah's hand and watching the thick water treacle past below.

'You know I love you, don't you?' he said.

'I know.'

She leant her head on his shoulder and closed her eyes. He listened to her breathe, feeling the weight of her head on his shoulder and the pressure of her hand in his. He closed his eyes and tried to relax.

8

Thurso

*'Wrap your cold and clammy arms around me
Soak into my bones
Whisper in my ear you'll never leave me
Make yourself at home'*

The Ossians, 'The Haar'

The van grumbled over the Kessock Bridge heading north to the Black Isle. Ahead of them a clump of dark hills mottled with snow disappeared into a muffle of thick, black cloud. The swish of passing cars as they sprayed along the wet dual carriageway was the only sound, until Connor couldn't stand the weight of the silence and the clouds and stuck on some vintage Teenage Fanclub to cheer them up.

Three o'clock on a Sunday afternoon and they were running late again. The Thurso gig was just a pub job so there wasn't a specific get-in time, but they had a long drive ahead and precious little energy. Connor was ragged. He tried to add up how much sleep he'd had since they left Edinburgh. He came to a different number each time, the highest of which was fifteen hours. That was over six nights. He had to get a grip. His bones ached with exhaustion but his mind was whirring like the workings of a great mechanical clock, thanks to all the amphetamine. Among all the drinking and weed smoking, speed was his anchor drug, a lifeline that kept him tethered to something like reality. But there's a reason why speed's under a tenner a wrap. Today's comedown was brutal, and he'd started getting stomach cramps to add to his headaches, which never seemed to go away except when he was extremely drunk. He'd taken more speed and a couple of hits of gin for breakfast just to take the edge off but he still felt like absolute shit. He tried to think of the last time he'd eaten properly. He could recall sitting down for a meal in Arbroath, but hadn't eaten any of it. How long ago was that? It seemed like that happened in a previous life, to a different person. He used his fingers to count back and realised it was only four days ago. Shit.

They crossed the Cromarty Firth over a low bridge and crawled up its northern edge as the rain fell in swirls. Massive oil rigs stood waiting to be repaired in the water like giant alien ships preparing to attack, crouching with their colossal legs in the slapping water and not giving a damn. Their vastness so close to land was unnerving, and all four of the band couldn't keep their eyes off them, watching silently as the road turned northwards towards Dornoch Firth and the wilderness of Sutherland.

The road took on a rhythmical pattern. For a while they would drive alongside the sea, raging waves sending spray on to the windscreen, large puddles filling the dips in the road. Then they would rise dramatically, snaking up a hillside as Paul dropped down the gears, their ears popping as the rain turned to sleet and patches of snow speckled the roadside. This continued for miles and miles, Paul complaining all the time about the state of the roads. As heads cleared and Teenage Fanclub did their work, things brightened in the van despite the weather outside. Connor was amazed at the bleak, brown expanses of heather and bracken. There were no trees anywhere.

They passed a sign saying 'Caithness Glass welcomes you to our county' and after a while the road headed inland towards Thurso on the north coast, the long straight stretch of tarmac cutting through a flat plain of low gorse and heather. They didn't see another car for twenty minutes.

'Jesus,' said Danny, 'this must be the arse end of nowhere. Where's all the traffic?'

They came over a rise and spotted the sea in front of them. The grey, hunched form of Thurso lay ahead, sheltering in a bay against the ferocious rain that battered the countryside into submission.

As they hit Thurso, Connor felt depressed. He didn't know what he was expecting from a town on the north coast of Scotland, but a smaller version of his hometown definitely wasn't it. Within two minutes they'd driven round the centre, a small grid of houses in mushy brown and splashy grey with shopfronts poking out on the ground floor, and a tiny pedestrian precinct that looked straight out of an Edinburgh housing scheme.

When they found the hostel they were booked into they couldn't believe it. It was a chippie. 'Sandra's Snack Bar, Takeaway, Internet Café and Backpackers Hostel', it said in curvy red and green lettering above the door. A sign to the side of the building said 'Hostel Reception In Snack Bar', except someone had changed 'Hostel' to 'Hostile'.

It was already dark and they dodged in through the rain, the slimy smell of chip fat hitting them instantly. Luminous orange cardboard signs with jagged edges covered all available wall space behind the counter; handwritten marker-pen scrawls advertising every conceivable combination of greasy food. A small, wiry, moustachioed man of fifty presided behind the counter, flanked by two chubby, goth-looking teenage girls squeezed into short skirts and bust-enhancing corsets. The girls looked like they'd rather be anywhere than in a chippie in Thurso. Two long-haired metalheads in biker jackets and a couple of spindly lads in Rangers tops and baseball caps stood in front of them in the queue. Once that lot had their fish suppers dished up – all of them eyeing The Ossians as they waited – Paul checked into the hostel with the boss.

Connor spotted a cupboard with the door half open, a pair of feet poking out and the flickering light of a screen inside. He wandered over to take a closer look and it turned out this was the 'Internet Café' advertised outside. A curly-haired skater boy was checking out surfing websites on an ancient PC, the three walls covered in scrawled website addresses. The cupboard was so small the boy had to sit side-on to the screen, his long legs sticking out the door. Connor chuckled to himself as Paul came back with keys and motioned towards the door.

Upstairs Hannah and Kate dumped their bags and checked for stains on the sheets while the boys dicked around in the other dingy room.

'Some place,' said Kate, thinking how little time the two of them had spent alone together since they'd started on tour. Kate had a lot of time for Hannah. She had her head screwed on properly, and didn't take any shit from anyone, especially Connor. She was a calming influence on him, although he did seem to be losing it on this tour. So God knows what he would've been like if it wasn't for her. It was strange for Kate to consider why girls were attracted to Connor, because of the brother thing, obviously, but also because he'd always annoyed the crap out of her. She realised he was good-looking, although she would never have told him so, it would've been too weird, and anyway, it would just make his head swell. So on that level, she could see why Hannah was first attracted to Connor. But he was an odd little bundle of energy, and she knew she would never have put up with all that hyper, high-maintenance shit from any boyfriend of hers. That's why she was happy with straight-forward, no-nonsense Danny. She admired Hannah's patience, in a way, her ability to soak up anything Connor dished out. Then again, perhaps Hannah had a completely different relationship with him, perhaps she saw a totally different side to him. Who knew what any couple was like in private? Who was she to judge them?

She and Hannah were two women in the idiotic blokes' world of rock, playing mostly to blokes, and hanging around with blokes all the time. Sometimes Kate thought that Scotland wasn't a million miles away from countries in the Middle East, the ones where women were expected to cover up and stay at home, while the menfolk sat around in cafés and village squares putting the world to rights. Any visit to a pub in a small Scottish town would tell you it wasn't like *Monarch of the Glen* or whatever new piece of scenic garbage was on Sunday-night telly. There was always a vast majority of men – ignorant, bigoted men – in these places. Which, of course, meant she and Hannah always got grief, which then meant Connor would overreact, go off the deep end, and the night would end in trouble.

Hannah hadn't spoken, and seemed in a dreamworld. Kate worried that the incident in Inverness had taken more out of her than she would admit.

'You all right, love?'

Hannah was sitting on the bed, the anaemic streetlight making her look sickly. She said, 'Yeah, fine,' in a way that sounded anything but. Kate sat down next to her and Hannah fiddled with a thin, leather bracelet on her wrist.

'Is it the whole fit thing?' said Kate.

'Yeah. Kind of.'

'Does "kind of" mean "no, something else"?'

Hannah laughed a little, more of an exhale than anything.

'Yeah. Kind of.'

'You can tell me. Is it that arsehole brother of mine? What's he done this time?'

'It's not him. Not really. It's just . . .' Hannah looked around the room like she was looking for a way out. 'It might be connected with the fit. Maybe I'm just worrying over nothing, but . . .'

There was another long pause.

'OK,' said Hannah finally. 'I haven't had my period.' She looked across at Kate's knees rather than her eyes.

'When was it due?'

'Just after we started the tour. Five, six days ago, maybe? It's no massive deal, I'm not particularly regular anyway. I figured with all the partying, and now this . . . fit, or whatever. It's probably just my body telling me to sort my shit out. I dunno. What do you think?'

Hannah looked up at her now, and Kate saw a worried face.

'You have to find out,' she said. 'Get a test. Just to be sure, if nothing else. You can't go the rest of the tour without knowing if you're pregnant or not, it'll drive you nuts. I'm sure you're right, everything'll be OK. Try not to worry about it. Do you want me to nip out now, see if I can find an open chemist?'

'No, no,' said Hannah quickly. 'It'll keep for a day, I guess. You can't tell Con, though. Promise? You know what he's like, he'd just worry like mad about it, which won't do any good.'

Kate smiled. 'What do you take me for?' she said. 'I won't tell him. But you'll have to find out one way or the other, don't you think?'

'Sure,' said Hannah, pushing her hair away from her face.

The door opened and Danny poked his head round.

'How are my two favourite ladies?'

'Fine,' said Hannah, standing up and heading for the toilet.

'You seen Con?' said Danny once Hannah left the room.

'Thought he was with you,' said Kate.

'He was, but he wandered off. Seems to be wandering off a lot.'

'Do you think he's upset about . . . you know . . . us?'

'Don't know. Don't think so. He seemed fine about it yesterday. How's he been with you?'

'His usual nippy self.'

Danny sat down next to Kate. 'And how are you?'

'I'm fantastic, Danny boy.' Kate leant over and kissed him on the cheek. She thought about Hannah and her late period.

'Yes, you are,' said Danny.

They looked at each other for a moment then started kissing.

Hannah sat on the toilet with her face in her hands and sighed. This was all she needed. What she'd told Kate was true, her periods had never been regular, and she quite often skipped them completely, especially if she was drinking, smoking and taking drugs. She didn't think she'd been hammering the drugs this tour, at least compared to the rest of them, but she'd still had a few joints, plus a wee bit of speed and coke. And she'd been tanning the booze and the Marlboro Lights the whole time. She didn't feel pregnant, but then what on earth did pregnant feel like? All that guff you heard women spout about knowing when they were pregnant before they took a test – that was crap, wasn't it? Every time she missed a period she worried a little, but she was usually pretty certain it wasn't because she was pregnant. It was the same this time. But then there was the thing in Inverness to think about. She hadn't felt any ill effects, except a little tiredness, much to her surprise. Was she epileptic? What if the fit had something to do with the missed period? Did the fit cause her to skip a period, or was it the fact she was pregnant which somehow made her have a fit? She'd never heard of anything like that before, but then she was no expert. She'd hardly even thought about pregnancy before now. Your mid-twenties were no time to be thinking about that sort of thing, not these days. Maybe when you hit thirty or something. What age had her mum been when she'd had her? Mid-twenties, right enough, but that was a generation ago, a different world. What if she *was* pregnant? She found to her surprise that she wasn't completely horrified by the idea. She was kind of nervous and apprehensive, maybe, but she could just about stretch her imagination far enough to the thought of having a baby. What would Connor think? How would he react? He was all over the place at the moment, like he was being spooked by ghosts. They'd never talked about having kids, not once, not even when they were steaming drunk, so she had no idea how he'd react. For that matter, she had no idea how she'd react if she took a test and it was positive. She couldn't stand not knowing, but then she couldn't stand the idea of finding out, either. Jesus.

She got up, flushed the toilet and headed out the door.

'Hey, lovebirds,' said Paul, 'leave it out.'

Kate and Danny were lying on the bed snogging when Paul came in. They quickly disentangled as Hannah followed Paul into the room.

'I take it you didn't find laughing boy, then?' said Paul, smiling.

'Got a bit distracted,' said Danny.

'So I see.'

'When's soundcheck?' said Hannah.

'About an hour ago,' said Paul. 'But it's only a pub gig with a vocal PA, so we'll get away with a quick one, or even just a line check. I'll give His Highness a call on his mobile.'

'He's got a mobile?' said Kate. 'Since when? I thought the Luddite was dead against them?'

'He told me he got it for the tour,' said Danny.

'I never knew that,' said Hannah.

'Keep up, people,' said Paul. 'Yes, he's got a mobile. And probably just as well, since he always seems to be doing a bloody disappearing act at the moment.'

Paul pulled out his own mobile and flipped it open.

'Shit, no reception. I'll try from outside. Can you head over to the venue, I'll catch you up.'

Hannah, Kate and Danny looked at each other before slowly trooping out the door.

Connor pulled the phone out as he walked. He recognised Paul's number, pressed cancel and stuck it back in his pocket. He wasn't sure where he was heading, but surely this two-bit town wasn't big enough to get lost in. He'd had a call ten minutes ago from Gav, telling him to head for the harbour and find the fish market. He grumped through a scabby pedestrian precinct, past a handful of cheap, weather-beaten houses, then found himself on a long stretch of promenade, with a large expanse of beach alongside and the roar of a livid sea in his ears. It was dark but a lemon-slice moon was out and he could see enormous pale breakers tumbling over the grainy shore. He'd never seen waves like it, except on television with people surfing on them. On television, though, the water was always an idiotic crystal blue, Hawaiian or Californian surf, full of chest-puffing young dicks and irritatingly beautiful, bikini-clad nymphets. These colossal beasts in front of him were untouched by human interference, and ashen grey, like a herd of watery elephants trumpeting their thundery arrival. Even from this distance he could feel the force of them, a shudder through his body that was elemental.

He dragged his eyes away from the surf. To his left the beach continued on till it was stopped by a stumpy headland. To his right was the tiny harbour and a solitary, flat, wide building with a rusted corrugated-iron roof. Beyond that Connor could make out the ruined remains of a small castle, and far beyond there appeared to be lights on a stubby finger of land way out to sea. Could that be Orkney? You got the ferry from around here somewhere, but Connor had no idea if you could see it from the mainland.

He made his way over to the harbour. By the rank smell, the building was clearly the fish market. He sheltered in the doorway, lit a fag and let the angry cacophony of the sea fill his ears and his mind.

'Connor?'

He jumped. The figure had appeared out of nowhere. He was young, short, wiry and seemed edgy. He was fidgeting and twitching, as if a low-level electrical current was see-sawing through his body.

'Gav?'

'Let's get this over with.'

'My thoughts exactly.'

Gav pulled a package about the size of a shoebox out of a Tesco bag. It was wrapped up tight in several layers of thin plastic waterproof sheeting. Connor couldn't make out anything inside the wrapping. He took the package and handed over the envelope with Gav's name on it. Gav looked nervously over his shoulder, twitching away.

'Tell Nick I don't fucking owe him any more,' he said, almost having to shout over the sound of the waves crashing on the beach.

'Tell him yourself, he's no fucking mate of mine.'

'Why are you working for him, then?'

'Why are you?'

'Fair point. See ya.'

'Wait.'

Gav stood there, his foot tapping on the concrete. Connor wanted to ask him what he was taking possession of, what this was all about. This was different from the other two deals, he was taking the bigger parcel and handing over the envelope this time, and he didn't like it. Not that he liked the other ones, exactly, but at least he'd felt like he knew what he was doing before.

'What?' said Gav impatiently.

'Nothing.'

'Right.'

Gav turned and was gone round the corner. Connor bent to put the package in the kitbag.

'Connor.'

The voice came from behind him, and he nearly shat himself. He was going to have to start wearing fucking nappies at this rate. As he straightened up and turned, his face went pale. A few yards

away was a tall, thin figure. He wore a long coat, his dark hair
flapping in the breeze, and he had a gaunt look in his pale eyes.
Connor recognised him. From his shape and clothes it was clearly
the person he'd chased on the beach in Aberdeen. But now that he
was up close, Connor recognised more than that. The face looked
drawn and tired, but it was definitely the same one he'd seen on
television, the one that kept appearing in news stories he kept
missing. And more than that, he realised, he'd seen that face in
person before. He remembered the first gig of the tour, that initial
triumph in Edinburgh, and the face he spotted in the half-darkness
of the crowd, the one he thought looked a bit like him. This was
the same person, the same boy. He was definitely a boy, now that
Connor saw him up close, although he had an effeminate air about
him, that androgyny emphasised by perfectly smooth skin and long
eyelashes. It was like looking at a younger, more feminine version
of himself, right down to the cheekbones and the green eyes. It was
unnerving, but also somehow comforting, strange but familiar. He
wondered briefly if it was a hallucination, something he'd conjured
up from his subconscious, but put the thought out his mind. This
boy was real, although there was something unearthly about him,
something dangerously angelic. He seemed almost too perfectly
good-looking to be real, but Connor realised that was a crazy
thought, and also a kind of creepy one. He wondered how old
the boy was. He was considerably taller than Connor, but maybe
around five years younger. Or maybe not. It was hard to tell.

They'd been staring at each other for quite a while, the raging
rhythm of the sea in the background.

'Who are you?' Connor asked quietly.

The figure just shrugged. It was a shy kind of movement of the
shoulders, and it made Connor warm to him.

'Who are you?' he said again.

Eventually the boy spoke.

'Just someone.'

'What kind of an answer is that?'

Once more the boy shrugged.

'What do you want?'

'I've been following you.'

'I know. I've seen you. What do you want?'

There was a long silence. Connor felt like shaking him, but was worried that if he reached out and tried to grab him, maybe this vision would evaporate into the ether.

'I've been following you.'

'You've said that. Why?'

'I've been looking out for you.'

'You think I need looking out for?'

'Maybe.'

'Well, I don't.'

'I've seen everything.'

Connor thought back. He felt strangely vindicated. All the times he'd thought he was being followed, but had doubted his own mind, yet here was his stalker, right in front of him, flesh and bone. He remembered having sex with Hannah in their flat in front of the open curtains, then looking out the window afterwards. He remembered the drug deals in Dundee, Aberdeen and now here. He remembered the gulls on the pier. He suddenly remembered the couple having sex in the toilets at Drummonds, and realised it was Danny and Kate. Why hadn't he pieced that together sooner? He'd heard them at it in Dundee as well, through the wall – it had been Danny after all. With his sister. What an idiot he was. Secrets, secrets. And here was this stranger claiming to know everything about him, all *his* secrets.

'What have you seen?'

'Everything.'

'Like what?'

'I saw you at St Andrew's Cathedral. I saw you meeting someone at the *Discovery*. I saw you having a snowball fight in Arbroath. I saw you kill those gulls. I saw you steal pills from that girl in Raigmore Hospital. I saw you in the Market Bar. I've seen all your gigs, all your fights. I saw you just now, taking a package from that guy. I've seen everything.'

This was more, much more than Connor had suspected. The hospital? How the hell was this guy in the hospital when he'd lifted those pills? Arbroath? He'd been watching them in fucking Arbroath? He tried to stay calm.

'And?'

'And what?'

'What are you going to do about everything you've seen?'

The boy looked confused.

'Nothing.'

'Nothing?'

'I told you, I'm looking out for you.'

'I don't need looking out for. Why are you doing all this anyway?'

The boy did his shrugging thing again.

'Are you a fan of the band?'

The boy was silent.

'Why do I keep seeing your face on television?'

The boy's pale face looked heartbroken, and his eyes were a little watery. The sound of the surf was still raging all around them, but it felt as if they were in a bubble, protected from the outside world.

'I have to go,' said the boy, backing off.

'Wait.' Connor reached out a hand, but then let it drop as the boy moved away.

'You're late for soundcheck,' said the boy as he disappeared round the corner of the fish market.

'What?' Connor looked at his watch. 'Fuck.'

'There's a great metal scene up here!'

Hannah and Connor were having their ears bent by the guitarist in Maelstrom, local support for the evening. The place was stowed and everyone was already steaming. The Newmarket was a jumbled clutter of a pub, every inch of wall space covered by some piece of branded, booze-related tat. Behind the bar hung a Miller Genuine Draft mirror and posters for Smirnoff, Gordon's and a handful of alcopops. The walls were pink, plastered with copies of the *Racing Post*, and the low red ceiling was broken up by thick black wooden beams with bar towels pinned to them. A scattering of chalkboards advertised the bar's promo offers as well as tonight's entertainment.

A string of weak, red fairy lights round the black wood bar was the only sign of festive cheer.

Connor tuned out as the guitarist slavered away. He scanned the crowd, looking for that familiar face, but couldn't see it. There seemed to be two main kinds of people mingling in the place. Half the punters were typical nu-metal, goth or emo types, all baggy black jeans, pocket chains, Muse or Slipknot hoodies, most of them well underage. When he'd come in, two girls were propping up a boy outside as he puked violently against the wall. Connor was impressed that the boy was back in the bar now with a pint of snakebite and black in his hand. Mixed in with the nu-metallers were a crowd of neddy types, the boys in checked shirts and baseball caps, the girls wearing as little as possible, showing as much pasty flesh as they could. Connor reckoned that pretty much all of them must still be at school. As soon as anyone turned eighteen they were surely out of here to somewhere less remote. But then what the fuck did he know about this place? It reminded him of where he grew up, but so what? Not all towns were the same, were they? Looking around at the pished-up mayhem, Connor suspected they were. He felt strangely straight compared to those around him. It's not that he wasn't drunk already – he'd been sneaking swigs of gin from a refilled water bottle since he got out of bed. But at twenty-four he was much more capable of controlling and hiding his drunkenness than a bunch of fifteen- and sixteen-year-olds. Plus there was the handful of joints he'd smoked with Danny, which always helped him chill out, the umpteen speed hits he'd taken to anchor proceedings, and the pill he'd just popped five minutes ago. Now he came to think of it, he was a fucking state. But to outward appearances he seemed pretty together, and he felt a kind of pride in that. He was dragged back from his thoughts by the incessant prattle of the guy next to him.

The guitarist made the mistake of asking Hannah about guitar effects and playing techniques. Connor smiled to himself. If there was one thing in the world he and Hannah hated, it was guitar wanks. In fact, muso wanks of any kind. All four of The Ossians hated going into music shops and only ever did so reluctantly when they had to, because they were full of know-it-all arseholes trying to impress you with tedious patter about this set of machine heads or that bridge action or some new crappy innovation that would make your guitar-playing sound more like Steve Vai or your drumming more like you were sitting in with fucking Van Halen. Who fucking needs it?

'Sorry, what was your name again?' said Hannah, interrupting the guy in full flow.

'Gordon.'

'Well, Gordon, I couldn't give a flying shit about the difference between digital and analogue delay pedals or any of that bollocks. I wouldn't be caught dead using a delay pedal for that matter. I just get on stage and play guitar, got it?'

Gordon appeared not to hear and kept talking about guitars and guitarists he rated. When Hannah turned her back on him and walked away without a word he focused his attention on Connor, who interrupted him mid-sentence.

'Is it always this busy?'

'Aye, Sunday's a heavy drinking night,' said Gordon. 'Part of the weekend, isn't it? This time of year there's not much happening at school, so hangovers are fine. It's not always this busy, mind, a band from Edinburgh's a big draw up here, you know. The good thing is, normally everyone would fuck off to Skinandi's later on, it's the town cattle market. But it's shut at the minute getting done up so everyone'll stay here until closing.'

'What kind of a name is Skinandi's?'

Gordon shrugged. 'Some Viking pish, don't really know. Anyway, the place is a fucking dump and there's always loads of fights there, so I'm pretty happy it's closed. Although it's normally open till three. But if we play our cards right we might get a lock-in here.'

Connor looked out the window. He could've sworn he was seeing the same cars passing again and again. A parade of tacky, souped-up nedmobiles, Fiestas or XRis, all with alloys, spoilers and go-faster stripes. He asked Gordon about it.

'They're doing the circuit.'

'What?'

'They drive down Traill Street then back up Princes Street, round and round all night.'

'Who does?'

'The neds that dinnae drink. They're showing off their motors. The girls around here fucking lap it up. They stand giggling to each other, eyeing up the twats in the cars, looking for a ride, if you know what I mean. You should see it in the summer, it's ridiculous. This time of year it's not too bad, but it's still fucking sad.'

Connor shook his head. What a place. A 'great metal scene', a primitive courting ritual involving showing off your shite car, and a hostel that's a chippie. He noticed that one of the cars he kept seeing was more expensive than the others, a Merc or BMW or something similar. 'How do they afford the cars?'

'Some of them work at Dounreay, maybe. That usually pays pretty well.'

'Is Dounreay near here?'

Gordon laughed. 'Aye, ten miles down the road. Just about everyone in town works there, it's the biggest employer in the area by far. It sits there polluting the whole fucking coastline with nuclear waste, and no cunt ever says anything because if the place shut down everyone would be out of a job and Thurso would turn into a ghost town.'

Something was nagging at the back of Connor's mind, something he'd seen on the news.

'Isn't there a radioactive beach around here? They found particles in the sand or something?'

Gordon nodded as he gulped down more lager.

'Sandside,' he said. 'It's just the other side of the plant. Lovely little place, but you cannae go on the beach now. Where are you headed tomorrow?'

'Durness, I think.'

'You'll go right past Dounreay and the turn-off for Sandside. Take a look at it, it's a fucking disgrace.'

A spotty, gangly kid with black eyeliner and incongruous rosy cheeks came up to them, staggering slightly and slopping his pint.

'Gord, we're on,' he said.

'Right,' said Gordon, then to Connor, 'see you on the other side.'

Connor watched as the pair stumbled onstage joined by two similar-looking kids, all four drunk as fuck. The mobile went off in his pocket. It was Nick checking up on how the drop had gone. He kept it monosyllabic as he supped his pint, watching Maelstrom shambolically try to get a sound out their gear. He wanted this conversation over, and so did Nick, it seemed, because he was off the other end in under two minutes, having ascertained that Connor had been successful. Connor didn't want to tell him about the guardian angel, the stalker, whatever he was. It was his little secret for now. And no one would believe him anyway. Least of all Nick. He finished his pint and headed towards the bar, thinking about angels.

'Another gig, another punch in the puss,' said Danny. He tilted Connor's head back, trying to stem the flow of watery blood from his nose. Connor blinked away tears from his eyes and pressed the scrunched-up ball of bog roll to his upper lip.

'I can manage, cheers, Danny. I've had the practice.'

'I don't know how you do it,' said Danny. 'You always manage to rile someone. Indie kids, students, metalheads, goths, neds or just a random bunch of people, you can say exactly the right thing to ensure a smack in the face. You could start a scrap in an old folks' home. Make some sarky comment about arthritis or colostomy bags and you'd get a Zimmer frame wrapped around your head in no time.'

Connor laughed and a small bubble of blood and snot escaped the bog roll.

'You do realise you're doing it, don't you?' Danny continued. 'What kind of a twat deliberately says things that guarantee a kicking? You got some kind of victim thing going on? Does getting knocked about give you the moral high ground? You realise Hannah and Kate have just about had enough of it all. This was supposed to be an adventure, getting ourselves geared up for the Glasgow show. In case you'd forgotten, that's the gig where we're meant to get signed? And what's happened? We've played a handful of crappy wee shows to a bunch of indifferent bastards, Hannah's not well, you've taken several kickings and then there was that whole thing on the pier in Aberdeen.'

Connor let the lecture soak in. He deserved it. What the fuck was he thinking, that this was going to be some journey of self-discovery, as they mapped out modern Scotland and their place in it through a bunch of triumphant rock gigs? Pathetic. And Hannah – why the hell were they even still on the road, when she'd had a serious medical incident? Fuck, he couldn't think straight, and the pulsing pain across his face wasn't helping. He took the bog roll away from his nose. It seemed to have stopped bleeding for now. He couldn't even remember what happened. What was happening to his memory?

The gig had gone well, they'd gotten over their hangovers and were raring to go after a day without playing. Songs like 'Justified Sinner' and 'Alcohol' had never sounded better, Kate and Danny, especially, nailing them down ruthlessly. He'd done his usual bit of banter between songs, nothing too insulting or dangerous, but then he seemed to be misjudging that line more and more often. As soon as they finished and walked to the side of the tiny raised area that passed for a stage, a guy in a Burberry baseball cap strode up and lamped him, catching him square in the face. The punch was so unexpected that Connor just stood there looking at the guy. He was only about eighteen with a sallow, grey face, the outline of thin, spindly arms underneath his pale yellow polo shirt, but by Christ that punch had hurt.

'You think you're so much fucking better than us, eh?' he said. 'You fucking poncy prick, I should get my mates down here to give you a proper fucking doing. Where do you get off, calling us fucking ignorant? You're fucking ignorant. Why don't you fuck off back where you fucking came from, and take your fucking shite band with you, you sad fucking arsehole.'

For the life of him, Connor couldn't remember calling anyone ignorant. But he couldn't speak. He felt the rush of pain, adrenaline and embarrassment in his face as he stood looking into the kid's eyes, full of anger and hate. He said nothing.

'Come on, Andy,' said another guy, appearing at Burberry's side. 'Let's just go to the Central, have a game of pool, eh? He's not worth it.'

They stood looking at each other for a few more seconds, no one saying anything. Finally the two guys moved slowly towards the door, both keeping their eyes on Connor.

'If I see you again, you're fucking dead, right?' Burberry snarled in Connor's face, pushing past him and out the door in a swagger.

Now, in the bogs with Danny, he still couldn't remember what he'd said on stage.

'I never said anyone was ignorant, did I?'

'I didn't hear anything,' said Danny. 'But I had no monitor, so I couldn't really hear anything except drums. It sounds like something you'd say, though.'

He laughed, producing a smile on Connor's face which made the pain shoot from his nose up to his forehead.

'What the fuck are we doing here?' said Connor, examining his face in the mirror.

'A very good question. Apparently we're bringing intelligent rock music to the masses of Scotland. Whether they like it or not.'

'What day is it?'

'Thurso, so it must be Sunday.'

'And when do we get home?'

'Friday night, after Glasgow.'

'How many more kickings do you think I'm going to get?'

'A few. Come on, I think we could do with a drink.'

'That's your answer to everything isn't it?' said Connor, smiling.

Back at Sandra's the post-gig analysis continued. Connor's latest meeting with a fist turned out to be from the only unhappy punter in the place, and they'd stayed till closing, soaking up the pissed, enthusiastic praise. As usual, Connor got most of the attention, with Kate and Hannah getting admiring looks from across the pub but little else, which suited them just fine. Connor kept looking for that face, his effeminate angel's face, but if the boy was at the gig, he couldn't see him.

'There's gonna be some headaches in double maths tomorrow morning,' said Danny, skinning up as the five of them sprawled around the boys' bedroom.

'I wouldn't want to be their teacher,' said Kate.

'I can't believe you got punched in the face again,' said Paul.

Hannah was sitting on a sofa cuddling up to Connor.

'Yeah,' she said. 'I wish you'd take care of that pretty face of yours. It's all right for you, but I'm the one who has to look at it all the time, and I don't want you looking like a bulldog chewing a wasp by the end of this.'

'Thanks,' said Connor, poking her gently in the ribs. 'I like to think of myself as a therapist-cum-punchbag. I travel round the country providing an outlet for the pent-up frustrations of small-town life, an easy target for arseholes to lash out at, representing, as I do, the exciting and glamorous rock 'n' roll life they can never have.'

'Shut up,' said Hannah. Her talk with Kate had brought everything into focus. Before that she'd been trundling along, not thinking about this late or missed period. But then she'd had the fit, and things seemed more serious. Now, everything was imbued with thoughts of pregnancy, of babies and all the terror that involved. She didn't want to think about it. She didn't want to know, because once she knew, that was it, all other options, all other possibilities were gone.

Connor got up to go to the toilet.

'Get me another beer while you're up,' she said, feeling Kate give her a look from across the room. She avoided looking in that direction as Danny passed her a joint and she inhaled deeply.

'Another day off tomorrow,' said Danny.

'Yeah,' said Paul. 'Not ideal in terms of money, but the next gig in Ullapool is a long drive, and we couldn't get it booked for tomorrow anyway, so I reckoned stopping halfway wouldn't kill us.'

'Where are we staying tomorrow night, then?' said Hannah, exhaling and passing the joint to Paul.

'Durness,' he said, taking a toke. 'A place called the Smoo Cave Hotel. I know absolutely nothing about it except it's cheap.'

'Have you got that road map handy?' said Connor, coming back in with a handful of beers and settling in beside Hannah again. Paul fished the map out his bag. Connor flicked to the page and traced the road along the north coast with his finger.

'Fucking hell,' he said. 'Durness is right next to Cape Wrath. Sounds good, eh? There don't even seem to be any roads there.'

'It's an MOD firing range or something,' said Paul. 'Probably some top-secret bollocks.'

'Oooh, could we have an adventure, do you think?' said Hannah. 'Maybe we'll uncover a drug-smuggling operation or something.'

'Seeing as how we've got the night off, yes,' said Paul. 'I'll pencil us in for a mysterious adventure. Just like Scooby Doo.'

'Scooby Smoo,' said Danny, giggling to himself.

Paul looked at him. 'That doesn't even mean anything.'

'I know that.'

'Maybe I'd better skin up next,' said Paul. 'Put in a bit less of that lethal grass.'

Connor was still examining the map closely, trying not to think about Hannah's drug-smuggling quip.

'Seeing as how we're in no hurry,' he said, 'I take it no one minds if we make an extra wee stop on the way?'

'Where did you have in mind?' said Paul.

'I'll tell you when we get there.'

'Oooh, we *are* going to have an adventure!' said Hannah, clapping her hands. 'Just like the Famous Five. How positively thrilling.'

'Yeah, right,' said Connor, patting her on the head. 'Whatever you say, dear.'

'And can we have lashings of ginger beer?'

'You've lost it,' said Danny, finishing a new joint he'd been working on. 'Here, want to start this?'

Hannah felt Kate looking again. She wished she hadn't said anything if this was how it was going to pan out. There was nothing to worry about, it happened to her all the time. It wasn't exactly unexpected under these conditions. She wasn't bloody pregnant, so there. She took the joint and sparked it up, sucking the sweet air into her lungs and feeling her head wobble slightly as she breathed out. There really was nothing to worry about, Kate should lighten up.

'Does anyone else get the feeling we're a long way from home?' said Danny.

'Yeah,' said Kate. 'Before, when we were playing Aberdeen and Inverness, well, they're still cities, aren't they? But now it seems like we're in the middle of nowhere.'

'We are,' said Connor. 'And we're going to be at the arse end of nowhere by tomorrow.' He pointed to the map. 'This road doesn't look like it'll be up to much. Probably single track for a lot of the way, it's going to take us hours to get to Durness.'

'Like you say, we're in no hurry,' said Paul. 'Assuming your little detour doesn't take us anywhere stupid or dangerous?'

'As if I would do something like that.'

9
Durness

'We stumbled on your grave, two thousand years too late
Rolled away the stone, found your bag of bones
The stones remember us, like the stars above
Under northern skies, we knew we had to die'

The Ossians, 'Magnetic North'

Cotton-wool clouds raced frantically overhead. The van sat rocking as a ferocious wind pummelled it. Despite the gale, the water seemed strangely calm in the small, enclosed bay. They were parked next to a large sign, the last of several they'd driven past down a narrow dirt track. The sign read:

WARNING

RADIOACTIVE PARTICLES ARE BEING
FOUND ON THE BEACHES AT SANDSIDE.

IT IS NOT ADVISABLE TO TAKE CHILDREN
OR ANIMALS ON TO OR DIG OR REMOVE
MATERIAL FROM THE BEACH OR DUNES.

Next to it Connor was absent-mindedly kicking at a pile of sand as the wind whipped his hair round his face. Behind him was a tiny stretch of sandy beach and a row of fishermen's houses lining a small stone quay. Across the bay sat Dounreay, a giant golf ball nestled beside towering chimneys and factory blocks.

'How much longer are you going to stay out there?' shouted Paul through a slit opening of the van's window into the tearing wind. Connor pretended not to hear and Paul wound the window up.

'Does he think we're stupid?' said Kate in the van. 'Does he think we don't get it? Oooh, look what they've done to our beautiful country, and all that guff. A lovely beach spoilt by the nasty, big man and his nasty, big nuclear power station. Of course it's bad. Bad things happen. Hanging about here isn't making any difference. Except that he's probably kicking up radioactive particles out there. Which I'm sure would cheer him up no end, martyr that he is.'

No one else spoke. They sat for a while, the Silver Jews' oddball country sounds playing on the stereo, struggling to be heard over the whistle and whip of the wind. Outside Connor tried to throw a stone into the sea, lost his balance and fell heavily on his arse. He sat there for a while before slowly getting to his feet, taking sideways swipes at the seat of his trousers to dust the sand off.

'Some adventure,' said Hannah.

'We've discovered a radioactive beach,' said Danny. 'That's like something the Famous Five would do, isn't it?'

'We hardly discovered it,' said Hannah. 'It's been in the news. Wasn't there some controversy about a possible increased rate of leukaemia around here? Scary, yes. An adventure, no.'

'It's pretentious,' said Kate. 'Standing on a radioactive beach, being all aloof like he's Bono in a fucking U2 video. He's got his priorities wrong. He's all about the big statement, the grand gesture – it's not all about tilting at windmills. There's friends, family, relationships to deal with – everyday life that needs managing. Not something Connor's particularly good at.'

'Preaching to the converted,' said Paul. 'You should tell all this to radioactive boy out there.'

The warning sign rattled as a strong gust made the van sway. The wind raged around Connor, roaring in his ears as he stared across the bay at Dounreay. From here it looked nothing special, just another factory sitting on a seafront. He tried to imagine the microscopic particles of radiation in among the grains of sand under his feet, but couldn't get his head around it. What an adventure those particles must've had, all the way across this windy bay, getting swept along in the sea, or swirling about in the air for days, weeks, months, not knowing where they would end up. Another big, dumb metaphor for something. Except it wasn't really. And metaphors suck anyway. Radiation on Scottish soil – so what? Wasn't Aberdeen more radioactive from all the granite? Fishermen obviously lived here, and they wouldn't do that if it was dangerous, would they? Then again, maybe they didn't have any choice. Perhaps this had been their livelihood for generations, and their homes and families were rooted here. Then one day some boffins detect deadly shit you can't see, and the next day they're hammering in signs warning you not to go on your own beach.

Connor looked back at the van. Four bored and mildly pissed-off people sat chatting inside. He felt guilty for dragging them all the way round the country on some stupid wild goose chase. For what? Some third-rate, muse-like inspiration for a shit, narrow-minded indie band, with pretensions of intelligence and a singer with a knowing self-destructive streak and a cowardly self-importance. He felt guilty for letting them think all this was about the band and the music, a record deal and show business and stadium gigs and fame, when all Connor really wanted to do was fuck it all up.

Maybe his stalker was here for a purpose. Maybe he was a guardian angel sent to look after him, deliver him from evil, from himself, from all the bullshit in his head. Or maybe the opposite – maybe he'd come to destroy him. Was he even real? Connor tried to remember their conversation. He could picture the haunting, beautiful pale face, and the quiet, effeminate voice, but what had they talked about? Nothing much, except that he seemed to know every fucking thing that Connor had done since they'd left Edinburgh. And maybe even before that.

He imagined telling Hannah he was being stalked by an angel, here to save or kill him. He was fed up of secrets, the kitbag full of drugs and drug money, the thoughts in his head that he couldn't talk about. Maybe the stalker would show up at the next gig, and Connor would introduce him to the rest of the band. He would turn out to be a harmless fan and they'd all get along great. He realised this was just more bullshit in a head already crammed with the stuff.

The wind was stronger and he was having trouble standing up. An insistent throb at the base of his skull made him reach for another two pills from his pocket. He washed them down with gin from his water bottle, hardly even noticing the burn in his throat. He wondered if he'd accidentally watered down the gin, then found himself wondering if there was anything stronger than straight gin he could be drinking to take the edge off. For fuck's sake. Let's get out of here.

Connor struggled to open the van door in the wind, then had to grip on to it to stop it blowing off its hinges. He shut the door with a whump, and the raging noise the others briefly experienced was sucked out the van, leaving only muffled rumbles and creaks.

'Can we fuck off out of here?' Paul asked.

'Of course,' said Connor, then didn't know what else to say as the van turned and bumped back up the track.

'You OK?' Hannah asked him.

Connor didn't answer. There wasn't an answer.

The wind was joined by bursts of sleet and snow. Past Dounreay the road became a rough single track, the 'Passing Place' signs swaying like yachts' rigging in the ferocity of the weather. It was slow going. At Kyle of Tongue they descended the lochside to cross the expanse of eerie green water over a causeway. The van was exposed to the raging storm, large washes of spray drenching it. An exhalation of relief could be heard once they were across. The road twisted up over high ground before looping slowly round Loch Eriboll, the large geometric shapes of fish farms implacable in the water below.

As they travelled, they saw the occasional Land Rover or farm vehicle and had to backtrack to the last passing place, Paul returning the other drivers' waves with a nonchalance he didn't feel. It was almost dark already, the storm bringing an early end to daylight. Driving a dodgy old van in these conditions, on a shitty road he didn't know, with farm vehicles looming out at him from the gloom, didn't fill him with confidence. At one point they drove past an expensive-looking executive car parked or abandoned in a passing place with no sign of anyone around, Paul tutting under his breath.

174

Cornering a headland they passed a string of sandy beaches getting hammered by the elements, then spotted a sign for the Smoo Cave Hotel, indicating a grassy farm track heading out on to a clifftop. They bumped along the track past a couple of squat, whitewashed houses huddling pathetically against the storm, then the road came to an end at a rusted gate, just a barren field beyond. They U-turned, drove slowly back down the track, and realised the last house they'd passed was the hotel. A disorientating shambles of a building, it seemed to have been built in several bursts, with low extensions jutting out at odd angles. Now they looked, there was a small sign. A chink of light appeared between the shutters at one of the windows.

'This is the end of the world,' said Danny, peering out at the building. Paul cut the engine, leaving just the raging whoosh of the wind and the spatter of sleet on the windscreen.

'Looks like it,' said Hannah. 'Why don't we take a closer look?'

As they opened the door they were hit by a breathy wailing sound. They stood in a brightly lit stone-walled bar with a pool table, a wood-burning stove crackling away in the corner and an old beaten-up piano next to it. Arranged in a semicircle to the side of the room were half a dozen primary school kids in uniform, all of them dwarfed by the glittery accordions they were struggling to see round. They grimaced as they heaved the instruments' bellows in and out, creating an aimless caterwaul that bounced around the room.

Admiring this racket from the bar were a cluster of men with pints of lager in their hands – two in golf jumpers, two wearing blue overalls, one guy in a dirty T-shirt and ripped jeans and a policeman with a giant whisky chaser on the go. A red-faced, balding man in his forties behind the bar spotted them loitering in the doorway and headed straight for them.

'Are you The Ossians, staying the night?' he shouted in a London accent over the howl of the accordions. He thrust a hand out.

'Yeah,' Paul shouted back at him.

'I'm Derek,' said the man. 'Me and the missus run this place.' He looked at the kids, who were lost in their own wee world. He stuck a thumb towards them. 'Accordion lessons, every Monday after school. Don't worry, they'll finish up soon.' He jerked his head over to the bar to indicate the men lined along it. 'It gives the dads a chance for a quick snifter.'

Connor watched the kids as they stuck their elbows out before jamming the two parts of the instrument back together. There seemed to be no semblance of a tune coming from anywhere, but as he listened he thought he could pick out something, a vaguely familiar lilting folk melody struggling to cut through the atonal mush around it. He looked along the line, trying to figure out which kid might be making music in among it all. He was distracted from his thoughts by the mention of alcohol.

'What?'

'Do you want to see your rooms, or do you fancy a quick drink first?' Derek asked.

'We've always got time for a drink,' said Connor, looking round at the threadbare carpet and the rough walls. The dads at the bar were eyeing them up. Connor couldn't work out if they were eyeing up the lads as out-of-town twats or eyeing up the girls, for obvious reasons. Whatever, he didn't feel threatened, maybe due to the presence of half a dozen schoolchildren, or maybe just because it wasn't a threatening situation. Not every situation had to be. As the kids continued to create their cacophony of wheezy madness, he noticed for the first time in God knows how long that he didn't have a headache. He had a good feeling about this place. He turned to the rest of them.

'What are we all having?'

'So are you a folk band, then?'

Derek's wife, Lynne, was a chatty little redhead with rolling hips, flushed cheeks and a wide smile, dispensing drinks and taking cash with one hand as she fussed over a tiny mongrel dog with the other. The Smoo Cave Hotel was full of dogs. An Alsatian, a collie, a pair of greyhounds (one of which was deaf, his owner having to click his fingers near the ground to get it to come), a Highland terrier and some indiscernible crossbreeds all mooched around for dropped crisps, sniffing at hands and trouser legs. The kids were still there although their accordions had been packed away, and they were now playing a complicated game of tig around the pool table. Where the kids had been practising there was now a ragtag ceilidh band made up of three accordion players, a fiddler, a lean woman in dungarees bashing away with a table leg at what looked like a home-made drum and a huge guy with an eye-patch and a beard dwarfing a mandolin. They were playing straggly, mournful laments that swayed with a sea shanty rhythm, at least partially due to the drunkenness of the players.

It seemed like half of Durness had turned up, as dozens of people crammed into the bright space of the bar. Pint arms got nudged, conversations eavesdropped and dogs' tails trodden upon. Connor had been getting the life story of the village from Lynne, as if it were her own tale. People here either worked on the fish farms or for the Ministry of Defence at Cape Wrath or did the occasional bit of sheep farming or else worked in the tourist trade like her. Plenty of people came through in the summer, but they hardly got any visitors in winter, that's why she'd been surprised by their booking, but it was nice to see new faces around the place, and such young, attractive faces, too. There were half a dozen of the most beautiful beaches within walking distance if this weather cleared up and, of course, Smoo Cave, which has one of the biggest cave mouths in Britain, and then there's the golf course past Balnakeil, the most northerly on the mainland and, oh, Balnakeil beach is absolutely gorgeous, but sometimes it's closed if there's missile or bomb testing going on, and then there's the craft village, with all sorts of interesting little arty shops and workshops, and did Connor know that John Lennon used to spend his summers up here as a child with his favourite auntie and there's a memorial to him in the village hall's garden, which featured in that *Beechgrove Garden* programme, hadn't he seen it?

'Only with a name like The Ossians I thought you might be a folk group,' she was saying now in a singsong northern accent placed somewhere between Shetland and Ireland to Connor's ears.

'You know, it sounds a bit Celtic or something. I'm just glad you didn't turn out to be protestors. You know, against the MOD test range along the road? We get some of these new-age types coming up protesting against the military, they always look like that Swampie from the telly a few years back. They've all got these dreadlocks and scruffy clothes and wear beads and things, but they're ever-so-well-spoken and all have proper jobs with posh companies and earn more than we do. What they don't realise is that the government and the army provide a lot of employment in this area. What would happen to Durness and Balnakeil if the range shut down? The school roll is dropping as it is, families are leaving to go to towns and cities, and pretty soon I don't know who'll be left except people catering for tourists and fish farmers, I suppose. Did I tell you about the fellow Henderson who used to work on the fish farms? Killed his wife. Put her in the water, just like that. They locked him up in that loony bin Carstairs, but he got out eventually cos he wasn't daft, not really, and you know what he did?' Connor shook his head, suppressing a smile. 'He only phoned up the Fisheries Commission, asking for his old job back. Can you imagine?' The dog under her arm yapped in agreement, then struggled out of her grasp.

'So what kind of group are you?'

'A rock band, I suppose.'

'Like that nice Travis lot?'

Connor laughed, finished his pint of 80 and moved on to the huge nip of whisky in front of him.

'A bit like them.'

'He's awful nice-looking, that fellow in Travis. Are you going to be as famous as them?'

'I wouldn't have thought so. We're not quite as mainstream as that.'

'Will you be giving us a song later?'

'It's our night off.'

'Och, I'm sure you could play us a wee something.'

'Honestly, I don't think it'd go down too well. Besides, this lot are pretty good.'

'Ach, they'll be falling off their chairs with the drink soon,' laughed Lynne.

'Are you planning on doing any work tonight?' Derek shouted jovially from the far end of the bar. 'Or were you going to yack on there all night? Poor bloke must have sore ears listening to you going on.'

'Please excuse my husband,' said Lynne, moving towards a waiting punter. 'He doesn't understand the concept of being a friendly host. Speak to you later, dear.'

They hadn't made it to their rooms yet. The five of them had stayed in the bar and soaked up the atmosphere as the pub gradually filled with locals. The mood in the room was a lot less reserved than they were used to from city pubs. As unfamiliar faces they were a magnet, locals pitching up and engaging them in conversation as if they were old friends. This was both a good and a bad thing. Kate and Danny got talking to a sweet elderly couple who ran a craft shop along the road and had nothing but nice things to say about the world. But later, Connor and Paul almost got into a fight with a mouthy prick of a salmon farmer who referred to an English footballer as 'that darkie bastard'. Later, Paul found himself laughing at the same arsehole, as he drunkenly lamented that he 'used to love that Gary Glitter, used to sing his songs and dance around the bedroom as a kid, but not now'.

Connor made his way to the toilets. At the door to the bogs, still attached to half a ton of concrete at its base, stood a diamond-shaped 'Passing Place' sign, the first 'a' changed clumsily to an 'i'. Connor chuckled despite himself. In the toilets he sucked speed off his fingers, swallowed a couple of large, oblong pink pills, and finished the last of the gin out of his water bottle. He wondered how he might be able to procure more gin without the rest of them knowing, and sauntered back to the table.

The wheezy sway from the ceilidh band cut swathes through the air. Connor looked around as he let the drunken rhythms wash over him. Everyone in the place seemed comfortable, content. They all seemed to know what they were doing here. He was jealous. Bursts of laughter rose over the sound of the band, and made him feel lonely. He watched Derek and Lynne, swapping banter and looks with each other, smiles on their faces. His gaze fell upon the small portable telly sitting at the end of the bar. It was switched on with the sound muted, but he recognised the Scottish news presenters. He was thinking how weird it would be if the boy's face appeared on the television and almost dropped his pint when it really happened. There were the boy's angelic features staring out from the television, right at Connor. He felt the hairs on the back of his neck tingle and laughed to himself. Had he conjured this up using the power of thought? Just how loaded was he? The picture on the screen was grainy, the boy seemed less radiant, less beautiful than he had in Thurso with the sound of crashing waves around them. Connor watched the news story and saw footage of a posh area of Edinburgh, a concerned-looking woman, then a shot of a dark executive saloon car and a registration number. It looked like a regular missing-person report. Did that mean the angel was just a boy who'd done a bunk from home with his parents' swanky car? Maybe that's what the angel wanted him to think. Maybe he'd arranged this little show specifically for Connor. He realised he would miss the angel if he wasn't around. He found himself worrying that he wouldn't turn up at the next show, wouldn't look out for him any more, would just give up and leave him to fend for himself. The news report ended and he looked around the room, hoping to see that face among the punters, knowing that he wouldn't, and knowing that he would be disappointed.

'Who you looking for?'

Hannah was watching him.

'What?'

'It's as if you're looking for someone.'

'Just soaking up the atmosphere.'

Hannah was still looking at him.

'Did you see that thing on the telly just now?' Connor said eventually.

'What thing?'

'A news report. About a missing boy, I think.'

'Connor, the television's not on.'

He looked round. He wasn't particularly surprised to see the television was off. Had Derek or Lynne just switched it off while he wasn't looking? Had it ever really been on?

'It was on a minute ago.'

'Was it?'

'Yeah. Wait here.' He walked over to the television and placed his hand on the back of it. Still warm. He wasn't going mad. He returned to his seat.

'Still warm.'

'OK, so the television was on. What missing boy?'

'I think a boy has run away from home, stolen his folks' car and is following me round the country.'

'You mean following *us* round the country, don't you? I take it you're assuming he's a fan of The Ossians.'

'I don't know.'

'Why else would he follow us? Or you?'

'Good question. Do you believe in angels?'

'Connor, you need to calm down on the drink.'

'Do you?'

'No, I don't believe in angels. Don't be daft. I take it from the question that you do?'

'I don't know.'

'I'm worried about you.'

'There's no need to be, I'm perfectly fine.'

'Apart from seeing angels and imagining news reports on television.'

'I didn't imagine it. The television was on, it's still warm.'

'Whatever.'

He wasn't upset that Hannah didn't believe him. He wouldn't believe him either, the state he was in. It didn't matter whether anyone believed him, he knew the boy was looking out for him, and it made him feel comfortable. He felt contented.

He looked across at Hannah, who had a frown on her face.

'You don't have to worry about me, you know,' he said.

'Don't I?'

'I should be worrying about you.'

'I'm fine.'

'Are you? What about the thing in Inverness? How do you feel now?'

'I told you, I'm fine.'

'You don't look fine.'

'Thanks. I love you too, fucknut.'

'That's not what I meant. You look great, just . . . worried or something.'

'The only thing I'm worried about is you.'

'Promise?'

Hannah thought about her missed period, her conversation with Kate and her fit in Inverness. She thought about Connor, sitting there loaded, talking about angels as if it was normal. She thought about bringing a baby into this world.

'I promise.'

There was an almighty bang and rumble from outside. The windows rattled in their frames and a whoosh of air was forced down the chimney. A couple of seconds later there was a lower, subsonic shudder, like an earthquake happening far away, that Connor and Hannah could feel through their legs. They looked at each other.

The band kept playing, while some of the punters gave each other knowing looks. Another bang and rumble shook the windows again, followed two seconds later by the earthquake shake.

'What the fuck's that?' Connor shouted over the band to Lynne.

'That'll be the MOD,' she said. 'I told you about the bombing range at Cape Wrath, didn't I?'

'I thought it was a few miles down the road.'

'It is,' said Lynne, coming round from behind the bar. 'But they sometimes fire at the range from navy ships out at sea. Depending on the weather we might be able to see something.'

She took Connor gently by the elbow and indicated to the rest of them to follow as she headed out the door.

*

The wind had dropped to a whisper and sleet clouds were clearing from a sky jammed with stars. They followed Lynne up the road and stood at the gate to the clifftop field. They could hear the sea beyond the cliff, now that the weather had calmed. In the field a small flurry of sheep broke into an aimless run. To their right were three blinking lighthouses along the coast, twinkling out of sync.

Suddenly there was a flash followed by a bang, and they saw the outline of a ship silhouetted against the horizon in the afterglow of gunfire. This happened again, then again, each time followed by a low, quaking rumble a couple of seconds after the explosion of light. The ship, maybe a mile out to sea, was repeatedly outlined against the blackness of the horizon like a shadow puppet.

'Looks like a frigate of some kind,' said Lynne, smiling as they all looked at her. 'You get all sorts of navy ships out here and you can tell them apart quite easily. There should be some aircraft bombing soon, they do both at the same time. Tornadoes or Harriers usually, but sometimes they fly American aircraft like Hornets. I think the idea is to simulate battle conditions.'

'What are they firing at?' said Danny.

'The naval guns fire at the Cape Wrath range, it's just a big stretch of empty land really. And the aircraft usually drop their bombs on Garvie Island, it's just beyond the headland here. It's the only place in Europe where they're allowed to drop live, thousand-pound bombs. You get quite a shake from those, I can tell you.'

The ship's guns had been quiet for a minute or two when they heard aircraft jets overhead. Connor craned his neck and felt dizzy as the stars birled round the sky. He couldn't see anything except the bright pinpricks of light from millions of miles away, millions of years ago. The engine roar got louder until it filled their ears, then just as quickly it eased away, fading into the blackness. Suddenly the earth shook and their ears popped and an almighty walloping explosion made them all jump. A few seconds later this was repeated, then again and again. Connor's ribcage shuddered and his heart raced. He held on to the gate, flakes of cold rust coming off in his hands as he clung on.

'Is this safe?' Danny shouted over the sound of another plane slicing through the air above them.

'Oh, we're fine here,' said Lynne calmly. 'They're very careful about where they're shooting and bombing. There have never been any accidents as long as I can remember.'

'What about that friendly fire you hear about?' said Kate, her eyes wide as another crumpling bang shook her guts.

'That's the Americans, isn't it? Not our boys, they know what they're shooting at.'

'Hmmm,' said Kate.

Connor was mesmerised by the noise and was settling into the rhythm of it. A rising crescendo of jet roar, slowly dying away then – wham! – a bowel-loosening explosion that made you jump no matter how much you were expecting it. He tried to imagine being a small bird flapping around in the shock waves from the explosion, or a tiny bug, flipped up into the air and fried in a microsecond.

'It's unbelievable, isn't it?' Hannah leant in and shouted in his ear.

'Just a wee bit.'

'It's like being in a war zone,' she said. 'Something off the news.'

A lot of the boys Connor was at school with in Arbroath had ended up joining the forces, that's what happened if you had a marine base just outside town. He wondered if one of them was flying a plane over their heads right now, or manning the guns on the frigate. What made people join the army? He couldn't think of anything in the world he'd rather do less. Didn't these folk always end up as drunken security guards or homeless junkies when they came out? They were supposed to get a sense of community from it, a sense of belonging to something, wasn't that the recruitment angle? But wasn't that what *he* was looking for? Maybe he should join up, that would give him a bit of discipline, a bit of backbone. And it would sort his drinking and drug-taking out. What a load of shite. He would die in the army.

But he felt he was dying now, standing on a dark clifftop, listening to bombs dropping, clinging with tensed knuckles to a rusty gate, the stars swimming above him. This was his country, a drunken dickhead making racist remarks in a pub. This was Scotland, a friendly wee woman with an expert knowledge of British navy ships and fish-farm murderers getting their old jobs back and dead seagulls on piers and Ecstasy and coke and angelic stalkers following your every move and ridiculous drug deals under cover of darkness and ketamine pills and punches to the face and swigging straight gin and dead seals on beaches and stealing pills from hospital patients and Christmas shoppers in November and speed and hash and bad weather and English students and beautiful landscapes and whisky and more gin.

He felt nauseous and began shivering. He vomited thick, stinking, dark bile on to the grass, the acrid taste of it stripping his throat. Hannah started rubbing his back gently. The rest of them looked at him as he spat and wiped his mouth with his sleeve and blinked away tears.

'I think we'd better get you inside, dear,' said Lynne, trying to loop her arm through his. Connor shrugged it off.

'I'm fine,' he said.

There was silence for a few moments as everyone looked at Connor, then at each other, then eventually shifted their gazes back out to sea.

'Well, the show's over anyway, by the looks of things,' said Lynne.

She turned and walked back towards the hotel, the shafts of light from the shuttered windows splayed out across the grassy track like grasping fingers. They followed, the silence after the noise of the bombardment unsettling and ominous in their battered ears.

10
Ullapool

'If I had a boat, I'd scuttle it for you
If I had your love, I'd try to sink that too'

The Ossians, 'Shifting Sands'

Connor hadn't slept at all. His face throbbed, a slicing pain cut across his brain, and now his stomach was aching – acidic, bitter cramps. His ribcage felt tight beneath the skin of his chest. Whether it was the retching from last night, the raw spirit he was pouring down his neck or the indiscriminate pill-popping – fuck it, it could even be stress, he thought – his guts were telling him they weren't happy. His mind streamed with thoughts like an old stock exchange ticker-tape display, constantly analysing and re-analysing things, worrying what might happen before they got back to Edinburgh where he could crawl into a bed that would maybe help him sleep properly for once. He knew all this was a trick of the speed, in that way you know the drugs are working but you kid yourself you're on top of things and you can stop your teeth grinding and your brain flitting from one idea to the next before the first one's even taken hold. He was so tired his bones felt made of lead. Exhaustion was turning him to stone and metal like a statue, hardening from the inside out, and he thought with an air of resignation that he might never fall asleep again.

It was painfully bright outside when they left. Thick, heavy snowflakes fell on to the onlooking sheep, The Ossians and their van, covering the world in an uncomfortable calm. They drove past the village hall and spotted the memorial to John Lennon, a stone pillar standing snow-capped among diggers, traffic cones and dirty, frozen patches of earth. They stopped at Smoo Cave and trudged down the steps like convicts chained together into the unsettling, mossy, stagnant green-black space. The brightness outside was all the more blinding from inside the cave, and the gush of a waterfall somewhere in the darkness was white noise in their ears. They drove past a closed hotel, a petrol station out of petrol and a smattering of guesthouses with no vacancies. They passed a sign for Balnakeil Craft Village that pointed to a strange gathering of boxy, white buildings with large, fat chimneys. They realised they must have taken a wrong turn when they came round a corner to a dead end next to a ruined church, graveyard and a beautiful curve of sandy beach. The snow was falling thickly now, and it struck Connor that he'd never seen snow on a beach before, which was odd considering he'd grown up in a seaside town. Tiny, individual flakes of snow mingling with the equally minuscule particles of sand – two disparate forces, made up of unimaginably small constituents, battling it out at a microscopic level. Then again, maybe it was just snow on a fucking beach.

Paul rustled the map laid out across the steering wheel. 'Took a right instead of a left somewhere. Wanna take a look, or should we just fire on?'

Nobody said anything so Paul turned the van round, making circular tracks in the snow, and headed back the way they came.

They pulled into the craft village in search of coffee and directions. The Loch Affin Bookshop and Restaurant – 'food for mind and body' – was surprisingly busy. As they entered, shaking snow off their shoulders and stamping their feet, a thin middle-aged man with thick glasses, low-slung cords and a plaid shirt was talking loudly on the phone in an Oxbridge accent about types of balsamic vinegar, and whether the person on the other end of the line's kaffir lime leaves were fresh or dried. A second man, shorter, thicker round the middle and with grey hair flapping out of control, scuttled about behind a counter, fixing coffees and teas and putting buns and cakes on plates.

The walls were lined with bookshelves. They plonked themselves down at a lurid Formica table and Connor noticed they were sitting next to the Scottish fiction section. He scanned the rows of books and they were surprisingly well stocked considering, as the sign declared on the door, they were 'the most northwesterly bookshop and restaurant on the British mainland'. On the back of the same door, Connor now noticed, was an A4 sheet of blue paper with a cartoon drawing of two men in a boat unloading boxes. The accompanying blurb warned people to keep a vigilant lookout for smugglers in light aircraft or small boats acting suspiciously, and there was a number to call if you saw anything. Fat chance, thought Connor, they're probably all cut in on the deal up this way. Maybe that's how the books got here, or maybe that's how the guy on the phone was having his balsamic vinegar and kaffir lime leaves delivered. Then again, the smugglers' booty was more likely smack, coke and hash, or booze and fags. Fuck it, he was part of that game now. The drugs he was picking up must be smuggled ashore up here. He didn't know that for sure, of course. He could've been picking up consignments of locally grown grass – you heard plenty rumours about quality cannabis operations up here in the middle of nowhere. Maybe that's all it was. If he was carrying around a supplier-sized stash of class As, he was well and truly in the shit if he got caught. At least if it was doob he might be in for less of a sentence. He would still get sent down, the amount that was surely in those packages. He tried not to think about it – the next deal wasn't until Kyle, so he had a day off from all that shit. Thank fuck.

The wild-haired man came to take their order, flirting with Paul, and flounced away to sort out coffees. A couple of young families were in, trying to keep toddlers and babies happy. At the table next to them sat three young new-agers making roll-ups from a tin. They were talking in West Country accents about a solstice festival they were trying to organise and wondering where they could get their hands on stilt-walkers and fire-eaters round these parts. Connor examined the bookshelf next to him. They really did have a decent selection. All the newly published stuff was here, but there were also plenty of classics – Hogg, Stevenson, Scott and Burns. He got up and perused the nearest shelves, which contained a bunch of anthologies and collections. He picked out something called *Scottish Ghost Stories*. He vaguely remembered a book like this being around the house when he was little, and felt uneasy, as if he'd been spooked by it at an impressionable age. Flicking through it now, it seemed a little pathetic. A bunch of typical spectre sightings, given a tartan twist, and written up in hammy style for tourist eejits. Without thinking, he stuck the book in his pocket. Immediately he regretted it and wanted to bring it back out, but he worried that someone might see him. He wanted to bolt out the door, but they'd just ordered coffees. He felt the book smouldering in his pocket, warm against his thigh. He looked round and a toddler with tight blonde curls was looking straight at him over a plate of biscuits. He wondered if she'd been watching the whole time, and if she could talk yet. He felt sweat on his forehead. He sat back down at their table.

Paul was chatting to the wild-haired guy, getting the gen on the road south. Apparently it was rough track for only a few miles, then it widened to a decent road, and it shouldn't take them more than a couple of hours normally, but in this weather, with the snow and everything, they'd better watch.

'I suppose we should fire on,' Paul said. 'Let's get these down our necks, eh?'

The blonde girl was playing with a doll but still looking at Connor, and the book was getting warmer in his pocket. He stuck his hand in to feel the texture of the pages and whirred them between his fingers. Outside the snow was getting thicker, heavier and slower, like it was settling in for the long haul of winter. They drank their coffees quickly – Connor burning his lips – then paid up at the counter, the blonde toddler keeping her eye on Connor but never saying a word. He was sure she'd seen him stick the book in his pocket. Maybe she didn't understand it was stealing, she was only two or three years old, after all. Nevertheless he felt her eyes burning into his back. A bell tinkled as the door opened and two oversized policemen came in. There was an awkward moment as The Ossians had to move aside to let them in. The police kept their eyes on the band as they squeezed past on the way to the till. Connor looked at them as he went through the doorway. One of them produced a piece of paper with a photograph on it, and showed it to the camp guy behind the counter. He wondered if it was a picture of his stalker. He rubbed the stolen book in his pocket, closing the door behind him with a tinkle.

They were outside in the white silence of the snow. Connor waited to hear the bell sound again, expecting one of the owners to rush out accusing him of stealing, or one of the policemen to grab him for shoplifting, or possession or drug-dealing. But it didn't happen. Everything remained still. So he was guilty of shoplifting. And he didn't even want the fucking thing. He scrunched through the snow towards the van, thinking to himself, what the fuck next?

The journey south wasn't too treacherous, despite the snow. Slack, white flakes fell thick around them, but a gritter had been through and the road was OK. They snaked through barren, undulating countryside, always dominated by large, looming masses of hills that seemed to suck light out of the sky. Large boulders peppered the ground all around them, and scree slopes appeared out of the snow, their scattered hillside debris like huge natural landfill sites. Lochs too small for names or maps appeared everywhere, some frozen, some not, the solemn inkiness of the unfrozen water defiant against the snow that sizzled in it and disappeared.

Connor glanced out the back window. Halfway down a slope was a dark blue executive car, an Audi or a BMW, with heavily scored tracks behind it. It was the car he'd seen in the television report about the missing boy, his angel. They'd driven past the same car parked in a passing place on the way to Durness. But was it the same car? Had it crashed? It looked in one piece, but it was lodged at an angle deep into the scree, with no possible way of getting back on to the road without a tow truck, and even then it would be tricky. What if the boy was still inside? What if he'd crashed and needed help? But the car didn't look damaged, so maybe the boy got out. Maybe it wasn't the boy's car at all – but how many posh bastard cars like that did you see driving round these roads? Fuck, fuck, fuck. He didn't know what to do, so he continued to do nothing. As they drove on, he started to convince himself it had all been a hallucination. His mind was playing tricks, that was it. Still, he wondered what the stalker was doing now, if he was OK, if he would appear at the Ullapool gig. If Connor didn't see him at the next show, then it was time to worry. But he hadn't spotted him at the Thurso gig, or the few before that either. Where did that leave him?

He took a few deep breaths, pulled the book from his pocket and started flicking through it to distract himself.

'Where did you get that?' asked Kate.

'Brought it with me,' said Connor, feeling his ears burn.

'I thought you had that book of Ossian's poetry with you.'

Connor remembered that book of impenetrable guff at the bottom of his bag, beneath the envelopes of money and parcels of drugs.

'I brought this as well. A little light relief.'

'I haven't seen it before.'

'Like you pay attention to what I'm reading.'

Kate bent the book round to look at the cover.

'Didn't we have something like this growing up?'

'That's why I bought it. I remember being shit scared when we were little, but it reads like a pile of boring crap now. Just daft local superstitions collected into a tourist-fleecing money-spinner.'

'So why read it?'

'Dunno. Something to do. Nobody seems to have much chat today.' Connor felt like the mountains were sucking the life from his body. 'Got any other suggestions?'

'OK, back to your ghost stories, smart arse. We'll let you know when we hit civilisation.'

'Civilisation? We'll be lucky. Haven't seen any signs of it yet on this jaunt.'

'Who rattled your cage?' said Hannah, drawing her gaze away from the moonscape outside.

'Sorry,' said Connor. 'Just talking shite. Ignore me.'

'If only,' said Kate, flashing her brother a sarcastic smile.

'What have you got there?' said Hannah, looking at Connor's book.

Kate rolled her eyes. 'Don't ask,' she said. 'That's what set him off.'

'Let me see,' said Hannah, taking the book from him.

'Do you mind? I was reading that.'

'Doesn't look like your kind of thing. Where'd you get it?'

'I brought it with me.' Connor wished everyone would stop talking about the fucking book.

'Any good?' asked Hannah.

'No,' said Connor. 'Shite. Keep it. I'm going to sleep.'

He closed his eyes and felt his pulse beating strongly in his throat. He felt Hannah and Kate looking at him and imagined them exchanging looks. Fucking witches coven, that's what they were. Trying to organise every little thing he said or did, watching his every move.

After a time he opened his eyes and they were heading downhill towards a cluster of small white buildings, threads of grey smoke rising up from chimneys into the snowy sky. The houses were nestled in the only flat part on the banks of Loch Broom. This was Ullapool. The town was arranged in a crescent shape around a rocky beach and a small harbour which seemed to contain a massive, semi-submerged ship, its snow-covered deck stark against the black water. Connor looked again and realised it was a submarine, and a huge one at that.

The town was full of Russians. Very drunk Russians. The Ossians pitched up outside the Seaforth, a large two-storey, whitewashed pub sitting opposite the ferry terminal. As they got out they could see two dozen young men with severe haircuts in dark-blue uniforms scuffed around the cuffs, with their collars loosened, clearly steaming. Despite the falling snow and blustery wind, they sat at the pub's outside tables puffing on roll-ups – some playing cards, two of them arm-wrestling and another pair swaying as they simply tried to stand up straight and have a conversation.

As The Ossians loaded in the gear they were greeted loudly in Russian, some of the men helping them with the heavier amps in a ramble of drunken enthusiasm. Inside there were another three dozen of them, many of whom were already in a shambolic state.

It was four o'clock in the afternoon. Like a Pavlovian dog, Connor felt his mouth salivate as he watched them knocking back shot after shot of vodka.

'Russians,' said the promoter, shaking his head but grinning at the same time. He was a short, squat troll of a man in his forties, with greying curly hair down past his shoulders. He wore a faded old Clash T-shirt, black jogging bottoms covered in what looked like paint and a pair of slippers. His shoulders were covered in dandruff, and he reeked of cheap sausages. He immediately focused on Kate and Hannah, who hung back, trying to avoid his stare.

'Their submarine broke down somewhere off the coast,' he said, looking Hannah up and down. 'So they docked here and are waiting to get it fixed or towed back to Russia. They've been here almost a week now. It's a bit hectic. They know how to drink. The way they get through vodka is unbelievable, and a lot of them have developed a wee thing for whisky, which they can drink like water. But they're running out of money so I don't know how much longer they'll be bringing in any business.'

'Isn't a gig in front of a bunch of fucked Russian sailors a bit risky?' said Paul.

'Whatever you do, don't call them sailors,' said the promoter. 'They go mental if you call them that. They're submariners. They've got a thing about sailors, absolutely hate them. The gig'll be fine. They've hardly been any trouble the last few days. Perhaps there were some high spirits to begin with, but they've settled into a routine now, and could do with a bit of entertainment, take their mind off things.'

Two submariners came in and approached the promoter. They seemed less drunk than the rest. They were both tall and fair-haired, their uniforms impeccably turned out, and they had serious expressions on their faces.

'We have the things you asked for,' said the taller of the two. 'From the ship. The brass and copper.'

The promoter had a brief look of panic in his eyes. 'Fine, Dimitri. Bring it round the back door in two minutes and we'll sort something out.'

'You're stripping the fucking sub?' said Connor as the sub-mariners disappeared smartly out the door.

'They have no money and they want to keep drinking,' said the promoter, shrugging. 'What am I supposed to do? I'm helping these gentlemen enjoy themselves, that's all. They don't owe the Russian navy any favours, some of them haven't been paid for months. Besides, I can shift that stuff for a packet. Now, you lads and ladies –' he said this slowly, looking again at Hannah and Kate before remembering he was mid-sentence – 'you can set up over there on the stage in the corner. The sound guy should be here soon, he'll sort you out. I've got some business to attend to, but I'll speak to you later on.'

He looked over at the girls again. Connor was ready to lamp the slimy fucker in the face by this point but the promoter was already scuttling through the back of the bar with a strangely effeminate walk.

'What an arsehole,' said Kate, turning to lift her amp.

The rest of them followed her to the six-inch stage in the corner of the pub. The Seaforth had a generic boozer feel to it. Booths lined the walls next to large windows overlooking the harbour, while a massive fireplace with a ship's wheel above it dominated the wall to their right. At the other end of the room was a short, dimly lit bar, row upon row of whisky bottles on the gantry. In front of them was a worn-out pool table and a table football game. The stage was tiny and there would be sod all space to move. They set up the gear, then pitched into one of the booths to keep an eye on the equipment while Paul went to sort out the place they were staying that night.

'Anyone else got a bad feeling?' laughed Danny.

'Know what you mean,' said Kate, looking at one of the booths of Russians as they heard the tinkle of smashing glass.

'And that promoter,' said Hannah. 'What a wank. The sooner we get through this one the better.'

Outside, the snow was falling in sleepy fashion, taking its time to reach the ground. The mountainous sides of Loch Broom loomed in the distance. The rippling water in the harbour was black and slick as slate. The snow was piling up on the road outside, sickly orange in the streetlight, and they saw some Russians start a snowball fight which looked dangerously aggressive. Just then the hulking presence of the Stornoway ferry slunk into view. Only thirty feet out from shore, it crept along, high in the water, lights sparkling against the blackness.

The presence of the sea so close calmed Connor. Despite some rank music channel like TMF blasting from the four televisions in the corners of the room, he imagined he could hear the gentle lapping of the waves against the pebbled shoreline, the greasy bladderwrack lifting and falling in time with the waves, as if it were a softly breathing lung. Why did such natural beauty always have to be spoilt by the arseholes who inhabited such places? He was appalled at the snobbishness of the idea, and felt ashamed. And why had no one bought him a drink? He sprang out his seat towards the bar. After downing a sly double whisky, he returned to the booth to see Paul coming in with a face like fizz.

'Fucking fuck,' Paul snapped, exasperated as he slumped into the booth. 'The place has shut down. The Ferry Boat Inn, just about the only pub in town with rooms. There's a sign saying they're closed. I collared some guy going past and apparently there was a massive fight two nights ago, all this bunch.' He flicked a thumb towards a booth of submariners. 'Most of the windows are boarded up, and the place is a tip. So I went to the tourist office – shut, obviously. Then the two backpacker hostels. Shut. Tried a handful of B&Bs down the road, and either everyone's left town or they're too scared to answer the fucking door cos of these cunts.'

'What are you saying?' said Hannah. 'We're sleeping on the street?'

'Well, it looks like the van at the moment unless we persuade some locals to put us up. That's if any locals turn up tonight. I've got a feeling that people have battened down the hatches and are riding out the storm of Russian pissheads.'

'Superb,' said Kate, shaking her head. 'This is a new high, a gig in front of pished foreign sailors, and nowhere to sleep.'

'Excuse me, I could not help overhearing your conversation.'

A tall, stringy teenager with a black, stubbly head and wearing a scruffy dark uniform was standing at their table, addressing Kate. The Russians from the next booth were nudging each other and smiling.

'My name is Vladimir. First of all, we are not sailors, we are submariners,' he said, slurring through a thick accent. 'It is a very different thing.' He waggled his finger first at Kate then around the table, as they all tried to suppress smiles. 'I can see you are not taking me seriously, but we hate those sailors, they are fucking cunts, as you Scottish say.'

Connor was impressed he'd picked up the local lingo so fast, but more impressed at the effortless way he waved a glass of vodka about without spilling a drop, while also pulling up a barstool and sitting down at the end of their booth.

'So, Vladdy boy, how are you enjoying sunny Scotland?' said Connor. The rest of them gave him funny looks for encouraging the lad, but he reckoned the Russian could only be about eighteen years old and his friendly face and thin build didn't suggest a dangerous killing machine. And anyway, maybe it made sense to get chatting to some of these bastards if they were going to be their crowd for the night.

'It is beautiful here, very beautiful,' said Vladimir. 'I come from industrial area in Russia, lots of factories and dirt. Ullapool is very clean. Scotland is all like this?'

'Not exactly,' said Connor. He thought about the little chocolate-box houses sitting on the lochside, the whitewashed walls and the snow falling like something out of a Hollywood Christmas schmaltz-fest. He thought of the picturesque view from the Scott Monument back in Edinburgh and how the city attracted swarms of tourists, even in winter, so that it didn't seem to have any character of its own any more. He also thought of the shitty, schemie parts of the city – Craigmillar, Wester Hailes, Sighthill – and decided that he really had no idea whether Scotland was a beautiful place or not.

'Russia, of course, is very big,' said Vladimir, knocking back some more from his tumbler. 'We have many very different parts, and of course, everyone wants their own little country, it is the way.'

Connor thought about devolved Scotland. If Scots had no deep-rooted connection with other Scots, who the fuck were they supposed to connect with?

Vladimir waved his glass at Kate and Hannah.

'Here you have very beautiful ladies, yes?' He nodded in a courteous gesture to the girls. It seemed an innocent teenage compliment, so Hannah and Kate raised their glasses in his direction and took a drink.

'I'll drink to that, Vlad,' said Connor, slapping the boy on the back a little too hard so that he choked on his vodka. 'Shit, sorry,' he said, but Vladimir waved away his apologies, downing what was left in his glass.

'I must go pee,' he said. 'Please excuse me. I'm sure we will speak again soon.'

As he watched the Russian get up, Connor realised he needed to pish as well, plus it had been a while since he'd had a decent hit of speed, and maybe he could try another of those mystery pills, see what sort of mess might keep him from caring when tonight's gig went tits up. He followed him to the Gents.

Hannah watched him go, then turned back to the booth. Paul was fiddling with his mobile while Kate and Danny sat flirting, oblivious to her. She watched them for a while. It had been like that with her and Connor at the start. The first flush of sexual excitement, the thrill of undiscovered secrets in someone else's body. She still loved Connor, but it was a different kind of love. What replaced that initial buzz? Had anything replaced it? He was making it bloody difficult to love him these days, always out of it, talking rubbish about angels and some missing boy. She couldn't remember a time since the start of this ridiculous trek when he hadn't been shit-faced. He needed to straighten out, so they could have a proper conversation. She still hadn't had her period, and she'd pretty much given up hope that she would. She'd either skipped it completely or was pregnant. Kate was right, she had to find out. If it turned out she was, she had to talk it over with Connor. But that wasn't a conversation to have now, with Connor off his face, in a pub full of drunken Russians, before a potentially disastrous gig. And anyway, she had to find out for sure first.

Watching Kate and Danny, she was envious of them. She wondered what they had in store over the next few years, if it would be anything like her and Connor. She didn't know if she wished that on them. But she was being unfair – most of the last five years with Connor had been a riot. It just didn't feel like that right now. Maybe Connor would straighten out, maybe he would stop acting weird and doing stupid things and they could get back to how they were. Maybe.

In the toilets, Connor stood next to Vladimir pissing in the trough. The Russian looked around theatrically, before stage-whispering, 'Do you have any money?'

Connor realised what a mistake this was. He was alone in a toilet with a skint, drunk member of the Russian armed services and unprepared to fight, what with having his pissing cock in his hands.

'How do you mean?'

Connor was suddenly ultra-aware of his surroundings. The orange wall seemed to vibrate before his eyes and the acidic smell of urine burnt his nostrils. Vladimir pulled a gun out his pocket.

'Jesus,' said Connor, trying not to piss down his leg as he finished and zipped up. 'You're mugging me? Is that it?'

Vladimir put his finger to his lips. 'Shhhh,' he said, shaking his head. 'No, no. I sell you gun. You like?'

Connor looked at the swaying Russian, who held a small, black handgun in the palm of his hand, offering it up for inspection. It wouldn't hurt to have a look at it. Just out of interest. He'd never handled a real gun before, only air rifles and the like.

'Is it loaded?' he asked, unable to take his eyes off it.

'Yes, but it is quite safe,' said Vladimir. 'Look, the safety catch is on. It is called a Grach. Very good Russian gun. Would you like to look?'

Vladimir lifted the gun to eye level. It was pitch black and sleek and glowed in the bright strip-light of the toilet. It seemed too small to be anything dangerous. Connor took it. It felt cold and dry, heavy and metallic and beautiful.

'How much?'

'Fifty pounds.'

Connor felt the metallic coolness of the gun in his left hand as his right hand rummaged in his coat pocket.

'I'll give you twenty quid plus these,' he said, producing a handful of pills from his pocket. He was careful not to include the ever-diminishing speed bag in the bargain. Vladimir's eyes widened.

'What are they?'

Connor shrugged. 'Uppers, downers. Does it matter?'

Vladimir considered the offer thoughtfully, then a wide grin spread across his face and he slapped Connor on the back, laughing as he did so.

'No, it does not matter. It is a deal.'

Connor tipped the pills into the Russian's hands, then handed him the money. He bounced the gun up and down in his hand as if trying to guess its weight.

'You want me to show you how to use it?' said Vladimir.

'I'm sure I can work it out,' said Connor, not at all sure, but unwilling to show ignorance. Vladimir pointed to a sliding switch near the top of the handle on the left-hand side. 'This is the safety. Leave it like this unless you want to shoot. It is fully loaded.'

He smiled again, then examined the handful of pills in his hand. Connor slipped the gun into his coat pocket.

'One thing,' said Connor. 'This is our little secret, OK? Don't mention it to them out there. Understand?'

Vladimir grinned that grin again, a smile Connor was really warming to.

'Our little secret,' he said. 'I understand.'

Of course the gig went badly. A handful of local kids turned up half an hour before the band were due to go on, the guys in buttoned-down collars, Hilfiger gear and baseball caps, the girls in micro-skirts that they kept tugging on, skimpy spangly tops and too much make-up. They made for the pool table. The guys, only just eighteen, eyed up the booths full of submariners, who were laughing and slapping each other on the back, singing songs and smashing glasses. Some of the Russians were admiring the girls' show of flesh.

When The Ossians started, no one paid them any attention – the Russians too drunk and the locals concentrating on the pool game in front of the stage. Not for the first time, Connor wondered why they bothered, and if they could cut the set short.

One of the submariners approached the pool table, putting money down to book a game. He began chatting to one of the girls, a petite lass with a plain face, bony, bruised knees and wearing a tiny mini-kilt. The Ossians filled the air with waves of jagged guitars and pounding drums, and Connor watched events unfold as he went through the motions of singing the words. It was like watching an old silent film, he half-expected dialogue to appear in front of his eyes between the action sequences. The Russian kept talking to the girl, who was playing with her hair and swinging her hips from side to side. One of the guys she was with came over looking like someone had pissed in his pint. He and the Russian had words. There was a shove to the chest, a shove back, a smack in the face and a pool cue was brandished.

Then everyone was in. Punches flying everywhere. Bar stools careened over people's heads and the sound of smashing glass could be heard over the music. The girls were screaming, the guys grunting and swearing in English and Russian, the pool table was upturned and the band stopped playing. It seemed almost comical, at least it would have, except a maul of wrestling bodies tumbled onstage, knocking over an amp and two cymbal stands as the band leapt out the way.

'Come on,' Paul shouted over the escalating levels of fight noise. 'Let's get the gear out of here before it's totally fucked.'

'Listen to that,' said Hannah. 'Unbelievable.'

The five of them sat in the van. They were parked on the lochside promenade at the other end of town from the Seaforth, where they thought they'd be safe from any trouble. They were wrong. They could hear gunshots and laughter outside, Russian swearing, drunken singing, then more gunshots. Every time a loud pop went off they all jumped. Danny was skinning up fast, only blow could make this bearable. Hannah was restless, wide-eyed and fidgeting, talking constantly, giving a running commentary of their situation.

'I can't believe we're sitting in a van in the Highlands, with nowhere to sleep, having just not been paid for a gig that ended in a brawl anyway, surrounded by insane Russian sailors who appear to be carrying out target practice on the whole fucking town.'

Another pop made her jump, then another. They heard some congratulatory whooping and singing.

'Could we not go and park somewhere else?' said Hannah. 'Somewhere miles away from these nutters?'

'They're at both ends of the street now,' said Paul peering out the steamed-up windscreen. 'I don't want to drive past any of them in case they take a shot at us. This is a fucking nightmare. We'll just need to wait for it to die down.'

'We're being held hostage here,' said Kate, as Danny passed a joint to her. She took a toke and deliberately missed out Hannah, passing it to Connor. 'Who's fucking idea was this tour, little brother?'

'Yeah, like I could've predicted a broken submarine full of lunatic Russians gone stir-crazy,' he said, inhaling deeply. 'Cos that's *always* happening to fucking Coldplay on tour.'

'This is pretty ridiculous,' said Danny, starting to chuckle. The sound of his deep, rumbling laughter made Hannah relax a little, and she pointedly took the joint from Connor and inhaled, looking at Kate. There were a few more pops from outside, sharp little noises, but she didn't jump. When the door of the van banged, however, her heart thumped like crazy.

'Fucking hell,' said Paul, wiping his hands on his trouser legs in nervous circles. 'Fucking hell.'

A muffled voice spoke from outside, the sound given a strange metallic ring from the acoustics of the van.

'It is me, Vladimir.'

Connor felt a tightening across his chest. What did he want?

Paul wound the window down and there was the Russian, his stubbled head covered in a snowy hood, his grin spread from ear to ear.

'I must apologise for my comrades' high spirits,' he said, and Connor sensed he was clicking his heels together, although they couldn't see below his chest. 'Things are a little out of control, but no one is in any real danger, I do not think.'

'What are you shooting at?' said Hannah, passing the joint to Paul.

'I do not have a gun,' said Vladimir, and Connor thought his heart was going to burst out his chest. He stared directly at the Russian, who was smiling but not even looking at him. 'Some of my shipmates think they see seals in the harbour, and are rather foolishly shooting into the water. I do not think the seals will still be there, if they ever were, but they keep shooting all the same. It is a waste of ammunition.'

'Jesus,' said Danny, as Connor regained his composure a little. Paul passed the joint out the window to the Russian, who eagerly accepted it and took a couple of deep tokes.

'I overheard earlier that you had nowhere to sleep tonight,' he said, passing the joint back into the van. 'I was wondering if you would like to sleep onboard? It may seem a bit rowdy at first, but really it is fine. The beds are comfortable and I can assure you that you will be safe and warm.'

They all looked at each other and it was clear from their faces they were all thinking the same thing. Connor spoke. 'That's very kind, Vlad, but we'll be all right here. It's warm enough, and we wouldn't want to leave the van and the gear for the night, considering everything that's going on.'

Vladimir kept smiling that implacable smile.

'I completely understand,' he said, looking away as more gunfire echoed down the street. 'Now I must go and make sure my comrades do not get into too much trouble. Also, I have recently acquired some substances which may make our stay here more interesting.' Connor felt his face fill with blood. Vladimir looked around the inside of the van and seemed to do that heel-clicking thing again. 'It has been a pleasure to meet you all. Maybe one day we will meet again. I hope so. Goodbye.'

Without waiting for a reply he turned and walked briskly but with a slight wobble down the promenade towards the sound of gunfire. Snow filled his footprints as he went.

'Nice lad,' laughed Connor. 'I take it nobody was up for a night on a Russian sub?'

'Thanks but no thanks,' said Hannah.

'What a loon,' said Kate.

'He's probably the sanest of the lot of them,' said Hannah. 'At least he said he didn't have a gun, which is something. Although what the hell was he on about, "substances"? Reckon he's drugged up?'

Connor shrugged and turned to Paul. 'Think we're going to be able to track down that promoter twat for the money?'

'I doubt it,' said Paul. 'I can't see him sticking his head above the trenches tonight or tomorrow, and we've got to be in Kyle of Lochalsh by tomorrow afternoon, so it looks like today's been another fucking write-off.'

'This tour gets better and better,' said Danny.

'Yeah, something to tell the grandkids,' said Hannah, and felt Kate's gaze fall on her.

Weak laughter spread for a few seconds in the van before petering out, each of them shaking their head at the situation. There was the occasional pop of gunfire. The windows were steamed up and snow fell outside, as the dark, lonely water of the loch absorbed bullets like they were stones thrown by little kids. In three days' time they would be back home, but that seemed impossible to imagine.

II

Kyle of Lochalsh

'I don't sleep
So I walk these dirty streets
Halfway to the grave'

The Ossians, 'The City of Dreadful Night'

Kyle of Lochalsh was a dead-end town. Hewn out of the dark, damp rock, the scatter of depressed houses seemed to shrug at their miserable fate. Once, Kyle had some purpose as the place to catch the Skye ferry, but when the bridge was built it became the stopping place no one in their right minds stopped in. The bridge, arching gently in the distance behind the sprawl of pathetic houses, seemed to mock the town, as did the omnipresent misty black bumps of the Cuillin Hills behind it. Cars sped along the town's main road, blurs of hope, heading for better things on the island. The snow of further north had turned to oppressive, ominous rain, the kind of rain that beats you down into the ground with relentless force, dissolving your head and shoulders, torso and legs until there's nothing left.

The windscreen wipers struggled to keep up with the thud of raindrops as they pulled up to the hostel in a thick fog of misery. The hostel was a large, dirty concrete brick of a building with a long, unpronounceable Gaelic name and a badly drawn cartoon wolf on its wall. Across the street a handful of teenage girls hung about a sheltered bus stop near the jetty. They wolf-whistled and cat-called any boys who came within a hundred yards, their shrieking laughter piercing the skin of the van and sending a shiver up Connor's spine. Occasionally cars stopped by the bus stop – teenage boys in pathetic souped-up Fiestas with spoilers and extra lights – and a short exchange of expletives and flirtations would take place, before the boys spun off in a screech of tyres and a flurry of bum-fluffed macho bravado.

No one had slept at all, so as soon as they checked in to the hostel they crashed out, all except Connor, despite pleading from Hannah and the rest that he really needed sleep. He knew he needed sleep, but it seemed so long since he'd closed his eyes and dreamt that he didn't think he could do it any more, and couldn't ever see a time when he would again. He dabbed some speed, rolled a joint, rubbed the handle of the gun in his pocket a few times and headed out into the wretched rain and the wretched town, a suitably wretched figure.

He bought a bottle of the cheapest gin at a corner shop and had the seal broken before he was out the door. He stood outside surveying the scene. Across the road was the jetty and the Lochalsh Hotel, a massive white building frayed around the edges, like the suit of a Scottish laird fallen on hard times. The large car park outside it was empty, and waterlogged picnic tables stood at the lochside next to a lone flagpole. To his right was Main Street and the Kyle Hotel. Christ, these people had some imaginations, he thought. Another squat, dirty white lump of concrete, its main body had ugly extensions sticking out at various angles. The Kyle was their gig venue for tonight and Connor grinned ruefully looking at its pitiful frontage. He turned to look past the hostel to the dingy, grimy train station. Two engines rested in the sidings pumping small clouds of black smoke up into the unforgiving rain. This was Kyle of Lochalsh, very possibly the arsehole of Scotland. If they had any sense they'd move everyone out of here and bulldoze the fucking dump, like they did the Gorbals.

He made for the shore. If in doubt, make for water to soothe the nerves. He headed across the road, dodging between cars as they fizzed continuously to and from the bridge, none of them willing to spend a second more than they had to in this shithole. As he walked towards the jetty, the girls at the bus stop started shouting a mix of obscenities and provocation at him, anything to get noticed.

'My mate wants to shag you, ya prick, will you no shag her? Are you a fucking poof?'

'Come over here and we'll shag your arse off.'

'We'll batter you, ya cunt, are you fucking scared?'

Connor had heard it all a million times before. He ignored them and sat at one of the soaking picnic tables outside the Lochalsh Hotel. The rain lashed down, drips turning to rivulets at his collar, drops mixing with snot as they dripped off his nose, dampness seeping through his jeans. He looked out across the water at the drenched island beyond and realised he couldn't feel the rain.

He swigged the gin and sucked his teeth. It occurred to him how rude it was not to have offered the bus-stop bitches a drink. He remembered how he would've done anything for booze when he was that age. He got up and headed back in their direction. As soon as they saw him they started.

'Here he is, the fucking gay cunt,' said one girl, her hair tied back so tightly in a ponytail it gave Connor a headache to look at it. He smiled calmly and took a big swig from the bottle, letting them see the label.

'Afternoon ladies,' he said. 'Fancy a drink?'

'Are you a pervert?' said Ponytail. 'A fucking child molester, aye?'

Connor stood holding the bottle out. There were four of them, dressed almost identically in pink or yellow cropped tops, blue pedal pushers and white shoes. They all wore cheap gold jewellery and watches, were caked in make-up and had their hair tied back in various arrangements. The abuse continued for a few more minutes, accusations followed by bursts of laughter that were too hard and forced. Gradually they quietened down until Ponytail warily said, 'It's just gin, aye?'

Connor nodded and waggled the bottle at her. Ponytail grabbed it in an ungainly lunge, like a newborn foal taking its first steps. She made a show of wiping the rim of the bottle on the hem of her top, then took a big gulp. One of the other girls made a grab for it, but Ponytail took another long drink before she passed it on.

'Keep it,' said Connor, walking away.

'We've got yer fucking bevvy, dickhead,' said Ponytail, but there was something in her voice which lacked conviction. 'Too scared to take it back, aye? Or did yeh spike it, ya fucking perv?'

Connor walked back up to the corner shop to get himself another bottle. The girls called insults after him, but he felt them bounce off his back like the rain, his wrecked body now shielded by an unseen force field. He walked into the shop and asked for another bottle of gin to raised eyebrows. As he stepped back outside, he saw the girls shoving each other as they fought over the bottle. He felt better than he had for a while. He stroked the gun in his pocket. It seemed to be giving off heat which spread through his body. A familiar noise came to him. It sounded comforting, but he couldn't place it. After a while it came to him – 'Smells Like Teen Spirit'. The phone. He took it out and answered as he downed gin and watched the girls at the bus stop. A wasted female voice babbled in his ear.

'Where are you?'

'Across from the Lochalsh Hotel.'

'I'll meet you there in five minutes.'

'Fine, I'll be at one of the picnic tables.'

'Outside? In this rain? Are you mental?'

Connor hung up. He crossed the road, taking a wide berth around the bus stop, where the girls were still fighting over the bottle. He sat down at the waterlogged table, the relentless splat of raindrops on wood for company. He thought of the angel. He hadn't seen him last night at the gig – was that a bad sign? They'd been occupied with saving themselves and their gear from destruction, and he hadn't given his angel any thought until now. He felt ashamed. If his angel was looking out for him, shouldn't he also look out for his angel? What if he was back in that car, up near Durness, and Connor could've rescued him? What if he'd decided to leave earth altogether, give up on Connor's soul? He didn't think he could take that. Having an obsessive, stalking evil angel look out for you was better than having no one look out for you at all.

'Connor?'

He recognised the voice from the phone call, but hesitated before turning round, hoping it was his angel.

He assumed this was Susie, since that was the name on the last package. She looked as if she was having a much worse time than

Connor. She looked scrunched up and soaked through, and wore a grey hoodie, tracky bottoms and skanky old trainers. Her eyes were sunken, surrounded by gritty bags, and her mouth and nose were rimmed with sores. The skin hung loose at her neck and hands, although she didn't seem old, just worn through.

'You got the stuff from Nick?'

'You got the money?'

'Of course, let's see the drugs first.'

Was this the first time someone had explicitly referred to these packages as drugs? He reached into the kitbag under the table and handed over the package. To his surprise, she ripped it open right in front of him, frantically inspecting the contents before smiling and closing the package. She wasn't like the others. They'd been in control and assured, she seemed like a totally fucked-up end-user. What was Nick doing dealing direct with someone like this? Maybe he owed her a favour, or maybe he was sweet on her or something, although it seemed unlikely anyone could be sweet on such a car crash. He was a fine one to talk.

'Where's the money?'

As soon as he asked it, Connor knew the answer. Susie was edging away from him, her body turning side-on, her eyes looking away.

'Where's the money?'

'The thing is . . .'

Connor waited. What was he going to do? Looking at the state of her, she wasn't going to give the package up without a fight. He didn't want to be in this fucking shithole, in the pissing rain, fighting over a drugs package with a junkie cow. Then he remembered the gun. He stroked the metal in his pocket. How would it pan out if he pulled the gun on her? He was taking the gun out his pocket, Susie watching in horror and realisation, when he heard another voice.

'Hey, cuntface.'

It was Ponytail and her mates. He pushed the gun back in his pocket. Susie edged further away. Ponytail and her mates were heading towards him fast, then all around him, right in his face.

'Who's yer girlfriend?' said Ponytail. 'Fucking junkie scum. Got any more booze?' The girls were between him and Susie now, she was getting further away and he couldn't do anything about it.

'Fuck off,' he said, pushing Ponytail. She stumbled, then came straight back at him, shoving him hard in the chest so that he lost balance.

Susie saw her chance and bolted. She was across the main road before Connor had even righted himself. Ponytail was screaming in his face, and the other three girls were shrieking as well, joining in the chorus of abuse and crowding round him. He looked across the road but Susie had gone, slipped behind some shop or house, disappeared under a fucking rock in this slimy little pisshole of a place. Fucking great. The bus-stop bitches were still screaming at him. How easy it would be to get rid of them just by pulling the gun out his pocket and waving it around. That would shut them up. But he didn't take it out. Instead he offered up his second bottle of gin to Ponytail, who shambled forward and grabbed it, swearing at him in triumph before turning and leading her posse back to the bus stop.

He would just have to tell Nick what happened. He wasn't to blame. But Susie would say she handed over the money, so it would be Connor's word against hers.

How had it come to this? He was standing in the pissing rain in the biggest scum-sucking shithole in the country, fucking up drug deals, giving away booze, and somehow expected to play a gig. He looked at the bridge in the distance and pictured himself jumping off it. He thought about stepping on to the road in front of a car, feeling the cold, hard kiss of metal against his body.

He heard a voice he recognised.

'Connor?'

He turned and smiled at his guardian angel, his runaway boy, his stalker. A strange glow seemed to be emanating from the tall, thin figure, and the rain seemed not to be making him wet. As he noticed this, Connor thought it was both ridiculous and perfectly reasonable.

'I could've used you a few minutes ago,' he said.

'Sorry?'

'I had a spot of bother.'

'What kind of bother?'

'You don't want to know.'

'No, go on.'

Connor waved a hand at nothing. 'Drugs, junkies, money, booze, schemie underagers . . .'

'Sorry I wasn't here.'

'Where have you been? I didn't see you in Ullapool.'

'I had car trouble.'

'Shit. Was that your car on the scree slope on the road down from Cape Wrath?'

'Yes.'

'Fuck, I'm sorry. I saw it, but it was too late, we'd already driven past it, and I didn't know anyone was in it anyway, let alone that it was your . . .'

The figure raised a hand slowly. 'It's OK. I slept in the car last night, then hitched a lift this morning.'

Connor stood with this serene figure in front of him, the rain thrashing the ground all around them.

'What's your name? You never told me your name.'

The figure seemed to consider this for a while.

'Martin.'

'Martin?'

'Yeah.'

'Tell me something, Martin, are you an angel?'

Martin laughed shyly, but didn't reply.

'Are you?'

'Are you serious?' Martin's smile faded. 'You're serious, aren't you? No, Connor, I'm not an angel. Not by a long way.'

'But you said you were looking out for me. I thought you were maybe my guardian angel.'

'I am looking out for you, but I'm no angel.'

'Then what? A stalker?'

Martin looked uncomfortable. 'I'm not a psycho, if that's what you mean.'

'No, no, I didn't mean it in a bad way.'

'You didn't mean "stalker" in a bad way?'

Connor didn't know how to explain that he'd liked the feeling of being followed.

'If you're not an angel or a stalker, what are you?'

'I'm just a fan,' said Martin, looking awkward.

'A fan of what? The band?'

The rain hammered the tarmac beneath their feet. Martin looked embarrassed, but didn't speak. Connor wanted to ask again, but didn't dare in case Martin ran away. He couldn't bear it if he made this kid run away. But he couldn't help himself from wanting to know more.

'Why do I keep seeing you on television? Have you run away from home? I've seen your parents, and the car you were driving, which must be theirs, and the area of Edinburgh you live in, which looks like Marchmont or Morningside. The police are looking for you, you know. I saw them with your picture in a book shop up north.'

Things began falling into place in his booze-soaked brain. This was just a kid who'd run away from home, and was following him and the band round the country for whatever messed-up reasons. He wasn't an angel, or a stalker, or some kind of saviour. He was just a fucked-up kid.

'Why don't you come and meet the rest of the band.'

'I can't.'

'Why not?'

'I just can't.'

Martin looked nervously around him, as if the whole thing was a set-up, and the rest of The Ossians might spring out of the nearby water and grab him. He started moving away from Connor.

'No, wait!' said Connor desperately. 'Don't go. Not again. I want you to stay.'

But Martin had already turned and was running away. It never even occurred to Connor to run after him, so heavy were his legs. He watched as Martin nimbly darted across the road, and off down Main Street into the godforsaken gloom of Lochalsh.

*

'Still nothing?'

Kate looked at Hannah, who looked ill in the yellow light of the Kyle Hotel. Hannah pursed her lips and shook her head, looking down at her lap.

'What are you going to do?' said Kate.

Hannah shrugged. 'What can I do? Wait and see. I can't get a pregnancy test here anyway, have you seen this dump? There's barely a shop, let alone a hint of civilisation.'

She looked around at the tattered brown walls of the bar. A handful of oddball punters were in, one man wearing wellies and a waxed jacket, another middle-aged woman in what appeared to be a Stetson and cowboy boots. Apart from them there was a handful of neddy types, inevitably clustered round the pool table. The young, muscular barman had a bored look on his face as he watched motor racing on a television mounted in the corner above the toilets. The smell emanating from that direction suggested the bogs hadn't been cleaned in a long time. The strip-lighting, sickly walls and urine stench seemed to create an unearthly mist in the place, Hannah thought, as if they were playing tonight's gig on Venus or something. She turned back to Kate, who had a worried look on her face.

'Fuck's sake, Kate, lighten up,' she said. 'It's not as if I've got cancer.'

'All right, but . . .' Kate trailed off, not knowing what to say. She nodded at the double vodka in front of Hannah. 'What about that?'

'What about it?' Hannah straightened in her seat. 'I've told you, we don't know anything for definite, and I've skipped periods before, mainly because of booze and stress. This is not a big deal.'

She realised she'd been prodding the table. She examined her finger, which was sticky with spilt alcohol and had a grey smudge of dust on it. That bloody barman could be cleaning these tables, she thought to herself. What else did he have to do in this dump?

'Fine,' said Kate. 'It's your body, do what you like. But Con is my brother, and I think you should tell him. What if you are pregnant? He deserves to know. I realise he's been an arsehole, but this is maybe just the thing to sort him out.'

'You're getting *way* ahead of yourself. There's no point getting him involved when we don't know anything.'

'But that's just it, he is involved. I assume.' As soon as she said it, Kate regretted it.

'What the fuck is that supposed to mean?' said Hannah, blood rising in her cheeks. 'What are you trying to say? That I'm sleeping around?'

'Whoa, whoa. I didn't mean anything by it,' said Kate, waving her hands as if trying to stop a runaway train. 'Sorry. Look, I really didn't mean that. Forget it. Fuck.'

There was a long, angry silence.

'I guess we're all a bit stressed,' said Kate eventually. 'This whole tour is a bit of a farce, isn't it? We haven't had any decent sleep and the gigs have mostly been terrible. Christ knows what we'll be like by the time we hit Glasgow. Wasn't the whole point to get up to speed for King Tut's? No one's even talked about that for days, it feels like we're just trying to stay alive, you know? I'm not even sure the band's going to hold together much longer. It feels like we're disintegrating.'

Hannah thought about it. She'd been feeling bad about the band, too. Now that someone else had voiced the opinion, it seemed a real possibility they might split up. The Ossians had always been Con's baby, and the more he lost the plot, the less chance they had of keeping their shit together as a band. As for Connor's state of mind, Hannah didn't even want to think about it. She knew she should try talking to him, but it seemed like such a huge effort, and she was busy trying to keep herself together. She didn't need to be sorting out his head as well. But then wasn't that what couples did for each other? And weren't they a couple? It didn't feel much like they were at the moment. She loved him but she was tired, so bloody tired of all the bullshit that came along with their relationship, the band, their lives. She just wanted to go to bed and forget about it. If only it was that easy. The next best thing to sleep, of course, was getting drunk. She downed what was left of her vodka and made for the bar, feeling Kate's disapproving look and not giving two shits.

*

213

Connor and Danny sat in their room at the hostel. Danny had been heading for the gig when he spotted Connor sitting on his own in the rain outside the Lochalsh. When he reached him, Connor was in a trance. He dragged him back to the hostel and got him out of his wet clothes, slinging them on the radiator, creating a humid stench in the room, like wet dog.

'Have you got any spare clothes?' he asked, but Connor didn't answer. Danny headed over to the bag Connor had with him outside – he seemed to be carrying that thing everywhere. As he knelt down and unzipped it, Connor came to life.

'Wait!' He was sitting in just his pants, a damp patch spreading on the duvet under his arse. 'I'll get that.' He moved quickly over to where Danny was kneeling and took the bag from him. Danny stood and watched him rummage through the bag for a while. Eventually he spoke.

'Is this something to do with me and Kate?' he said quietly.

Connor looked up from his bag like a fox caught raking through bins.

'What?'

'The way you're acting. Is it because of me and Kate?'

Connor looked confused. 'How am I acting?'

'Weird. Fucked up. Seriously fucked up.'

'I might be fucked up, but it's got nothing to do with you and Kate.'

'Why were you sitting out in the rain?'

'Getting some fresh air.'

'Don't be an arsehole. When was the last time you slept? Or ate anything?'

'What is this, the Spanish Inquisition?'

Danny sighed and sat down as Connor carefully pulled a T-shirt and jeans out the bag and put them on, almost falling over as he stuck one leg then the other into the trouser legs. As he was zipping up, they both heard Connor's phone going in his coat pocket.

'Who keeps phoning you?'

'Probably just Paul wondering where we are.' He took the phone out his coat pocket. It was Nick. He switched it off with a furtive thumb press, then held it to his ear and made a face at Danny.

'No one there,' he shrugged. 'Must've rung off.'

Danny watched as Connor put the phone away.

'Con, what the hell's going on?'

'What do you mean?'

'I mean with you. You keep disappearing, and getting weird calls. You don't want me near that bag of yours, and Hannah said you were talking bollocks about angels yesterday.'

'I fucking hate that Robbie Williams song.'

'Very funny.'

'It's no joke. I really do hate that song.'

'Connor . . .'

But Danny didn't know what to say. Connor looked at him with a kind of mugging clown face, pursing his lips and raising his eyebrows. Danny could see he was fucked up, worse than he'd ever been before. They only had two days and two gigs to go before Glasgow, but turning up there with Connor in this shape seemed like a disaster waiting to happen. He felt helpless.

'Come on, we should get to the gig,' he said, pulling his jacket on.

'Need to freshen up a bit. I'll catch you up in a minute.'

Danny looked at him. 'I'll wait.'

'I'm not a fucking baby, I can make my own way to the gig. Go get the pints in.'

Danny eyed him a final time, then reluctantly headed out the door.

When he was sure Danny was downstairs, Connor phoned Nick.

'Did you just switch the phone off when I called?'

'No.'

'Fucking liar. How did it go?'

'What?'

'The meeting with Susie, dickhead.'

Connor stood thinking about what happened outside earlier, the static of the phone line in his ear.

'Well?'

'Nick . . .'

'Oh, Jesus. Tell me it went OK. Please. For everyone's sake.'

'She got the package, but didn't hand over an envelope.'

Silence.

'Tell me what happened.'

Connor talked him through it, the state of Susie, the handover, the interruption by the bus-stop bitches, Susie bolting it.

'So what you're saying is you let a couple of little girls get in your way, then Susie ran off.'

'That's about the size of it.'

'Why the fuck should I believe you?'

'I don't know. Why the fuck should you believe Susie?'

'How do you know I've talked to her?'

'I don't, but if you haven't already, you will soon, and she'll tell you that she gave me the money, then it's down to who you trust more.'

'I don't trust you, that's for fucking sure.'

'Thanks.'

'Welcome. But I don't trust that fucking slut either.'

'Well, then.'

'What's that supposed to mean?'

'I guess you're in a bit of a situation, aren't you?'

'You're really pushing it, Connor. If I were you I'd keep my fucking mouth shut.' There was a deep sigh in Connor's ear. 'Jesus fucking Christ, I knew this was a bad idea.'

'Working with me, or dealing with Susie?'

'Both.' Another sigh. 'Look, just bring back what you've got. Two envelopes and a package, right?'

'Right.'

'I'll see you when you get back to Edinburgh. And I'll think about whether to break your legs in the meantime.'

'Great. One other thing.'

'What?'

'I'm being followed.'

'What?'

'I told you before I thought I was being followed – well, I was right. I am.'

'Who by?'

'Some kid, a fan of the band, maybe.'

'Jesus, you gave me the shitters, there, Connor. I thought it was something important.'

'Thing is, I think he ran away from home.'

'Boo hoo.'

'You don't get it. The police are looking for him. He took his folks' car. Some expensive shit. It's been in the news. He's following us, and the police are looking for him. Which means the police are indirectly following me.'

'Can't you shake this kid off?'

'How would I do that?'

'Tell him to fuck off home.'

Connor didn't say anything. He didn't want to tell Martin that. He wanted Martin to stick around and look out for him.

'Look, Connor, just keep cool. The cops have no reason to suspect anything unless you give them one.' Connor thought about the unlicensed gun in his pocket. 'They don't have any reason to nail you on anything else, do they?'

'Of course not.'

'If you're lying to me . . .'

'I'm not.'

'Just try and hold your sorry arse together until you get back to Edinburgh, OK?'

'Sure.'

Connor hung up and pulled his coat on. He felt the gun in his pocket, took a hit of speed and a random pill, and headed out the door to face the music.

The gig passed without incident. Connor was blind drunk but the speed kept him upright. He felt like he was sleepwalking through the tunes. His legs were made of stone, his heart was full of lead and he regularly had to take big, deep breaths to make sure he was still getting air into his iron lungs. He clung to the mic stand, missing out most of his guitar parts as a result. As soon as they finished he slumped on a stool next to the stage with his hands on his thighs, his head bowed and his lank hair pointing at the floor.

Around fifty folk had turned up, an odd mix of clueless teenagers and older weirdos. Connor suspected this was just the usual turnout in the Kyle Hotel on a Wednesday night – it was Wednesday, wasn't it? He couldn't even raise his head to look around, it seemed too heavy to lift by willpower alone. He was in a fucking mess and he knew it, but he felt helpless. He sat feeling like shit with his eyes closed, listening to dizzying sounds all around him, voices incessantly chattering, the television in the corner now blasting out football commentary.

'You all right?'

It was Kate sitting next to him, rubbing his back. With a monumental effort, he lifted his head to look at her, his eyes taking a couple of seconds to focus.

'Yeah, I'm fine,' he said with a gentle laugh. 'Just a bit fucked. Not much of a crowd tonight. Not enough songs from *The Commitments* soundtrack for their liking, probably.'

Kate was staring at him with what seemed a mixture of pity and anger.

'I think you should talk to Hannah,' said Kate, with the look of a schoolteacher reprimanding a pupil. Connor nodded. He did have to speak to her. About all sorts of stuff. About how he loved her but he was so tired he could hardly keep his head up. About how he wanted to stop drinking, but didn't know where to start. How he'd been blackmailed into being a bungling, half-arsed drug courier. How he was almost out of speed, and that put the fear into him more than anything. He tried to shake his head, shake it free of alcohol and speed and pills and hash and worry. With another struggle, he spoke.

'You're right,' he said, Kate going in and out of focus in front of him. 'I need to speak to Hannah. You're right. I love her, you know. I really do. I love you, too.'

'That's beautiful, really it is. Now try telling her that,' said Kate, as Hannah sat down at the table and Kate left to start packing away the gear.

The sight of Hannah produced a kind of clarity in Connor's head, an anchor for his thoughts.

'Kate says I should tell you I love you,' he said, trying to sit up. 'But I realise I'm absolutely fucked, and you'll just think I'm saying it because I'm drunk.' He was rambling a bit, and maybe slurring a little, but it was going OK. 'Anyway, I just wanted you to know that I know I'm drunk, and I know you think I'm just saying I love you because I'm drunk but I'm not, because I really do love you, you know, and I am drunk, and that's maybe making it easier to say, but it's not the reason I'm saying it, the reason I'm saying it is the fact I love you to bits and I always will and you're beautiful and kind and generous and all the things I'm not and I love you.'

He felt like his lungs were collapsing. There was a burning in his chest that he tried to ignore, and pain in his stomach and face and head and his aching legs and he wanted to curl up and go to sleep, but he knew he never could. Hannah was looking at him, but he couldn't work out what the look on her face meant.

'I know you love me,' she said. 'And I can see you're fucked.' She let out a little laugh. Connor thought it was the most beautiful sound he'd ever heard. She was shaking her head and smiling. 'What a fuck-up of a boyfriend I've gone and got myself, eh?' She reached across and stroked his hair gently out of his eyes. 'What did I do to deserve you, Connor Alexander? What did I do?'

Connor wanted to say so much to her, stuff he couldn't untangle, feelings he couldn't unjumble, long threads of meaning and purpose that might always remain mixed up.

'No,' he said, swaying towards her. 'What did I do to deserve you?'

He tried to reach out to her face but she cut him off, taking his hand and holding it across the table. Then he suddenly remembered something important. Kate had gone to get drinks, hadn't she? She was taking her time. Where was she with his drink? He looked around but couldn't spot her, then turned back to Hannah. She was scanning the pub, too, and Connor thought at first she was searching for Kate as well. But then it seemed she was miles away, lost in her thoughts. She wasn't smiling any more and looked sad. He wanted to tell her it would be OK, that everything would be OK, but he didn't know how. So he just sat there in silence, holding her hand and wondering where the hell his drink had got to.

12

Fort William

'Brother we're in trouble now
We are lost and cold
Brother we are dead and gone
Welcome to the fold'

The Ossians, 'Justified Sinner'

'It says this is the most popular film location in Scotland,' said Danny. He wiped snow off the sign. '*Bonnie Prince Charlie, Highlander, Loch Ness, The Master of Ballantrae, The World is Not Enough* and many others,' he read out in a corny American voice-over voice. 'Jesus. *Highlander*. What a pile of shite.'

'A Frenchman playing a Scot and Sean Connery as a Spaniard,' said Paul. 'What the hell were they thinking? Mind you, it's still better than *Loch Ness*. Some schmaltzy Ted Danson crap about finding love in the Highlands with Nessie in the background. Christ.'

'Why didn't they just use Loch Ness?' said Danny. 'Why film this place pretending it's somewhere else?'

'It's probably the ideal of what Americans think Scotland looks like,' said Paul.

'Imagine they'd filmed it in Kyle of Lochalsh,' said Danny. 'That would decimate the tourist industry at a stroke.'

The five of them stood in the gentle snowfall looking at Eilean Donan castle. It perched on a rocky outcrop jutting into Loch Duich, connected to the mainland by a small stone bridge. They were in a large gravel car park by the side of the road, on their way to Fort William. Four large tour buses and a handful of cars were parked and gangs of tourists in lurid waterproofs and backpacks swarmed over the area. The castle stood impervious to it all, its small, high windows peaking slivers of light out into the afternoon gloom. Connor had never seen this place in real life before but he recognised it from films, television and tourist brochures. It seemed unreal that this was actually a place in Scotland, a place where people had presumably once lived, but which had been reduced to a caricature, tailor-made for tourists and their two-dimensional idea of the country.

'Fuck's sake,' said Danny, reading to the bottom of the sign. 'The current castle was built in the nineteen twenties. Here was me thinking this was some proper old place. Why don't they just paint the thing tartan and be done with it.'

Connor thought he'd quite like to see it painted tartan. And maybe wrapped up in a big ribbon. At least that would be more honest. Here's your Scotland, delivered just the way you like it, straight off a fucking shortbread tin or postcard, with snow-peaked turrets, a bridge and the lapping waters of the loch, and only eighty years old. In Scotland, you either had this piece of twee tourist bollocks, or you had Kyle of Lochalsh up the road – nasty, ugly and depressing. You either had Edinburgh Castle and *Brigadoon* or you had *Trainspotting*. But then *Trainspotting* had become another version of the same thing, hadn't it? They ran *Trainspotting* tours of Leith, for Christ's sake. Didn't that just misrepresent the country as much as *Highlander*? But then what the hell was the answer? Parts of Scotland are beautiful, and people like to look at beautiful things – where's the crime in that? Why not show a beautiful castle in a James Bond film, what the fuck does it matter if it was only built eighty years ago? Would it have been better to leave an eighteenth-century ruin? Or a twelfth-century one? How far back do you have to go before you have something authentic? What the fuck does 'authentic' even mean?

Connor couldn't really remember last night's gig, only tiny snapshots of being onstage, then arguing with Hannah back at the hostel, and Kate's angry face in front of him as he skinned up. Then it was morning. Had he slept at all? The fat, wet flakes of snow seemed to soak straight into him today, waterlogging his bones and making it almost impossible to put one leg in front of the other.

He imagined what it would be like to pull the gun out his pocket and start shooting at the castle, trying to make those lit windows blink out of existence with each bullet.

They passed a couple of lochs then turned right at some two-bit village and headed south to Fort William. A few miles down the road Connor, sitting up front with Paul, spotted a figure walking along the roadside. He was tall but hunched in the snowfall, white patches collecting on his shoulders and hair, and he had his thumb sticking out.

'Pull over.'

'We're not picking up hitch-hikers,' said Paul.

'I know this guy,' said Connor, grabbing Paul's arm. 'Pull the fuck over.'

'All right, Jesus. Take it easy.'

The rest of them looked at one another as Paul pulled in alongside the hitcher. Connor watched as the figure turned to look at the van. There was a moment of simple pleasure on the stalker's face as he saw he'd snared a lift, a look which turned to a fevered kind of panic when he realised who was in the front seat, and who the van belonged to. He stood there, eyes wide.

Connor wound down the window and was about to speak when someone beat him to it.

'Martin Gill!'

It was Hannah. She pulled open the door of the van and jumped out, making straight for Martin, who cringed as she approached. Connor was right behind her.

'Martin, what the hell are you doing out here in the middle of bloody nowhere?'

Martin stood there, a look of abject horror on his face.

'Wait a minute,' said Connor, 'you know this guy?'

'Of course I do,' said Hannah, 'he's one of my pupils. How the hell do you know him?'

Connor stood there not knowing what to say.

'Hang on,' said Hannah. 'This is your angel? The boy you said was following us round the country?'

'Em . . .'

'Christ, Connor, he's in one of my classes.' She turned to Martin, who looked as if he was ready to take a hit. 'Have you run away from home?' Martin stayed silent but eventually nodded. 'And you've been following us for the whole tour?' Another slow nod. 'We need to get you to Fort William, phone your parents and the police. They must be worried sick.'

'Hold on,' said Connor, as Hannah turned to face him. 'He's old enough to do what he wants, isn't he?'

'How old do you think he is?'

'I don't know. Seventeen?'

'Fifteen. Big difference. It's going to look fucking dodgy that he ran away from home, then turned up ten days later in Fort William with his young, female history teacher, isn't it? I can't believe this is happening.'

'Sorry, Miss Reid.' Martin's voice sounded thin and pathetic.

'Oh, for Christ's sake, Martin, call me Hannah. We're not in the bloody classroom.' She looked at him closely. 'Do you want to tell me what this is all about?'

Martin stayed quiet. Looking at him, Connor understood and felt disappointed. All along, he thought he'd been the focus of Martin's world, he'd been the subject of his stalker's adoration, the centre of his angel's universe. But that was bullshit. The truth was Martin was a schoolboy with a crush on his teacher. He hadn't been looking out for Connor, he'd been following Hannah, and worried about Connor as the romantic competition in some fucked-up way. Was that all it came down to? A schoolboy crush? Connor was amazed at his own self-centred assumptions, and depressed that the truth could be so bland, so boring. A thought flitted across his mind. What if it wasn't all one-sided? What if Hannah and Martin were having an affair, she'd led him on or something? That's why he was out here on the other side of the country chasing down his history teacher, having stolen his parents' car and probably their credit cards. He dismissed it. He couldn't believe Hannah would do such a thing. It was sick to even think it. But then, she hadn't been getting much satisfaction from their relationship recently, so why not look elsewhere? But a fifteen-year-old boy? A pupil from school? Insane. Just fucking insane.

As he watched, Hannah was already ushering Martin into the back of the van.

The snow turned to sleet as they unloaded the gear at the nicotine-yellow back door of the Ben Nevis Bar and Restaurant. Behind them cars and lorries sloshed up and down the A82 creating an edge of traffic noise that cut right through them. Martin sat on a low wall with a face like fizz, his hands rammed deep into the pockets of a coat which looked remarkably like Connor's. He hadn't spoken a word on the drive down, refusing to answer a string of questions from Hannah.

As soon as the gear was in the pub, Hannah declared she was taking Martin to the local police station, which the bar staff said was at the bottom of the High Street. She asked Connor to tag along. He thought about the gun and the pills and the bag of drugs and drug money. He didn't say anything and didn't move. Hannah glared at him, grabbed Martin and headed out the door.

Once she was gone, Connor announced he was off to get pain-killers from a chemist. He felt himself trembling and thrust his hands in his pockets so they wouldn't see. Immediately the feel of the gun in one pocket and what was left of the speed bag in the other comforted him, and he felt the tremors in his body subside.

He stormed up the High Street wondering what would happen to Martin, what Hannah would say to the cops. Gradually, he slowed down and let his mind soak up Fort William's commercial thoroughfare. A handful of gift shops lined either side of the cobbles, with names like The Hebridean Jewellery Shop, The Whisky Shop and, Connor's favourite, House of Scotland. Pubs and cafés advertised special deals that didn't sound too special.

He stopped. Nestled between a bookie's and a charity shop, right there in front of him, was a small wooden door and a wrought-iron awning overhead with Ossian's Hotel written on it in a cheesy Gaelic script, shamrock green. He stared for a few minutes. He didn't believe in signs or any of that superstitious crap, but this was a sign. Around him Christmas shoppers – a mix of bright-eyed tourists and darkly shuffling locals – flitted by in a blur of chatter and clattering feet.

There were no lights on in Ossian's Hotel. Connor went up to the doors, looked around, then rattled the handles. Nothing. He spotted a small sign which said the place was shut for winter, giving contact details and summer opening hours. He thought about breaking in, but passers-by were watching him suspiciously.

Ossian's Hotel. He couldn't unscramble what it meant. There seemed nothing to do but walk on. Two doors down was an offy. Maybe cooking whisky would help. He went in, bought a bottle and started necking it in a disused doorway. Shoppers watched him cautiously as he began sauntering down the street. He spotted the tourist office and decided on a whim to step inside.

It was roasting. He felt sweat bead up on his forehead and his armpits get warm. The place was bustling with visitors, and five middle-aged women stood behind the counter in matching sweatshirts and slacks. Connor slunk over to the large display wall, feeling dizzy and disorientated by the heat and noise. His gaze fell on a wall-mounted map. He felt a tightening in his stomach, and glanced around. No one was looking at him. He turned back and stared at the map.

It was a map of the area around Fort William. A few feet to his left sat the town, nestled at the top of Loch Linnhe, with the Nevis and Leanachan forests leaching out from it like blots of spilt green ink. Closer to him, fawn contours tightened over the peak of Ben Nevis, before spreading again to follow Glen Nevis. At the eastern end of the valley sat Loch Treig, which met the railway line as it headed south. Connor's eyes followed the railway line down until he was staring straight ahead at the thing he'd seen first of all. Loch Ossian.

He gazed at its small, oblong form for a long time. The blue shape was peppered with tiny dots of green at its western end. A small red triangle sat at the loch head and a double dotted black line led to a similar-sized red dot sitting on the railway line, with Corrour Sta and the number 408 printed beside it. He looked for a key to the symbols, but couldn't find one. He had no idea what scale the map was, but it didn't look far from Fort William to Loch Ossian. If this wasn't a fucking sign he didn't know what was. It was beautiful and teasing.

It was getting hotter and he felt sweat drip down his cheek. He walked over to the rack of maps and rifled through them, his fingers slippy. He couldn't read the numbers as sweat stung his eyes, but eventually he found the correct one. As he held it, it seemed to give off an ill, orange glow. He slipped it into his pocket, looking at anything except what his hands were doing.

The map seemed to give his body strength, and he powered towards the door, bumping into a postcard stand, then stumbling against a large woman who eyed him warily. The door was just a few steps away. Connor imagined that alarms would ring and security gates would come crashing down any second.

But then he was out, and nothing happened. He stood in falling sleet and streetlight glare. He took a deep breath, filled his body with shocking cold air, and headed back to the gig.

A chalkboard at the Ben Nevis announced the live entertainment. This week they had already missed Johnny Rebel, Powerhouse and the Ski Vixens. Jesus, how many covers of DJ Ötzi had been played within these four walls, thought Connor. Well, they wouldn't get singalong crap tonight. It used to be that Connor revelled in gigs like this – The Ossians against the world and all that shite. Nothing to lose, you could just get up there and go for it, and if ninety-nine per cent of the bastards hated you, who cared? As long as the other one per cent decided you were the best band that ever walked the fucking planet.

But the last two weeks had ground him down. He could feel his skin merge with the motes of dust that swirled around. He felt himself disintegrating into his constituent molecules, like an inverted big bang. The big suck. He laughed. That was his life, the band, this tour. A big suck. Whatever it was he'd been hoping to find out here, whatever the big idea was at the beginning, it hadn't happened. They'd drifted like phantoms round the edge of a country, barely interacting with the places and the people they'd encountered. They'd haunted Scotland for two weeks, and now Connor felt as immaterial as a ghost. He imagined going onstage tonight, an apparition barely even noticed by the poor souls in the place. A semi-solid presence, trying to entertain.

Entertainment? Was that what The Ossians did? Not here it wasn't. They wanted 'Mustang Sally' and a bunch of Oasis songs, stuff they knew and could sing along to. That's why karaoke was so popular, people didn't want to be sung to, they wanted to do the singing themselves. Why not? Maybe that could bring a community together. That's what used to bring communities together – that's what folk music was. If it happened to be songs that Connor couldn't stand, that was just his tough fucking luck. The Ossians were elitist. He only realised it now. They were musical snobs. Maybe not the rest of the band, but him, his songs and his attitude, it was all about snobbery. He was sickened by it.

He felt bad about Martin. For a while it seemed Martin would be his saviour, a strange spirit appearing at opportune moments to lift him out of whatever hole he'd dug himself into. But Martin was just a wee boy who fancied his teacher. He tried to think what it was like, being fifteen and so infatuated with Hannah that you'd steal a car and money and travel round the country. He couldn't imagine it, which depressed the absolute shit out of him.

'Where are the ladies?' he asked Paul, sitting with Danny.

'Hannah never came back from taking Martin to the police, so Kate went to see what the story was,' Paul replied.

'Thank fuck this is the last show before Glasgow,' said Danny. 'No offence, Con, or Paul, whichever one of you cooked up this bloody tour, but it's been pretty useless.'

'It's been an adventure, hasn't it?' said Paul hopefully. He looked at Connor, who was thinking about the tourist office. He couldn't get the image of Loch Ossian out his head. That small blue shape kept swimming in front of his eyes, and he felt the edges of the water throb in anticipation of his arrival.

'Fuck adventure,' said Danny. 'Next time, can we do a few shows where there are people who actually like our music?'

'We've made a few converts,' said Paul. 'The east-coast shows were cool. What about Aberdeen? That was a laugh.'

Danny looked at Connor at the mention of Aberdeen, but Connor ignored him.

'I suppose,' said Danny reluctantly.

'You're overreacting,' said Paul. He looked at Connor, who still hadn't spoken.

A bouncer came over to their table, wheezing with the effort of lugging his body around.

'You lads in the band?' he said in an Australian accent.

They nodded.

'On in ten minutes.' He was huffing and his face was wet with sweat.

'Fuck, where are the girls?' said Paul, looking around.

'They'll be here,' said Danny. 'I suppose I better get a round in. What're you after, gents?'

Connor thought of the whisky he'd drunk before returning from the tourist office. A whole bottle. It struck him that in the past he would have considered someone who drank that much an alkie. Ah. But he wasn't nearly loaded enough to play yet.

'Gin, cheers,' he said. 'Make it a double.'

As Danny headed to the bar, Kate and Hannah came in the front door.

'How'd it go with the police?' said Connor.

'What do you care?' said Hannah. 'If you were so concerned, why didn't you come?'

'Don't be like that. I just needed to clear my head, and I didn't think a police station was the place to do it.'

'Bully for you. You could've helped, you know. You'd seen Martin a few times, you could've told the police when and where. I was left trying to explain it all to the cops without really knowing what the hell was going on. They believed me in the end, once they'd got in touch with his folks. But it still looks bloody suspicious that I'm his teacher, and we're hundreds of miles away from home, and we just happen to be in the same place. They took my details. They wanted to take a longer statement now, but I explained we had a gig to do, and Kate arrived to back me up. At least someone gave a damn.'

'Hannah, I'm sorry. I thought . . . I thought it would be best if you handled it – you're better at that kind of shit.'

'That's just it, isn't it? I'm the one who always has to handle everything, cos you can't deal with the real world. You knew that kid had run away from home and was following us, but you did nothing.'

'Did he say why he did it?'

'Only that he was unhappy at home. Which could be said for ninety-nine per cent of fifteen-year-olds. They're all pissed off over something.'

'But why follow us? Does he have a crush on you?'

'I don't think so. He never showed any signs of having one in class, and they're usually pretty obvious to spot. I didn't ask him directly, of course, he'd die of embarrassment. He and some mates did come to a couple of our gigs. Maybe he just really likes the band.'

'That seems unlikely.'

'Who knows what goes on in a teenager's head? He liked the band, he hated his parents, he felt like an illegal adventure – maybe that's all it takes.'

'How was he funding it?'

'Had his dad's credit card. They knew, of course, but didn't want to cancel it, since it was his only means of food and shelter. They were following the trail of his charges to the card, always one step behind.'

'So what happens now?'

'His folks are driving up to get him. They'll be here in a few hours. And when he gets home he'll probably be a bloody hero to his classmates. Either that or have the piss mercilessly ripped out of him for following his teacher around the country. Probably a bit of both.'

'Poor kid.'

'Don't give me that. You were happy enough keeping him a secret all the way round this stupid tour.'

'But I didn't know who he was, or how old he was.'

Hannah fumed as she watched Connor play nervously with a beer mat. She was furious with him, for all this shite with Martin, for always being drunk. He was drunk now, for Christ's sake, she could see it in the cloudiness of his eyes. He'd deteriorated beyond belief in the last two weeks. She felt like she didn't even know who he was any more, looking at the shambolic figure across the table.

Kate had bought her a pregnancy test. She felt it in her pocket. She knew she'd have to use it, but not yet. She didn't know if she could handle the news. How could she bring it up, with Connor in this state? She would take the test after the gig, or maybe tomorrow, and keep her fingers crossed. Christ, what about the fit? That would have to wait until they were home. One crisis at a time.

Danny arrived at the table with a handful of drinks. 'We're on,' he said, then headed for the stage.

Connor watched Hannah as she left the table. She was angry, he could see that, but his brain was too mashed to do anything about it. So the adventure with his angel was finished. Now he just wanted to get this gig over with. And after that, he needed to work out how the fuck he was going to get to Loch Ossian.

The gig was another blur. Drenched in booze and speed, Connor drifted through the music like a wraith. He hadn't slept in as long as he could remember, he was awake but dreaming, a kind of ultra-awareness sweeping over him in waves, in between bouts of nausea and dizziness. His stomach hurt and his head pounded to the rhythm of Danny's drumming. At one point he saw Martin Gill in the crowd, but the unearthly way the figure drifted around the back of the room made him realise it was a hallucination.

Loch Ossian sat in the front of his mind. Why had he stolen the map? Why hadn't he told the others there was a place nearby named after the band? It was his place, his haven. A refuge from all the vacant faces staring at him and all his friends and their smothering, suffocating concerns.

When they finished a shortened set with no encore, the four of them couldn't even be bothered packing the gear away and just sat at a corner table drinking in silence. Connor imagined Loch Ossian and the lapping waves on its banks, the beautiful heather-strewn moorland, the hills falling away in the distance, maybe an eagle soaring high overhead, barely recognisable as he blinked and shaded his eyes from the bright sunlight. Even as he thought it, he knew how ridiculous it was. He was drawn back to the table by Paul talking.

'So. Glasgow tomorrow. All set?'

There was a pathetic silence among the four band members, as they looked at each other.

'Yeah, then home,' said Hannah. Connor noticed she wasn't drinking, but didn't say anything. She hadn't nipped outside for a fag either. Maybe she was still worried about the incident in Inverness.

'Forget home,' said Paul. 'We've got to focus on tomorrow night. Remember, if we kick ass, we could be offered a deal.' He paused. 'OK, Connor?'

'What?' Connor drifted up to the surface and looked around. 'You think I can't fucking hold it together, is that what you're saying?' He felt a knot of anger in his stomach, but knew Paul had a point. He was barely holding on to the edge of the world as it was.

'I'm just saying we need to be focused on Glasgow, it's got to be the absolute bollocks if we're going to impress this guy.'

'Fuck that,' said Connor. 'We're always the bollocks, aren't we? If this arsehole, whoever the hell he is, doesn't like us, then fucking tough.'

He realised he was shouting, and his hands seemed to be waving about in front of his face with a life of their own. He didn't really believe the words coming out his mouth, but he resented being told what to do.

'Paul was just saying we need to be on the ball, that's all,' said Kate. 'He's got our best interests at heart.'

'He was saying I can't be trusted not to fuck up, weren't you, Paul?'

Paul spread his arms out in conciliation. 'I just want it to go well,' he said softly, 'and for you guys to get the deal you deserve.'

'Maybe we don't deserve a deal. Maybe we're elitist, miserable indie pish, and we're just like every other two-bit bunch of chancers with guitars.'

'You don't believe that any more than I do,' said Paul. 'So don't give me that shit. The Ossians are the best fucking band in the world. I should know, I manage you bastards.'

Connor felt sick to his stomach. He had to get away from the table, from these people.

'I'm off for a pish,' he said. 'Want to come hold my dick for me, Paul?'

'There's no need for that,' said Hannah, reaching out for Connor's hand. Paul just sat with a rueful smile on his face.

'Why are you taking your bag?' asked Danny.

Connor pulled his hand away from Hannah's, turned and headed for the toilets.

He sat in the trap, dabbing speed with one hand and feeling the glowing gun in his pocket with the other. He got the map out and unfolded it to Loch Ossian. He stroked the blue water with his finger, feeling the coolness of it spread up his arm and through his body. It felt good. He'd always loved maps as a kid. He started to trace a line west from the loch, a tiny, black dotted line that headed through the valley floor of Glen Nevis, before twisting north along woodland until it came out at the east end of Fort William. He wondered how easy it was to get there. He sat like that for a while until he became aware of a dryness in his mouth. He folded the map, flushed the toilet and headed back out.

Except somehow he got lost. He emerged in a different part of the bar, brighter and noisier, with a pool table and a television in the corner of the room. When he tried to find his way back to the rest of the band, he turned one corner then another and found himself at the delivery door at the back of the pub. No one was about. He pushed open a side door and inside was the cellar, stacked with kegs of lager, and crates of beers and spirits. He looked around. Still no one about. He grabbed two bottles of gin, stuffing one into the kitbag, then headed out. He pushed open the back door and was outside in the car park overlooking Loch Linnhe.

It was snowing lightly, a flutter of flakes disappearing as they landed on the main road and the still water beyond. He sat on the wall, broke open the seal on the bottle and took half a dozen gulps. The burning in his throat, then stomach, seemed to warm him from the inside out, and he felt calm spread over him.

He thought about that fucking idiot Paul, mollycoddling him for the last two weeks. The whole lot of them doing it, in fact. He was twenty-four years old, for fuck's sake. He could look after himself. All his life, it seemed, these fucks had been wrapping him up in cotton wool, trying to protect him from what? Himself? The world? It was fucking pathetic.

He put the bottle down and took the gun out his pocket. It didn't mother him. He knew it was stupid and childish, but he really *did* feel better when he held it. Like it was made for his hand, moulded to his fingerprints, even, right down to a microscopic, molecular level. Some fucker in a pub once told him that according to quantum physics the molecules at the edges of touching objects actually interact, intertwine with each other a little. At the moment his hand and the gun were so close that part of his hand was the gun, and part of the gun was him. He didn't even think this was strange. It felt completely natural, as if the gun had always been an extension of his arm. It had just been misplaced for a while. After a time he put the gun back in his pocket and pulled out the map again. It was folded open at Loch Ossian and he rubbed it with his fingers, imagining the molecules of his hand merging with the glacial blue waters of the loch, the rugged browns of the mud, the greens of the grass and the trees.

Just then two German bikers on large BMW motorbikes pulled up and dismounted. Connor watched as they removed their helmets and examined their bikes. He folded up the map and stuffed it into his pocket. He picked up the gin bottle, took a few swigs and walked towards them.

'Excuse me.'

They turned from the bikes to look at him. He must be a

wretched sight, he thought. Wet, exhausted, drunk, strung out, unwashed, with his dirty coat, his lank hair and his wired, red eyes. He pulled the gun out his pocket and pointed it at them.

'Sorry, gents, but I need to borrow one of your motorbikes,' he said quietly, swigging from the bottle without taking his eyes off them.

Controlling the bike was simple once he got used to the bulk of it. A few early skids, then he had it sorted and was heading out of town. The turn off for Glen Nevis was easy to spot and he wobbled down it. Small, lonely houses appeared occasionally on the right and the wiry tangles of trees to his left hid the Nevis River, its burble drowned by the hum of the engine beneath him.

He laughed as his headlamp lit up a sign for 'Braveheart Car Park', then he passed a squat, square building which seemed to be some kind of visitor centre. Snowflakes were like ray-gun fire in the bike's headlamp, zooming at him and making him feel dizzy. The bike skidded and he felt sweat form on his forehead then instantly dry in the wind. The road took him over the river and the ominous, colossal bulk of Ben Nevis rose up in front of him. He continued a few more miles until the road ended in a gravel car park. He pulled up and swung the front of the bike round, using the headlamp to examine where he was.

There was only one path out of the car park apart from the way he'd come. A small wooden signpost said Corrour Station 15 Miles. It rang a bell. He took out the map. Next to Loch Ossian, there it was, Corrour Sta – that must mean station. And he could just ride there from here. He traced it once more with his finger, small fluffs of snow landing on the page as he did so. There was a path, a small black dotted line, all the way from here to there. It was that simple.

He revved up to the path entrance. He could see now it was rocky, winding and steep, impossible on motorbike unless you were a scrambling champion. So he would walk it. He'd read somewhere that the average human walks five miles an hour, so fifteen miles would take him three hours. Add a bit extra because of the terrain and he could be there in four. And there was this station, Corrour, where he could shelter. Sorted. He would need a torch. He searched the panniers at the back of the bike and sure enough there was a torch, along with two bars of Kendal Mint Cake that he stuffed in his pocket. Perfect. He imagined Hillary checking provisions before setting off from Everest base camp. Torch – check. Kendal Mint Cake – check. Map – check. Handgun – check. Bag of amphetamine sulphate – check. Bottle and a half of gin – check. Kitbag full of drugs and drug money – check. He knew this seemed idiotic, heading off into the hills at night in winter, but he knew how to walk and read a map, didn't he? And judging by the map, most of this looked pretty flat, so what was the problem? He switched the torch on, gave it a bang to make sure its rubber handle was sturdy, hoisted the kitbag on to his shoulder and set off into the snowy darkness.

He felt spooked by the loneliness of it, but happy about being spooked. This was what he was after, for fuck's sake, a bit of peace and quiet. He kept the torch on the path for the most part, whirling its beam up occasionally into the treetops where the wind sounded like wailing spectres. After a while the snow got heavier and the wind died as he clambered up an incline into a flat, open meadow. A waterfall roared in the distance, and he felt his head beginning to pound, so took some gin and a whack of speed. His feet were soaking already and caked in mud, but he could hardly feel them, and what he couldn't feel couldn't hurt him, right?

He followed the path along the side of the meadow, the trickling river somewhere to his left drowned out by the increasing rush of a waterfall up ahead. He waved the torch about hopefully in the din, but couldn't see anything so he trudged on, still feeling pretty good despite the thickening snow. He came to a ruined cottage. Who the hell would live out here? Half a dozen sheep lay sheltered in the tumbling stones, their heads sunk into their bodies against the elements. Weren't sheep supposed to be taken inside on winter nights? As if he knew anything about sheep farming.

He pushed on, feeling the speed buzz through the marrow of his bones, warding off the fat snowflakes, the icy mud underfoot, the sticky blackness of the night and the wind whistling down the glen into his face. The funnelled wind sounded like high-pitched voices, and several times he turned, thinking that someone was calling him, only to stare back into the blackness and hear nothing. He finished what was left of the first gin bottle and slung it with all his strength over his shoulder. As he walked on, the mountains on either side closed in. It felt claustrophobic, but in a good way. He enjoyed being flanked by the land, millions of years old, unchanging, unflinching and uncaring. The path became less well defined and large muddy puddles appeared. Rather than find a way round, Connor just sploshed through them, keen to get to Loch Ossian and the peace and quiet he imagined there. He was kidding himself, he knew, and even now he thought, why the fuck am I doing this?

'This could turn out to be the dumbest thing you've ever done,' he said out loud. The sound of his voice surprised him in this inhuman place, the darkness soaking it up like a sponge. He screamed as loud as he could, just to see what would happen. The sound disappeared as soon as it was out his mouth, as if the land were sucking it out of him. Could he turn back? Should he? What was back there, anyway? Just irritation and white noise, that's all. Just a country full of fucking morons. A bunch of people held together by absolutely nothing. Hadn't someone said there was no such thing as society? Well there wasn't any fucking society out here, just individual bundles of nerve and sinew and idiotic thought, like him.

He trudged on for what seemed like hours. The weather got worse, closing in, the snow somehow wetter and the wind a continual slap in the face. As long as he kept the river nearby he was all right. He checked the map again – it was getting soggy with the continual snowfall – and seemed to be on track. There were no obvious landmarks on the map, which was just as well, because since the ruined cottage he hadn't seen any. That seemed like a fucking lifetime ago.

He walked on. What else was there to do? Lie down and die?

'Get to fuck,' he shouted, and the world soaked it up without a blink. 'You think this is ridiculous, don't you?' he shouted at the darkness. 'Don't you!' Silence.

He walked some more, enough for four more hits of gin, two of speed, a slab of mint cake, which he chewed with a sarcastic grin on his face, and five more checks of the map, which looked increasingly sodden and sorry for itself. At one point he spotted another ruined cottage across the burn in front of him. It looked as fucked as the last place, but somehow the sight of it spurred him on. He walked faster now, the path hugging the waterside as the burn turned up to the left and twisted back round on itself.

After a while the steep hills at either side fell away and he was faced with a huge expanse of water. He could sense the calmness of its size, the immensity of it. He checked the map, which was almost falling apart at the sodden creases. This must be Loch Treig, he thought. Yeah, there was the small island, and the loch seemed to taper off into the distance, flanked by massive mountains on either side. That meant Loch Ossian wasn't far away. He measured along the map with his finger. He had already walked three quarters of the way! Piece of piss. Get it up you, nature. Hill walking was a fucking doddle. Why did everyone make such a fuss about it? He figured he'd earned a rest, so removed the kitbag and threw it to the ground, then plonked his soaking arse down on the sandy edge of the loch, drank some more gin, had a piece of mint cake and a dab of speed. The speed was beginning to get wet and cake up in the bottom of the bag. He tied the top of the bag tightly and stuffed it down the front of his trousers into his shorts underneath.

Right, time to get moving. He brushed the sand off his arse and headed east, with what could almost be called a spring in his step, despite the snow which was falling thickly again, a swirling wind that was getting stronger and an all-pervasive darkness.

But as he left the banks of the loch and headed what he thought was south, his high spirits quickly ebbed away. He started on the path, which was little more than a line etched in boggy marsh amid the whirl of snow and darkness. He was surrounded by sludgy peat bog, as featureless as the ocean. The snow was thick on the ground where it had drifted, but bare patches of brown still showed through. He headed for these areas initially, but found himself knee-deep in mud, so returned to heaving his solid legs through the deepening snow. The path had completely disappeared. He looked behind him and all he could see was the same featureless spread of brown and white. The light from the torch seemed dimmer now, sporadically flashing brighter for a moment, then weaker. He banged the front of the torch hard with the heel of his hand but the beam didn't change. He pulled the map out his pocket – it was in several pieces now, the folds an incomprehensible mush. He swigged more gin, the last of the second bottle, which he hurled into the void in disgust, losing his balance and falling as he did so. He landed with his face in a pool of icy mud. He fished the speed bag out his pants. It had crystallised completely in the soaking wetness. He smudged out a pinch of the mulch and swallowed it, which made his stomach sear with pain for a moment. He felt the unnatural burst of energy to his brain and used it to drag his limbs out the mire and continue.

There was supposed to be a path here, for fuck's sake, and a railway line nearby. If only the weather wasn't so fucking terrible, he might be able to see where the hell he was going. He figured that if he just kept heading in this direction – it was south, wasn't it? – eventually he would find this bastard loch, or at least the train station where he could rest for a bit. He felt his head throbbing and went to his pocket for the gin. It took him a few seconds to remember that he'd hurled the empty bottle away.

'Fuck,' he said quietly. He felt like screaming but there didn't seem much point. The land wasn't going to listen to his screams, it didn't care about him, wandering about in a blizzard in the wilderness. He trudged on a short distance, his legs like anchors in the sludgy mush of mud, snow and ice. The wind was blowing a gale now and he frequently had to stop in his tracks to let huge gusts play over him. He couldn't walk into it, not with these fucking legs. He wondered if he was getting frostbite. Maybe he should go back. But the wind and the snow were all around him now, and he didn't know any more which way he'd come. The ground had levelled off under the layers of mud, and he had no idea where the hell he was. He took the map out again but when his hand emerged from his pocket all it held was paper mush that slipped through his fingers and mingled with the swirling snow around him. No fucking map.

Great. This was looking like the most brainless fucking idea yet. The rest of the band would gloat over this one. They'd all be chortling to themselves around his grave saying 'I told you he was an idiot', 'What a stupid way to die' and all that shit. Well, fuck them, he wasn't about to die out here. He pulled his sodden coat tighter around him and struggled on, one torturous step after another, his bones and muscles and sinews and marrow and brain all aching with every step. The torch got dimmer and dimmer, either the battery was dying or water was getting in. Connor desperately wanted a drink to steady himself. He felt the burning cold in his feet and legs, his ears and nose. The wind roared around him, and he had to stop for longer times to let gusts blow past. He tried to keep moving when the wind died down, but as soon as he'd gone a few steps it would rage in his ears again. Snow spiralled in the inky nothingness around him and he screamed at it, swearing at the top of his voice for it to stop.

A few more steps, another rest, this time sinking to his knees in snow and mud. He felt dizzy and sick, and had lost all feeling in his fingers. He tried to reach into his trousers to get the speed but couldn't get his fingers to work, and dropped the torch in the process. The effort to bend down and pick it up seemed monumental, like he was a giant stone statue coming to life for the first time. If anything, the wind was getting stronger and the snow heavier, and he had to take individual steps, one at a time, resting in between, the blinding pain now pulsing incessantly through his whole body, making him even more desperate for a drink that would numb it all.

He couldn't go on. He felt as if his legs were set in concrete. He stood wavering in the gales. The only thing keeping him upright was the mud and snow his limbs were anchored in. He waved the pathetic beam of the dying torch around but could see nothing, just black night and white snow stretching all around him. His knees gave way and he pitched forwards into the soft whiteness. He imagined the snow as a large frozen pillow. Eventually he struggled on to his elbows and looked up.

In front of him only ten yards away was a large, reddish-brown stag, looking straight at him with impassive eyes. With its shoulders arched back and its antlers proudly displayed, it reminded Connor of a painting he'd seen somewhere. He tried to get up and move towards the animal but his legs wouldn't work. The stag seemed to be looking smugly at him now, impervious to the blizzard that battered against them both, the storm that had sucked all the life out of Connor's body. He reached for his pocket and managed through the burning pain to fish the gun out. The metal against his fingers was the first sensation he could remember feeling in a while and it felt good. He lay in the snow propped up on his elbows, the feeble torch beaming out from one hand, the gun, now pointing at the stag, in the other. He pulled the trigger. Nothing. His brain sluggishly thought about what he was doing. The safety. The safety was on. He dropped the torch and fumbled with the gun in both hands, trying to find the switch at the top of the handle, then fumbling to flick it. There. He readjusted his weight, picked up the torch, which was virtually useless now, and steadied himself.

Bang! Even in the raging storm, the noise of the gun shocked him. It was as if the bullet had gone through his brain, severing the synapses from each other, ripping their delicate connections apart like tearing fresh bread. At the sound of the gun the stag tensed its body but stayed absolutely still, looking right into Connor's eyes. He'd tried to kill it and missed. The two of them looked at each other for a long time, Connor imagining a look of pity coming into the stag's eyes. Then suddenly it leapt off into the terrible blackness, leaving him alone.

He started to cry. The tears ran down his cheeks and were whipped away in the wind, mingling with the relentless snow. He lay there weeping to himself. After a time he banged the torch pointlessly against the snowdrift. No light. He was utterly alone in the dark and he realised he was going to die out here, a pointless, idiotic death. He felt angry as hell. He hurled the torch up into the air and as it arced away in the night he fired wildly at it, using his free hand to steady the top of the gun. One, two, three shots rang out, the sound of each one puncturing his head before being quickly sucked away. He heard ringing in his ears and felt a new, excruciating pain in his hand. He brought it up to his face and in the blackness somehow sensed it was sticky with blood. He licked it and the bitter, ferric taste felt good on his tongue. He felt disorientated again and more tired than he'd ever been. He vomited thick, bloody bile next to where he lay. He put his head back in the snow and closed his eyes for a second to stop the world spinning, the wind raging and the snow swirling. His mind drifted off into complete nothingness, oblivion, and his body relaxed.

13

Corrour

'It's the hope that kills us
But it's the hope that keeps us alive
With our heads in our hands
And smiles on our faces
With a song in our hearts
And blood on our lips'

The Ossians, 'The Hope That Kills Us'

Scarlet shadows danced across his eyelids. The sweet, warm smell of burning wood came to him. He could hear the spit and crackle of a fire. His body throbbed with pain and, as he became more aware of it, the focus seemed to be his left hand. He opened his eyes.

He was wrapped in blankets and lying on a threadbare crimson sofa in a cluttered living room. A large open fire threw out reckless heat and an ornate wooden clock on the mantelpiece said it was nearly eight o'clock. The sound of breakfast being prepared started up in another room – sizzling, the clatter of pans, a kettle boiling. He had a blinding headache. A deeper pain was pulsing in his hand. He lifted it up to his face – it was bandaged tight. He turned the hand, examining it from all sides as if it was something he didn't recognise.

'You'll need to get that seen by a proper doctor.'

A short, round elderly woman of about seventy stood in the doorway. Her grey hair was pulled back in a bun and she wore a plain white apron over a dark dress.

'I'm a retired nurse, you see, so I bandaged it up for you, but you'd better get it seen to just in case.'

Connor wanted to speak but didn't feel his brain was up to speed,

243

so just watched the woman, who came into the room and started clearing things from a dining table.

'You're very lucky,' she said. 'You could easily have died, you know, out here in winter, in this awful weather. Just as well your friend found us.'

'What?'

The old woman was looking back at the doorway, and Connor followed her gaze. What he saw made his mind stall. Standing there looking serene and angelic as ever was Martin Gill. He started helping the woman set the table.

'We thought we heard shots,' said the woman as she bustled around with cutlery and placemats. 'Just as we were wondering what to do, whether we'd maybe imagined it, or if we should head out into the blizzard and have a look around, there was a knock at the door, and there was young Martin, saying we had to come quickly because his friend had collapsed on the moor. Turned out you were only fifty yards away, lying in the snow. Do you remember?'

Connor shook his head, feeling stupid. He looked at Martin, who was avoiding eye contact, busying himself with putting salt, pepper and glasses on the table. The woman looked at Connor.

'If you don't mind me asking, what on earth were you two doing out here?'

Connor thought about the question for a long time but didn't say anything.

'Martin never told me either,' said the woman. 'It's none of my business, I suppose, you don't have to tell me anything. Although I strongly advise you don't do anything as daft as that again.'

A large, broad bulk of a man in his late sixties came in from the kitchen. 'Ah, the dead has arisen,' he laughed. He smiled widely but there was concern in his eyes. 'And have we found out what the wanderers were up to yet, Selma?'

'Leave the boys alone, Donald. This one's only a laddie, and that one's still in shock.' Selma nodded towards Martin then Connor. 'How's breakfast coming along?'

'Breakfast is in hand, dear,' said Donald, heading over to a drinks cabinet. Then to Connor, 'I suppose you could do with a wee dram for the shock, son?'

'That would be grand,' said Connor.

'And for you?' Donald looked at Martin, who shook his head silently. 'Fair enough.'

Donald poured two large nips, handed one to Connor and sat down opposite him in an armchair. They clinked glasses. 'Slainte.' They took a drink, Connor downing his in one and feeling the slow creep of warmth spread outwards from his chest. They remained in silence for a while, just the crackle of the fire and sizzling from the kitchen in their ears. Donald sat looking at the fire, while Connor couldn't take his eyes off Martin, watching him as he quietly glided around the table, helping Selma lay it out for breakfast, never looking up. Once the table was set Selma and Martin headed back into the kitchen. Connor sat looking at the doorway for a while, still unable to get his head round anything. Eventually he spoke.

'Where am I?'

'Corrour Station House,' said Donald, refilling both glasses. 'Selma and I are employed by the estate owners to keep this place ticking over. You're bloody lucky, son. If it wasn't for young Martin there, you'd be a dead man. This is the middle of nowhere, you know. What the hell were you two doing out here?'

'Looking for Loch Ossian,' said Connor. The words sounded pathetic.

'You nearly found it. Just under a mile east of here. Where did you come from?'

'Fort William.'

'Jesus wept, son, that's nearly twenty bloody miles. Did you walk the whole way?'

Connor thought about the stolen bike, and nodded sheepishly.

'In that weather? Christ, you're a pair of madmen.'

Connor suddenly thought about the gun, and felt below the blanket for it. He noticed he was only wearing shorts and a T-shirt. The man watched him for a moment.

'If it's the gun you're after, it's safe. It's over on the mantelpiece. I didnae think you'd be needing it before breakfast. I'll not ask if you've a licence for that thing. That's your own business, I suppose.'

Connor finished his whisky. He felt his hand throbbing and held it up to examine it in the firelight.

'Powder burns, apparently,' said the man. 'You'd need to ask Selma more about it, she dealt with it. Happens when you don't fire a gun properly.'

Selma and Martin came back in carrying plates heaped with food – sausages, bacon, eggs, toast, tomatoes, haggis, mushrooms, beans and black pudding.

'Are you up to a wee bit of breakfast?' Selma said to Connor. He didn't feel at all hungry, but thought he should at least make the effort. He noticed that his clothes were drying next to the fire. He wrapped the blankets around his shoulders and sat at the table.

'I'm Connor, by the way,' he said as they started eating.

'We know, Martin told us,' said Selma. 'It's a pleasure to meet you. We don't get many visitors this time of year.'

Outside, the sky was lightening to a translucent grey colour as high, feathery clouds broke up, exposing patches of clear sky.

'Looks like it could be a fine day,' said Donald.

Connor watched Martin getting stuck into his massive plateful of food, shovelling large forkfuls into his mouth. Connor's brain and body still felt like they were thawing out, although the drams had helped. His hand hurt like a bastard. He tried to think about how he'd got here, how the fuck Martin was here, too, and how they came to be sitting with a charming old couple having breakfast as if life was normal. He couldn't work anything out, so he just sat looking out the window at the massive expanse of sky.

By the time they'd cleared the breakfast things away it was bright outside. Connor had eaten nothing but had drunk four cups of coffee, despite a burning sensation in his stomach with every sip.

'I'm just away to let the dogs out,' said Donald. 'Are you two up for the guided tour?'

Martin nodded shyly at Donald. Connor was feeling a lot better thanks to the whisky, the coffee and the spread of daylight filling the room. 'Sure,' he said to Donald as Selma gathered his clothes, checked they were dry and presented them to him. She disappeared into the kitchen. Connor dressed quickly, slipping the gun into his coat pocket, aware that both Donald and Martin were watching him. The three of them headed outside.

There was a snap in the air which burnt Connor's lungs as he breathed deeply. They stood outside the station house, a neat building in racing green and whitewash with a tiny spread of saplings lined up like midget soldiers outside. A railway line stretched off into the distance in either direction, dead straight, as far as he could see. In front of them, the track divided in two and ran either side of a small hut and a larger bunkhouse on an island platform. Beyond that the view was stunning – miles and miles of snowy moorland, with white peaks off in the distance. The sense of space was unbelievable. Connor felt minuscule in the face of the colossal stretches of land and sky all around him.

Donald had let two collies out the house, who were snuffling around the saplings and each other, their paws making fresh patterns in the snow. To their left a small wind turbine flicked round and a thirty-foot aerial emitted a low buzz. On the right was a path over the railway, a battered old signpost too weather-beaten to read and a dead tree, spindling into the crystal sky.

As Connor looked down the track he felt as if he'd been here before. There was something definitely recognisable about the place. He sensed deep in his mind that he'd seen this place, this exact place, sometime in the past, but he couldn't place it. He thought about it for a couple of minutes.

'This place looks familiar,' he said.

Donald and Martin turned.

'You would remember being here before, don't you think?' said Donald. 'It's the most remote railway station in Britain, they say, so it's not the kind of place you just stumble across. Present company excluded, of course.' He spoke with a little laugh as he looked first at Connor, then Martin. The three of them stood absorbing the view for a while as the dogs played with each other. Then Donald seemed to remember something. 'They did use this place in a film a while back,' he said. 'A trendy, young folks' film. You might have seen that.'

'What was it called?'

'Now, it had a funny name. It was all about drugs or something, but it had an odd title. What was it, again?'

Connor knew what it was. He remembered the scene almost exactly. He laughed.

'*Trainspotting*?' he said.

'That was it,' said Donald. 'Did you see it? Any good?'

'Yeah, I saw it,' said Connor. 'It was pretty good.'

It's shite being Scottish. This is where they filmed that scene, the one where Ewan McGregor does his rant about Scotland. The lowest of the low, the scum of the fucking earth, all that. And Connor had ended up almost dying here, trying to find a loch that was named after some fake ancient Scottish bullshit-merchant warrior poet, the same figure he'd named his pointless little band after. A smile spread across his face as he looked at Donald and Martin, then down the railway line into the distance, as if he expected his own personal train to come into view any second and carry him away.

'Christ, Connor, where the fuck are you?'

Paul was fuming.

'Corrour.'

'Where the fuck is that?'

'I'm not sure.'

'Is your mobile on? I've been calling all fucking night.'

'There's no reception here.'

'We were about to go to the police, you daft bastard. What happened last night? You just went to the bogs and never came back.'

'I went for a walk and got a bit lost, that's all. You know how it is.'

'No, I don't. Try telling Hannah and Kate that. They've been going out their fucking minds, Hannah especially. Where are you? We'll come and pick you up.'

'You can't.'

'What do you mean?'

248

'There are no roads.'

'No roads? How the hell did you get there?'

'I walked.'

'Is this a village or something?'

'It's really just a house and a railway station run by some old pair. Look, I'm fine, OK? Apparently it would take hours to get back to Fort William. There are two southbound trains through here every day, both of which stop at Glasgow. The quickest thing is for you to head down to Tut's and I'll catch you there.'

'This is fucking insane,' said Paul, exasperated. 'You want me to tell the rest of them that you've phoned and we can't pick you up cos there are no roads, and we'll just meet up in Glasgow? You think that'll go down well?'

'It's the most sensible option. Tell Hannah I'll speak to her tonight at Tut's. This is the easiest way of doing things. I'm sorry I never came back last night, but things got on top of me. And I really did get lost in the middle of nowhere. Actually, I was pretty lucky Martin found me.'

'The kid? What the fuck has he got to do with anything? Please don't tell me he's there with you.'

'Em . . .'

'Jesus, Con, he's supposed to be at home in Edinburgh with his folks by now. Hannah left him at the cop shop, for fuck's sake. What's he doing with you? What the hell's going on?'

'I'm not sure, to be honest.' Connor could hear Paul exhaling deeply. 'Look, the train is at half twelve, I can be in Glasgow by five. It'll take you that long to drive down anyway, won't it?'

'Probably, but . . .'

'In that case, I'll see you there. I'd better go, I'm using this old couple's phone. I'll speak to you in Glasgow. Cheers.'

He was relieved to put the phone down. He walked back through to the living room. No one was about and the drinks cabinet was open. He was about to take a bottle of single malt when Donald and Martin came in.

'Where can I find this Loch Ossian, then?' he said to Donald.

'Out the back door, straight ahead for about a mile.'

Connor turned to Martin.

'Fancy a stroll?'

They walked the short distance without speaking. Now, sitting on the bank of Loch Ossian next to Martin, the quietness was overwhelming. Back at the station house the wind turbine, aerial and generator all created background noise. Here, there wasn't a single sound in the whole world. The bank was mossy and slushy underfoot, and the water was a blue so dark it seemed like tar. Without a cloud in the sky, the day seemed too bright, the edges of things too defined. He'd never seen anywhere so in focus before. Out in the loch were half a dozen tiny islands, each with a spread of scabby conifers clinging to its surface. Beneath his feet, jutting out of the water at angry angles, were broken, dead tree stumps, the wood slowly decaying and sinking into the peat all around. The station house was behind them, but over the brow of a hill so that from here they could neither see nor hear it. The water was so calm it looked like glass, and Connor dipped his finger in to check it was liquid. The tiny ripples played out from the epicentre and disappeared into the distance.

So this is what he'd been looking for. Big deal. It was just another beautiful, scenic place. Scotland was full of them. Christ, ninety per cent of the country was probably as gorgeous and peaceful as Loch Ossian. The band had been touring round shitty towns on the edge of the country and even they'd seen some beautiful sights. Scotland was a big place. The middle of the country was a massive expanse of hills and forests and Christ knows what else. Peace and fucking quiet, plain and simple. It wasn't so complicated, was it?

But what did he need peace and quiet for? He was a kid of twenty-four and in a rock band, for fuck's sake. If anyone should be enjoying big cities with late-night bars, drugs and drink and partying, fighting in the streets on a weekend night and eating too much cheap carry-out food and watching football and going clubbing and taxi rides home and skinning up to come down, it should be him. But he was sick. Sick of it. Sick to fucking death of that world already, and only twenty-four. It was going to kill him.

Or, more accurately, he was going to kill himself. He'd almost done it last night. He felt ashamed as he swigged from the bottle of malt Donald had handed him silently back at the station house. Fifteen-year-old, cask-strength Laphroaig. Very nice. It tasted so peaty it was antiseptic. That's what he needed, antiseptic for the soul. To clean out the festering wound, the abscess in the heart of him, the big fucking infected hole in his heart.

He turned to look at Martin. In this perfect winter light the boy seemed more pure and unsullied than ever. He was naïve and innocent in a way Connor never could be again. He was untainted by the world, and Connor envied him. It struck him once more how much Martin looked like him – the same mess of black hair, the same green eyes, the same hollow cheeks and spindly limbs. They could be brothers. But Martin somehow put it all together better, didn't have any of the poisoned shit in his mind that Connor had, the stuff that ended up contorting Connor's face into a sight he hated. The stuff that made Connor feel like he'd unravelled, that his being was made up of disparate body parts barely held together by fragile threads of sinew and vein. His body and mind were fucking wrecked, almost beyond repair, and that realisation slowly started to creep through him as he watched this perfect, untouched, beautiful version of himself sit next to a serene loch, picking at bits of moss and stick on the ground.

'Martin.'

Martin looked up, but didn't hold Connor's gaze.

'Want to tell me what happened?'

There was a pause.

'How do you mean?'

'Last night.' Connor waved a finger behind him. 'Out there.'

Another pause.

'I found you unconscious.'

'Come on, Martin, I'm not a fucking idiot. We're fifteen miles from anywhere. You were following me, right?'

Martin moved his head slightly in agreement.

'Look, why not rewind back to Fort William. Start at the beginning.'

Martin hesitated, then looked away as he spoke.

'I was in the police station. My parents were driving up from Edinburgh. I didn't want to go back. So I walked out.'

'Just like that?'

'I wasn't under arrest or anything. I was just in an interview room. I waited till they were busy with a couple of drunks, then sneaked out. It was easy.'

'Then what?'

'I came back to the pub. I was almost there when I saw you in the car park with those bikers. Pointing a gun at them.'

Martin looked Connor in the eye now, and it was Connor's turn to look away.

'I saw you take one of the bikes. As you were leaving, the two guys ran into the pub, presumably to get help. They must've panicked, because they left the key in the other bike. I took it and followed you.'

'I didn't see you.'

'I came off the bloody thing at the Glen Nevis turn.' Martin lifted his right leg and Connor saw there was a large rip in the knee of his jeans and scrapes down the thigh. 'I've only ridden wee scramblers before, that was a big beast of a thing. Anyway, I got back on, but by that time you had quite a head start. I got to the car park at the end of the road, and saw your bike next to the start of the Corrour path. I put two and two together, and set off to find you.'

'Just like that.'

'I got some provisions from my bike's panniers. Food, a torch, these boots which happened to fit and this big dorky jumper.'

'But how did you know where I'd gone?'

'There was a path. I just followed it. After a while I found an empty gin bottle, so guessed I was on the right track. It was like you were leaving a trail for me. Then I heard you shout a few times as well. I tried shouting back, but you mustn't have heard me.'

Connor tried to remember. Had he thought he heard shouts or screams? Most of last night was a blur, a mush of visions jumbled together. 'But I got lost, there didn't seem to be any path after I stopped at that big loch.'

'Really? I followed the path up the hill all right. Then I found another gin bottle. So I just kept going.'

'But how the fuck did you find me in the end? I mean, there was a blizzard and miles and miles of fucking moor.'

'I heard shots. One shot at first, so I headed in that direction. Then a few more as I was getting closer. But it was just luck that I found you, I suppose. I almost stumbled over you on the ground. Maybe it was fate.'

Connor didn't believe in fate. Although fate was doing a pretty good job of changing his mind at this rate.

'And what about the station house? I didn't see it and I was only a few yards away. How did you know it was there?'

'Maybe the visibility got better, or the snow eased off or something. I saw a faint light, then what looked like the outline of a house. I tried to drag you that way, but I couldn't lift you. So I went and got help.'

Connor was having trouble taking it all in. It seemed too fluky to be real. By rights, he should be dead. Is that what he wanted? Was that why he'd come out here in the middle of a snowstorm at night? To die? Well, if it was, it hadn't worked. Martin had saved him. His guardian angel came good after all. He really had been looking out for Connor all along. Through some sort of ridiculous, corny miracle, or some piss-taking divine intervention, he was still alive. Wasn't that a kick in the fucking crotch.

'I guess I should thank you for saving my life.'

'It was nothing.'

'It wasn't nothing, it was everything.' Connor put his hand on Martin's shoulder, as Martin looked away at the loch, embarrassed. 'Thanks.'

They sat in silence, looking out at the elemental, primeval stillness of the world in front of them. Eventually Connor spoke.

'There's something I don't understand.'

Martin looked at him but said nothing.

'Why?' said Connor.

'What do you mean? I just did what anyone else would've done.'

'No, I don't mean why save me, I mean the whole thing. Why

run away from home, why follow us round the country? Why follow me into the wilderness? Why?'

Martin just shrugged.

'Were you unhappy at home?'

Martin stayed silent for a while. 'Yeah,' he said finally.

'Was someone hurting you or something? Abusing you?'

'Nothing like that.'

Martin suddenly looked like a typical teenage boy, confused and unsure of himself. Connor had always assumed he was older than fifteen, but now, if anything, he looked younger.

'Then what?'

'It's just . . . it's difficult to explain. I have these . . . thoughts, I suppose. Feelings. I don't know, it's confusing. If Mum and Dad knew what goes on in my head, they'd freak.'

'Come on, everyone has weird thoughts. It's nothing to get worked up about.'

'That's easy for you to say.'

Connor thought about everything that had gone on in his head, all the ridiculous crap that had brought him here, to this beautiful, lonely place next to this worried teenager.

'I've probably had weirder thoughts than you.'

'I doubt it.'

'Remember in Kyle, I told you I thought you were an angel.'

Martin looked at Connor and a quizzical grin spread across his face.

'But that was a joke, right?'

Connor shook his head. 'I kept seeing you – at gigs, beaches, on television. I seriously thought you were an angel come down from heaven or something, visiting me for some reason, trying to tell me something. And I don't even believe in God.'

'You're not serious.'

'I'm deadly serious.'

'That is weird.'

'Told you.'

More silence between them.

'Was it something to do with Hannah?'

254

Martin looked uncomfortable.

'Not exactly.'

'Lots of kids have a crush on their teacher, it's normal.' Connor put a reassuring hand on Martin's leg. 'And Hannah is pretty cute.'

'I don't have a crush on her.'

'What then?'

Martin looked down at Connor's hand on his leg, then back up at his face. He was blushing. He leant in and kissed Connor on the lips, forcefully, quickly, then pulled away and held his gaze for a moment before looking away at the expanse of Loch Ossian.

'Jesus Christ,' said Connor, taking his hand from Martin's leg. 'What the fuck?'

Then he twigged. Everything seemed to slot into place, although Connor could scarcely believe it.

'Me? You fancy me?' Connor was almost laughing, it was so ridiculous, but tears were welling up in Martin's eyes. 'Fuck, Martin, I'm flattered and everything, but I'm not gay.'

'I know that. Neither am I.'

'Aren't you?'

Martin was crying now.

'I don't know. Maybe I am. I don't know. If my dad knew, he'd fucking kill me.'

'Don't be stupid, it's perfectly normal.'

'That's not what he thinks.'

'I'm sure he'd be fine with it if you were.'

'I don't even know if I am, you know. Gay. That's what's so bloody confusing. I haven't felt like this about other boys. Or girls. Just you.' He turned to look at Connor, tears streaming down his face. 'I love you, Connor.'

The words floored him. He didn't know what to say. This was totally fucked up.

'No, you don't, Martin. It's just a crush.'

'Don't say that, it sounds so trivial and stupid.'

'That's not what I meant. Of course it's not trivial. But you know I'm going out with Hannah, so you know I'm straight, right?'

Martin nodded, sniffling as he wiped his eyes with the backs of his hands.

'And anyway, I'm – what – nine years older than you? You're just a kid.'

'I can't help the way I feel.'

'Martin, I . . .' Connor just didn't know what to say.

'I've felt this way for months,' said Martin, blurting out the words. 'Ever since I first saw The Ossians. A few of us came along to a gig to see Miss Reid – Hannah – see what her band was like. The first moment I saw you it hit me like a punch in the chest. You looked so amazing up there on stage, totally cool and, I don't know, in control.'

Connor laughed, but quickly stifled it when he saw the look on Martin's face.

'Don't laugh at me.'

'I'm sorry, Martin, really. I'm not laughing at you. But, in control? Me? Are you sure you've got the right guy?'

Martin looked away.

'Martin, look. You've seen me acting as an unwilling drug courier for a twat I owe money to, unwittingly take part in a gull massacre, get more fucked up on drugs and booze than any human should, steal a motorbike at gunpoint and almost kill myself in the middle of the Scottish wilderness. I *would've* killed myself if it hadn't been for you. You're the cool one, you're the one in control. I'm the biggest fuck-up you're ever likely to meet. I'm a complete arsehole, a selfish wanker, a pretentious dickhead. Just ask the rest of the band if you don't believe me. Ask Hannah. I don't know why she puts up with me.'

'If you're an arsehole, what does that make me? I stole my dad's car and credit card and buggered off round the country chasing after you like a . . .'

'Like a what?'

'A silly little schoolboy. Which is what I am.'

'Jesus, Martin, I should be learning from you, not the other way around. You're a fifteen-year-old kid who's independently travelled round the country on your own for two weeks, all the while keeping your head together. You trekked fifteen miles in a snowstorm and saved my life. Hey, wait a minute – how are you able to drive?'

'I just am. It's easy.'

'But you can't have a licence.'

'No.'

Connor shook his head.

'Anyway. You saved my life, Martin. You saved my fucking life. I'm in your debt for the rest of my sorry little existence. I should be learning from you. You're the mature person here.'

As he spoke, Connor realised the depths he'd sunk to. He really could learn about how to be a proper human being from this kid. Here was a boy who'd followed his heart, taking him round the country on a trip he didn't understand, all the while being level-headed and smart along the way. What had Connor done over the last two weeks except run away from shit? Take more and more pills and speed and whisky and gin and beer and hash and coke and more pills just to keep the real world at bay. He'd been abusive to friends and strangers alike. He'd been rightly beaten several times for being a total wanker, and he'd brought that on himself deliberately, so he could play the battered victim, a martyr that only he believed in. It was all so pathetic. Seen through Martin's eyes, he must look like the sorriest cunt in the history of the world.

He'd wrapped this whole thing up in a flag. From the band's name, which now seemed like a puerile joke, onwards, he'd been banging on about looking for the real Scotland, a tangible nation, something he could call home at least. But he'd missed the point. He hadn't even been able to read more than thirty pages of that book of Ossian's poems, what the fuck did he know about the history of this sorry little country anyway? It wasn't a matter of inventing or denying some romantic, made-up ideas about nationhood or homelands, or worrying about borders or the fucking English, it was just about getting on with life, getting on with people, and being honest and kind and trying not to fuck up too much. It wasn't much of a life philosophy, but it was a fucking start.

But how could he start again? His body was a wreck and he

needed alcohol and drugs to stay alive. That's how he felt, deep in the marrow of his bones and in the tainted blood running through his veins into his brain, which was in worse shape than his body. He was sitting here with a fifteen-year-old schoolkid, in the middle of nowhere, swigging from a bottle of cask-strength whisky as if it was fucking juice. He didn't know what to do, and he felt like he didn't have the strength to sort himself out. But he wasn't going to run away any more. He was going to Glasgow to face up to everything. Face up to himself.

'What's going to happen with the band?' said Martin quietly.

'What?'

'The Ossians. Reckon you'll get signed?'

The Ossians couldn't go on. He realised now that he didn't want to get signed. What would happen if they did? Relocation to London – a bigger, brighter shithole to crawl about in like a lab rat and slowly kill himself? No thanks. Endless promotion and gigging, talking and explaining about the band, and all the while hating everyone who was idiotic enough to be interested in them and their dumb-arsed, pathetic, insular tunes? Fuck that. He hated The Ossians. He hated what he'd become as frontman of the band, a self-important dickhead playing at being ironic about the whole thing, but secretly loving the shallow praise, the adoration of kids like Martin, the puerile, meaningless nature of everything they did, which was nevertheless lapped up by fans and critics who didn't know anything about anything.

'The Ossians are splitting up.'

'What? Why?'

'I hate this irrelevant, shitty little band. It's been my excuse for being an arsehole for years now, and I don't want an excuse, I don't want a hand-fed reason to fuck up, to act the cunt for the rest of my life. We'll play this gig tonight, then it's all over.'

'That's a shame.'

'Why?'

'I love The Ossians. I think you're great.'

'We're not, we're shite. Do you play an instrument?'

'No.'

'Learn one and form a band. I'm sure you'll be a lot better at it than me.'

'I doubt that.'

'Give it a go. If you're shit, it doesn't matter, as long as you enjoy yourself. I haven't enjoyed being in The Ossians for years.'

With the realisation that the band was finished, Connor felt a huge surge of relief. He wouldn't have to do this shit any more, the tour was almost over, the band was almost finished, he could go home soon and sleep for a month. He could try to dry out, stay off the pills and blow, maybe he and Hannah could go away somewhere for a holiday, or even a new start. Maybe they could come and live somewhere like this. But that was running away, and he'd had enough of running away. Besides, it was a joke, thinking he could live somewhere as remote and quiet as this. For all he moaned about his life in the city he would be lost in a place like Loch Ossian. It was easy to sit here for a few hours and glamorise life in the country. He could walk the dogs, maybe start smoking a pipe, Hannah by his side as they mended fence posts or whatever the fuck people did around here. It was pathetic. That was just as useless a life as the one he was living now, if he didn't sort his shit out. And that's what it came down to – straightening himself out. For the first time in as long as he could remember, he wanted to do it. The desire was there. But he doubted he had the strength of character, the will to face the world without drugs, and with only reasonable amounts of booze. See? Already he was moving the goalposts, ruling out the idea that he could do without alcohol completely. Fuck, this was going to be impossible. Life was going to be impossible from now on, no matter what he did.

Something came to him from last night.

'Shit, the bag. What happened to my fucking kitbag?'

'I don't know.'

'Didn't I have it when you found me?'

'No.'

Connor tried to think back. Had he kept it until the end? He couldn't picture himself having it later on, but then he couldn't remember much. Christ, he must've left it somewhere out there, maybe when he stopped at that bigger loch. Maybe he'd put it down and just completely forgotten about it, or had he chucked it away in a pointless rage? Fuck.

'We have to look for it.'

Martin gave him a sceptical look.

'We'll never find it. There are miles of blanket bog and frozen moorland out there.'

'You found me, didn't you?'

'That was a fluke.'

'Maybe we'll get lucky again.' Connor said it, but looking around at the colossal expanse of gorse, heather and moss, he knew it was pointless. The bag was gone, the drugs and money were gone. Nick was going to fucking kill him. In a way, he was relieved. Now he could really start afresh, without all this hanging over him. What's the worst that could happen? They wouldn't actually kill him, would they? So, what, they'd badly beat him up? He'd be in hospital for a while, but eventually he'd get out and be able to start again from scratch.

'I don't think we've got time for a search,' said Martin. 'Your Glasgow train's in half an hour.'

'Maybe you're right,' said Connor. 'Hang on, what do you mean, *my* Glasgow train? Aren't you coming, too?'

Martin looked steadily and confidently at him.

'No.'

'Don't you want to see The Ossians' last-ever show?'

'I think maybe I've seen enough of The Ossians.'

'I know how you feel. But I'd like you to be there. For the last one.'

'I don't think so.'

Connor looked at Martin, who seemed sure of himself. He felt a swell of admiration.

'What are you going to do?'

'I'm not sure.'

'Are you going to meet up with your folks in Fort William?'

'I don't know.'

'They'll be worried sick. You should call them at least.'

'I could stay here with Donald and Selma. They seem nice.'

'I'm sure they are, but that's a pipe dream.'

'You think?'

'You can't stay here forever. You can't run away from your life, that's one thing I've learned on this senseless tour.'

Martin smiled. 'Maybe just a while longer, though. The train the other way goes as far as Mallaig, where you can get a boat to one of the islands. I've always fancied a ferry trip.'

Connor shook his head, but was smiling.

A high-pitched roaring sound came from far off, and in the distance they spotted a low-flying military jet heading straight down the loch towards them. The plane was overhead then gone, the whining scream of the engines peaking just as quickly then trailing off into the piercing blue of the winter sky.

'Come on, we should head back,' said Martin, getting up. 'You've got a train to catch.'

Connor rose and followed Martin away from Loch Ossian, stopping to look back at the serene, inky waters that had lured him into almost killing himself. It was a beautiful place, all right. Another flash of something came to him from last night.

'Did you see a stag?'

'What?' said Martin, turning back.

'Last night. When you found me. Did you see a stag?'

'No.'

Martin looked at him. Connor just shrugged and shook his head. They headed back to the station house, and the trains that would carry them to different futures.

They heard the train before they saw it, the clank and chug of the engine in that sharp, rarefied air sounding to Connor like a harbinger of doom. He turned to Martin, who was smiling beatifically at him in a way that was almost unbearable.

'I don't know what to say,' said Connor.

'Don't say anything.'

'I owe you everything.'

'Don't be ridiculous.'

'I owe you my life, at least. And probably my sanity.'

'Your life and sanity are in your own hands now.'

'Oh fuck,' laughed Connor, 'don't say that.' He turned to Donald and Selma and thanked them, promising to repay their hospitality and the lend of a train fare, a promise which they waved away. He turned to Martin as the train slowed for its approach to the platform. 'Are you sure you don't want to come and witness the ignominious end of The Ossians?'

'I don't think so.'

'I could use the company.'

'You don't need me any more.'

'You don't need *me* any more, Martin, that's not the same thing.' Connor was close to tears at the thought of his guardian angel about to head in the opposite direction, away from this solitary place. 'Maybe we could hook up in Edinburgh sometime in the future, when things have settled down?'

'Maybe.'

'How will you find me?'

'I'll find you.'

The train stopped, and the handful of punters on board were staring at the foursome on the platform. Connor hugged Martin, squeezing his thin shoulders, then stepped on to the train.

'Enjoy the islands,' he said as the automatic doors closed between them.

As the train started, he felt like a naughty kid being sent back to boarding school. He didn't look back. He slumped in his seat and felt an overwhelming bout of nausea wash over him. Out the window the sky was a blinding blue, painful to look at, and the light skited off the snow-covered moorland, filling the carriage with unearthly illumination. Connor closed his eyes. They passed some trees and the quick flickering of dark and light on his eyelids made him feel even more like vomiting. He thought of Hannah having her fit in Inverness and tried to will himself to lose control in similar fashion. He relaxed his body, hoping something otherworldly would sweep in and take control, some rush of extraneous force that would make his mind stop working for a moment and let him slip into the void of epilepsy.

But nothing happened. After a while he opened his eyes. Sitting opposite him was a sinewed and leathery man of about forty, with bags of fishing and camping equipment and a small border collie looking up at him obediently. Connor went to pet the dog.

'Careful, I reckon he might have ticks,' said the man. His accent was northern England somewhere. 'The deer are riddled with 'em, you see, and I reckon he might've picked 'em up out there.'

Connor withdrew his bandaged hand and examined it. It seemed to be pulsing a message to him, shards of pain shooting up his arm. He took out a packet of painkillers that Selma had given him and dry-swallowed four.

'A lot of deer about?' he said.

'Loads of 'em this time of year. They come down from the mountains in winter, better feeding, you see.'

Connor looked outside and winced at the sharpness of light on snow. He fished out Donald's whisky bottle and offered a drink to the man, who smiled and glugged down a mouthful, handing the bottle back.

'Been fishing?'

'Sure have. I work as a woodcutter nine months of the year, that way I earn enough to spend the winter fishing. Can't beat it, being out there with no one else about, just you, the water and the fish. And this little fella, of course.'

The dog's tail thumped the carriage floor. The thought of ticks leaping about in its fur unsettled Connor and he imagined tiny beasts launching themselves at him. The thought made him itch all over and he started to scratch at the back of his bandaged hand, then up his arm. He suddenly couldn't stand to be opposite this man and his dog. He felt itchy and trapped, hot and sweaty. He got up, saying he was going to the toilet, and headed down the carriage, bumping from side to side with the movement of the train, until he reached the doors he'd stepped through getting on board.

Out the window, he saw two scruffy kids playing in the snow

beside a green corrugated-iron hut. They were descending now, down off Rannoch Moor, and in the distance Connor saw little reflective glimmers as cars trundled along a road, bouncing sunlight and snow glare back off their metallic bodies. He wondered if one of those glimmers was The Ossians, heading south to meet him in the sweaty, dank confines of King Tut's.

His thoughts were interrupted by the sound of his mobile. As the train descended, the reception must be coming back. It kept beeping with all the messages that had been left for him in the last twenty-four hours, time he'd spent blissfully out of contact, trying to kill himself in the Scottish wilderness, or whatever inane shit he'd been doing. He let the phone burble in his pocket until eventually it stopped. There were ten phone messages and seven texts. Half were from Paul, half from Nick. He didn't bother to read any of the texts, or listen to any of the messages. He'd already spoken to Paul, and he didn't have anything to say to Nick, at least not anything Nick wanted to hear. As he was standing with the thing in his hand, it started ringing. He jumped. That fucking tinpot tune. He looked at the screen. Nick. He'd had enough of him and the stupid phone calls and this whole fucking escapade. He pressed answer and shouted into the mouthpiece, 'I've lost your fucking bag full of money and drugs, get over it.' He opened the window and hurled the phone out as hard as he could. He watched its curved trajectory as the train sped away, then saw it land with a flump in the snow, before the train turned a corner and it disappeared out of sight. He wouldn't be able to listen to 'Smells Like Teen Spirit' ever again, Nick had fucking ruined that song for him. He felt relief now the phone was gone, but an undercurrent of worry at what Nick and, more importantly, Shug would do to him when he returned from this little jaunt empty-handed. Fuck it, he couldn't do anything about it now. He'd have to take what was coming to him, either that or avoid them for the rest of his life, which wasn't exactly likely. He'd worry about it after tonight. One shitty little thing at a time.

He went to the toilet and necked four more painkillers, a final pill he found deep in a pocket and a lump of crystallised speed, downing them with whisky. He felt better, despite a burning in the pit of his stomach. As he left the toilet, two girls about four years old came running down the corridor towards him. Both wore pink dresses and had their hair tied in bunches with pink ribbon. Connor thought they were the cutest things he'd ever seen, the snow glare lighting up their perfect faces. As they got closer he heard one of them shouting over her shoulder, 'Last one there's a rotten egg.' He couldn't believe kids were still saying things like that.

'Where are you running to, girls?' he said, crouching down and feeling unsteady on his haunches. Their eyes widened as they stood looking at him and he saw himself through their eyes – stinking of booze, bleary-eyed, hand bandaged, unwashed, unsteady, in a dirty long coat standing outside the toilet accosting them. He felt ill.

One of the girls nudged the other, and they ran off quickly without saying a word. He looked down the carriage and they were standing talking to a woman and pointing back in his direction. He felt his face flush and the pain in his hand got stronger as blood coursed through it. He turned and walked the other way, feeling his back burning. Towards the rear of the train he picked an empty seat. He sat down feeling nervous. Jesus, fuck, now he was scaring little girls on trains. What the fuck was wrong with him? He had to try and hold his shit together for one more night.

Outside, clouds were predictably gathering. Of course, it would be raining by the time they got to Glasgow. It always rained in Glasgow, as if that blighted city had invented the stuff. They were travelling through heavily conifered land now and thickly packed pine trees lined the railway track, throwing sodden, murky light into the train as they sped past. They stopped somewhere, shunting back and forth to attach or detach carriages, the only view out the window being hundreds of already logged trees, awaiting collection.

Next stop, Ardlui, they waited ten minutes. Passengers got off to stretch their legs and have a fag, despite a thin smir in the air. Connor stood at the back of the platform, the heavy, sweet smell of wet pinewood in his nostrils, avoiding the stare of the pink girls' mum, swigging whisky and massaging his sore hand, which seemed like an alien extension of his arm. A train heading in the other direction stopped, too, the passengers sauntering on to the platform to mingle and smoke fags, chat and stretch. Connor felt like switching trains, heading back up to Corrour, Loch Ossian, Martin and peace. But he couldn't go back there, he'd been through all this already, it was a fucking joke to think that he'd be able to survive up there. And what? Play happy fucking families with Donald, Selma and Martin? Aye, right. Martin was probably gone from there already, heading fuck knows where.

The people from the other train had the same vacant look in their eyes as the herd from his train. The same resigned acceptance of their lot, the same automaton shuffle. He was standing on the platform with a bunch of hapless drones, all moving slowly round each other, never interacting, never communicating, all of them living in their own little worlds. But he wasn't any better than them, he was worse, because he scorned their ambitions, belittled their dreams, objectified their lives until they were nothing to him, because that was easier than getting involved. He went back inside and drank some more whisky on his own.

The train snaked south, barbed-wire fences appearing either side of the track. They sped past large signs reading 'MOD Property Keep Out'. One large loch stretched into another, as the water gradually widened, becoming the Clyde. Miserable, grey, two-storey box houses sprouted out of the wet landscape, their insipid colour like damp stains on the land. As they trundled along the waterside the weather worsened, the rain becoming heavy and flecking the river surface with spots. Despite this, Connor spotted three boys ripping planks of wood from a rickety old quay, and a middle-aged man smacking golf balls into the river from a rubbish-strewn beach. Bottles, glass and plastic crap were everywhere now, washed up on the shore from fuck knows where. Dingy tenements and high-rise flats appeared on the horizon and they passed a parade of warehouse shops, DIY stores and electrical retailers, all squatting by the river's edge as if getting ready to jump in.

The end was approaching. They crawled through Glasgow, the rain relentless from a sky the texture of burnt wood. Connor downed the last of the whisky and slung the bottle under his seat.

He looked at his ticket, which he was fiddling with in his seemingly uncontrollable bandaged hand, and only then realised it was the thirteenth. Friday the thirteenth. He smiled grimly as the train pulled into Queen Street Station. He remembered sitting backstage at the Liquid Room, all those days ago, and laughing that the final gig was on Friday the thirteenth. It seemed back then like a big joke. Now he wasn't sure. The train came to a juddering halt and people started to get off. He sat. The guard came down the train emptying bins and told him this was the end of the line.

Feeling the weight of the overhead storm clouds pushing him into the earth, trying to crush him into the dirt, he got off. He slowly made his way out the station feeling the ache of his throbbing hand by his side. He headed out into the bleak, oppressive, treacherous city, his mind as dark as the winter streets.

14

Glasgow

'We hit the wall drinking
But we drank straight through it
We drank ourselves stupid
What else were we trained to do?'

The Ossians, 'Alcohol'

By Christ his hand hurt.

He needed a drink. He was in no hurry to get to King Tut's, apprehensive about meeting the rest of them. What could he say about Corrour and Loch Ossian? How could he tell them The Ossians were splitting up? What about these A&R guys that were coming? He needed to talk to Hannah, but couldn't think straight, distracted by the incessant pain pulsating in his bandaged hand. It seemed to be scudding messages to the rest of his body that his brain didn't know about, taking over his limbs and his heart, as if that injured hand was an invading army, infiltrating his system and taking charge of this hapless shell of a body. He imagined it as a coup, his brain being ousted from power by his malevolent hand. What ridiculous pish.

Tut's was getting closer as he trudged his way up St Vincent Street in the dreary, pishy rain. He saw a shabby, downmarket boozer off a side street and headed towards it. Before he entered he could hear the karaoke, some poor cow murdering Robbie Williams' 'Angels'. He went in and ordered a pint and a double whisky. He looked round. The pub was full of weegie dregs, all seemingly having the time of their lives. Connor felt like an alien beamed down from another fucking planet. There were smiles on faces everywhere he looked, as a young woman squeezed into a short skirt and tight top two sizes too small got up onstage and started caterwauling through 'Dancing Queen'. Her mates bounced around, waving Bacardi Breezers, all of them laughing their arses off. The pain in his hand thumped in time with the music as he downed the whisky and started on the pint. His stomach was agony with every sip, but he drank on regardless. He thought about Martin, standing on a ferry with the winter wind blowing his hair about, a sly smile on his face as he headed for new adventures in a place Connor would never visit. That stupid confused bastard had saved his life, all because of a daft gay crush. How ridiculous was that? Connor was still alive because a young boy fancied him enough to chase him round the country. Yet here he was killing himself again in a pub full of cheery idiots. He was going to turn it round, though. He would explain it all to Hannah tomorrow, when he was straight, once this gig was over, and he could draw a line under everything from the last two weeks.

But then he thought of Nick. He'd no idea how much money and drugs had been in the kitbag. It didn't matter. It was gone. When he got back to Edinburgh, he was a marked man. Maybe if he went to the police? But that wouldn't work, what evidence did he have? And anyway, he'd be implicating himself if he grassed Nick up. Perhaps if he just came clean to Nick about what happened, the wee shite might have a rare attack of conscience and let him off with only a small beating. That was bollocks and he was kidding himself. But he couldn't think about Nick yet. He had to stay focused on tonight.

The 'Dancing Queen' girl finished, and a young lad got up and started laying into 'Smells Like Teen Spirit'. He could only have been about sixteen, no way he would remember Nirvana from first time around. Jesus Christ. How fucking depressing. Connor downed what was left of his pint, retching at the acidic pain in his stomach, and stumbled out the door, desperate to get away from that fucking riff and those happy people.

He was soaked through by the time he got to Tut's but didn't bother shaking himself off as he entered the bustling downstairs bar. He made his way unsteadily past the tables and jukebox and headed for the upstairs club area. He was scared of what the rest of the band would say. Scared of talking to Hannah, the one person he loved more than anything else, the one person he'd been the biggest arsehole to.

Fuck, his hand hurt like hell. He couldn't concentrate.

Upstairs was empty apart from Hannah, Kate, Danny and Paul, sitting in a booth with plates of hot food. Connor saw the look of relief in Hannah's eyes as he appeared and felt a terrible sickness wash over him.

'We thought you were fucking dead,' she said.

'No such luck.'

'You look like shit,' said Danny, sticking a forkful of something in his mouth.

'You too.'

'We were worried sick, you stupid bastard,' said Kate. 'What the hell happened?'

'I explained it all to Paul,' said Connor, already wanting the interrogation to end. 'I went for a wander and got lost.'

'He said there were no roads and you were up in the hills somewhere,' said Hannah. Christ, why wouldn't they all just shut up about it? 'There was a storm last night, you could've been killed.'

He wanted them to please just shut up about it. He saw the look in Hannah's eyes, now wet with tears, and felt sick again.

'It wasn't Hurricane Hannah, was it?' he said, and instantly regretted it. 'Look, I'm fine now.' He sat down in the booth and eyed up the unattended bar opposite. 'Shouldn't we be soundchecking?'

Paul gave Connor a look somewhere between furious and relieved. 'We didn't know when you'd turn up. Or if. So we soundchecked already. The man from K2 Records is in town, he's getting here later.'

Connor should've said something. He wanted to explain that it didn't matter a toss if a hundred A&R guys turned up, the band was finished. But he didn't know how to start. He bottled it, and felt ashamed, telling himself he would break the news later, once the gig was over, or maybe tomorrow once he'd straightened out a little. Yeah, that's what he would do.

Paul was still talking.

'. . . so please just try and hold it together until then, eh?'

'I'm fine.'

'You don't look it.'

'Neither would you if you'd spent all night in a snowstorm in the fucking mountains.'

'Shit, what happened to your hand?' said Kate, grabbing his wrist and lifting his bandaged hand to the centre of the table. He pulled it back, worried for a split second that it might lash out of its own accord. He was losing it.

'It's just a scrape,' he said. 'I caught it on a fence. The woman who found me was a nurse so she bandaged it up. It's fine.'

'It looks like more than a scrape,' said Danny.

'Well, it's not.' When was this conversation going to fucking end?

'Can you still play guitar?' said Paul.

'As badly as ever,' he said, trying to laugh, but a strange gurgling noise came out instead.

'Where's Martin?' said Hannah, a look of steel in her eyes.

'What?'

'Paul said Martin was with you. Is that right?'

'Yeah.'

'Want to explain that to me? I left him at the police station in Fort William, waiting to get picked up by his parents.'

'He just walked out, apparently. Came back to the pub, spotted me leaving and followed me.'

'Wait a minute, you said you got lost.'

'I did.' Connor didn't have the first fucking clue how to explain everything that happened at Corrour and Loch Ossian. He didn't want to admit that he would've died if it hadn't been for Martin.

'You didn't see any gun-toting lunatics on your little walkabout?' said Danny.

Connor felt queasy, and squeezed out a nervous laugh.

'How do you mean?'

'Two foreign guys came in the pub at one point after you'd gone and said some fucking nutter had taken one of their bikes at gunpoint outside.'

271

'Really?' So this was his new start, lying through his fucking teeth with every word that passed his lips. But what else could he do?

Danny was laughing. 'Idiots left the key in their other bike, and when they got back outside it was gone as well. Shouldn't laugh, but what a pair of dolts.'

'Never saw anything like that,' said Connor with a nonchalance he was sure sounded completely false.

'Anyway,' said Hannah. 'About Martin?'

Christ, he was getting it from all sides. Why couldn't they all just shut up?

'What about him?'

'If you were lost, how did he follow you?'

'I don't really know. He just did. I was up in the hills and he eventually caught up with me. Then, with the storm and everything, we both made for this nearby station house, where an old couple put us up for the night.'

Hannah looked far from convinced. Connor didn't blame her one bit.

'So where is he now?'

'Sorry?'

'Where is he now?'

Connor didn't answer.

'Connor, no. Please tell me you made sure he got together with his parents. Or at least got in contact with them.'

Connor looked down. The pain in his hand was pounding as he felt the colour rise to his cheeks.

'Jesus Christ, Con. Do you know how dodgy this looks? A fifteen-year-old boy ran away from home and followed his female teacher round the country for a fortnight. And you knew about it all along. When I finally realised what was going on and got him to a police station, he then did another runner, and ended up on some bloody *Kidnapped*-style trek across the bonnie fucking moors with you in the middle of a snowstorm. Then the next day, you didn't even make him get in touch with his parents, and let him swan off to wherever he likes.'

'He had some shit to sort out.'

'Oh, grow up, Connor. He's a mixed-up fifteen-year-old kid. They've all got shit to sort out, but they don't all steal cars and leave home for a fortnight on a wild goose chase. Any idea where he actually is?'

'Not sure. He was heading to Mallaig. Then the Outer Hebrides, maybe.'

'God Almighty.' Hannah shook her head. 'Any suggestions what to say when I go back to school? "Sorry Mr and Mrs Gill, but my boyfriend let your son fuck off to the Outer Hebrides, despite the fact you were out your minds with worry about him for two solid weeks, after he bizarrely decided to follow me round the country." How does that sound?'

There was no answer, so Connor just sat there, watching Hannah fume, trying to ignore the excruciating pain radiating from his hand.

'I could lose my job over this, you bloody idiot,' she said. 'I can't even look at you right now.'

Hannah squeezed out the booth and stormed down the stairs. Connor let her go. He deserved everything she'd said. The speed, pills, painkillers, whisky and incredible throbbing pain in his hand were all making his head rage and his sight blurry.

'Are you just going to sit there?' Kate asked Connor. He couldn't concentrate on what she was saying. What was he meant to do?

'Jesus,' said Kate, getting up. 'I guess I'll go and see how she is, shall I?'

She trooped off down the stairs. After a while Connor turned to Danny and Paul.

'Either of you pair got money for a round?'

'I think you've had enough,' said Paul.

'Who are you, my fucking mother?'

'Here,' said Danny, chucking a twenty across the table. 'Mine's a pint of cooking.'

As Connor approached the bar, two staff materialised. He ordered pints all round and a double gin which he downed at the bar. The doors must've opened downstairs because punters started filtering into the club, some of them positioning themselves to get the best view for tonight's gig, others hanging around at the bar chatting. Connor stuck the drinks on the table.

'I've got to go for a pish.'

'Don't get lost this time, eh?' said Paul.

'I'll try not to.'

He headed downstairs to the toilets where he locked himself in the first sit-down. He sat with his head in his hands for a long time.

In the other toilets, Hannah and Kate were in a cubicle, Hannah sitting wiping her eyes with a piece of toilet roll while Kate stood, gently touching her back.

'Come on, babe, he's not worth it.'

'You've got that right.'

'He's king of the arseholes.'

Hannah sniffed. 'I thought he was fucking dead, you know. When he went missing like that, I thought maybe he'd done something stupid. You know how he's been. Then he just swans in today, already totally loaded, and tells me he's been with Martin and probably lost me my job into the bargain.'

'Try not to let him get to you.'

'I can't help it.'

Hannah's breathing slowed. She put her hand in her pocket and pulled out the pregnancy test stick. She waved it at Kate, who took it and examined it coolly.

'Congratulations?'

Hannah laughed a sniffly laugh. 'Thanks.'

'Come here,' said Kate, kneeling down and hugging Hannah firmly, the two of them awkward in the tight space of the cubicle. She straightened up, handing her back the stick.

'How do you feel?'

'You mean physically or emotionally?'

'Both.'

'Physically fine, despite that episode in Inverness. Emotionally, I'm all over the place. I have no idea how I feel about it.'

'When are you going to tell him?'

'When on earth can I? I've been putting off the test because

I knew that if I was, I'd have to confront him. But he's so bloody wasted all the time, I can't face it.'

'Maybe once tonight's over,' said Kate. 'Maybe once the tour's finished, things will settle down.'

'You don't believe that any more than I do.'

Hannah loved Connor, but she'd had enough of all the crap that went along with him. Either he sorted his shit out, or they were finished, baby or no baby. She didn't even know if she wanted it. She might not have a fucking job as of next week, how the hell was she going to bring up a kid? But that was no excuse, millions of people did it all the time. She was scared shitless of the future, and couldn't see a clear path ahead of her. Maybe Kate was right, maybe after tonight things would settle down, Connor would straighten himself out and they could sit down and talk about it. Yeah, right. She wasn't holding her breath.

She got up and flushed the loo.

'We'd better get back up there,' she said.

'It'll be OK,' said Kate, giving her another hug. Hannah wasn't convinced.

Connor sat in the cubicle. How was it everything that had come out his mouth since he turned up this evening was a pack of fucking lies? He wanted to bolt out the door and run down the street, away from the people he loved, the people he knew he was hurting, but seemed unable not to. He was going to hurt them some more, once he split up the band. Maybe then he'd be able to sort himself out. Go home, relax, finally get some sleep. But home was Edinburgh, and Edinburgh was Nick and Shug. Hannah was the key, he needed her to believe in him. After this gig he'd be able to tell her everything. He needed to tell her everything. Maybe she would help him, maybe not. He needed help, that was for fucking sure.

There was a knock on the door. How long had he been in here?

'Con?'

Danny.

'Con, come on. We're onstage in five minutes. I don't know what the hell's the matter with you, but you better get it together.'

Connor opened the cubicle door.

'Sorry,' he said. 'I needed a bit of time to myself. I'm fine now.'

'Once this is over, you really need to take a look at yourself. For Hannah's sake, if nothing else.'

'I know.'

The thought of the gig made his stomach tighten. He couldn't imagine being onstage and singing those songs he'd dug out of somewhere inside him, and yet he was letting himself be led back upstairs, into a hot and sweaty venue where an eager crowd was waiting to be entertained.

He felt into his pocket, stuffing the very last of the speed carelessly into his mouth and licking the powdery bag as he mounted the stairs. He let himself be led like a zombie, then somehow, suddenly, they were on the tiny Tut's stage being greeted with cheers and whistling from three hundred fans as he automatically picked up his guitar.

All he wanted was some peace and quiet. He thought briefly that he might be able to lose himself in the songs, in the rhythms pulsing around him, this one last time. Sometimes that happened, and he'd drift off somewhere else. Not this time. Not any more, not ever again. Right there, on that cramped stage in front of three hundred people, The Ossians seemed like the most pathetic, played-out joke of a band on the planet. A useless waste of space who spent their time disturbing the air with their tedious sounds and hackneyed, clichéd, half-baked sentiments. Halfway through the opening song Connor's monitor started feeding back. Nothing he hadn't experienced a hundred times before, but this time the sound cut right through him. He imagined the noise as tiny particles, the reverberating molecules of air interacting with the atoms in his body, raising them to an excited state, a state in which his body could dissolve into sound itself. He felt his body reacting with the high-pitched whine from the monitor, the noise swirling around him and in him and through him as if he was a ghost, a wraith, trying pathetically to communicate with the living through the impenetrable vacuum of space. He knew he was destined to pass through this world alone, drifting like a lost spirit from place to place, never understanding or being understood, always looking for something real to latch on to.

Then suddenly everything seemed too real. The red and green lights flashing onstage were tearing at his eyes and his brain, the feedback was creeping over his skin and inside his body, wrapping itself around his chest and squeezing until he felt like his heart would explode. He realised amid the noise and the flashing that he hadn't sung a note or touched the guitar, which hung limply round his neck. The guitar was creating unearthly shrieks of feedback as if trying to talk to the monitor at his feet, one of its own kind, like whales communicating over many miles of sea, locating each other in the murky depths of the world's oceans. He was hanging on to the mic stand with his eyes shut tight. Why couldn't they all just shut the fuck up? Why wasn't anyone doing anything to stop the noise and the lights and the chaos?

He imagined himself falling through the floor, descending into a pit of hell, white hot and brutally bright, the end of every nerve in his body alive with pain, desperate for anything that would stop the sensation of living, the ability to feel. His hand pulsed with excruciating pain and hung limp at his side. It felt like it was the size of a baseball mitt, throbbing and red as if hit by a hammer in a cartoon. He opened his eyes and was shocked to see the faces of the crowd watching in confusion, looking at the frozen statue on stage. His face contorted as if he was seeing demons in front of his eyes. He felt alone. His eyes searched the crowd, looking for Martin, looking for a saviour from all this madness. He knew Martin wasn't here, but that didn't stop him. Then he saw him, moving slowly among the stragglers at the back of the room, gazing back at him and radiating pure, angelic light from his simple, beautiful face. Connor felt the warmth emanating from Martin right across the room, and closed his eyes to bask in it. When he opened his eyes again, Martin was gone, and he knew he'd been imagining it all along, willing Martin into existence here in this place, wishing he would come and take him to safety. Nevertheless his eyes still searched the room for that face, the maelstrom of feedback all around him and ringing in his ears.

Then he saw two other familiar faces, and his chest tightened so much he thought he might pass out. Making their way slowly from the bar towards the stage, excusing themselves through a sea of punters, were Nick and Shug. Nick was staring straight at him as he put a hand on successive shoulders to squeeze past, while Shug followed in his wake with his head down. The two of them made their way to the steps at the side of the stage and stood there, Shug stony-faced, Nick with a smile on his lips but a look of hate on his face. Connor closed his eyes for several seconds, suddenly more aware of the cacophony around him, the pounding pain in his hand. He opened his eyes, but this time the vision hadn't disappeared. Nick and Shug were really there, and they clearly meant to do him some serious harm.

He felt like crying. The feedback from the monitor pierced through him and his hand raged in pain, desperate for relief. The sound of the wailing, the dissonance around him was making his hand worse, it was pulsing with angry life. He had to stop the pain and the noise he was immersed in, buried in, swamped in, drowning in like quicksand. If he didn't do something right now he would spend the rest of his life with the mangled sound of it tearing at his ears.

His left hand went into his pocket and pulled out the gun. Immediately he felt some of the throbbing from his hand transfer to the gun as if the vibrations had been transmitted to the solid, cool metal, soaking up the pain from this monstrous extension of his feeble arm. But the sound, the swirling storm of sound, remained. He aimed at the monitor and fired once, twice, three times, surprised at how easy it was. He felt large bolts of pain shooting out from his hand with the bullets and into the monitor.

Around the edge of his vision, he vaguely sensed panic. The crowd seemed suddenly to be performing a complicated Scottish country dance at double speed. The monitor in front of him wasn't laughing its banshee howl any more, its wire-mesh front contorted into vicious, sharp shapes. But the noise continued around him. All he wanted was some fucking peace and quiet, was that too much to ask? He turned towards his amp, but Nick came into his line of vision. He stopped. Nick was pointing a gun at him with a look which said he was more than happy to use it if it came to the crunch. Connor was pointing his own gun straight at Nick. He saw Shug behind Nick, frowning, as if he didn't really understand what was going on. Connor felt nailed to the spot. He stood there looking at Nick, the two of them pointing guns at each other, and he sensed the panic increasing all around him, the caterwauling feedback still whirling around his body. After a period of time that Connor had absolutely no concept of, he slowly turned towards his amp and fired. The amp exploded in a shower of sparks like tiny indoor fireworks. And the feedback was gone. At last. That's all he wanted. How simple the solution had been. They could all get on with their lives now.

He looked around. Kate, Danny and Hannah had stopped playing and were staring at him. He couldn't understand the looks on their faces. They seemed nervous, maybe scared. Yeah, they were afraid of him. He wanted to explain there was nothing to be frightened of, he'd sorted out all the horrible noise and mess, they were now free to get on with things. He wanted to tell them everything was fine. If they all just looked out for each other from now on everything would be OK. But he couldn't speak. And besides, he couldn't think of the words that would make any sense of all this. He looked back at Nick and Shug, and was confused to see them being wrestled to the ground by half a dozen other guys.

He looked down at his left hand. He was still holding the gun. A small patch of blood was seeping through the bandages and he could make out a smear of sticky darkness on the gun handle. He looked up again. Hannah was staring at him and the look on her face made him want to gouge his eyes out. He felt a spasm in his stomach and his legs began to shake, as if the earth was moving underfoot. The tightness moved up to his chest making it difficult to breathe, then into his throat and he vomited. His throat convulsed, spilling out thick, nightmarish bile which dribbled pathetically down his front and on to his bandaged hand and the gun, dripping like dirty engine oil on to the floor. His legs gave way and he sank to his knees. The sickness had released him like the first drops of rain from a storm cloud, and he sat on his knees sobbing like a child too tired to sleep, wishing for all the world that he could curl up and die right there.

He felt himself being slung around as Paul pulled the van recklessly on to the M8 heading east. His head was bursting with pain, and he needed a drink. His body felt like it had spent several tides getting battered against dangerous rocks. The pain in his hand was down to a dull throb, but the bandage was soaked through with blood.

'Do you see anything?' Paul asked Danny, who was hanging out the window.

'Nothing.'

'Are you sure?'

'No one's following us.'

The last thing Connor remembered was being onstage, surrounded by feedback, then he had the gun in his hand . . . fuck.

'What happened?' he said.

'What, you mean after you went mental and started shooting up the place?' said Paul, urging the van down the motorway. 'Or after those guys at the side of the stage started waving badges about and shouting that they were cops and no one was to leave the premises? We fucking bolted, what do you think? Me and Danny grabbed you, then the five of us legged it out the stage door. You think we'd hang about after what you did, with a bunch of police around? Any chance of explaining what the fuck you were up to, you complete fucking psycho?'

'This should be good.' Kate sat opposite him with arms folded and lips pressed together. Next to her was Hannah, who'd been crying. When he saw the look in her eyes he knew he had to tell her everything. This whole sorry tour had been full of lies and secrets, and if he was going to have any chance of starting over, of making a go of life, he would have to come clean. Part of him dreaded it, but part of him felt an amazing sense of relief.

'What do you want to know?' he said.

'Good question,' said Kate. 'Where do we start? How about where the hell you got a gun from?'

Connor took a couple of deep breaths.

'Off that Vlad guy in Ullapool.'

'The submarine kid? Why on earth would he give you a gun?'

'He didn't give it to me, he sold it to me.'

'And why the fuck did you want to buy a gun?'

'I don't know. It seemed like a good idea at the time.'

Kate shook her head. 'Unbelievable.'

'Who was that guy tonight?' said Hannah quietly.

'Which guy?'

'The guy in Tut's. You were pointing the gun at him. He was pointing a gun at you.'

The memory came back. Connor could see the hatred in Nick's face, the two weapons pointing at each other in a pathetic stand-off. But it was all too real. They could've died. Someone else could've died. Hannah could've fucking died. Anything could've happened. This had all gone way too far.

'That was Nick.'

'Who's Nick?'

'He's a drug dealer I owe money to.'

There was silence for a moment.

'Did I hear that right?' said Paul from the front.

'Depends,' said Kate. 'Did you hear that Connor owes a drug dealer money?'

'Yeah.'

'Then you heard right.'

'That probably explains why those plain-clothes police were all over him and his mate like a fucking rash,' said Paul. 'Had them pinned to the floor sharpish after the guns came out.'

'What else?' asked Hannah, ignoring Paul.

'How do you mean?'

'Connor, he wouldn't point a gun at you just because you owe him some money.'

Connor sighed, but the words came easily now that he'd started.

'To pay off the money I owed, I did some work for him.'

'This just gets better,' said Kate.

'What sort of work?' asked Hannah.

'I was delivering packages for him in exchange for envelopes, round the country, all through the tour.'

Kate put her head in her hands, but Hannah sat motionless looking at Connor.

'Jesus fucking Christ,' said Danny. 'Is that why you kept disappearing all the time?'

'Yeah.'

'And all the weird phone calls?'

Connor nodded.

'That still doesn't explain why he was pointing a gun at you,' said Hannah.

'I lost the packages and envelopes last night, up in the hills.'

'So, let me get this right,' said Kate. 'You were acting as a drug courier for some midget dealer prick you owed money to, you bought a gun, then you wandered into the wilderness and lost all the guy's drugs and money, then thought you'd come to Glasgow and have a fucking shoot-out with him?'

Connor didn't know what to say.

'You've been watching too much *Scarface* or *Goodfellas*. You're unbelievable, you know that?'

Connor sat in silence.

'Is there anything else?' said Hannah.

'Like what?'

'You tell us,' said Kate. 'You weren't pimping that kid Martin as a rent boy, were you?'

'Don't be stupid.'

'*I'm* being stupid?'

Connor thought about stealing pills from the girl in the Inverness hospital, and from his parents' bathroom cabinet. Something else came to him.

'It was me who took that motorbike in Fort William.'

'Outside the pub?' said Hannah.

He nodded.

'At gunpoint?'

He nodded again.

'Holy fuck,' said Danny.

Kate counted on her fingers. 'So, we've got possession of an illegal firearm, using that firearm in a public place, drug-dealing and armed robbery. Anything else to add to the list?'

Connor could see Danny looking at him. He was no doubt thinking about the seagull thing. What would be the point in owning up to that? What was that in the overall scheme of things? He looked at Kate and shook his head.

He looked at Hannah, but she'd turned away, unable or unwilling to look at him. He didn't blame her. Faced with everything he'd done, he felt like the dumbest, most wretched arsehole in the world. Apart from that, he must look like a total mess. He hadn't shaved or washed since they started this farcical trip, his clothes were a shambles, his eyes bloodshot, teary and exhausted, his hand wrapped in dirty, bloody bandages. But it was nothing to how he felt, as if his body would pack in at any minute. He was on the brink of collapse, and had to rest his head on the cold steel of the van wall and close his eyes to stop everything spinning.

He opened his eyes. Hannah had her head in her hands, and her shoulders moved as she began sobbing.

'Hannah . . .' He got up to head towards her but lost his balance and fell on his arse.

Kate slid along and put her arm around Hannah.

'Leave her alone,' she said. 'I think you've done enough, don't you?'

She gave Connor a look full of venom, which he fully deserved.

They sat quietly for a few minutes amid the rumble and clatter of the van bouncing along the M8, heading home.

Connor looked at Kate comforting Hannah, and wondered if he'd ever be allowed to get that close to her again.

15
Edinburgh

'We used to think
The mountains would stand tall
The seas would never boil
The land would never flood
We were wrong'

The Ossians, 'Geometry'

Hannah looked at Connor.

'How have you been?'

'Not bad, considering. You?'

'Same.'

The afternoon twilight had given up and turned to darkness around them. Below their Ferris-wheel carriage, Christmas Eve shoppers hurried around as if buying last-minute presents was the most important thing in the world. The sound of kids shrieking on fairground rides drifted up to them, mingled with the relentless thump of cheesy house from the skating rink. Connor could smell cheap burgers and onions being fried somewhere down below. The Scott monument looked grimy next to them amid the luminous bustle of Princes Street, its dark shape skulking in the gloom. Connor tried to remember being up there a few weeks ago with his sister but the details escaped him. He'd been drunk. He'd been drunk for as long as he could remember. But not for over a week now, and counting. That fact amazed him. He'd not been wasted for the last ten days. Of course, he hadn't been totally sober either. To begin with, the speed was the worst thing. He missed the amphetamine buzz something fucking terrible, and had smoked a lot of grass to take the edge off the cravings. But he'd gradually eased off on the blow, and now hadn't even smoked a joint in two days. Two fucking days. It was a similar story with alcohol. He tried cold turkey to begin with, but it was killing him – passing out, the shakes, vomiting, the fucking lot – and after twenty-four hours he'd resorted to a few beers and a whisky in the house each day, just to keep him going. He'd somehow managed to restrict it to that. He'd gradually reduced that amount, and now hadn't had a single drink in over twenty-four hours. He felt weird. Why the hell was it called being straight? It felt like the most fucking warped thing in the world, walking around with a clear head and a pumping heart and momentum in your legs. He was no idiot, he knew it wasn't over. It would never be over. The one-day-at-a-fucking-time cliché, and all that.

The first night had been the worst, not helped by the fact he'd spent it in the cells of the local police station. When they got back from Glasgow, Hannah jumped straight into a taxi to her mum's, saying she needed time away to think. He let her go without a fight. Half an hour later, with Danny walking Kate home and Connor alone in the flat looking at a bottle of whisky, there was a knock at the door. The police had found him easily enough. He was the lead singer in the headline band, for Christ's sake, even the most moronic copper could've tracked him down in five minutes. They took him to the station for questioning. Neither Paul nor the band knew he was there, which was how Connor wanted it. It was nothing to do with any of them, he would have to get out this shit on his own.

They spent a few hours interrogating him, and made him spend the night in the cells, but had to let him go come morning. There was little they could pin on him. His gun had disappeared in the chaos of King Tut's, some opportunist chancer obviously lifting it in the mayhem. Turns out the cops at the gig were from the Scottish Crime and Drug Enforcement Agency, and had been following Nick for months, waiting for him to fuck up. When they saw him pull a gun in public, that's all the excuse they needed to go in heavy, get the appropriate warrants, and go to town on him and his drug operation which, judging from the cops' hints, was far more widespread than Connor had imagined. They clearly hadn't been doing too good a job of tailing Nick, however, because they didn't seem to know anything about Connor's involvement, or his activities on tour. There was no evidence of his connection to Nick. The drugs and money were somewhere in the wilderness near Loch Ossian, and the phone Nick gave him was lost. Connor couldn't believe his luck. He kept quiet, and denied having seen Nick before. He was physically and mentally wrecked in the interview room, barely able to string a coherent sentence together, drained to absolute empty. The police hadn't been that interested in him, anyway. They had who they wanted, and believed they had enough to put him away for a long time. Since they didn't have the evidence of Connor's gun, they decided to let him off with a caution. He was surprised they hadn't made a connection between him and the bike theft in Fort William, or the patients' pills in Inverness, or the thing at Aberdeen pier. But then why should they? They weren't interested in him, all they wanted was Nick in jail, end of story. That's the impression he'd been given as he stood blinking in the early-morning light outside St Leonard's police station, and he wasn't about to complain.

The walk home across the Meadows in the sharp morning air, through the stretch of barren trees, was an odd mix of elation and misery. He was free and clear of trouble with the police, and Nick and Shug were in jail for the foreseeable future. But what about Hannah and the rest of them? That was all fucked. Hannah was gone, and he didn't know if she was ever coming back.

But here she was sitting next to him.

Hannah examined Connor while he gazed down at the melee below them. She was partly relieved and partly annoyed to find he was looking pretty good. He was clean-shaven and clean-clothed, and his eyes were clear, although tired-looking, with lines around them she'd never noticed before. He was painfully thin. She'd heard through Kate that he'd gone to the doctor, who prescribed antacids for what turned out to be stomach ulcers, presumably because of all the speed. More extensive test results for liver damage and the like were still pending. The powder burns on his hand had healed enough for the bandage to come off. Hannah could see an angry red blotch of a scar in the crescent between his forefinger and thumb which looked like it was going to be permanent. A nice wee reminder of everything.

She didn't know what she was doing here. She'd holed up at her mum's as soon as they got home. She didn't tell her mum anything about the tour, Connor, or her condition. Connor left messages with her mum every day, but she didn't reply or speak to him until now. It was only now, after ten days, she'd decided to face him, arranging to meet here on neutral ground.

She'd got in touch with the school as soon as possible. It'd been decided she should go on paid leave for a while. She couldn't blame them. Thankfully, Martin turned up safe at home in the middle of that week, singing Hannah's praises, and blaming no one but himself. His parents were so relieved, they forgot all about being angry at anyone, and Martin received a hero's welcome from his classmates for his, by then, notorious adventures. The Fort William police backed up his and Hannah's version of events, and she was free to return to work in the New Year. Whether she would or not, she didn't know yet. Everything was up in the air. Her, Connor, the baby. The baby. Thinking that to herself freaked her out. She'd gone to the doctor, who confirmed the pregnancy. She was now waiting on results from a CT scan, to hopefully determine the cause of her fit. In the meantime, she'd been advised to relax, enjoy the pregnancy. Easier said than done. Maybe that's why she was here now, after ten days away from Connor, because there was something altogether bigger linking the two of them, something he still didn't know about, something she had to get off her chest. She had to tell him, but she didn't know where to begin.

Connor watched as Hannah gazed out at nothing. She looked great. Clearly the time away from him had done her the world of good. She was wrapped up in her big suede coat with the furry trim. Connor could see her knee-length leather boots, and wondered what she was wearing under the coat. A brief flash of the two of them having sex, her still in those boots, flitted across his mind. God, he loved her. Why had he treated her so badly? In the last ten days he'd thought about her constantly. Throughout the police interviews and detox sweats and sickness and stomach cramps, all he thought about, the focus of everything, was Hannah. Looking at her now, her face seemed somehow more luminous. Maybe it was just the cold wind biting down Princes Street into their faces. She was wearing a woolly hat with side flaps, and without her hair to frame it, her face was exposed. He realised how beautiful and kind that face was, full of compassion, hopefully even for the likes of him.

'Did you go to the doctor?' he asked.

'What?' she said, flustered. Shit, maybe Kate had said something about the pregnancy.

'The fit in Inverness,' said Connor. 'Did you get it checked out?'

'Oh, yeah. They did a CT scan to see if it was epilepsy. Still waiting on the results. I reckon it might just've been stress.'

'Right.' Connor looked miserable. 'I guess I caused that.'

'Me having a fit wasn't your fault.'

They were silent for a moment.

'Hannah, I know this sounds completely pathetic and insubstantial, and it's only words, but I really am *so* sorry. For everything.'

Hannah looked at him, and could see tears welling up in his eyes. She didn't know if he was crying or if it was this bloody freezing wind.

'I know you're sorry.'

'But?'

Hannah sighed. 'It's difficult. Sorry is just a word. I know you mean it, that's fine. But you have to prove you mean it every day from now on. There's no deadline on this, it goes on and on and on, as long as we do.'

As long as we do. There was promise in that phrase.

'I know. I know it does.'

The wind blustered around them in a huff. Connor noticed that the sky was clear of clouds, but starless. The sound of festivity below them felt like it was being beamed in from a far-off planet.

'Kate and Danny seem to be doing well,' said Hannah. Why was she bringing this up now? Didn't they have more important things to discuss?

288

'From what I hear.'

The new couple seemed to be flourishing, from what little Connor knew. Kate was still hardly talking to him, but she and Danny had spent almost all of the last ten days in each other's company, according to Danny. They mostly kept out of Connor's way, for their own sake, no doubt, as he was so miserable around the flat. He was glad they stayed away, because despite wishing them all the best together, the sight of them in the first stages of love only highlighted how bad his relationship with Hannah was. If there was even still a relationship there.

'How was the police stuff?' said Hannah after a while.

'Fine. I didn't tell them anything, they didn't have any evidence on me, and they let me off with a warning.'

'What about the other stuff? The bikes and everything?'

'They never mentioned it, so neither did I.'

'And what about that dealer and his mate?'

'Locked up for a long time, as far as I can gather.' Connor looked Hannah in the eyes. 'Did you want me to confess everything to the police? All that other shit? Because I would, if that's what you wanted.'

'Don't be stupid,' said Hannah. 'What would be the point? You got lucky, Con, make the most of it.'

'I intend to.'

'Speaking of which, I hear you're trying to dry out.'

'Trying.'

'How's it going?'

'OK.'

Hannah looked at him pointedly.

'Really?'

'Yeah. Do you want specifics or something?'

'Actually, specifics would be good.'

Connor hesitated a moment. He didn't have a leg to stand on, now or ever.

'No speed, coke or pills at all since we got back. Smoked a lot of weed to begin with, but cut down, and haven't had a joint in two days. Same with booze. Haven't had more than four or five drinks a night, gradually cut down, and had my first dry day yesterday.'

'I'm impressed.'

'And surprised?'

'And surprised.'

'Not as surprised as me.'

'How do you feel?'

'Strange. Everything is so sharp and in focus. My body feels like it's been battered to fuck.'

'Your body has been battered to fuck.'

'That's true.'

'I heard about the stomach ulcers.'

'Yeah, the middle-aged businessman's medical complaint.'

'Are you taking anything for them?'

'Some big, chalky tablets. Tried snorting them, but didn't get anything. That's a joke, by the way.'

Hannah smiled, and the sight of it made Connor's brain fizz.

'I realised that was a joke. I know you pretty well, Con.'

'I guess you do.'

She looked him up and down.

'You could do with putting on some weight, you know.'

'I know. But I don't have much appetite.'

'You're not about to go anorexic on me, are you?'

Now it was Connor's turn to smile.

'I don't think so, somehow. You look amazing, by the way.'

'Thanks.'

'I mean it.'

'I know you do.'

They didn't talk for a while, letting the sounds of Christmas revelry and traffic noise wash over them. The lights on the Ferris wheel began flashing different colours.

'What about the band?' asked Hannah.

'The band's finished.'

'I assumed as much.'

Connor hadn't officially split up The Ossians, but everyone knew it was over. As if through some kind of telepathy, they'd all clearly realised it was finished, without having to mention it. Paul phoned Tut's after a couple of days, trying to get their gear back, but the manager told him they were hanging on to it, payment in kind for the damage done and the mayhem caused. What were they going to do, complain to the police? It was also made perfectly clear that The Ossians needn't try to play anywhere in Scotland ever again. A day later, Paul received a light-hearted phone message from the head of K2, saying that while he'd enjoyed the, ahem, full-on nature of the show, he just wasn't into the music enough. It didn't matter, of course.

'I heard you lost your job,' said Hannah.

Connor hadn't bothered going into the record shop or phoning in since his return, too busy trying to keep it together, and thinking about Hannah.

'No great loss,' he shrugged.

'What are you going to do?'

'Something'll turn up.'

'Tell me something. Did you find what you were looking for? With the band and the tour?'

Connor thought for a moment.

'No, I don't think I did.'

Hannah looked at him. 'What are you smiling about?'

'Actually, I was just thinking I learned something from Martin.'

'What's that?'

'I think I learned how to grow up.'

'You learned how to grow up from a fifteen-year-old boy?'

'Yeah.'

His smile dissolved. The Ferris wheel continued to turn and the world turned with it. In the sky beyond the Scott monument a solitary plane banked, its lonely lights blinking softly in the nothingness.

Hannah had run out of avoidance tactics.

'Connor, I've got something to tell you.' She couldn't look at him while she spoke, and felt her pulse thumping in her ears and her throat, making it hard to get the words out. She'd imagined this moment a thousand times over the last ten days, but she'd never once worked out what Connor's reaction might be, or what she wanted it to be, for that matter. 'I'm pregnant.'

Connor's head swam and the world seemed to go blurry. He felt the blood moving through his veins a little faster as he looked across at her. She was looking down and picking at her knees.

'That's great news,' he said. 'Isn't it?'

'I'm not sure. I think so.'

She looked up at him and Connor saw tears in her eyes. He wouldn't blame her if she never wanted to see him again. He'd been a pathetic little shit for so long he doubted that he knew any other way to live. But he wanted to sort his shit out, he *was* sorting his shit out. He wanted to look after her and love her and do all the things that normal people do. But he also knew that just saying those things wasn't going to make any fucking difference, not after the way he'd behaved. He had to show her. He was determined to do that.

Hannah didn't know if she and Connor had a future together, but she'd already decided she had a future with this baby. She was keeping it. Whether the three of them could be a family, after everything that had happened, she just didn't know.

He reached out for her hand and she let him hold it. Their carriage reached the top of the Ferris wheel and they could see the Christmas lights strung out down Princes Street like glistening threads into the unknown. Connor didn't know what to do next. He watched her as she looked into the distance. After a while he turned and followed her gaze. The plane had disappeared from view. They sat in silence for a long time, staring at nothing.

Acknowledgements

Eternal gratitude to Judy Moir and Lucy Luck for their incredible passion and astute advice, and to everyone at Penguin for their enthusiasm. Immeasurable thanks, as always, to my wife, Trish, for her love, encouragement and belief.

The writer acknowledges support from the Scottish Arts Council towards the writing of this book.